---

★

---

Tippett appeared at the top of the grand staircase, his sparsely grey-haired head sitting above a freshly pressed tuxedo. The actor replied, "Here I am, Mr. Rick," and started down the staircase.

About halfway down, Tippett paused, broke into a broad, toothy grin, raised his finger as if about to make a point and was about to speak, when he suddenly jerked, hit from behind. His body trembled, his eyes flicked down to the spot of red that had abruptly appeared where his mortal heart used to be. Then he pitched forward and fell facedown on the stairs, a crossbow bolt jutting angrily from his back.

Backstage, a woman screamed, "Son of a bitch!" Donovan swore, and began to run down the center aisle.

---

★

---

*Previously published Worldwide Mystery title by*
*MICHAEL JAHN*

MURDER AT THE MUSEUM OF NATURAL HISTORY

*Forthcoming from Worldwide Mystery by*
*MICHAEL JAHN*

MURDER ON FIFTH AVENUE
(in A NEW YORK STATE OF CRIME)

# EDGAR AWARD WINNER

# MICHAEL JAHN

# MURDER ON THEATRE ROW

# WORLDWIDE®

TORONTO • NEW YORK • LONDON
AMSTERDAM • PARIS • SYDNEY • HAMBURG
STOCKHOLM • ATHENS • TOKYO • MILAN
MADRID • WARSAW • BUDAPEST • AUCKLAND

*For David Aaron Jahn*

## MURDER ON THEATRE ROW

A Worldwide Mystery/April 2000

First published by St. Martin's Press, Incorporated.

ISBN 0-373-26346-5

# Author's Note

Several persons helped with research for this Bill Donovan mystery. Thanks go to David ("Iolo") Watson of New World Arbalest, Austin, Texas (http://beacon.moontower.com:80/crossbow), for help with the weapons lore. The staff of the Westwood, New Jersey, Public Library was helpful, as always. Several others chimed in with thoughts, quips, and trivia. I am indebted to Mark Crane, Paull Giddings, Barbara Klink, Bill Millard, Berkeley Rice, Cindy Starr, Lauren Walker, and Barbara Weiss.

A special tip of the hat goes to my publishing crew: Neal Bascomb, Meredith Bernstein, Elizabeth Cavanaugh, and Tom Dunne. Ed Gorman is a special friend. A long time ago, Dick Shepard offered gentle wisdom to a young music critic. Much further back, O. Henry and Voltaire said things that one day would prove irresistible to an old novelist.

Thanks also to my eldest son, Evan, and my mother, Ann. And to other family members: Vivien and Julian Lebetkin, as well as Marty, Barbara, Ben, and Joe Mayer. And my deepest gratitude to my loving and supportive wife, Ellen, and our miracle baby, David Aaron Jahn, born February 25, 1995, to whom this book is dedicated.

Michael Jahn
January 10, 1996

# ONE

## A PARTICULARLY INTERESTING CORPSE

TEDDY ROOSEVELT WAS President and preparing to dig the Panama Canal in 1903 when the thirty-inch water main was laid down below Forty-second Street in New York City. The Wright Brothers had just flown the first airplane when the cast iron main was buried in its trench between the just-built Interboro Rapid Transit subway station and the basement of its neighbor in Times Square, the Old Knickerbocker Theater. And one frosty Monday night, the fourth of December ninety-plus years later, Bill Donovan, newly appointed captain in the New York Police Department, was riding the subway home from his office at One Police Plaza when the water main—untended lo those many years—burst.

It did so in the spectacular way known well to New Yorkers, who are long accustomed to the thrill of life in the world's most complicated and fragile infrastructure. Like a dirty brown Old Faithful, the water blasted out of the street and sidewalk a crater fifty feet long, thirty feet wide, and twenty feet high that reached into the basement of the Old Knickerbocker. It shut down the city's busiest crosstown street and flooded its largest subway station.

Because three lines met beneath Times Square, "the Crossroads of the World," underground traffic came to a virtual standstill across the dense and throbbing city. Because the rush of emergency vehicles to the scene blocked not only Forty-second Street but also Broadway and Seventh Avenue, almost the entirety of midtown was gridlocked. Because the world below streets in Manhattan is so densely packed, not only water but also gas, electric, and steam lines were torn asunder. For the length of a long, cold, and memorable night, the Great White Way went dark. The rescue workers sent to evacuate the three-thousand-some-odd subway passengers trapped up to their knees in freezing water had to do so using emergency lights. Apart from those beacons and a seeming thousand flashing red lights, the only illumination in Times Square came from the votive and hurricane candles hastily lit in storefronts and restaurants.

It was, in fact, the presence of two emergency candles on top of Sardi's bar that allowed Donovan to see while he put down his briefcase—until then clutched to his chest to keep it dry—and wrung out his pant legs. He had been on the wagon for years, and though he welcomed the tender refuge of Sardi's bar, he considered a water main break and major civil disturbance insufficient reason to resort once again to tormenting his liver. Still, Donovan rued the fact that the well-earned pleasure of one of the establishment's famous Bombay martinis was denied him. It lurked nearby, though, in the hands of a preoccupied man of about fifty years whose ponytail was marked by twin streaks of white—one on either side—giving his square head the appearance of a '54 Buick that had been racing-striped. He was the only other customer at the darkened bar.

"A brave refugee," said the fat and ancient bartender, approaching with a cocktail napkin to lay in front of the captain.

"Can I get a cup of coffee?" Donovan asked.

"You want a shot of Irish in it?"

"Not tonight, thanks."

A moment later a carafe was placed before him. "You might as well drink it all. There's no electricity to keep it warm. But if you want a shot of Irish in there, you just yell."

Donovan sighed and said, "I would sooner have my flesh ripped by demons."

At which remark the other customer turned briefly and waggled his glass. Donovan wondered if the man was volunteering to be a demon. Donovan swiveled around and looked out into the dark of Forty-fourth Street.

The red lights made traces on the brickwork of the buildings across the street. The white emergency lights that now lit up Times Square cast a twilight glow down the side street between Broadway and Seventh Avenue. Even through Sardi's plate-glass window, he could hear the crackle of police radios and the curl of sirens. A small portable radio set on the maître d'hôtel's lectern carried one of the local all-news stations. It was reporting, in tinny tones suitable for a disaster story set in that neighborhood, the extent of the damage.

Several million gallons of water had already poured out of the broken main, one of 5,760 miles of such conduits within the city that never sleeps. Water flooded the tunnels as far south as Herald Square, shutting down Macy's right at the start of the holiday shopping season. A quarter million subway riders had their evening rush hours disrupted. As for surface traffic, all of midtown from Thirty-fourth to Fifty-seventh west of Fifth Avenue was gridlocked. Getting into the Lincoln Tunnel for escape to New Jersey was out of the question. Commuter buses piled up at the Port Authority Bus Terminal. As many as a million people were wet, tired, cold, in the dark, or otherwise inconvenienced. All were mad as hell.

Donovan swiveled back to his coffee and, unconsciously, began singing the chorus to "New York, New York." The man down the bar chuckled, then joined in for a moment. When the impromptu singalong had become embarrassing for the man who started it, Donovan stopped and set his cup back down.

"Stuck here and can't get home?" the man asked.

Donovan shrugged. "I can always walk."

"Where do you live?"

"Riverside and Eighty-ninth. You?"

"Riverside and One-sixteen."

Donovan said, "Well, I got a shot at walking home wet and freezing, but that's kind of far for you."

"Never mind. I'm supposed to be working anyway."

"I'm off for the day."

"What do you do?"

"I'm a cop."

"A cop?" the man said, a bit scornfully, looking Donovan up and down, the way young people did in the 1960s. "You don't look like a cop."

Donovan felt like saying, "You don't look like an idiot, but..."

In the name of civility he restrained himself. Instead, he asked, "What do you do?"

"I'm a writer," the man replied.

"Where?"

"At *The New York Times,* but I can't work."

"Oh. Hurt your fingers on that martini?" Donovan grinned vengefully.

The man huffed and ordered another. When it was delivered and the bartender once again had retreated to his stool at the far end, the man said, "All the computers are down. My laptop is in the shop. And I can't find a typewriter in the joint."

He nodded in the direction of south. The Times building was on Forty-third between Seventh and Eighth, just a block away. It was after the newspaper that the Times Square area, the one-time Longacre Square, was named, a fact an amazing number of New Yorkers seemed not to know.

"My old editor used to keep an old Underwood, but he died a year ago and took it with him."

"I use a notebook computer."

"Cops know about computers?"

"I have it in my briefcase. I hope it didn't get wet."

"If you're a cop, how come you're not out there working?" He nodded in the direction of the street.

"I'm a fellow victim of this particular tragedy," Donovan said. "Anyway, I'm a homicide investigator and off duty until such time as they turn up a corpse." He extended his hand. "Bill Donovan...Captain Bill Donovan."

"Good to meet you," the man said, apparently unaffected by meeting such an elevated police personage.

"If you're a reporter, how come you're not outside reporting, computer or no computer?" Donovan asked. "I seem to recall reading about this guy covering the Johnstown Flood by using his house key to scratch notes on a piece of paper."

The man said, "I'm not a reporter. I'm a..." He cleared his throat. "A rock critic...a music reviewer."

"You sing nice," Donovan said agreeably.

"Lucien Schadenfreud. You can call me Luke." They shook hands.

"I've seen your byline, but can't remember what the story was about."

"And the reason I'm not working is I was supposed to interview Pearl Jam but they're stuck in traffic and had to cancel."

It was Donovan's turn to look blank.

"Uhh...Pearl Jam?" the man said again.

"You got me: Is that anything like silver polish?"

"No," Schadenfreud laughed. "The rock group."

"Sorry. I don't rock and roll."

"But you must know who Pearl Jam is."

"I have spent nearly all my fifty-some-odd years avoiding rock and roll."

"I seem to have spent most of my fifty-some-odd years in it," Schadenfreud said, with more than a trace of bitterness.

"How long have you been reviewing rock concerts for a living?" Donovan asked.

"How long ago was 1968?"

"About four hundred years, politically speaking."

"Well, that's how long it's been."

"You poor guy. How are your ears? More to the point, how is your liver? Tell me, is it true no rock stars can speak in words of more than one syllable?"

Schadenfreud thought for a moment, then smiled and said, "Backstage at Woodstock, Janis Joplin called me a 'bastard.' "

"I *am* relieved," Donovan replied.

"It was only a few months later I wrote her obituary. God, I can't believe you don't like any rock."

"Is Tom Waits rock?"

"No. He's an intellectual saloon singer."

"My kind of guy—a drunk who thinks too much."

"Hear, hear," Schadenfreud said.

"Give me a singer leaning on a piano at three in the morning belting out 'One for My Baby' and you'll see before you a happy man."

"I'll drink to that, too," Schadenfreud said, and did so.

As they had been speaking the man had moved closer and, in so doing, came closer to one of the candles that burned brightly on the bar. That gave the captain a good look at his face, which was red and puffy from years of drinking. Schadenfreud's eyes were bloodshot, with capillaries that looked like the street map of the Bronx. His thick white fingers shook each time they approached the thin-stemmed martini glass, forcing Schadenfreud to steady them by pressing down against the bar before lifting the glass for a sip. He also bent forward quite a bit, thus to hold down the amount of spillage that could precede the glass reaching the lips.

Donovan thought, This guy ought to either get straight or drink right out of the bottle. No doubt one or the other was the next step for the man. Twenty-five or thirty years going to rock concerts for a living! A new definition of hell, in Donovan's opinion. Still, the man dressed respectably enough, if a bit old fashioned. In a brown corduroy suit, the jacket of which didn't come close to covering his swollen gut, Schadenfreud resembled a gone-to-seed professor of English literature.

The captain's musing was interrupted by the ringing of his cell phone. Embarrassed by this public display of expensive technology—he had once told his assistant, Detective Sergeant Brian Moskowitz, to shoot him should he ever be caught using a cell phone ostentatiously—Donovan took the instrument from his pocket.

After listening for a terse moment, he said, "Okay, I'll meet you there," and hung up.

"Let me guess: Your wife is complaining dinner is getting cold and wants you to meet her at the Carnegie Deli," Schadenfreud said.

"I'm not married," Donovan replied, getting to his feet and leaving several bills on the bar. He also handed the critic one of his cards.

"Call if you hear of a crime," he said, adding, "I guess I have to go to work after all. The rescue workers manning this catastrophe found a corpse—an interesting one—and that's my specialty."

# TWO

## LINEAR ECCHYMOSES AND THE TATOO OF A PARROT

THE BODY IN QUESTION belonged to a male Asian in his mid-twenties. He was found forty feet below street level, where the rampaging water had collapsed a ten-foot segment of the ancient brick wall that separated the basement of the Old Knickerbocker Theater from the subway tunnel. To the south of the chasm was the basement, now used mainly for storage and, apparently, as a repository for debris from the construction workers who were renovating the floors above. In particular, the work of installing a pneumatic lift to move massive sets up to and down from stage level had left tons of as-yet-uncollected plaster, concrete, and wood splinters lying about in four-foot-high piles that had been turned by the floodwaters into grey mounds of glop. To the north of the hole made by the water main break was the subway tunnel used by the IRT Flushing line. A hastily abandoned train sat axle-deep in water. The water had finally been shut off to the broken main, so it was safe (but wet and still freezing) for emergency workers to go into the area. Gigantic emergency pumps worked overtime to suck the water that remained below street level up to Forty-second Street, where it ran westward finally to spill into the Hudson River not far from the Intrepid Air and Space Museum.

When Donovan arrived on the scene he picked his way down the subway platform to the collapsed wall, then stepped gingerly over a pile of bricks. When he got inside the basement of the old theater, he found Sgt. Moskowitz crouching next to the body, which was dressed in new black jeans and a black sweater someone had hiked up to the armpits. The man lay on his stomach, his head turned to one side, a patina of grey concrete dust covering him except where forensic technicians had brushed it off.

"The last time I was on that subway platform I was on my way to Shea Stadium to see a Mets game," Donovan said.

"What one?" Moskowitz asked.

"I only remember they won."

"I'm too young to recall those days," Mosko said, using the edge of his notebook computer to point out curious lines in the body of the deceased. The victim's back was marked with blue-black stripes in a pattern that approximated his ribs. The lines radiated from twin vertical marks that ran parallel to the backbone.

"What the hell's that?" Donovan asked, handing his briefcase to a uniformed officer and squatting beside his aide and close friend.

"I don't know, but he has the same thing on his stomach. We looked. That and the tattoo of a parrot."

"What kind of parrot?"

"How the hell should I know? I grew up in Canarsie, not the damn rainforest. Ask me about chickadees and pigeons."

"Are those stripes painted on his skin?" Donovan asked.

"Nope. They look like bruises."

"Linear ecchymoses."

"Say what?"

"Bruises, and in lines. What do you think's going on?"

Moskowitz stood, and so did Donovan. "Beats me. A ritual something, maybe. Since you handled that case of ritual murder in Riverside Park I thought you could tell me."

"How do you think he died?"

"Preliminary observations suggest being hit on the head and drowned. He has blunt-force trauma to the back of his skull, but there was a lot of water in him."

"Any ID?"

"Not a thing. No wallet. Twenty-two bucks in fives and ones in a pants pocket."

"Whose footprints are those around the body?" Donovan asked, looking at the array of overlapping footprints that had been left in the grey mud.

"Most of them belong to cops. There are a few unidentifieds, probably the anonymous civilians who spotted the body and dialed 911."

Donovan said, "Okay, this guy was killed by the water main break. Let's go home."

"He looks Chinese," Mosko observed.

Donovan stepped over the body and bent over it once again. This time he peered closely at the man's slim limbs, clean hands, and what appeared to be a cheap wristwatch, one of those electronic ones that included a tiny calculator or computer, Donovan couldn't be sure which without touching it. There were a series of buttons, all too small to be pressed with anything larger than a pencil point. Then Donovan concentrated on the man's face. After a moment the captain stood again and shrugged. "It's hard to tell where this guy is from. He could be Chinese, except his face is a little thin. I'm no expert on Asian ethnic groups. He looks like he doesn't shave, and a lot of Asian men don't grow facial hair."

"The Maharishi has plenty," Mosko said.

"Far-Eastern men, I mean. He doesn't look Mongolian or Siberian, so I guess China or somewhere in that vicinity is about right. Let's see if we can find out."

"Right, boss."

"Did he work in this building?"

"Could be, but I can't tell you until the morning."

"Bag that watch and after you check it for prints, save it for me. I also want color photos of the bruises and the parrot."

Donovan waved his hand as if to brush the smell of wet concrete and plaster dust from his face. "What's he doing in this place?" he asked. "Where are we?"

"In the sub-basement—they call it the 'B-level basement'—of the Old Knickerbocker Theater, a porno house."

Donovan drew himself up to full height, those of his genes that controlled indignation bristling. "You call the Old Knickerbocker a porno house?"

Mosko was instantly aware he had stepped in shit. Two things remained for him to determine—what kind and how deep? He cast his eyes downward.

Donovan said, "Perhaps elsewhere atop this boulevard of broken Broadway dreams are topless bars and smoky back rooms that sell dirty books in front and offer live sex shows in back—"

"I apologize," Mosko said, hoping in vain to cut short the inevitable polemic.

"Maybe down the block a piece—on that part of it not yet turned by the relentless hand of commerce into the Mall of America, Times Square Substation—a sleazy theater is showing Debbie Does Dubuque...."

Like many lifelong New Yorkers, Donovan was deeply suspicious of the campaign, costing hundreds of millions of dollars (many of them from the Walt Disney empire), to reclaim the Crossroads of the World from the depths of sweaty depravity—drugs on the sidewalks, porno in the storefronts—to which it had sunk in the decades following World War II. As much as he was repulsed by X-rated movies, and as much as he was of the firm—and hard-won—belief that life was best lived using the fewest chemicals possible, Donovan worried that replacing Debbie with Goofy wasn't the ideal fate for the crossroads that gave the world New Year's Eve.

He continued: "You are standing on hallowed ground. In the century since it was built, this theater saw the likes of Sarah Bernhardt, the Barrymores, and the Times Square Follies—the cream of vaudeville—before falling into the unfortunate disrepute that sometimes comes with old age."

"Jesus, it was just an offhand remark."

"It is true pornographic films were shown here in recent years. But during the 1950s and 1960s, long after the prime of the Old Knickerbocker, I came to escape summer's heat and catch Richard Widmark westerns—three for a buck, as I recall. The day's entertainment over, you could wander down Forty-second Street and get a complete meal at Tad's Steaks: a steak, baked potato, and garlic bread for a buck-nineteen. And if you didn't live in such a hot neighborhood, there were stores where you could pick up a nifty implement of destruction for modest cost. I bought a neat machete right across the street from here for fifteen bucks."

"A machete?" Mosko asked brightly, sensing the tirade was winding to a conclusion.

"I used it to clear weeds from Riverside Park when we wanted to play ball," Donovan said. "So look, my knowledge of this hall ends about two years ago. When the Times Square renovation project began to show signs of succeeding I stopped paying attention. What's become of the Old Knickerbocker? I see construction going on.''

Moskowitz scrolled down a few pages on his notebook. His just-turned-cheery-again face resumed its downcast look.

''What's the matter?''

''Maybe you should hear this sitting down,'' Mosko said.

Donovan shifted his weight nervously, sensing another indignity.

Moskowitz read from his notes: ''The Old Knickerbocker is being renovated by producer Sir John Victor Holland and will reopen on New Year's Eve as the new home of his latest megamusical that just proved itself in trials in London—*Casablanca: The Musical*.''

Donovan turned white. He looked about him, down at the body, then off at the dunes of concrete dust. He said, ''If it turns out this guy died of flesh-eating bacteria, can I shut down the show?''

''I don't think so, but I'll check in the morning.''

''My God, *Casablanca: The Musical*. I read about that and assumed it was a bad joke. You know, one of those stories the *Post* runs every so often to stir things up. About the same time, I heard Sylvester Stallone was trying to turn *Rocky* into a Broadway musical. Now, as horrible as that may seem, it ain't a bad idea compared with the prospect of Rick and Ilsa singing a duet to 'We'll Always have Paris' while waltzing down the grand staircase.''

Mosko chortled.

Donovan looked once again at the body, then said, ''I'll bet flesh-eating bacteria can leave a pattern of bruises like that.''

''I'll check that out, too.''

''This burns me up. This bum Holland tortures the American stage with a string of megamusicals with hundred-dollar ticket prices and plots that make *Snow White and the Seven Dwarfs* look like *Who's Afraid of Virginia Woolf?* and the goddamn queen knights him. Previous queens knighted previous criminals for doing things some of my ancestors eventually ran the British out of Ireland for doing. It seems the least I can do is run Sir John out of New York.''

''Can we remove the body first?'' Mosko asked.

DONOVAN SPENT another hour in that basement, poking around the body and making handwritten notes he would type up later at home. His gut reaction that the victim was killed by the flood, no more, was tempered by his fervent desire to somehow embarrass Sir John Victor Holland. Donovan left only after his forensics team arrived. It was led by the redoubtable Sgt. Howard Bonaci, who, like Moskowitz, had followed Donovan from his old command. The West Side Major Crimes Unit was now under the capable leadership of newly promoted Lt. Thomas Jefferson. Donovan's near-decade-and-a-half of leadership of that busy and, recently, trendy neighborhood's crime-fighting unit was over, and now he served the entire city as chief of special investigations. His well-proven expertise in solving high-profile homicides—often involving exotic weapons—was due to be tested on a larger playing field. But nothing about that night was high-profile: Donovan left the basement of the Old Knickerbocker still wet, quite cold, and very hungry, and got a squad car to drive him uptown.

It was just after eleven, and the kitchen of Marcy's Home Cooking had just closed for the night. When Donovan walked in, his suit pants wrinkled from the knees down, the modest-sized room was half-filled with diners finishing their coffees and desserts. Marcy sat at the bar, alternately gazing wistfully at the piano player—at that moment, doing an instrumental version of "Stormy Monday"—and glaring at George Kohler, who was behind the bar. As usual, something of emotional complexity was going on.

She jumped up when she saw her fiancé, tousled his hair, and gave him a kiss.

"Hiya, doll," he said, sliding his briefcase onto the bar.

"You're wet and cold," she said. "You got caught on the subway in the water main break, didn't you?"

"Up to the knees. They shut down the local and express starting at Times Square. Then I got called to Forty-second Street: business."

"Who died?"

"Don't know. A nameless corpse with some interesting pin-striping. Is there anything left to eat? I'm starving."

"I saved you a burger. Beef. Do you mind? All the turkey sold out early."

"At this point I will even eat it raw," Donovan said as he took a seat at the bar and watched as a bottle of Kaliber was placed before him. Marcy disappeared into the kitchen, appearing two minutes later with a warmed up platter of burger and fries. The beeping of the microwave told him his longtime girlfriend still carried a torch.

"I would have something made fresh for you but the cook *just quit!*" she said, spitting the last phrase in the direction of George.

"I thought there was something in the air," Donovan said.

"I just ain't cut out for slinging hash," the tall, burly, and, despite approaching his sixtieth birthday, still-hairy bartender-turned-cook said.

"I don't serve hash," Marcy said.

"It's a figure of speech. What I mean to say is the Big Guy upstairs intended me to be a bartender, and who am I to argue?"

"He got a job downtown," Marcy said.

"You can't leave this neighborhood," Donovan said. "In case I fall down the twelve steps I'll want to see you at the bottom."

"You can visit me at the Hotsy Totsy Club. In fact, you can fall down the twelve steps there. It's the ideal place."

"My friend, the Hotsy Totsy Club went out of business in 1929."

"It's coming back."

"How?" Donovan asked, "Reincarnation?" The Times Square speakeasy, on Broadway between Fifty-fourth and Fifty-fifth streets, was owned by the legendary gambler Legs Diamond until two people were shot to death inside it—an argument over a prizefighter, the story goes—and a passel of witnesses met similar fates. The club had become a dim memory shared by historians of crime and those New Yorkers old enough to remember the Roaring Twenties.

"The place is reopening as part of the Times Square renovation project," George said. "I start next week."

Donovan swallowed a gulp of Kaliber, pretending for a moment it had a significant dose of alcohol in it. "What will it have, a wax-figure Legs Diamond propped up at the bar?"

"Maybe. I don't know. I'm only a bartender."

"The original barkeep was one of casualties of the Hotsy Totsy

Murders, along with the waiter, the cashier, and the goddamn hatcheck girl. So what are they doing, having Madame Tussaud's recreate it? Jesus, they really are building the Mall of America, Times Square Substation, down there. And I thought that was just a bad joke made by a man who was wet, cold, and hungry. Look at the lineup: Disney, MTV, Madame Tussaud's, megaspectacles such as *Casablanca: The Musical*, and, before we can all catch our breaths, *Rocky: The Musical*, and twenty or thirty sanitized ten-plexes showing G-rated features to German tourists who have come to New York because they're afraid of being gunned down in Miami.''

"Finish your burger, William," Marcy said. "Your tummy is rumbling."

"I am deeply suspicious of this whole Times Square rehab thing."

"*The Times* is all for it."

Said Donovan, "I don't suppose that could in the least be related to raising real estate values in *The Times'* neighborhood."

"You would prefer hookers?"

"You know what the city should do? Go all the way and turn all of Times Square into an actual mall. Just slap some plexiglass over the whole thing. Get Madame Tussaud's to replace the real hookers, drug sellers, and three-card monte dealers with wax-figure ones. I mean, why stop at Legs Diamond? Let's recreate that sailor and nurse who were photographed smooching on V-J Day, just prop them right up in the middle of the square. How about having Damon Runyon writing *Guys and Dolls* on a manual typewriter, itself now virtually unknown to Americans under the age of thirty; Dick Clark introducing rock bands on New Year's Eve. Let's go all the way—strew some imitation crack vials on the sidewalk. For that authentic look, hire some real homeless guys to play themselves. They'd love it. They could still lie around drinking cheap wine but this time they wouldn't get rained on. Hey, Marlowe!''

The one he called was Richard Marlowe, a white-bearded Columbia English professor and crossword-puzzle devotee who had an encyclopedic knowledge Donovan envied and tried to emulate through reading. Marlowe was also one of those Manhattan curiosities: *New York Times* buffs. These persons kept track of the comings and goings of Times reporters the way others tracked baseball players. Marlowe was sitting a little ways down the bar, finishing a puzzle.

"Twelve minutes," he said proudly, waving a Bic pen.

"To finish the *Times* puzzle? That's pretty good."

"Pretty good? Can you do better?"

"It ain't a contest to me, but one of these days I'll keep time. Tell me one thing: You read the paper cover to cover every day— you ever hear of a Lucien Schadenfreud?"

"Oh, sure. He covers pop concerts. He was the paper's folk music reviewer in the sixties and then became famous for covering Woodstock and other things of that ilk. He still does it, if you can imagine that. I know you never read the pop coverage."

"I take note of the ridiculous amount of ink given to rap," Donovan snarled.

"Why do you ask about Schadenfreud?" Marlowe asked. "Is he the body you mentioned before?"

"No. I mean, he's not dead yet. I ran into him tonight. He strikes me as being a self-destructive, alcoholic nut. But occasionally entertaining."

Marlowe brightened, saying gleefully, "Well then, invite the doomed sonofabitch up for a drink."

"I think we're all past living our lives that way," Donovan said.

"Maybe," Marcy said, plucking a french fry from Donovan's plate and feeding it to him. "But every so often it's good to remind yourself what might have been."

# THREE

## OR MAYBE HIS THREE FAVOURITE LOTTO PICKS

DONOVAN HAD PLANNED to spend the morning in his office at One Police Plaza, poring over reports from the detectives on his staff. There were thirty or forty active cases going on all over the city, invariably the ones local precinct and borough investigators found troubling for one reason or another. Often those reasons involved exotic weapons as well as bizarre or unusual circumstances. They were the high-profile cases, not the ones wherein janitors stabbed their lovers to death. Several of them interested Donovan enough to get personally involved in—that is, when he wasn't ducking his nemesis, Deputy Chief Inspector Paul Pilcrow. Pilcrow feared, not without some reason, that Donovan—who attracted reporters the way other men attracted bill collectors—would make him look bad. Donovan was so associated with high-profile cases that he was surprised and a bit irritated to find himself back in the basement of the Old Knickerbocker Theater, listening to Moskowitz explain the need for his presence.

"You got to be here to talk to this guy," Mosko said, calling up notes on his computer. The soft clicking of the keys was in sharp contrast to the grey and moldy basement, which overnight had acquired a waterlogged stench Donovan hadn't smelled since spending a wet February day poking around a corpse on a rotting Hudson River pier.

"Who is he?"

"Jack Derrida."

"Sounds familiar. Should I know about the man?"

"He owns the outfit hired to rebuild this theater. They're almost done with the job, despite the mess you see before you in the basement."

"Is he a mob guy?"

"He says no, absolutely not, couldn't be, 'how dare you defame me?' "

"He's as dirty as last week's laundry," Donovan translated.

"That's what the Organized Crime Control Bureau says. But they can't prove it."

"So what am I doing here? It's not exactly unheard of for the Mafia to be in the construction business. I have other things on my plate. The murder in Jackson Heights with the Filipinos and the chickens, for example. Did you turn up anything on the Asian body found down here last night?"

"I'm thinking the victim was an undocumented alien on the payroll of Derrida Construction. I have no proof yet, but last summer when this theater project started Derrida was picketed by the South Bronx Boys."

"The ones who came roaring down Forty-second Street with baseball bats and nine-millimeter automatics and got into a gunfight with the black group from Corona?"

"The same. It made the front page of the Post: SHOOTOUT IN TIMES SQUARE."

What had happened was that a Hispanic group had quarreled, shall we say, with a black group over who would get to extort money—in the guise of no-show jobs—out of Derrida Construction, all in the name of equal opportunity for minority construction workers. A different operation was out there now, holding up movie companies—those trying to film on the streets of New York—for no-show jobs for "disadvantaged film students." In the episode mentioned by Moskowitz, rival extortionists had fired at one another as well as at several Derrida security guards. No one had been killed, and the handful of arrests were for minor offenses. No one did hard time for his involvement in the event, which did little to dispel the perception, across the land and abroad, that the Big Apple was Dodge City incarnate. In fact, following the Forty-second-Street shootout, the mayor of the real Dodge City went on TV to brag about the old gunfight-capital's tiny per capita crime rate.

Mosko continued, "One of the beefs articulated by the South Bronx Boys was that Derrida was hiring illegals."

"From Asia?"

"From wherever."

"We've come a long way in this country when the Hispanics are complaining about illegal aliens," Donovan said. "What happened to that watch the victim was wearing?"

"I got it right here," Mosko said, pulling a small evidence bag from his jacket pocket and handing it to his boss.

"Any prints?"

"Yeah. All of them belonged to the victim."

"Did you get a match?"

Mosko shook his head. "No. If this guy ran afoul of the law, he was wearing gloves at the time. He also never applied for a job or a license—not in this city anyway—that called for fingerprinting. It's possible his prints are on file somewhere in this wide world, but they're not in any database we hook up with."

Donovan turned the watch over and over in his hands, inspecting it from every angle. Finally he used the tip of a ballpoint pen to poke at the assorted buttons, all the while watching the liquid-crystal display. In less than a minute, a long number appeared:

10 45375832648 002447

"Write this down," Donovan said, and his assistant did so.

"What is it?"

"It looks like a bank account number."

"My number isn't that long."

"It would be if you included the bank and branch code," Donovan said.

"You got that off the watch?" Mosko asked.

Donovan nodded. "This computer watch has a little memory function. It's formatted to recall important phone numbers. But the victim used it for the number I just gave you. That's all there is in memory, so it must be important."

"I'll get one of the men on it."

Donovan put the watch back in the evidence bag and returned it to Moskowitz, who reciprocated by handing the captain a bunch of photos of the unidentified body. Donovan scanned them.

"Did you get a medical opinion on that pinstriping?" Donovan asked. "Tell me it didn't come out of an auto body shop on Coney Island Avenue."

Mosko scrolled further into the file currently displayed on his notebook computer, then said, "The marks are linear icky...how do you pronounce that word?"

"*Ecky-mow-sees.* It means bruises."

"Whatever it is, the medical examiner has never seen the likes of it before. His only suggestions are abuse of some kind or a ritual involved in the death."

"Any idea how long before death those marks were made?" Donovan asked, warming to the case considerably.

"Not long before, no more than a day. The marks could have been made within the hour of death. It's impossible to tell for sure."

"So the victim could have been tortured. But what killed him?"

"He suffered blunt force trauma to his skull. But it was drowning that killed him. There are water-borne concrete dust particles—similar to those you're standing in—in his lungs."

"Any idea what the poor sonofabitch was hit with?"

Mosko bent over, picked up a red brick from a pile of them, and said, "Considering the circumstances he was found in, I would say one of these. Or several of these. I've got some men coming down here to look for the exact one."

"So what you're telling me is, there are a number of possibilities. For one: The victim was tortured, hit with a brick, and drowned after the water main broke and blasted down the wall."

Mosko picked up the thought. "Another is that the victim was abused in the comfort of his own home and merely standing on the platform waiting for a train when the water main broke, throwing him through the hole it had just made in the wall."

"And, once inside the basement of the Old Knickerbocker, he drowned," Donovan said.

"If you can think of any other possibilities..."

"Other than the chance of Bigfoot having done it, no. The most likely explanation is the second one. The victim was on the platform waiting for a train when the main broke. Adding to that likelihood is the fact the number seven IRT is the only train that comes into this platform."

"The Flushing line," Mosko said.

"Yeah, and there's a huge Asian community in Flushing. Have you been there recently? Half the store signs are in Korean or some such thing. See if you can't tie that number I gave you to a bank in those parts."

Mosko nodded, but said, "Then again, that number could be his three favorite Lotto picks."

Donovan grumbled at that very real possibility, then took advantage of the daylight that poured through the hole in Forty-second Street to illuminate the B-level basement of the Old Knickerbocker. As he did so, several strings of bare bulbs, hanging loose and netlike from the pipes and girders of the ceiling, flickered on. A new day had dawned—with a sizeable new problem in the basement—for Derrida Construction.

In the combination of artificial light and filtered sun, Donovan could see the whole of the area where the body was found. The B-level basement of the Old Knickerbocker was built around a wide hall—wide, Donovan assumed, to better permit the moving of sets and other equipment—that ran from beneath the theater entrance to beneath the stage, paralleling the center aisle. At the far end of it, he could see the stage-lifting equipment; beyond that was the freight elevator and a small Dumpster. The hall itself was used mainly to store debris, and the rest of the B-level basement— a maze of rooms large and small, interconnected in apparently random fashion—seemed to have no use at all anymore and was as dark as the labyrinth explored by Theseus. The water had broken through at the spot where the hall widened even more to form a large storage area. The few locked filing cabinets within were coated with flood debris.

The dunes of concrete dust that seemed so pervasive the night before now looked puny. Overshadowing them in the distance at the end of the hall was the massive hydraulic machinery— shrouded in plastic to keep it clean until the surrounding dust was hauled off—that would raise and lower the even bigger stage. Beyond the machinery was more rubble and, around the rim of the basement, the unaltered remains of the theater's bowels. Brick alcoves held ancient and moldy wooden crates, old steamer trunks, rusting barrels, and the remains of sets and props that might, at one point, have served Bernhardt or the Barrymores. In an ink-dark corner just down the wall from where the water had broken through, water damage had caused a section of floor to buckle, toppling several old crates.

Donovan had turned his attention to the hydraulic stage, wondering what they would lift on it—the main floor of Rick's Café Americain, he assumed, complete with Sam's piano—when Moskowitz brought over the man the captain was there to see.

Jack Derrida was a small and wiry man of forty or so years with carefully coiffed, prematurely grey hair. His skin was smooth and tanned—and the color ran well down beneath the unbuttoned front of his shirt, not just on the forearms, as was so often the case with construction men. He wore new designer jeans and an expensive black leather jacket. Donovan felt the man gave at least as much thought to his outfit as he did to his work. The jacket and several gold chains seemed, to the captain, intended to accent the tanned chest. And that told the onlooker that Derrida was in shape, and that he had enough leisure time and money to sit in the sun—for to do so in December meant going to an island.

"This is a nightmare, just a nightmare," Derrida said, after the introduction was made.

"If you're referring to *Casablanca: The Musical,* I couldn't agree more," Donovan said.

"I mean this building. It's haunted, you know."

"No doubt by the ghost of P. T. Barnum."

"Whoever."

"Tell me about this ghost. Have you seen him?"

"No. But my people talk, you know?"

"Construction guys talk about ghosts? Most of the ones I ever knew talked mainly about women."

"That too," Derrida said. "Look, they tell me this theater has a famous ghost and the ghost is responsible for all the trouble we've had."

"Such as being shot at by the South Bronx Boys?"

"Yeah, that. And the water main break. But mainly I mean all the aggravation I've gotten from the owner."

"That being Sir John Victor Holland?" Donovan said.

"Yeah, the producer. He bought the place over the summer

and—get this—wants it ready by Christmas so he can do a week's worth of previews and then open on New Year's Eve. He wants to start dress rehearsal the day after fucking tomorrow."

"This B-level basement is all I've seen of the joint, if you don't count some summer matinees 'round about 1959. Is upstairs done?"

"Basically, apart from some fixing up. Do you know how much work goes into renovating a landmark theater?"

Donovan shook his head.

"You got any idea how many fucking permits you got to fill out to get this past the Landmarks Commission?"

"A lot, I guess," Donovan said. He found himself softening toward a man he initially disliked. Anyone appalled by the volume of paperwork needed to get anything done in New York City was an ally of the captain. He asked, "Are you faithfully restoring everything?"

"Oh, you bet your ass I am. I even have a team of French art restoration experts repairing the terra-cotta beavers that decorate the first-balcony boxes. I got a group from Cornell University making sure all the animal restorations are true to the way animals looked in the seventeenth century."

One of the design elements that made the Old Knickerbocker Theater famous when it was built was the inclusion of murals and terra-cotta reliefs that showed every wild animal known to populate the isle of Manhattan in the 1600s, when Peter Minuit bought it from the Indians. There were beaver on the boxes, fox on the stairway railings, wolves and bear on the lobby walls, and eagles on the proscenium arch. The tapestries on the lobby walls romanticized the aforementioned transaction, and depicted all the animals of Manhattan looking on as the Dutch handed over the trinkets that bought them the property. With nary a thought as to whether the gesture would seem incongruous, the designers attempted to blend colonial American with classical European motifs. The immense dome of the ceiling was graced with decorations from the Sistine Chapel and illustrations of key moments in Shakespeare's dramas. Mark Antony eulogized Caesar not far from the spot where Macbeth worked, in vain, to wipe the blood from his hands.

"I got into this business because I like putting up buildings,"

Derrida said, "not to become a damn art historian. And, of course, Holland treats me like an idiot. I tell you, captain, nobody likes construction men."

"I worry more about the deconstruction men," Donovan said.

"Yeah, well, I agree with you there. Demolition guys are a strange bunch. I knew this one brownstone demolition specialist, an Irish guy who went to India when the Beatles did and studied Zen or whatever and came back to the States with a parrot on his shoulder."

"All just to be better at tearing down brownstones?" Donovan asked.

"That's the story he gave me. It was one of those yin-yang things—you gotta know how to build up to tear down. Now I suppose I got to hire a gang of these weirdos to move this crap outta here."

"Did the water do much as much damage as it looks?" Donovan asked, looking around at the mess.

"I'll tell you in a couple of hours what the damage is. But I can tell you now it will slow down renovation for a couple of days or a week while I get the sludge shoveled out and the wall bricked back up." He smiled and added, "Holland may want his dress rehearsals to start the day after tomorrow, but he sure doesn't want people just walking in free off the subway platform, you know?"

"What's the ticket price going to be for this farce? A hundred a pop?"

"You'll have to ask him," Derrida said. "I'm sure, though, that he's gonna go apeshit when he finds out I have to delay renovation because of the water main break. He'll be here in a few hours. Stick around and you can talk to the big man yourself."

"You don't like him much, do you?" Donovan asked.

Derrida gave the palms-up gesture of ambiguity seen on street corners all over the city. "I like him, I don't like him. I got to work with the guy. What can I tell you? Stick around and talk to him yourself."

Donovan said, "No, not me, thanks. I got more interesting things on my plate. Let me get down to business and then get out of here before Holland shows up. What he's got might be catching.

I'm afraid if I spend any time with him I'll wind up on Roller-blades, skating around One Police Plaza singing 'Round up the usual suspects.' " He handed Derrida the photos of the body. "Did this guy work for you?"

"Not a chance," the man said quickly.

"How can you be sure?"

"Hey, Captain, I work in construction. My men have their shirts off a lot. Anybody who showed up on the job with marks like that would spend the rest of the day explaining himself. So the bottom line is, I never saw anybody with markings like that. What the fuck are they, anyway?"

"Linear ecchymoses," Mosko said proudly.

"Come again?"

"Bruises."

"What was he, tortured?"

"It's a possibility we're looking into," Donovan said.

"So this is why the famous Captain Donovan is here in my basement?" Derrida asked. "Because of strange marks on an un-identified body?"

"That will usually get me here," Donovan said. "So tell me, where were you last night?"

"Here working until seven. Then I went home to my house in Port Washington."

"In Nassau County," Donovan said. "And there are people who can back them up when I send men around to ask them?"

"You bet."

"You're sure the man in the picture he doesn't work for you? Do you have any Asians working for you?"

"Not one. All my workers are Americans."

"Judge Ito is American," Donovan said irritably. "This is a multicultural country, and that's what makes it strong."

"I don't hire anyone of Asian descent," Derrida said, with an air of finality. "I was in Vietnam, captain. Slants make me nervous. Where were you during the war?"

Unfazed by this assault, Donovan said, "At a peace rally smoking dope with Bill Clinton. You got a problem with that?"

Either Derrida didn't have a problem with that or realized he faced an immovable object, for he shook his head and kicked idly at one of the piles of wet concrete dust. After talking with the man a while longer, Donovan decided he really disliked him after all. But the captain was known for his strong opinions and was well aware that they, plus a token, would get him a ride on the subway. He didn't make crucial decisions based on his own prejudices, just used them to amuse himself and, when he thought it might be helpful, to unnerve suspects. Derrida didn't seem particularly unnerved, and on top of it knew when to shut up, so Donovan let him go after a while. A short time after that Donovan abandoned the case—once and for all, he was sure—as insufficiently interesting or challenging. He headed south to his office, where he would spend an uneventful week.

# FOUR

## THE FLETCHING LOOKED BRAND NEW

IF THERE WAS one thing he missed about his old, cramped office over the Chinese restaurant and the donut shop on upper Broadway, it was the steaming, clanking radiator to which he occasionally handcuffed difficult suspects. This practice didn't exactly qualify as suspect-torture, at least not sufficiently to stand up in court (although several defense attorneys raised the matter). Rather, Donovan's favorite ploy served to bring those high-and-mighty among the lowlife down to earth—almost literally. For to be handcuffed to the radiator meant having either to sit on the floor or to bend low while seated in a chair. And it also required that a man thus shackled be ever vigilant, in winter, in order to avoid being burned by the hot pipes. (In other words, no dozing off.) In summer, the bent-over position forced the suspect's nose close enough to the wide-open window to enable the suspect to see, on the sidewalk one floor below, the freedom being denied.

There was no radiator in Donovan's new office on the twelfth floor of One Police Plaza. The automatically controlled climate was produced as if by magic from vents in the ceiling that made no noise at all. It was cool in summer and warm in winter. The window didn't open even a crack, and from that height you could scarcely see the sidewalk at all. There was a Chinese restaurant down there, however—a particularly good place, One Police Plaza being on the borderline between Chinatown and the municipal district. And when Donovan looked out the window, he had a magnificent view of the East River, including the Brooklyn and Manhattan bridges. In the morning the sun rose over Long Island and Donovan could watch jetliners from around the world make their approaches to Kennedy and La Guardia airports. At night the moon—and those brighter stars lucky enough to shine through the hole in the ozone layer—looked in on the gleaming computer screen atop Donovan's desk.

Some years back Donovan had given up drinking himself to death, calling it a lost cause. His constitution had proved too strong to allow him the traditional self-immolation that, for a long time, he felt was his due. He had never been a heavy drinker as a young man, but after his father—also a prominent policeman—was murdered, Donovan had given in to the temptation the Irish often write off with the phrase, "the poor man has a fondness for the whiskey." To Donovan, that seemed to suggest not an evil but a choice—like preferring the day to the night, or cold cereal to oatmeal.

But at an average of twenty dollars per night the drinking life was costing upwards of six hundred dollars a month, eating up Donovan's money and wasting countless hours that could otherwise be spent in accomplishing things—such as being promoted to captain, getting a citywide command and, maybe one day, tracking down his father's murderer. Learning was another passion long overlooked. So Donovan abandoned the bottle and started building his career and his library.

He spent the hours he once wasted propped on bar stools prowling the bookshops of Manhattan and patronizing the many used book vendors who lined Broadway on the Upper West Side. He also turned a onetime suspicion of computers into another passion. Books lined the shelves and monitors glistened in both his downtown and home offices, and the notebook computer he carried in his briefcase was capable of communicating with his other PCs by way of a cellular modem. While some at police headquarters thought the latter gadget made Donovan a techno-cop, the captain liked pointing out he got the modem after seeing it advertised on TV during the Superbowl.

"I don't see why the Chief of Special Investigations for the City of New York can't be as well equipped as some yuppie who wants to fax the office from the Hamptons," he told the commissioner when he bought the equipment for Moskowitz and himself.

No, it was not the sudden infusion of technology that gave Donovan pause. It was the loss of the steaming, clanking radiator. No longer, after nabbing someone, could he issue his famous, if only half-meant command: "Kick the shit out of him and cuff him to the radiator in my office."

That was a phrase he picked up from his father, who issued it often and meant it. In embracing midlife sobriety and by dedicating his off-duty hours to the pursuit of knowledge, Donovan intended, one day, to solve the crime that had so altered the course of his life. He worked on the old file detailing his father's murder, using computer links as well as personal contacts, when he got the chance. It was a lonely pursuit conducted after midnight. And, considering Donovan's new position as chief of special investigations, it was a pursuit frequently interrupted.

This Tuesday night, the twelfth of December, was one of those occasions. After leaving Moskowitz behind at a stakeout near the Bronx Terminal Market, Donovan went over reports from his detectives in the field. The Filipino matter was stalled. The three bodies found floating in Arthur Kill, Staten Island, were apparently unrelated. The mysterious disappearance of two teenagers who had been riding the Cyclone at Coney Island had some cult aspects that made it more than usually interesting, however, and Donovan pored over that file until well after seven in the evening. He had ordered lunch in from the corner deli but wanted something hot for dinner. Consequently, by nine he had finished a plate of grilled chicken with grits, accompanied by a health salad, and was having a cup of tea with Marcy at her restaurant when his cellular phone beeped ominously.

"I guess this means I'm sleeping alone tonight," Marcy said.

Donovan answered the phone, listened for a moment, then said, "Give me half an hour," and ended the conversation.

Marcy said, "Let me have a man such as sleeps o' nights. You think too much. And work too hard. Where are you going now?"

"Back to the Old Knickerbocker. Sorry."

"I thought that case was over, as far as you were concerned."

"Apparently it refuses to die. I better get down there."

"What are you doing, auditioning for the part of Rick?"

Donovan stood and pulled on his suit jacket. "I can't sing or dance. But I could really deliver that line about all the gin joints in all the world. If Sir John Victor Holland wants to build a show around one sentence, I'm his man.''

"What happened that you have to go back?" Marcy asked.

"There's been another death. This one unquestionably murder.''

"Was the body also pin-striped?''

"I didn't ask, but I think Mosko would have mentioned it.''

"Who's the stiff?''

"A guy the contractor brought in to clean up the B-level basement. He was shot in the heart.''

"How ordinary," Marcy said.

"With a crossbow," Donovan added.

THE BODY was spread-eagled across an old wooden packing crate and looked very much like a mannequin that was intentionally put there, by a stage designer, to create a dramatic effect. It was off to the right of the hole the water main break had made in the wall. In the week that had passed since Donovan last visited the spot, that hole had been covered by four-by-eight-foot plywood sheets in preparation for being rebricked. The wet grey debris Donovan had been forced to walk around the week before was gone, swept up and carted off by a small army of hands hired in the desperate attempt to get the theater open and the production started on schedule.

This time he entered the theater not from the subway platform, but more conventionally, through the loading dock in the back of the building that faced Forty-first Street.

The strings of lights that illuminated the long and broad hall had been augmented by several others. The sheets of plastic that covered the stage elevator machinery were gone, and Donovan could better see the massive hydraulics designed to carry entire sets to and from the stage. The stage was up in place at that moment, as a result of which the sleek steel tubes that were the main vertical elements of the elevator gleamed at the end of the hall. Donovan was reminded of the lifts in auto repair shops— multiplied by a factor of ten, big enough to raise and lower a house.

Several detectives, a handful of uniformed policemen, and two or three forensic technicians—led by the redoubtable crime-scene guru Howard Bonaci—buzzed around the corpse. The victim was twenty-something and wore faded jeans over steel-toed Doc Martens. His muscular chest was covered by a white Camels T-shirt, the front of which was soaked with blood that poured from around the protruding shaft of the arrow. That gruesome dart stuck straight up toward one of the bare lightbulbs that hung from the cobweblike wires. About three inches of arrow and two stabilizing black feathers protruded from the chest wall.

"Who is he?" Donovan asked Moskowitz.

"George Mooney of Inwood."

"Ginwood," Donovan said, acknowledging the nickname of the old Irish neighborhood that sits atop the northern tip of Manhattan.

"That's the place. He's twenty-two and lives with his cousin on Broadway and Two-hundred-fifteenth Street."

Said Donovan, "You go the length of Manhattan, from Wall Street to Ginwood, and you can't get away from Broadway. I seem to have lived my life along it."

"Mooney is a native of County Tyrone, Ireland."

"He's an Orangeman."

"As in a fan of Syracuse?"

"As in someone from Northern Ireland. Which doesn't make him a bad person. Maybe a little battle-scarred."

"He's a lot more than that now," Mosko said, pointing a corner of his notebook computer in the direction of the arrow.

"Tell me about that arrow," Donovan said. "Crossbows are out of my area of expertise."

"But not for long. By midnight you'll be on the Internet talking to the world's leading authority. Am I right?"

"I had other plans for the evening, but they seem to be as dead as this gentleman here. You're a bright lad, Brian Moskowitz."

"I don't know *bupkes* about crossbows," Mosko said, his words and inflection unmistakably Brooklyn. "That info came from Bonaci."

"Bonaci!" Donovan called, and presently his crime-scene chief showed himself.

"How you doing, Cap?" he asked.

"Howard, my son, tell me about crossbows."

"They're medieval instruments, but date back to Roman times.

Lately there's been a boom in sport-hunting models and crossbows for use in medieval tournaments.''

"Is this arrow from one of those?" Donovan asked.

Bonaci shook his head. "I don't think so. For one thing, it looks short. And old.''

"It's a lot shorter yet than a regular arrow. That I can see myself. Unless, of course, this particular one goes right through the dear departed and into that packing crate.''

"It doesn't," Bonaci said. "Once we get it removed—the mex wants us to transport the body with the arrow still in it—I'll give you a better assessment of its age.''

The "mex" was the medical examiner.

Bonaci continued, "This arrow definitely has a few years on it. The fletching looks new, though.''

"The who?" Mosko asked.

"The fletching," Donovan said. "The feathers. A fletcher is a man who puts the feathers on arrows. Why don't you read more?''

" 'Cause I work for a walking encyclopedia; who needs to read?" Mosko said.

"So the late Mr. Mooney was killed by a crossbow, the arrow of which may be a few years old. Tell me more. You were going to say something about that packing crate?''

"Yeah, he wasn't killed on top of it. He fell there after being shot off a stepladder we had to take away to get at the body.''

Bonaci pointed out taped marks on the stone floor.

Mosko said, "Mooney was assigned to the detail that was stringing up lights across the ceiling.''

He pointed up and Donovan followed with his eyes, noting both the recently suspended work lights and the strips of old asbestos fireproofing that hung, carcinogenic ribbons, around them.

"He must have been standing on the third step of the ladder when he got shot," Bonaci said. "That's about the only way he could have landed where he did.''

Donovan eyeballed the site, circling the body atop the box and peering both at it and at the tape marks on the floor.

"Where's the ladder?" he asked at last.

"Over against the wall.''

"Are you done with it, evidence-wise?''

"We're done with it. We printed it and photographed the blood-spatter pattern. You want to finish stringing up the lights?"

"Get the ladder and set it up again."

Bonaci did as he was told. The captain peered at the ladder, the blood spatters, and the body, circling the latter again, both clockwise and counterclockwise. He climbed up to the second, then the third step of the ladder, all the while making frequent glances back at the body behind and below him. He also reached up to touch the electric wires.

Then he got back down and peered through the rungs of the ladder.

"I see where you're going with this," Mosko said.

"Good lad. Mooney looks about my height."

"He's six feet even," Bonaci said.

"Close enough. To get shot in the heart while standing on that ladder and to fall back the way he did he would have to have been on the second, not the third step. That means the arrow had to come between the rungs of the ladder, coming from there."

He pointed to the dark corner he had noted the week before, the ink-dark corner where water damage had caused a section of floor to buckle. Despite the amazing work done elsewhere in cleaning up the B-level, several old crates remained topsy-turvy and untouched.

"Get me a flashlight," Donovan said.

After a moment, one was produced. He took it and made a cursory examination of the inky nook, peering around crates and at the stone floor where it had been partly torn up by the water. There were several oddities—small stones that either had fallen out of a crate or had been carried in from outside, and what looked like the remains of old, dried flowers. Donovan pocketed one of the stones.

"Did you look for evidence here?" he called back to Bonaci, who remained with Moskowitz by the body.

"Yeah. There's nothing."

"Who is Milos the Magnificent?"

"One of the czars?" Mosko called back.

"Sorry I asked. It was a name on two of those crates."

"Maybe some old show guy."

"No doubt," Donovan said, returning to the others and giving back the flashlight. He added, "Not only did that shot come from that corner, it hit the victim when his chest—the target—was in shadow. I looked down when I was atop that ladder and noticed the area in question was in darkness."

"That was an impressive shot," Mosko agreed.

"Were there any witnesses when Mooney got killed?"

"Not one. Mooney was finishing up in this area and was running behind the rest of his shift. He shouted when he was shot and made a noise when he landed, and the rest of his crew came running."

"Guess who was among them?" Mosko said, gesturing with his left hand to get Jack Derrida to come over.

The contractor had just walked down the hall, appearing wilted in comparison with the week before. His previously well-groomed look had given way to a dose of exasperation. By the time he got to Donovan, his hands were already gesturing, palms-up.

"What does a guy have to do?" he exclaimed. "I'm trying to make an honest living..."

"And it's proving to be harder than the textbooks would have you believe, right?"

"No shit, Sherlock. I tell you, you can blame this on the ghost."

"Him again," Donovan said.

"My men didn't want to come down here at night to begin with. They sure don't want to now. And these ain't superstitious guys, Captain. This place is spooky, I tell you."

Donovan pointed at the body. "Did you know this man?"

"I know I hired him the other day. He's a union carpenter..."

"Born in Ireland."

"... who had a green card. He's no illegal alien, Captain. You can't get me on that one."

"Tell me what happened tonight. Are you the one who found the body?"

"Yeah, that was me. My foreman—Del Wilcox—and a few of the guys were right behind me, though. Mooney was staying behind, finishing up. We had B-level hallways and other open areas all cleaned up with the exception of that corner."

He indicated the black nook Donovan had just finished glancing at. Then Donovan said, "This basement is big enough to hide an infantry batallion in. You cleaned up all of it since last week?"

"We did the areas that are important to us—this hall, the big room where the stage lift machinery is, and a few storage areas."

"How many rooms are there down here?" Donovan asked.

"Dozens. Most of them are filled with junk. Some are still locked and have been for years. When we think we're going to need one we open it and clean it out. But you got to understand, Captain: This is a new project that's going top-speed. We don't have time to make it all neat and pretty."

Donovan stared suspiciously at the dark nook from which the arrow had come. "I agree with your men," Donovan said. "I wouldn't be caught alone here at night if I had a S.W.A.T. team and an armload of Uzis."

"I told Mooney to finish running the work lights over there so we could see better to finish the job," Derrida continued. "The rest of us were sitting back by the stage hydraulics. We had a coffee station set up there. A few of us went upstairs to watch the rehearsal."

"The rehearsals have started already?" Donovan asked. "There's a body in the basement—there's been two bodies in the basement, in all, something of a record for Broadway—and Sir John Victor Holland is upstairs singing and dancing?"

"He isn't doing it now. They finished for the day an hour before you got here. The man wants to have his grand premiere on New Year's Eve, and that's only two weeks off. What can I tell you? So anyway, I was having a cup of coffee when I heard this shout and this crash. I ran down the hall—like I said, with some of my men behind me—and found Mooney on top of that crate, where you see him."

"Did you see anyone else? Did you see who did it?"

Derrida shook his head. "There wasn't anyone else," he said.

"The killer had to be down here someplace," Mosko insisted.

"But where?" Donovan asked. He scanned the area one more time. He noted the assortment of shoe- and bootprints and eyeballed in particular the heavy plywood sheeting nailed up to cover the hole in the wall.

There were shrugs all around from his men, a few of whom were poking around the storage area looking for escape routes.

"How many ways are there out of this level?" Donovan asked.

Mosko said, "Three. The first is the stairs you came down just before from the backstage area."

"Which my men were using," Derrida said quickly.

"The second is the stage lift."

"Which was in the up position," the construction chief said.

"And then the freight elevator. There's a passenger elevator, too, but the renovation work on it hasn't been finished yet."

"And where is the freight elevator?" Donovan asked.

"At the far end of the hall behind the stage lift."

"Where was that elevator when Mooney was shot?" Donovan asked.

"On the fifth floor," Derrida said.

"What's there?"

"Executive offices and Peter Minuit's Penthouse."

"Which is?"

"A restaurant and bar with an open-air brick terrace overlooking Forty-second Street. We finished the renovation on it two weeks ago."

"Thoughtful of you to do the bar first," Donovan said idly.

"Holland likes to have a drink now and then."

"To drown his guilty conscience, I guess."

"It's eleven already," Derrida said, checking his watch. "He's probably having one now."

"Tell me how you know the elevator was on the fifth floor if you were having coffee by the stage lift at the time."

Derrida paused to think, then after a moment said, "I guess I don't. I mean, it wasn't on any of the bottom three levels. Holland rode it up to five just before the murder, and I assume it stayed there."

"How many levels are there in this joint?"

"Seven."

"Let's hear what the floors are—from the top down," Donovan said.

"Five: executive offices and Minuit's Penthouse. Four: top balcony. Three: middle balcony and cheaper boxes. Two: lower balcony and fancy boxes. One: main lobby, orchestra, dressing rooms.''

"That leaves you with two levels to go and only one basement.''

"The basement is divided in two. Basement one, above us—the A-level—is where the moveable stage goes when it's in the down position. Also on that level are shops and dressing rooms. We stand in the B-level. It's for hydraulics and storage these days. My understanding is this lower level was also used for dressing rooms during the theater's vaudeville days.''

"So the stage elevator never comes all the way down here?'' Donovan asked.

"How could it? You got to put the hydraulics somewhere below it.''

Donovan nodded, feeling a bit stupid for not having realized that. Then he said, "We've got to look in all these rooms. Let's get them open one way or another.''

"I'm no detective, but it looks to me the only way out of here for the killer was past me and my men,'' Derrida said.

"You don't mind if we unlock some of these rooms along the hall just the same, do you?''

"Be my guest.''

Donovan told Bonaci to bring in the police locksmith to work with his counterpart on Derrida's payroll. Each door in the B-level would be opened and the rooms searched and photographed. It would take the rest of the night, so Donovan moved on to other matters.

"Did you check out Mooney before you hired him?''

"Hell, no. My crew chief made sure he had a union card and a green card and that was all I cared about.''

Donovan thanked Derrida for his help and let him go. The man returned to the work of supervising the renovation, which continued unabated on the upper floors.

"What did you find out about Mooney?'' Donovan asked Moskowitz.

"Not much. He was fingerprinted by Immigration and that's it. No run-ins with the law I'm aware of.''

"No IRA connection? No bad debts? No cuckolded husbands running around out there with crossbows?"

"He was twenty-two. Just a kid. Only in the country a short time. Not a lot of chance to make enemies. But we'll check it out in the morning."

"See if you can find any connection to the Asian victim," Donovan said.

"What connection did you have in mind? He was killed with a brick. The report is on your desk."

"I read it this morning. The M.E. couldn't pinpoint the murder weapon itself; only knew that it was at least an inch wide and probably wider. The dirt particles found in the wound included brick, so the M.E. went along with your idea that a brick was the murder weapon."

"They must have been flying all around during that water main break," Mosko said.

"Yeah, but we never found one with blood on it. The victim could have been killed by a Louisville Slugger or a two-by-four. There is only one definite thing. Our still-unidentified Asian victim was hit over the head and drowned. Listen to me: A killer who uses an elegant weapon like a crossbow ain't likely to beat someone over the head. But I don't suppose there are hard and fast rules about these things."

"We're ready to haul the body to the morgue, boss," Bonaci said, arriving at the head of a handful of coroner's men.

Donovan nodded and watched as the body was zipped into a bag and loaded onto a stretcher. The arrow made the black plastic stick up, and the whole arrangement looked something like a pup tent.

"It seems to me when you go out of your way to kill someone with a crossbow you're trying to make a point," Donovan said.

"What point would that be?" Mosko asked.

"I'll tell you when I catch the guy that did it."

Mosko looked up sharply from his notebook. It had been a while since the captain had seemed so interested in a case.

"So this is the case you're going to take personally?" Mosko said.

Donovan nodded, then said, "Where can I find out more about this ghost?"

"Don't tell me you believe in that stuff," Mosko said, although he was not entirely surprised by his boss's interest in the matter. It was common knowledge around headquarters the cases involving weird suspects and exotic weapons didn't land on Donovan's desk entirely by accident.

"Not for a minute," he said. "But ghosts can walk through walls, can't they?" And Donovan looked warily at the dark and brooding walls that had been sitting largely undisturbed for nearly a century.

# FIVE

## A JUGGLING PIANO PLAYER,
## A HEAD-HUNTING SAVAGE, AND A CRAZY SERB
## WHO SHOT APPLES OFF PEOPLES' HEADS

AN HOUR HAD PASSED uneventfully. It was midnight. Donovan's men had begun opening doors along the hallway that must, he thought, have served as the killer's escape route. At least two dozen doors, all unmarked or bearing handwritten paper signs made illegible by age and the seepage of water from the ceiling pipes, lined the corridor that began by the stage hydraulics and ended in the storage area that had already given up two bodies. These were black metal doors that were, in some cases, reinforced with steel crossbeams. Not even the layers of rust and a few generations' worth of dirt and mold could hide the original designers' intention to provide security.

"Whoever built these wanted to keep people out," said the police locksmith as Donovan, ever fascinated with old, locked doors, peered over his shoulder.

"Or else wanted to keep something in," the captain said, his hand slipping unconsciously to his Smith & Wesson.

"Here goes the first one," the technician said, removing the cylinder from the lock and manually opening it.

The door cawed like a crow as it pulled open. Another policeman shined a large flashlight into the black interior, which was heavy with dust and mildew. Packing crates like the one Mooney had died upon filled the room, leaving only space for a two-footwide passage that led to the back wall. Donovan took the flashlight and shined it around, picking up the body of a rat, mummified by age, against the back wall.

He pulled his fingertips away from his revolver and stepped into the room. Dust puffed up beneath every footstep and ancient cobwebs tickled his face. He said, "One of these days I have got to get that degree in archaeology."

To which Mosko replied, "You never even went to college."

"Me and the president were elsewise engaged those days." Donovan shined the flashlight on the packing crates, then pulled a handkerchief from his jacket pocket and wiped the dirt off the label on one of them.

"Who the hell is Ragtime Willie?" he asked.

The response was shrugs all around.

"Another vaudevillian, I guess. Never mind, I can access the bibliography of the Performing Arts Museum and look him up."

Donovan turned the flashlight onto the wall behind the crate and found, to his delight, that the surface was covered with tacked-up, yellowing press clips.

He recited an old headline: "HE TICKLES THE IVORIES WITH TEN PINS."

"Say again?" Mosko replied, stepping cautiously into the room and bringing another flashlight beam to bear on the wall.

Donovan leaned closer to the clipping and brushed more dust from it. "Apparently, Ragtime Willie played piano while juggling bowling pins."

"Neat trick. Guys used to get paid for doing this sort of thing way back then?"

"Sure, and not even that long ago. Do you remember the 'Ed Sullivan Show'? No, of course you don't."

"He was on TV before David Letterman, right?"

"Don't quit your day job, kid," Donovan said. "This clip is from the *New York Graphic*. That paper went out of business a long time ago. I think it was the one that covered Rudolph Valentino's funeral by posing someone in a coffin and taking a picture of him. Those were the days. Men were men, women were women, suspects were scum, and reporters never let the truth stand in the way of a good story."

"You wouldn't have lasted a minute," Mosko said.

"If that's your way of saying I think too much, you're probably right. Let's open the next storage room and see what's in there. Somehow I doubt a juggling piano player is our homicidal ghost."

It took less time, only fifteen minutes or so, to open the adjacent door. This room was notably smaller than the previous one—despite appearing, from the outside, to be as large. That gave Donovan pause, and he looked at the inside and outside walls with furrowed brow.

Noting the consternation, Moskowitz asked, "What's the matter, boss?"

"Did you ever watch 'Dr. Who?' " Donovan asked, scratching his head.

"He's a wrestler, right? Had a grudge match with Jake the Snake last year."

Now Donovan shook his head. "He's a character in British science fiction. I catch him on late-night cable every so often."

"My wife hates science fiction. She says it makes her nervous. The only way I got to rent *Predator*—you know, the Schwartzenegger movie—was to tell her it was a *National Geographic* special. When she goes to bed early I turn on 'Star Trek' reruns, but that's about it. So why are we talking about this doctor?"

"He's a time traveler," Donovan said. "On the outside, his space ship is a London police call box. Call it a big phone booth. But on the inside it's as big as Buckingham Palace. The explanation involves spatial displacement or the like."

"Spatial displacement," Mosko said blankly.

"This room is spatially displaced, but in reverse. It's bigger on the outside than on the inside."

"I know what you mean. My first apartment was like that."

Donovan shrugged, then tired of exercising that group of muscles and stepped into the room. Instead of packing crates he found orange crates, or something like them. Piled up were large, slatted wooden containers plastered with dirty markings that listed exotic place names: Sarawak, Sulawesi, Java, and Bali. The crates appeared to contain clothes and trinkets. Three fake palm trees, complete with wooden coconuts, were crammed in at an angle. Donovan was peering at them when he heard Mosko suck in his breath and then gasp, "Jesus Christ!"

Donovan wheeled toward the sound to see Mosko gawking, hand on revolver, at a display of shrunken heads. The six brownish-yellow, softball-size heads were hung by the hair from a plank that had been covered with Spanish moss and suspended from the ceiling. The dust and cobwebs that coated the stage props made them look like the mummified cats sometimes found in Egyptian tombs.

Donovan used his hankie to wipe off another sign. "sabah, THE WILD MAN OF BORNEO," he read.

"This is what people did before there was television, right? So tell me how bad the box is."

"This basement is a museum of cheap thrills," Donovan said. "If the rest of the storage rooms are like these two, Holland will move the contents right upstairs and install them in the mall."

"The mall? Oh, the one they should build over the whole of Times Square."

"Madame Tussaud's will buy the whole lot," Donovan said, giving the oddly sized room another once-over before retreating to the relative comfort of the hallway.

He got there in time to meet Derrida, who came down the hall reeking of vodka and looking sweetly satisfied for the first time since the captain met him.

"Yo, Captain," he said, "Whatcha find?" He was drunk as a New Amsterdam skunk that had just finished a guilder's worth of Dutch beer. He glanced at the open door, but without seeing anything inside. That was good, for his sake, Donovan thought.

"A juggling piano player and a head-hunting savage," Donovan answered jauntily.

"That's great," Derrida replied, paying not the slightest bit of attention.

"I see the sun has gone over the yardarm."

"At last."

"And almost certainly in Peter Minuit's Penthouse."

"You caught me red-handed, officer," Derrida said, extending his wrists in parallel as if to be handcuffed.

"How is Doctor Faustus tonight?" Donovan asked.

"Who's that?"

"Sir John."

"Oh. Sir John is dandy. His word, not mine." Derrida smiled and said, "He wants you to come up for a drink."

"Why would I want to do that?" Donovan asked.

"Because he says he can tell you all about the ghost that haunts this theater."

Mosko rolled his eyes. Donovan smiled, though, and clapped Derrida on the shoulder. "As long as he promises not to make a musical out of it," Donovan said, and headed off toward the elevator.

PETER MINUIT'S PENTHOUSE contributed its own colorful heritage to the lore of the Old Knickerbocker. The Penthouse was built, those many years ago, to serve as an outdoor tea room and forum for light entertainments. In those days, it looked down on most of midtown Manhattan and served light fare to theatergoers and socialites. It became a speakeasy during Prohibition, its rooftop location and single passenger elevator allowing good, early warning of police raids. During the late 1930s and for a while after World War II, the facility was a swing club, featuring the top dance bands of the era.

When the Old Knickerbocker bottomed out and showed pornographic films, the rooftop club opened for a time as an adult sex club. But again the aging building's physical limitations were felt. In addition to having but a single passenger elevator, the Old Knickerbocker was woefully short on ladies' rooms. (In the 1890s and the first decade of the twentieth century, it was considered bad form for a woman to go to the bathroom outside her home.) So in the 1970s the Peter Minuit room finally followed the example of its namesake and died.

Following Derrida's renovation, however, the room appeared in its original splendor—one that repeated the nature motifs seen in the theater itself. The long mahogany bar was decorated with carved beaver; trout swam above the back bar mirror, while round, white, wrought-iron chairs and tables shared the outdoor terrace with potted spruce and holly. A stuffed bear reared menacingly, fangs and claws at the ready, by the fireplace, which roared comfortingly. Above the mantelpiece loomed the head and antlers of a bull moose.

"This would be a great place for an NRA rally," Donovan said to the thin functionary who pointed him in the direction of the producer. Dressed in a white cashmere sweater over a black turtleneck and black jeans, the aide offered in reply only a sort of hoot that sounded, to the captain, like derision.

Sir John Victor Holland was thin himself, and tall to boot. He had the pasty white skin of an Englishman who had devoted his entire life to indoor pursuits. That complexion contrasted with a black silk Italian suit worn over a white-on-white formal shirt, open necked, which was decorated with a string tie. A prominent Adam's apple bobbed up and down with every sip of scotch—served, as Donovan might have expected, at room temperature. Holland sat staring into the fire, his narrow frame halfway disappearing into a plush black leather easy chair, one of a pair that flanked a round cocktail table.

Donovan walked over and introduced himself. Holland didn't shake hands, but waggled his glass and pointed a slender fingertip at the flames.

"He's in there, you know."

"Who is?"

"The ghost. I'm very intuitive about such things, and I heard you expressed interest in him, so maybe you are, too. You can see him in the flames."

"Is that really why you invited me up here?"

"You don't believe in ghosts, do you, Captain?"

"Show me one who's capable of winding, aiming, and shooting a crossbow and I'm a believer. Can I sit down? It's been a long couple of hours."

At that, the man showed the first sign of animation during the encounter. He rose halfway out of the chair and, after giving Donovan a limp and clammy handshake, said, "John Holland. Pleased to meet you."

"Bill Donovan."

"My contractor tells me you're a man to be reckoned with in this city. Why haven't we met before?"

"Probably because this is your first murder. It is your first, isn't it?"

"Most assuredly. That poor man, Mooney. And the Asian chap also, of course. But I know nothing about him. Mooney worked for my contractor, as you know. That's really all I know about him, actually. Killed with a crossbow, was he?"

"So it would seem."

"That's grotesque. I need another drink." He drained his glass to prove it and, by waving it in the air again, summoned his aide. "Anton, another scotch please, and something for the captain. What's your pleasure, Captain?"

"Kaliber."

"And who makes that?"

"Guinness."

"Do we have Kaliber, Anton?"

"We have everything," the man replied.

"A bottle, please."

When the man left, Holland sank back into his chair. Donovan sat on the edge of his. Holland said, "Have you heard of the ghost of Barton Hill?"

Donovan hadn't.

"That's in York. Do you know anything about Yorkshire?"

"I've had one of their dogs and several of their puddings. What about the ghost of Barton Hill?"

"He was a fifteenth-century Englishman named Walter Courtenay, a distant cousin of the Archbishop of Canterbury who was an expert at the longbow. You do know about the English longbow?"

Donovan nodded and thanked Anton for his beer, which arrived in a crystal glass. He said, "It won the battle of Agincourt. Changed history. Ended the age of chivalry. Made for a memorable half hour on The Learning Channel."

Holland continued, "While he was fighting in France in 1415, his ancestral home at Barton Hill was taken by a rival. He got home to find his land stolen and his wife murdered. He challenged the villain to a duel, but before it could happen was slain in the night by the man's agents."

"And you've never trusted agents ever since," Donovan said.

"Very good, Captain. You have a sense of humor, not to mention a basic knowledge of show business. I should offer you a part."

"I can't sing or dance."

"Neither can Elena Jordan, one of the stars of my show, but that didn't stop her agent from holding me up for a million dollars," Holland said, his tone turning catty. "Please don't tell her I said that. The poor woman is a nervous wreck trying to get her voice in shape for Broadway."

"We never talk shop," Donovan said, sinking a bit into his chair. Holland didn't seem so bad, the captain thought. At least he's easy to talk to. One of Donovan's guiding principles was if you keep a suspect talking long enough—about anything, really—eventually he'll say something revealing. Donovan knew that was also a guiding principle of psychoanalysis—one that fit in with his long-held belief that shrinks and detectives were two sides of the same coin. He added, "Let me guess: Walter Courtenay became the ghost of Barton Hill, returning every so often to haunt the descendants of the man who killed him."

"Close, but no cigar. He does return, but not to seek vengeance against a particular family. He haunts the site where his house once stood, appearing whenever something happens to disturb it. Several other homes were built there, but the owners always fled once faced with Courtenay's presence. Two men were killed—a real estate agent, and a construction foreman on a highway the government built through the land once people gave up trying to build houses on it. In both cases, the murder weapon was a longbow."

"That's a hefty weapon for a ghost," Donovan allowed. "And hard to conceal as well."

"It surely is. But no suspect was ever caught, so it must be the ghost that's doing it. Well, that's my story of the ghost of Barton Hill."

"Are you suggesting Walter Courtenay is loose in the basement of the Old Knickerbocker?"

"Of course not. This is a different ghost. Only the M.O. is similar. Have you heard the name Milos the Magnificent?"

"I saw it on a packing crate recently."

"That's the man. His stuff was stored on the B-level. I went down there myself and saw the crates."

"Who was he?" Donovan asked.

"Milos Tryvomanic, a thoroughly mad Serb who came to this country after a member of his family was instrumental in starting World War I. He fancied himself a Serbian nobleman, a descendant of the warrior who claimed the title of 'King of Bosnia and Serbia' during the fourteenth century."

"But his blue blood wasn't."

"Precisely. He was, in reality, a Sarajevo music hall entertainer—a trick shot with the crossbow."

"Crossbow?" Donovan asked, his brow furrowing.

"Indeed. Tryvomanic was very good with the weapon. He used to shoot apples off the heads of audience members, among other tricks, on stage as well as out there, on the terrace."

"How and when did he die?" Donovan asked.

"In 1933, at the height of the Depression. He had fallen in love in late middle-age. It hit him quite hard, according to the stories. His fiancée was a young chorus girl from Iowa who stood nearly six inches taller than him. They were just planning their wedding when the accident occurred."

"Accident?"

"The original stage lift had immense machinery that included a gigantic turnscrew. Milos's trademark white scarf became caught in it and he was dragged into the works."

Donovan winced.

"Think of being sucked into a meat grinder. There was barely enough of the poor man to bury, but they reconstructed his corpse and did it nonetheless. They buried him in the basement, by the way."

Donovan nearly choked on his beer. "In the basement. You're kidding me."

"Not in the least," Holland replied.

"How did they get permission to bury someone in the basement of a Broadway theater?"

"Well, remember the Old Knickerbocker had fallen from grace rather severely, and was then an aging vaudeville house. In addition, Milos had done quite well financially and bought himself an equity stake."

"He owned a piece of the theater?"

"Only ten percent, but that was enough to get him buried in the basement."

"Did you have to pay anything to his estate when you bought the building?" Donovan asked.

"What estate?" Holland laughed. "The man was a vaudeville performer who died sixty years ago, leaving no heirs. The theater subsequently went through a succession of owners, and I bought it from the last one. They owned clear title."

Donovan twirled his beer around in his glass, then said, "You mentioned Milos shot apples off peoples' heads on the terrace?" He nodded in that direction.

"Oh yes, the original terrace was much more extensive than the modest recreation outside. When first built, it had two levels, a waterfall and fish pond, a Dutch windmill, and an aviary that held several thousand songbirds."

"A windmill," Donovan said.

"My understanding is, it was fake," Holland said.

"Like so much around here," Donovan replied, growing weary of the conversation. A crazy Serb who shot apples off peoples' heads for a living and was buried in the basement after being turned into ground meat by the old stage machinery wasn't his idea of an interesting ghost. To him, decent ghosts were victims of the Spanish Inquisition or Indian war chiefs whose sacred gravesites were disturbed by twentieth-century builders. And ghosts Donovan could entertain the notion of believing in howled in the night or, at the most, rustled the curtains on still October eves. They didn't assassinate passers-by with crossbows. The whole thing was ridiculous, Donovan thought, and he was ridiculous for listening to Holland's yarn. There could be only one reason for Sir John Victor Holland's interest in the gentleman buried on the B-level.

"So who gets the role?" Donovan asked.

"Which role is that?" Holland asked, a bit thrown by the change in the direction of the conversation.

"The role of Milos the Magnificent."

Holland smiled. "You are a good detective. I am thinking of Hugh Grant. I'm sure he can do a Serbian accent but have no idea if he can sing."

"Doesn't matter," Donovan said. "Neither can Elena Jordan. And he'll love the nightlife on Ninth Avenue. Have you written the script yet?"

"No. This is only in the development stage. I consider Milos the Magnificent to be mainly an interesting, serendipitous find I got when I bought the building. My main interest now is to get *Casablanca: The Musical* opened on New Year's Eve. You will help me, won't you?''

"You want me to help you?"

"I want you to find the person who killed two people in my basement.''

"I thought you were sure Milos killed Mooney," Donovan said.

"Milos makes for amusing conversation. Maybe he will make me another hit musical, but no more. Find me the real person who used a crossbow to kill Mooney and a whatever to kill the other chap. Do not let this unfortunate crime interfere with my plans to reinvigorate the Old Knickerbocker. We start paid previews next week. Already thousands of tickets have been sold.''

Donovan finished his beer, and said, "You're about to remind me how important the successful rebirth of this theater is to the City of New York, which pays my salary.''

"I see you understand perfectly," Holland laughed. "Think of it, Captain. The show has its grand premiere on New Year's Eve. It's the Great White Way, the Crossroads of the World! A million people are in Times Square, waiting to ring in the new year! In front of the Old Knickerbocker, gigantic spotlights sweep the sky! The celebrities arrive by limousine while the TV cameras whirl! And after the curtain goes down, the cast, led by megastars Kurt Sharkey and Elena Jordan, leads the star-studded procession—all in costume, mind you—through Times Square to the Hotsy Totsy Club—''

Donovan swallowed hard.

"—where we all have a fantastic cast party. The networks will carry it live, and it will make all the newspapers in the world the following day. Have you ever heard of such a spectacular launch?''

Donovan shrugged, and said, "The *Titanic?*"

Holland stopped dead in his tracks; then, after a few seconds of silence, he laughed. "You disapprove of my production."

"Who gave me away?" Donovan said with a smile.

"I expected this from the *Times Literary Supplement* and doctoral candidates in drama, but not from a New York policeman.

Now I see you are one of those New York intellectuals who believe Broadway theater began and ended with Tennessee Williams.''

"Make it Eugene O'Neill and you got me cold," Donovan admitted.

"You are a man who would pay fifty dollars a ticket to see *Long Day's Journey into Night* on Broadway."

"Yes, but not with Hugh Grant singing it," Donovan said.

"You don't like musicals at all, do you?"

"I saw the revival of *Guys and Dolls* and I love Rodgers and Hammerstein. What does that make me?"

"Old fashioned but respectable," Holland said.

Donovan stood and straightened his jacket. "That's fair enough. Look, Sir John, I don't have to like turning *Casablanca* into a musical in order to catch this murderer. Whether he's a ghost or a real person is only detail. What I need is access to you when I need it as well as the run of the house."

"It's yours," Holland said, rising and shaking the captain's hand, a bit more firmly now that the producer had another scotch in him.

"I need carte blanche to go anywhere, at any time—even on-stage if it comes to that—for me and my assistant, Sergeant Moskowitz."

"Feel free to sing a duet with Elena if it so moves you," Holland replied.

"And there's one more thing."

"Name it."

"Just where the hell in the basement was Milos buried?" Donovan asked.

"I don't know. I learned what I told you from Roger Bock's *Legends of the Broadway Theater,* a rather old and very out-of-print book that I would be glad to loan you."

"I'd like that."

"Bock repeated an old story about Milos being buried on the B-level, but offers not one word about just where. The basement is fairly extensive, as you have seen."

"I noticed half the legends of vaudeville left something or other down there."

"I know," Holland said. "They're taking up a lot of what I had hoped would be storage space. Anton tells me there are shrunken heads! I really should contribute all that stuff to a museum, but there is simply too much to do right now. Maybe after the opening."

A commotion at the door heralded the arrival of Moskowitz, who—in addition to being a cop—was a weightlifter and a forceful presence in any company. Anton was swept aside.

"Hey, Captain, there's been a crime," Mosko called out, striding across the bar.

"The story of my life," Donovan said.

"Not here, I hope," Holland said. "I've had quite enough for one week."

Donovan made the introductions. Then he asked, "What crime?"

"Last week you gave your card to that guy Schadenfreud, the *Times* critic? Well, he called to report a crime and the call was switched to me."

"What sort of thing is he talking about?"

"He won't say."

"Where is he?"

"Inaugurating the bar at the renovated Hotsy Totsy Club."

"I think I know what the infraction might be," Donovan said with a sigh.

"Excuse me for intruding, Captain, but you know Lucien Schadenfreud?" Holland asked.

"We only met last week."

"The man is a troglodyte, an absolute beast."

"Nobody's perfect," Donovan said.

"He savaged my rock musical, cost me millions of dollars, and derailed my career for years. It took me forever to get back on track. I could kill him."

"He appears to be doing that to himself."

"If you mean his drinking problem, that's legendary. The man has the constitution of a steam engine. Do try to get him out of the Hotsy Totsy bar before my opening night party, won't you? You only have three weeks."

"I'll get right on it," Donovan said.

# SIX

## OUT OF THE SACK AND IN FRONT OF THE HOTPOINT

"FOUR DOLLARS and fifty cents for seven-eighths of an ounce of Jack Daniel's is too much," Donovan said.

George the bartender glared at him with coal-black eyes that were made not a bit less sinister by being forced to peer out from beneath hair that was slicked back, 1920s-style. Beneath the scowling lips was a bright red bow tie that adorned a tuxedo shirt that might have graced a servant in *The Great Gatsby*.

George said, "Donovan, I've said it before and I'll say it again: I liked you a lot better when you were a lush. Please, fall off the wagon so I can throw you and this here drunk out of my bar."

He nodded at the *Times* critic, who held his customary Bombay martini more steadily this time and, in addition, wore a sly smile.

Donovan said, "The man from the newspaper is right. A crime is being committed here—certainly the biggest one since Legs Diamond rested his elbows on the mahogany bar that this Formica slab attempts to emulate. At four-fifty a shot, a quart of Jack Daniel's will cost a customer one hundred and sixty-five bucks. I should arrest you right now." He switched his notebook, which sat atop the bar, from calculator back to communications mode.

"You've been breaking my balls about the price of Jack Daniel's since 1982 and never once have you had any," George said.

"And I'm not going to start."

"Then order something or get the hell out."

"I'll have a Kaliber."

"We ain't got any," George said gleefully. It seemed clear to Donovan that the man refused to stock his favorite brand merely to aggravate him.

"Buchler, then."

Fetching a bottle of the Dutch nonalcoholic beer, George

snarled, "I thought I was getting a break when I got away from your better half."

"I thought you weren't married," Schadenfreud said to Donovan.

George answered, "He ain't. He's been thrown out by some of the hottest women in New York. The bottom line is always the same: He gets the old heave-ho. Same as I plan to do any minute now."

"So what are you talking about, his 'better half?' "

"The one who's thrown him out more times than any of the others," George said.

Donovan explained, "I got this guy a job as cook in my girlfriend's restaurant and he thanked her by quitting to come work in this phony speakeasy."

He looked around in disgust at the recreation of the Hotsy Totsy Club. From the fake wood panelling to the discount-store imitations of 1920s lamps to the framed, sepia-toned photographs of athletes—every one of them white—the club reeked of a Hollywood set. The famous back room contained even more excesses than had marked the original. That was where Legs Diamond had held court, gambled and, when the situation called for it, had his enemies killed. (The bodies were carried out through the bar and dining area, and nobody ever challenged the yarn that the victims were drunks being put in cabs.) The renovated back room of the Hotsy Totsy Club was lined with photos and newspaper clippings—death notices, in many cases—of the gamblers and gangsters who had hung out there and at such other Times Square watering holes as Lindy's, the Stork Club, and the Silver Slipper. Among them: Lucky Luciano, Arnold Rothstein, Herman Rosenthal, Red Cassidy (whose murder therein closed the Hotsy Totsy Club), Hymie Cohen, Waxey Gordon, Gyp the Blood, Whitey Lewis, Titanic Thompson, Nigger Nate Raymond, Dago Frank, and George McManus.

All and all, the rebuilt club looked cheap and temporary, something to be folded up and relocated to a permanent home in Kansas City once the tourists visiting New York were done with it.

"I am not a cook," George said in his best Nixon imitation. He poured himself a draft beer, ignoring the two Japanese customers who were trying to get his attention. "Besides, I got sick of the constant kvetching."

"Marcy doesn't kvetch," Donovan said.

"Maybe with you she's miss personality, but back in the kitchen it's bitch, bitch, bitch all day long. If you once got her out of the sack and in front of the Hotpoint you'd know what I'm talking about."

"I'll tell you if it ever happens," Donovan said.

"Who's gonna cook when you two get married?"

"We'll work that out. Of all the things to worry about."

"I mean, she told me you got another marriage license. What is this, the second one?"

Twice before, pregnancies had caused Donovan and his lady to plan for marriage. Both were children of the 1960s—Donovan more than Marcy, he being twelve years older—who were prone to do things in a certain order. But two miscarriages made them so upset that the marriage plans had got lost in the cycle of sorrow and anger.

"The third."

"Don't you at some point have to get married?"

"We're trying to fit it into our schedules," Donovan said. "She's trying to run a restaurant without a cook, and I've got crimes to solve."

"You can't nail me for charging four-fifty for Jack Daniel's," George said. "I can name you three other places that charge five."

"Jesus, it's a regular crime wave. I better call for backup."

He angled his notebook so the others couldn't see the screen, then lost himself in work for ten or fifteen minutes, going over notes from Mosko and others.

After a time, Schadenfreud began to maneuver himself closer, so Donovan killed the screen.

"What are you doing?" Schadenfreud asked.

"Making a note to ask you what you were doing the evening of December twelfth," Donovan said.

"What day of the week was that?"

"Tuesday."

"Umm...I was up Broadway, at the Beacon Theater, watching people throw shotgun shells at Courtney Love."

"Who?"

"The widow of Kurt Cobain, who blew his brains out with a shotgun last year? Her fans like to remind her of the event."

"You know," Donovan said, "I can recall a time, and not so long ago, when *Times* men moved in circles that included presidents and prime ministers."

"A few still do. Anyway, I decided to call the number on your card after I found out what the prices are like in this tourist trap and this guy here—" The critic indicated George, who had finally deigned to serve the Japanese down the bar. "—said he knows you. But the price of whiskey isn't the only crime I had in mind."

"Tell me about it," Donovan said.

"I was sitting at my desk an hour ago, trying to think of something pleasant to say about Porno for Pyros..."

Donovan's eyes were glazing over, so Schadenfreud said, "Never mind. Better you don't know. Anyway, I happened to glance at my calendar and realized today is the twenty-sixth anniversary of the day I killed Elvis Presley. You have heard of him, haven't you?"

Schadenfreud stuck his hands out to be cuffed, but Donovan said, "You couldn't have killed him ten years earlier and we could have been spared *Viva Las Vegas?* Out of simple curiosity, how did you do it?"

"It was late 1968 and I had just joined *The Times.* Presley hadn't sung a note in seven or eight years, unless you count the songs he recorded for those horrible movies he made at a rate of three a year. But he was healthy, wealthy, and, insofar as it was possible, wise. Then he did a TV special where he sang, and was toying with the idea of coming out of retirement and reentering the world of rock and roll."

"And you encouraged it," Donovan speculated.

"Not me so much as the copy desk. I interviewed Presley's people and wrote a piece that lead with the line, 'Elvis Presley is thinking about appearing in concert again.' They refused to say he would definitely do it. The copy desk called me on the carpet, saying 'thinking about' isn't a very strong statement. Can we say he's *planning* to come out of retirement?

"I said, 'no, planning is definite, thinking about is conjectural. Learn to live with ambiguity.' "

"And they refused."

"They insisted on 'making plans.' I gave up and went out for a drink. The next morning the paper comes out and the headline reads, ELVIS PRESLEY TO MAKE PERSONAL APPEARANCES."

"I love the press," Donovan said.

"Anyway, *Time* and *Newsweek* picked up my story and ran it. A few days after they hit the stands, Presley called a press conference to announce he was coming out of retirement and going back into rock and roll."

"How long before it killed him?" Donovan asked.

"Seven or eight years. I've always blamed myself for not fighting harder to have the story come out the way I wanted."

"It's a heavy burden that rests on your shoulders," Donovan said.

"I'm an only child, and we never fight hard enough for what we want," Schadenfreud mused.

That was drifting too far in the direction of analysis for Donovan, who changed the conversation by saying, "I'd buy you a drink, except I don't want to contribute to your death."

"Don't worry about me, Captain. I have the constitution of a steam engine."

"So I heard tonight," Donovan said.

"From whom?"

"Sir John Victor Holland."

Donovan swore he saw the man's cheeks turn redder than they were and puff out. "You want to talk about someone who should be dead, that's him."

"He feels the same way about you."

"Let me explain something. Being hated by John Victor Holland is like being hated by Mussolini—it's a badge I wear with honor. On the day his wretched corpse is found rotting in a Broadway gutter, I will exult. On that day, you may as well go to a ball game, for there will be eight million suspects. If and when a perpetrator is ever caught, he will be honored as the savior of the

American stage. A special Tony Award will be presented for Best Performance by an Actor in Defense of His Craft.''

Donovan smiled.

Schadenfreud wasn't done. "Let's perform a little experiment," he said. "You're a man who likes jazz. I'll bet you know a good tune when you hear one. Hum me a John Victor Holland song."

Donovan was silent for a moment, then shrugged. "I can't think of one," he admitted.

"Nor can anyone," Schadenfreud said. "His songs are trite, bland, and forgettable. I have given this little test all over town and have yet to meet someone who can hum or whistle something Holland composed. But there isn't a soul in this city who can't remember half a dozen Rodgers and Hammerstein or Lerner and Loewe songs."

Without meaning to, Donovan began quietly whistling "I Could Have Danced All Night."

"See? See? What did I tell you? And it's not just those composers. It's Bernstein—I bet you can whistle me the entire score of *West Side Story*."

"Of course. It's close to my heart. I used to play stickball with some of the West Side hoodlums that show was written about. And my dad was the model for the character of Officer Krupke."

"Did you ever read *Murder on the Orient Express?*"

"I saw the movie."

"Holland's murder will be like the one in that story. The murder weapon will be passed around on the IRT. Everyone will want to plunge the knife into the body."

Donovan said, "Holland claims you cost him millions of dollars and derailed his career for years by trashing his rock musical."

"He said that? There is a God! Damned if I didn't try. That must have been twenty years ago if it was a day. And he's still pissed off about it? Well, I credit the man for perseverance. Bill Graham—you know, the rock impresario—tried to get me fired one time for pointing out that the manager of a certain famous rock group hid in his office during the American debut because the sound was less painful there."

Donovan raised his beer in a toast.

"But *The Times* dismissed his demand with dignified scorn and a few years later we made up. I agreed I could be an asshole now and then and he made the same admission about himself and, after that, we were friends. A shame about that helicopter accident. I told him not to fly in rent-a-choppers. So Holland is still mad at me? That's the best news I've heard in a week.''

''Just play it safe and don't get caught in a dark alley with him. Or in the basement of the Old Knickerbocker. The place seems to be lethally jinxed lately.''

''Why on earth would I go there? I won't be reviewing his latest travesty. The drama critic will, although if I were culture desk editor I would assign a critic who was acquainted with professional wrestling. Because that will be the level of the entertainment. Let me tell you how Holland writes songs.''

Schadenfreud put down his glass and, a bit unsteadily, got off the bar stool and arranged himself as if onstage and preparing for a solo. ''I never heard a note of the score to *Casablanca: The Musical,* but I can tell you exactly how the main title will go. I'm Kurt Sharkey. I'm getting too old to keep making action films in Hollywood, so here I am on the Great White Way trying to summon up a baritone voice and hit the notes.''

Gesturing like a ham actor trying to impress a small-town audience, Schadenfreud sang, in a surprisingly deep and clear voice, *''I came for the wa-ter, but I'll find love in Casa-blan-ca.''*

Donovan laughed, but George came rumbling down the bar, shouting ''That's it! You're outta here, the two of you.''

''Shut up, George,'' Donovan said, finishing his beer and putting his notebook back in his briefcase nonetheless.

''When the drunks start singing, that's the time to throw 'em out.''

''I have to go to work anyway,'' Schadenfreud said, finishing his martini.

''Work, in your condition and at this hour?'' George said.

''That's my time of day. If I catch a cab I can just make the last show at the Bitter End.''

''To see whom?'' Donovan asked cautiously.

''Shanghai Love Motel,'' Schadenfreud said, even more cautiously. ''They're a literate nouveau-punk band.''

Donovan drummed his fingers on top of the bar.

"And Jeff Buckley."

"He sounds normal enough."

"He's an art singer, sort of, like his dad, Tim. I always told that man the heroin would kill him, but did he listen to me?"

"Where do I get the impression everyone you ever wrote about has died horribly?" Donovan asked.

"I never thought about it that way," Schadenfreud replied.

"Is your life going to include any deaths tonight?"

"I don't think so, but the evening is young," the man said, and slipped out into it. Schadenfreud staggered out beyond the door, just missing a collision with Marcy, who slinked in wearing a smile and a black mini.

"Hello, sailor," she said, slipping her arms around Donovan's neck and kissing him on the cheek. "You know, for a man who doesn't drink anymore, you spend an awful lot of time in bars."

"You meet more interesting people than you do at Starbuck's. How'd you find me? Slip a homing device in my pocket?"

"I have a spy on the Great White Way."

"Oh, him," Donovan said, casting a wary eye at his old friend.

"I dropped a dime on you, Donovan," George said. "One way or another, I want you out of my place before you get me fired."

Marcy told her former cook, "So this is what you threw me over for? A Formica bar filled with tourists?"

"This is where the action is," George said. "Times Square is coming back. Would you please take this guy home before it gets here?"

"With pleasure," she said, grabbing Donovan's arm and tugging him toward the door. As he let himself be led out into the bright night of Times Square, Donovan heard George yelling, "Get her in front of the Hotpoint!"

WEDNESDAY, DECEMBER TWENTIETH, saw the first matinee of paid previews for *Casablanca: The Musical.* The first day of previews was a mammoth event that had been advertised widely—both in the States and abroad—and which had drawn a bustling, milling crowd of tourists. Dozens of chartered buses—most of them yellow school buses bearing the names of suburban school districts—also brought hundreds of suburban theatergoers to the first preview performance. The matinee was the dress rehearsal for the really big bash scheduled for New Year's Eve. And with that exquisite timing known all too well to New Yorkers, that Wednesday afternoon in the Big Apple also featured a massive demonstration at the United Nations, a speech by the president at the Javits Convention Center, and, for good measure, a five-alarm fire in a warehouse area along the Hudson piers. In addition, the holiday shopping season was in full swing on Fifth Avenue and in Herald Square. The net result was gridlock throughout midtown. That day was, of course, the one that Donovan, still stung by his experience in the subway during the water main break, chose to drive to the scene of the crime.

It took him only half an hour to drive uptown from One Police Plaza to Thirty-fourth Street, but after that it was a slow crawl. Midtown was thoroughly saturated with cars and people. In a vain attempt to bypass the worst congestion, he swung west toward the Hudson, forgetting the morning's advisory from the Secret Service to stay away from the route covered by the presidential motorcade. Consequently, Donovan was brought to a bumper-to-bumper standstill in front of Ninth Avenue's Chelsea Clinton Diner (named after the two neighborhoods the border of which it straddled). It was from that rundown eatery that Moskowitz emerged, red-faced from the frigid wind blowing in off the nearby river, and hopped into the passenger's side of Donovan's Buick.

"How long have you been stuck in this?" Mosko asked, unbuttoning his coat and fumbling behind his back for the seat belt.

"An hour so far. Half an hour to get to Thirty-fourth and another half an hour to go the three wonderful blocks that brought me here. How long did it take you to get here on mass transit?"

"Fifteen minutes."

"Don't tell me. I don't want to know the details."

"Ten minutes to take the E train uptown and five minutes to walk over to the diner. I had time for a cup of coffee waiting for you." He stopped fumbling for the seat belt long enough to hand his boss a container.

"Decaf with a spritz of real coffee and a dollop of half-and-half. You got to watch the caffeine and cream, boss. I think you're slipping. When we began working together all you would eat was bean sprouts and all you would drink was bottled water. I'm trying to promote health and safety here—where the hell's the seat belt?''

Irritated, Donovan said, ''Hey, Evel Knievel, what accident are you planning on getting into?'' He pointed out the windshield at the sea of taillights ahead of him.

''A guy can't be too careful,'' Mosko said.

''Read my lips: We're not moving. That noise you hear is cobwebs forming on the gas pedal.''

Moskowitz frowned, but settled down and, after a moment, pulled his notebook out of his briefcase and set it up on his lap.

''Tri Ng Dinh,'' he said after a screen came up.

''Spell that.''

Mosko did as he was told.

''Vietnamese?'' Donovan asked. ''Our Asian stiff is Vietnamese?''

''You got it,'' Mosko said proudly.

''How did you get his name?''

''As you suspected, that number you found in the memory of his computer watch was a bank account—at the Chase branch in Flushing Meadows.''

''Does he have any money there?''

''Yeah, a bit over seven thousand bucks.''

''Well, that's more than I had in my bank account until I made captain. And this guy had no wallet or ID?''

''He had twenty-two bucks on him. As for a wallet, there's always the chance it was taken by whoever killed him. Or was robbed off the body after he died.''

''Robbed off the body? In the middle of a deluge that ripped up the pavement on Forty-second Street and punched a hole in the wall of the theater basement? Not even Times Square has bionic muggers.''

Mosko said, ''I'm telling you what I know, and as yet it ain't much. I'm kinda proud we found his name at all.''

''Bless you, my son,'' Donovan said, patting his partner on the knee. ''Tell me what you do know.''

''Dinh was twenty-six and had been in the country for a year.''

''The same as Mooney,'' Donovan observed.

''Yeah. Think it's a coincidence?''

"Maybe," Donovan said. "What else?"

"He lived in a rooming house for Vietnamese in the shadow of Shea Stadium."

"Living that close to the Mets would have killed me, too."

"He went to work every morning and got home at night."

"No doubt by the number seven IRT, which would account for him being on the platform the night of the water main break."

"True, he could have been going home from work, but we have no idea where he worked. He didn't have a social security number."

Donovan said, "He could have worked for Derrida, no matter what the man says about not hiring illegals."

"It's possible," Mosko allowed.

"However, Dinh didn't look very much like a construction worker. He was on the slight side, with clean hands and no calluses. And the same concrete dust that was on top of him was also under him, so he didn't land in that spot before the water main break. What do they say at his rooming house?"

"They claim to know nothing about him. He came here a year ago, they say, and that's all they say."

"Have you seen his room?"

"Yeah, but there's nothing revealing in it. Just an address in Quang Yen."

"Where's that?"

"It's a coastal village in extreme northeastern Vietnam, not far from Haiphong and right near the Chinese border."

"Interesting," Donovan said.

"He also had some old coins. All his clothes were cheap knockoffs of good stuff. You know, fake designer jeans probably bought from street vendors."

"Do you think his fellow roomers are hiding something?"

"They were kind of nervous about talking," Mosko said.

"People who used to live in a police state tend to be jittery when talking to cops," Donovan said. "Run the address of the rooming house past Immigration and see if they've heard of it."

"I'm already doing that."

The conversation was interrupted by a burst of sirens and a flash of lights. Up Ninth Avenue's middle-of-the-road fire lane swooped a procession of black Jeep Cherokees and limousines, one of which carried the fender-top flag of the president of the United States. In less than a minute, the motorcade was gone and traffic began to inch forward, the sirens replaced by a cacophony of angry horns.

Mosko aimed his mouth in the direction of the motorcade and said, "Hey, Prez...the peasants are revolting."

"You ain't kidding," Donovan said, switching the radio to WBGO, the New Jersey jazz channel, and turning up the volume.

As his Buick began to move slowly up Ninth, Donovan said, "See if we have a Vietnamese officer who can go out there and talk to them."

"Will do."

"And another thing. Just for the hell of it, find out when Derrida was in Vietnam."

"Derrida? What are you thinking?"

"Nothing in particular. I just want to know."

"The victim was twenty-six. He came to the U.S. of A a year ago. He would have been a little kid when Americans were in Vietnam."

"Humor me," Donovan said, sipping his coffee.

"You're the boss. You want to know the latest bulletin about Mooney?"

"Yes."

"Our friend from Ginwood was indeed killed by a crossbow bolt—they're called 'bolts,' by the way..."

"Thank you for correcting my usage."

"—to the heart, coming from a ten-degree angle below the horizontal. That corresponds to the shot coming from where you said it did. That was a pretty nifty shot. It takes a marksman—or a lucky break—to get someone in the heart from that distance in the semi-darkness."

"The rungs of the stepladder would have been in Mooney's own shadow, made by the light he was stringing up," Donovan said. "So Milos could have done it."

Mosko gave his boss a weird look, so Donovan shrugged and drank some more coffee.

"I hate to tell you this, 'cause it will only get you all worked up, but Bonaci traced that bolt."

"Did he?"

"Yeah, and to a manufacturer of crossbow equipment that went out of business..." Moskowitz paused as one does when delaying the rest of the message. "... in 1932."

Donovan's eyes widened. "And Milos died a year later! Just as he might have been running out of ammo. Such was the state of manly combat in the middle of the twentieth century."

Perhaps seeking to head off a polemic on the subject of manly combat, Mosko said, "Of course, that was too long ago to trace the bolt to a specific customer."

"My friend, think of it. You have the body of a man who's been killed by a crossbow bolt. This body is lying in the basement of a theater that also holds the grave of a noted crossbow marksman. The death bolt is traced to the era in which this marksman operated. Futhermore, the lethal shot came from the direction of his old packing crates."

"Ghosts don't kill people with crossbows," Mosko said. "Pursuing this line of thought will make you look ridiculous downtown."

"For the first time, right? Today we get into those packing crates. We also try to find the grave of Milos the Magnificent."

"Who's this guy we're meeting who's supposed to take us there?"

"Roger Bock, author of Legends of the Broadway Theater. He's going to show us around while we look for Milos's grave."

"This is just wonderful," Mosko said.

"Do you remember anyone—I'm thinking of Derrida in your case—mentioning the Old Knickerbocker Annex?" Donovan asked.

"Nope. What is it?"

"An office and studio building that is, or was, attached to the rear of the theater."

"On Forty-first Street?"

"I guess. It's in the book."

"No one breathed a word."

"See, I find that interesting. According to Bock, the annex is an essential part of the story of the Old Knickerbocker. One goes with the other. Several of the legends he wrote about lived or worked there."

"I never noticed the place. But then, I was looking at the basement and not the neighboring buildings."

"Holland seemed pretty proud of buying the theater. Derrida liked renovating it. But neither of them mentioned the annex, and I asked Derrida to give me a floor-by-floor description of the joint."

"Do you think he's hiding something?" Mosko asked.

"I intend to find out," Donovan said.

# SEVEN

## ENOUGH TO RAISE THE DEAD

THE SCHOOL BUSES that brought the suburban theater parties to the Old Knickerbocker for the first day of paid previews were lined up on Forty-first Street. Some were pulled to the curbs in the no-parking zones that took up so much of midtown Manhattan, their drivers keeping the engines on in anticipation of being chased off by a traffic enforcement officer. Others were flat-out parked illegally; Donovan pulled to the curb and parked behind a bus marked WESTWOOD REGIONAL HIGH SCHOOL.

The line to get into the theater began on Forty-second, wrapped around the corner down Seventh Avenue to Forty-first Street, and went a few school buses down that block. Donovan and Mosko-witz skirted the tail end of it, then walked west toward the stage door and loading dock. Before showing their credentials to the stage door security guard, they stepped out into the middle of the street and surveyed the old and narrow building next door. The six-story, granite-trimmed, brick facade seemed never to have been cleaned. It wore that coat of brown that made Manhattan's dingier streets look like the depths of February even in the height of June. Several families of pigeons made their home atop the stone pro-trusion that served as a lintel over the door. Bird droppings soiled an ancient sign reading OLD KNICKERBOCKER ANNEX.

"No wonder nobody ever mentioned this building," Mosko said.

"What a dump," Donovan agreed.

"I wonder if anyone lives in there."

"Well, this block isn't zoned for residence, but you never know."

Donovan led the way to the door and pushed his way into the tiny foyer, which was barely large enough to fit two men and the mailboxes. Donovan ran his finger down the scratched-up brass plate that held the names of tenants. All the spaces designed for tenants to fill in their names were scratched out save one. It bore a name, typed recently on an old, manual typewriter: GITTELSON PROMOTIONS.

"Somebody hangs his hat here," Mosko said.

"I wonder why we weren't supposed to know about this building," Donovan said.

"Maybe Holland and Derrida were embarrassed by it."

"That's entirely possible," Donovan said, as the two men went back onto the sidewalk and walked the few paces down the block to the stage door. They were met there by a man of about sixty years, well-dressed in *Town & Country* duds: a brushed suede jacket over wide-wale brown corduroy slacks, a tucked-in blue button-down Oxford shirt, and Docksiders.

Donovan stuck his hand out and said, "Roger Bock...Bill Donovan."

"The pleasure is mine, Captain," the author said, betraying a slight Boston accent. "And this must be Sergeant Moskowitz."

"Nice to meet you," Mosko said, extending a beefy hand.

"I'm grateful to you for coming down here to help us solve this mystery," Donovan told the writer. "I hope I'm not taking you away from something important."

"Actually, this is work for me. I'm writing the authorized biography of Sir John."

"He didn't mention that."

"It was one of several things he didn't mention," Mosko added.

"In his defense, the news isn't out yet. There will be a press announcement on Monday, however."

"So that's why he was familiar with your book on Broadway legends."

"He liked it and felt I was the man for the task."

"What do you think of him? Is he a legend?"

"Of course. He's too big not to be a legend."

"Ah, the King Kong theory of immortality. Talent is optional. If you're big enough, you go down in the history books."

"Or you have them written yourself," Bock said. "Let's face it, Captain, my biography of Holland won't include anything the man himself doesn't want. But that doesn't mean I won't try to dig up the dirt on him.''

"Why bother if you can't write it?"

"Because I will confront him with the evidence and try to talk him into letting me print it. Some of it, anyway. A good biographer does that."

"What sort of things are you looking for? Old girlfriends? Old boyfriends? Odd sexual habits?"

"No, no. I was thinking more about his ethical shortcomings."

"Such as?" Donovan asked, his eyes widening.

"I assumed you knew about the Mark Twain thing."

"It must have slipped by me."

"When Holland turned *Huckleberry Finn* into the biggest musical of the 1980s, most theater lovers assumed he would give credit to Mark Twain. But he didn't, preferring instead to claim he had changed it so much it now belonged to him. I know Huck Finn was in the public domain and Holland didn't have to pay anything for it. But you would think he might have tacked Twain's name on it, you know, 'based on a story by Mark Twain.' But he didn't. He called it *John Victor Holland's Huckleberry Finn.*"

"If he set the Koran to music, the mullahs in Iran would have laid a *fatwa* on his head and he'd now be in hiding for his life," Donovan said.

"What a thought! So it's my hope I can get Holland to address this issue in his authorized biography. But he probably won't." Bock sighed.

"Maybe you can find some other kind of dirt," Mosko said.

"I only just got here but I'm willing to try," Bock said. "Maybe something juicy will happen at the party tonight."

"Party? What party is that?"

"The first-night-of-paid-previews party," Bock said.

"Will this one be at the Hotsy Totsy Club, too?" Donovan asked.

"No, no. Just upstairs in Peter Minuit's Penthouse. Holland is inviting a lot of his old pals from show biz on both sides of the Atlantic."

"Let's get to the subject of where Milos the Magnificent is buried," Donovan said. "Do you know the exact location?"

"Of course. His old dressing room. I'll take you there."

The three men entered the building through the stage door and immediately found themselves at the periphery of a maelstrom of activity. Off in the bowels of the building, just audible through several layers of stairways, corridors, equipment areas, and sets, the orchestra was tuning up. Dancers and extras loitered in the wings or scurried down corridors. Enough of them wore Arab garb or Nazi uniforms to make Moskowitz visibly uncomfortable. Stagehands hurried about carrying all sorts of things. In a dimly lit stairwell, slightly over-the-hill Hollywood star Kurt Sharkey paced up and down in his white suit, practicing smoking an unfiltered cigarette, Bogart-style—the lit end cupped under the curved fingers. Donovan inched into the stage left area just far enough to catch a glimpse of the back of the grand staircase.

"Didn't I tell you there would be a grand staircase?" he said to Mosko.

"Holland always has a grand staircase," Bock interjected. "Don't think it didn't take some imagination to get one into *Huck Finn*."

"I bet," Donovan said, thinking about Lucien Schadenfreud's impression of Sharkey singing and breaking into a smile.

The trio made its way down toward the B-level, with Bock leading the way. As they descended below the stage level the numbers of actors grew less and the presence of stagehands increased. The cacophony decreased, as did the lighting level. When finally they reached the lower basement, the sound of a busy theatrical production was almost entirely gone. The orchestra could be heard in the distance, much like the sound of a neighbor's radio playing after midnight—just close enough to let you know life was being lived somewhere, but too far off to let you make out the tune. The only noise Donovan could hear that came from nearby was the low-frequency humming of a motor or generator—a large one. Donovan looked toward the sound and found himself staring at the machinery that worked the massive stage elevator.

Bock said, "That noise is the stage hydraulics on standby. Wait till you hear the racket when they push the button to raise or lower the stage."

"You were down here earlier?"

"I beat you here by an hour. Run into traffic?"

Donovan growled and nodded.

"I took advantage of the time to prowl around the theater. Like you, I have the run of the joint. I'll need it if I'm to do a good job on Holland's biography."

"Did you find Milos's grave?"

"There wasn't *that* much time, but I got a general idea. Let me show you."

He led the way down the corridor that connected the stage hydraulics with the widened storage area in which the bodies of Dinh and Mooney were found. Donovan was surprised to note that almost no work had been done since the locksmiths had finished opening doors for the detectives' inspection of those dozens of rooms. Ribbons of grey hung everywhere, and other construction debris remained where the workmen had left it.

Most of the rooms had proved, following the search, to be long-forgotten storage spaces. A few held more old junk left behind by more old vaudevillians. But most held stage props from the Old Knickerbocker's days as a legitimate theater. There were fake hurricane lamps, phony guns, knives and swords, a warehouse's worth of couches, tables, and chairs, and a vast, largely moth-eaten wardrobe that included suits, dresses, capes, and robes. None of this treasure trove of theater arcana meant much to the detectives, who chronicled it nonetheless and fed the data into a computer file. You never knew what might turn out to be useful.

"I guess Derrida wasn't that eager to get this cleaned up," Donovan mused.

"Maybe the ghost scared him off," Mosko replied.

"Where did you hear about Milos turning into a ghost, anyway?" Donovan asked Bock.

"Some old vaudevillians told me about it. They were a suspicious bunch in general. You know, the act that appears second on the bill is always doomed. Such-and-such an agent is jinxed. The Old Knickerbocker has a ghost. Of course, it would be the ghost of an old vaudevillian."

"What happened to vaudeville, anyway?" Mosko asked.

"The talkies killed it."

"Say again?"

"Movies didn't always have sound," Donovan said.

"No shit. What a bummer."

"When the talkies became popular in the late twenties, they pushed out vaudeville. People wanted movies, and they were cheaper for a theater to book than were vaudeville performers. By 1933, when Milos died, the art form was basically dead. The better performers went on the radio or into the movies. A few, like Milton Berle and George Burns, wound up on television. Some of the lesser comics lingered on in burlesque, jammed in between strippers. Milos wasn't big enough for any of the good options open to him, so he died embittered."

"Ghosts are usually pissed off about something or another," Donovan said idly.

"According to the legend, Milos's ghost rises now and then to seek vengeance against anyone who defiles this theater, where he had his greatest successes," Bock said. "Most of the time, murder isn't in his ghostly repertoire?"

"What is?" Donovan asked.

"Oh, the usual. Weird noises at night, especially coming out of dark corners. Strange smells. Objects disappearing."

"If that's true, Holland should be careful," Mosko said. "His leading lady could disappear."

Donovan nodded and watched as Bock led the way into the storage area where Dinh and Mooney died. The strung-up lights were on, although the setup was no more complete than the week before when Donovan was last there. The death of Mooney clearly had caused renovations to be suspended in the basement. The stage machinery was working, Donovan realized, and that was all Derrida needed for the time being.

Bock stood in the center of the room, not far from where Mooney's body had been found, hands on hips, looking around. "This is it," he announced.

"This is where Milos's dressing room used to be?" Donovan asked.

"I'm sure of it. His dressing room was one of the bigger ones—remember, the man owned a piece of the theater—and located below the main entrance. Milos fancied himself an artiste, you realize, not a run-of-the-mill vaudeville performer. He thought himself a legend of show biz—him and his five famous crossbow bolts."

"Let's hear that one more time," Donovan said. "Five famous bolts?"

"Yes. It was another superstition, one Milos brought with him from Serbia. He was crazy about the pentacle."

"The five-pointed star."

"Actually, the pentacle is any convergence of five lines that appears starlike. It was given mystical significance by wizards and astrologers during the middle ages."

Donovan said, "It also has some role in vampire lore."

"I think you mean werewolf lore, boss," Mosko said. "You're getting your old movies mixed up."

"Maybe I am," Donovan allowed.

Bock continued: "Milos incorporated the pentacle into his act. He had his volunteer subjects stand onstage in front of a backdrop that was painted with a pentacle and decorated with garlic cloves. The pentacle was, you know, a star with all sorts of weird shapes on it—astrological signs and the like. And then Milos used five bolts to shoot things out of their hands, off their heads, you can just imagine. He had a specially built crossbow with five—and only five—bolts. The weapon and the bolts were buried with him."

"Were they?"

"Yeah, he had that stipulation put into his will. The man was crazy as a loon."

Donovan crossed his arms impatiently and said, "Are you sure all this isn't being manufactured by Sir John to pump up the value of his screenplay?"

"You mean the one on Milos? No, this is all real. I researched Milos for the man."

"Why?"

"Isn't it obvious? I want to write the screenplay and become rich and famous myself."

"Oh, so you have more of a stake in this than just writing Holland's biography," Donovan said.

"Everybody around Holland stands to make a ton of money off

him," Bock said, without a hint of shame. "You should get in on it, too."

"Thank you, but I'll pass. I have a rent-controlled apartment in a good neighborhood, a good job, a steady girl—well, we're getting along this year—and no interests I can't afford. I'd rather keep my soul pure."

"You make me feel like I'm entering into a Faustian bargain."

"Anyone who would dare to set the greatest American film of all time to music is akin to Satan in my book," Donovan said. "I put Holland right up there with the man—who I once admired, by the way—who stooped to colorize this fine black and white film. Look what happened to him."

"What happened to Ted Turner that's so bad?" Bock asked.

"Jane Fonda."

Bock nodded grimly and began prowling the storage space, carefully skirting the yellow crime-scene tape that lingered around the packing crate atop which Mooney had died. At the same time, Donovan pulled a Mag-Lite from his pocket and repeated his examination of the crates that had been there for so many decades, including the one that had recently borne a body. The crates were of rough-cut pine and some of the boards were warped from age and moisture. Many of the nails were rusted out; dirt covered part of the lettering that identified the boxes as belonging to the long-dead crossbow marksman. On the Mooney box, Donovan uncovered a hidden inscription that bore a street address in Sarajevo. In the dirt alongside another crate, he found a steamship tag marked:

RMS *Franconia*
From Gibraltar
Pass bearer from ship to shore.

On the line left blank for the passenger to fill in his name was written, in a cramped hand using a fountain pen, "Milos Tryvomanic." It gave an address: 985 West Forty-first Street, New York City.

Donovan stood and handed the tag to Moskowitz, who said, "That address is next door."

"The Old Knickerbocker Annex," Donovan said. "Milos must have lived there."

"Or had an office there."

Bock said, from a slight distance, "Most likely that was a combination studio and office. Performers both lived and worked there in the old days."

"You know about the annex, too?" Donovan asked.

"I did write about the legends of Broadway, remember? Many of them lived and worked there."

"Really? Ever hear of Gittelson Promotions, the last living tenant?"

"Oh God, yes. Everyone knows Sy Gittelson. He's one of the legends."

"I never heard of him."

"Have you ever seen the Woody Allen film *Broadway Danny Rose?*"

"Ten years ago."

"That's Sy Gittelson. He's Broadway Danny Rose. The genuine item. He's an old friend of mine. I like him a lot. He knows absolutely everybody, and that makes him a valuable source."

"He's a talent agent?"

"More than that. He's also an old-fashioned promoter, one who represented guys who would do things like play 'The Battle Hymn of the Republic' on the kazoo while riding a unicycle. Do you remember the days when PR guys would stage wild publicity stunts—what comes to mind is having a girl in a bikini take a bath in a wading pool in the middle of Times Square—just to get in the papers?"

"That's before even his time," Mosko interjected.

"Just how old is Gittelson?" Donovan asked.

"Eighty if he's a day. Maybe older."

"So he might have known Milos?"

"Sy was his agent."

"You got to be kidding me," Donovan exclaimed.

"And the man who introduced him to his fiancée."

"That would be the chorus girl who was six inches taller than him?"

"The same. Sy took over the promotion business from his father, the legendary Broadway promoter Abe Gittelson, who used to book acts for Oscar Hammerstein's Palace at the turn of the century. Abe represented Titanic Thompson, who inspired the character of Sky Masterson in *Guys and Dolls*."

Donovan shook his head in amazement. Then Bock said, "Captain...I think I found the grave."

"Where?" Donovan asked, hurrying over.

"Here." Standing in the dark, crate-filled corner from which the fatal shot had come, Bock pointed down at the crack where the floodwaters had buckled the concrete. When he had inspected the spot the week before, Donovan had stepped gingerly over that crack, which was from six to eight feet long, as many as three feet wide, and filled with rubble. At one end, the crack narrowed to an inch in width and disappeared below the brick wall about twenty feet from where the brick patch job had recently been completed.

"The water main break buckled the concrete over Milos's grave?" Donovan asked.

"Another reason for him to be pissed off," Mosko added, not quite as amused as he had been in the past.

"This is where I am sure the grave is," Bock said. "How long will it take us to uncover it?"

"About an hour," Donovan said, telling Moskowitz to "call and get us some guys down here on the double."

"You got it," the sergeant said, whipping out his cell phone and wandering off to make the call. As he did so, Donovan heard the opening strains of the overture to *Casablanca: The Musical*. If the tune sounded forgettable, the music was loud and strong. On cue, the stage hydraulics began to roar. Donovan and Bock couldn't help but gape in the direction of the sound, which resembled the heavy machinery inside a steel mill. How that industrial roar could be hidden from the audience two floors above was a fine testimonial to the strength of the building, Donovan thought. He watched as the massive steel gear rose, presumably moving the main set from the floor above to the stage level.

"Well, if that ain't enough to raise the dead," Donovan said, to no one in particular, "my men will just have to take jackhammers and do it."

As IT TURNED OUT, no such equipment was required. Led by Howard Bonaci, a team of six field detectives and evidence technicians removed the shards of concrete that covered the grave of the old vaudevillian. The chunks ranged from fist-sized rocks to pieces as large as bricks. And, Bonaci noted before too long, "This isn't the first time they've been moved."

"What are you talking about?" Bock asked.

"He's saying grave robbers were here before us," Donovan explained.

"How could that happen?"

"Beats me," Bonaci said. "All I can tell you is, we aren't the first ones to lift these chunks out of here." To augment his point, the crime-scene chief hefted a piece of concrete the size of a grapefruit. Then he tossed it onto the floor a few yards away. It broke in two and sprayed some fine white and grey dust in a corona about it. The pieces came to rest amidst the stones Donovan had noted earlier, as well as the remains of some flowers that had dried, been soaked by the water main break, and dried again, crumbling into bits.

"You see that dust? It's consistent with other dust I noted around this whole area when we investigated the Mooney homicide."

"What do you think happened, Howard?" Donovan asked.

"I think the water main break partially exposed the grave—assuming that's what we find when we get to the bottom of this rubble heap. Not too long afterwards, someone came along and shoveled these chunks out of the crack. Then they shoveled them back in."

"That makes no sense," Bock said.

"It does if the perpetrator found what he wanted—or else found nothing—and filled up the hole to cover up the fact that he had been interested in the site," Donovan said.

"We'll know better when we get to the bottom," Bonaci added, standing back to let his men finish the job.

They did that in less than twenty minutes after arriving. With the orchestra above coming to the end of act one and the stage hydraulics humming in preparation for a set change, detectives restrung the ceiling lights. The bare bulb Mooney had died while hanging now swung slowly atop the gaping wound in the foundation of the Old Knickerbocker. Donovan and the others gathered around and peered into the hole as a technician lay on the floor and reached down to toss out the last of the rubble. "I got something here," he announced at last. "Pieces of wood. Old wood that's been stained and varnished or something. The concrete was poured right over it. Some of it's been ripped up. I'm getting pieces of concrete with wood embedded on one side. It's a coffin, all right. And you know what, Captain? I'm not the first one to be doing this. Someone has been here before me."

"You were right about this being the grave," Donovan said to Bock.

The author didn't answer, but stared down nervously into the hole.

"Can you see the body?" Donovan asked.

"Yeah. The guy is still in there, Captain."

Donovan felt a slight sting. Word had gotten out he was looking for a ghost, or was at least discussing the subject. A certain scorn was one of the prices Donovan paid for drawing so many of the exotic cases.

The technician rolled out of the way to let the others see in. Milos the Magnificent had been buried in a frock coat that now lay collapsed over his bones and bore their outline. The bones of his hands remained crossed across his chest. A top hat teetered above a gaunt skull. A garland of desiccated garlic bulbs lay like a string of dirty pearls over the collarbone.

"Where's the crossbow and bolts?" Donovan asked.

The technician rolled back into position and angled himself so he could better reach into the grave. After a moment spent exploring the inside of the coffin with his hands, he announced, "They ain't in here. But there's a depression in the blue-black dust that lines this box. It's in the shape of a crossbow. Beneath it I can see the black velvet the guy was laid out on."

"Where did the crossbow and bolts go to?" Mosko asked.

"Taken by whoever beat us to the grave," Donovan said.

"Who would that be?"

"Maybe the ghost," the technician said. "Didn't folks used to leave garlic around to ward off ghosts?"

"It was to ward off vampires..." Donovan said.

"Werewolves," Mosko corrected.

"... and sarcasm is unbecoming to one of New York's Finest," Donovan continued. "When you're through being a wise guy, get samples of the dust in that depression you told me about. I want to see if it turns up anywhere else—such as on the bolt that killed Mooney."

"You got it."

"Whoever killed Mooney took the weapon and its ammo," Donovan said. "Maybe Mooney interrupted him in the act and died for his bad luck. Bock, you said Milos used five, and only five, bolts."

"Absolutely. It was an essential part of his act," the author said, looking a bit stunned by the turn of events. In a short period of time they had uncovered not only a grave, but a grave robber.

"And one of them was used to kill Mooney," Donovan continued. He was talking to the dank basement air, suddenly made still by the arrival of intermission. The slight rumble of thousands of feet milling about in the lobby came down from above. And the music was gone. In the center of the B-level the stage hydraulics burst to life again, making a racket that soon stopped entirely. The basement of the Old Knickerbocker was as still as death.

"I wonder what the killer intends to do with the other four," Donovan said.

# EIGHT

## JEEZ, WHAT A FUCKIN' NIGHTMARE!

THE CAPTAIN wasn't sure what prompted him to go upstairs to catch act two of *Casablanca: The Musical.* Maybe he wanted to see the abomination for himself, the way people can't stop themselves from looking at car wrecks no matter how grisly the sight. But maybe something else, some premonition of a more tangible disaster, drove him upstairs, leaving Bock to wander off by himself and Moskowitz to remain in the basement, watching as technicians took pictures of the just-opened grave.

Donovan mingled with the audience as members drifted back to their seats following intermission. He picked up a playbill and flirted with the girl who was handing them out. He prowled the lobby, eyeing the newly restored artwork. Then as the music began he stood at the rear of the orchestra and watched. He saw Sir John Victor Holland settle into his private box to the right of the stage. With him were Derrida and a handful of unfamiliar retainers, all of them smiling, too readily and too broadly, at The Great Man. Then the lights went down and the curtain came up on the main floor of Rick's Café Americain.

It was a dark and stormy night. The impression of clouds and the sound and visual effects of thunder and lightning filled the theater. Donovan wondered if there was thunder and lightning in the desert. That was the sort of question, surely, to keep him from sleeping that night. Still in his white linen suit, Kurt Sharkey paced back and forth, smoking furiously. Donovan was impressed with the man's ability to imitate Humphrey Bogart's manner of smoking. However much time Sharkey had practiced backstage was time well spent. Donovan looked at the man's receding hairline, which also recalled Bogart, and wondered if he could sing. If Sharkey's Hollywood movies were to be believed, he surely could emerge unscathed from bomb blasts, flaming crashes, and automatic weapons fire. But could he carry a tune? That, too, would soon be revealed.

After pacing back and forth for a moment, Sharkey consulted his watch, looked around, and called out, "Sam! Sam! Where the hell are you?"

According to the playbill, Sam was played by Henry Tippett, a black character actor of about sixty years who was best known for supporting roles in big-time movies. Among them were three buddy movies in which Tippett was the comic foil for Sharkey's wisecracking, macho cop. Those action films grossed hundreds of millions of dollars, and Holland's casting of the pair was considered, in show-biz circles, to be something of a coup.

Tippett appeared at the top of the grand staircase, his sparsly grey-haired head sitting above a freshly pressed tuxedo. This isn't in the movie, Donovan thought. The actor replied, "Here I am, Mr. Rick," and started down the stairs, which were at stage left and led down just to the right of the bar at which, sooner or later and at a properly dramatic moment, the assembled would sing the Marseillaise. Donovan wondered if Holland planned to claim the French national anthem as being his own work, too.

Sharkey turned toward the sound of Tippett's voice. He stood with hands on hips and watched his old friend and pianist descend the stairs. About halfway down Tippett paused, broke into a broad, toothy grin, raised his finger as if about to make a point, and was about to speak when he suddenly jerked, hit from behind. His body trembled, and his eyes flicked down to the spot of red that had abruptly appeared where his mortal heart used to be. Then he pitched forward and fell face down on the stairs, a crossbow bolt jutting angrily from his back.

Backstage, a woman screamed. Sharkey threw his cigarette down onto the stage. Members of the orchestra as well as the conductor and a few members of the audience rose to their feet, staring transfixed. "Son of a bitch!" Donovan swore, and began to run down the center aisle. More audience members stood, and there was more screaming. Holland got to his feet, gaping at the stage. Donovan skirted the orchestra pit and scrambled onto the stage, shoving into the orchestra's kettle drum a security guard who failed to recognize the detective and tried to stop him. There was more screaming backstage and it spread to the audience. The curtain came down.

Donovan got to the base of the stairs, flashing a badge in Sharkey's face and snapping, crisply, "Police." The actor was frozen in place, unable to move. Donovan dashed up the stairs, followed closely by the stage manager and several stagehands. He knelt beside the body and felt for a pulse. There was none. He whipped his phone from his pocket and dialed 911. He said, "Captain Donovan needs EMS at the Old Knickerbocker Theater, 987 West Forty-first Street, on the double." Then he grabbed a stagehand and said, "There are some detectives on the B-level. Get them up here." The man ran off.

"Is Henry...dead?" the stage manager asked, his face ashen.

"It looks that way, but maybe we'll luck out with the ambulance," Donovan said. "Nobody touches him. Nobody touches that arrow." Then he drew his Smith & Wesson from its shoulder holster, causing several gasps, and ran up the rest of the stairs.

The top led him through a curtain to a catwalk that ran from one side of the stage to the other. The catwalk connected at both ends with metal stairs used by the workers who raised, lowered, and otherwise tended the riot of curtains, lights, cables, and other fixtures suspended above the stage. Donovan thought quickly: The shot hit Tippett in the left back at a moment when he was standing angled to the right. The bolt had to come from stage left. Donovan got onto the catwalk and ran in that direction.

Two stagehands stood, white knuckled, on the stairs. "Did you see anyone?" Donovan barked at them.

"Like who?" one answered.

"Someone with a crossbow."

They looked at one another and then at the captain. "There were people around—extras, you know? We didn't see a crossbow."

"Extras were on the catwalk?"

"There was one guy."

"What was he—a stagehand?"

"No. An actor. An extra dressed like an Arab."

The other stagehand nodded in agreement.

Donovan's heart sank. You could easily hide a crossbow below one of the robes the several dozen extras wore backstage. The killer was, no doubt, long gone.

"Tall or short?"

"Uh...I couldn't say...but he had a mustache."

"Carrying anything?"

"No, but he had his arms folded and came barreling through like a fullback carrying the ball."

"Where'd he go?"

"He ran out this way."

The man pointed out the backstage door at the end of the catwalk.

"He nearly knocked me off the catwalk," the other stagehand said.

"Stay here," Donovan snapped.

The metal stairs were bolted to the brick wall that formed the barrier between stage left and the assortment of corridors and regular stairwells in that part of backstage. Every ten feet—roughly equivalent to a story—was a door that connected the metal stairs to the backstage corridors. Donovan hurried in the direction the killer had run, and found a door crowded with theater people, actors and stagehands alike. Fully half of them wore varying Arab robes. "Did anyone come running through here a moment ago?" Donovan asked.

Several people said they hadn't noticed. One extra, wearing a World War II French police uniform, had seen a mustached extra, dressed as an Arab, running down the corridor a moment before all hell broke loose. "But lots of people are running down these halls all the time," he said. "You have to get to your position."

Donovan nodded in glum acceptance of the fact that the killer would be hard, if not impossible, to catch that night. But he still asked the "policeman" to stay put, waiting for a real one to take his statement.

"Was Henry really shot?" someone else asked.

Donovan said "Yes," causing several more gasps, and returned to the stairs.

Sounding muffled from its source on the other side of the curtain, Holland's voice attempted to calm the audience.

Donovan put his revolver back in its holster and walked back out on the catwalk. The two stagehands whom he had met there were gaping over the rail at the scene below. Donovan took out his cell phone and dialed Moskowitz's number.

"Where are you?" he asked.

"With the body," was the reply.

"He's dead, then?"

"As a doornail."

"Is that one of Milos's bolts in him?"

"Bonaci hasn't gotten a close look yet. Where are you?"

"On the catwalk where the shot might have come from. I need a few guys up here to take statements. And get this whole area sealed off, would you?"

"The whole stage? Holland is screaming, 'The show must go on.' "

"My God! Just seal off the catwalk, then. Far be it from me to halt this entire production."

"I thought that's what you wanted."

"It is, but I also want to keep my job, and Holland has a lot of pull in this town. I'll leave it to the critics to stop the show. I'm sure they will."

"Did anyone see the perp?" Mosko asked.

"Three guys, but the sonofabitch was dressed like one of the Arab extras and there are dozens. Seal off the backstage doors and get the names of everyone who tries to leave for the rest of the night. Confiscate all the damn Arab robes and interview everyone in them. We're looking for a man with a mustache."

"That only describes half the Arab world."

"I'm gonna stay up here a minute and look around. Tell Bonaci to get some men up here ASAP. I want every kind of evidence there is—hair, fibers, prints—taken from this catwalk."

"That's where the shot came from?"

"I think so. But you never know." He eyed the old brick wall suspiciously.

Mosko said, "The stage manager wants to lower the stage— with Bonaci and me, the stairs, and the body on it—and have the staircase taken off and replaced with another."

"They have two?" Donovan asked.

"The other is an earlier version. He said they can put this one back exactly where it was once the performance is over."

"Let him do it, and I'll join you," Donovan said. "But first—go up two steps above the body and stand there for a minute."

"You got it," Mosko said, and did as he was told.

Donovan took that minute to spot his assistant and take note of everywhere on the catwalk from which Tippett could have been shot. Donovan also looked over his shoulder to see if there was another vantage point, from the stage-left utility stairs, perhaps, from which the shot could have been made. There appeared to be none, but a thorough look would have to wait. It was always possible that the Arab extra seen on the catwalk was just that—an extra who panicked and ran off after Tippett was shot.

Finally, Donovan went back down the catwalk and descended the staircase to where Moskowitz and Bonaci stood around the body. The stage manager stood by the foot of the stairs, impatiently checking and rechecking his watch. A few paces from him, seemingly frozen in the spot he occupied when Tippett was killed, was Kurt Sharkey. Donovan wondered if, at that moment, the man didn't wish he had never left Hollywood. From behind the curtain, Holland's voice uttered such words as "calm," "tragic incident," and "be patient."

Donovan said, "Lower the stage," and held on to one bannister—made of cheap pine that had been painted gold, he noticed—as the machinery lowered the stage to the construction level. The stairs vibrated ominously as the main floor of Rick's Café Americain slipped below the stage and clunked to a halt on the construction level below.

The A-level of the Old Knickerbocker was a broad, high-ceilinged area that resembled nothing so much as a large carpenter's shop. It smelled of sawdust and machine oil. The ceiling was a riot of ropes, pulleys, and other rigging. Three men stood to one side, ready to remove one stage and substitute another. The original "grand staircase" was, to Donovan, indistinguishable from the one on which he stood. But he assumed it was flimsier or had some other flaw.

Repeating for a new audience his admonition not to touch the body, Donovan led Mosko and Bonaci down the stairs. The three detectives got out of the way as stagehands rushed out of the shadows to roll the staircase—the corpse with it—off the platform. As Moskowitz and Bonaci followed Tippett's remains, Donovan sidled up to Sharkey, who was beginning to show signs of coming out of shock.

"Captain Bill Donovan, NYPD. Sorry I got in your face before."

Sharkey looked startled, but only for a moment. He said, "Forget it, pal. So Henry is really dead? Jeez, what a fuckin' nightmare."

Donovan knew "Jeez, what a fuckin' nightmare" was a phrase that cropped up in all three of the Dead Eyes movies made by Sharkey and Tippett. It was Sharkey's equivalent of Schwarzenegger's "I'll be back." So Sharkey had reacted to the tragedy by snapping back into his Hollywood persona. So much for the truly human reaction Donovan always looked for, but seldom got, when observing someone responding to death. It was then that he spotted the tiny diamond-stud earring, partly hidden by makeup, that decorated Sharkey's left lobe. That, too, was a Hollywood affectation, but one that would have appeared somewhat anachronous in 1941 North Africa. So much for taking a role seriously. Well, how seriously can you take a Holland musical, Donovan wondered.

"But you're going on with the show anyway," Donovan said.

"Yeah. You know what they say. Wish me luck. My friends tell me I sing like a bull moose in heat."

"Good luck," Donovan said, good-naturedly.

"I'll see you after the show? You'll come upstairs for the postmortem?" Sharkey caught himself, then smiled grimly, and continued, "Jeez, what a way to put it! I mean, you'll come upstairs for the first-night party?"

"I'll be there. I need to know if you saw anything."

"I saw Henry fall and that's it. But yeah, we'll talk later."

A rumble of steel wheels heralded the arrival of the replacement staircase. Donovan watched the stagehands lock the stairs in place, then scurried out of the way as Tippett's stand-in hurried onto the stage. He was a black man in his late sixties, noticeably older and taller than Tippett. His embrace and exchange of condolences with

Sharkey was interrupted when he made eye contact with Donovan and the two men recognized each other.

"Harry Spalding," Donovan said. "The last I saw you, it was at the Village Gate and you still had your trio."

"Young Bill Donovan. It's been too many years."

Amazed, Sharkey said, "You guys know each other?"

"We sure do," Spalding said. "We closed a few clubs together in the old days, Bill and me. The man knows his jazz, all right."

The stage manager came up and said, "Time, gentlemen."

"Later," Donovan said, and allowed the stage manager to lead him off into the wings of the A-level. There he watched as the stage once again was raised. Shortly thereafter came a roar of applause that seeped down to the A-level. Through muted loud-speakers, Donovan heard Sam's piano begin to play. Then the orchestra swelled up and, at last, he heard Sharkey sing. The words that stuck out were *"I came for the wa-ter, but I'll find love in Casa-blan-ca."* Exactly as Schadenfreud predicted, Donovan thought; not bad for a critic who had never heard a note of the score.

"Jeez, what a fuckin' nightmare," Donovan said. He thought he said it to himself, but Mosko had sidled up.

"You ain't kidding. I called downtown for help, 'cause there are reporters all around this building."

"I was referring to the show."

"That too. Look, Bonaci is taking care of the body, and Holland wants to see you."

"Is smoke coming out of his ears?" Donovan asked.

"You bet. Brits are funny when they get pissed off. You know they want to punch someone out but got no idea how to do it. So they stand there stiff-spined and sort of shake."

"Where is he?"

"On his way down here."

"That's just great. First he apologizes to the audience because murder held up the show. Then he comes down here to yell at me for not preventing it."

"Prevent it? What were you supposed to do, shoot the ghost?" Mosko asked.

They walked off the main floor of Rick's and into his "apartment and office." Ready to be rolled into place when needed, it sat to one side of the moveable stage. Adjacent to that set was Rick and Ilsa's apartment in Paris. On the other side of the stage was the hangar at the airport, in the background of which was the nose of a plane. Donovan looked at the sets in amazement. He had never been backstage at a Broadway theater, and for a moment allowed himself to be awed by the theater's ability to create illusions. Illusions are important in this world, he thought, wondering again where the bolt that killed Tippett might have come from.

The mood was broken when Holland appeared, not stiff-spined so much as red with rage. He was about to launch into a tirade when the captain, having survived many such tantrums on the part of VIPs, decided to launch his own—a preemptive strike.

"I want you to close this show down," he snapped.

Caught off guard, Holland stammered, "What? What?"

"This theater is still under construction. The walls have holes and someone is shooting crossbow darts through them. Two people have died so far. I won't let your lax security cause another death."

"My security?"

"Is laughable," Donovan said. "Today a killer proved that being on the Broadway stage does not protect one from being murdered. A week ago, the same murderer—presumably—proved you weren't safe being a construction worker in the basement, either."

"I can't shut down my show," Holland pleaded, his tone having lost its angry edge and turned pathetic.

"You've pulled out all the stops in order to give this show its grand opening night celebration in Times Square on New Year's Eve. The flood of workmen coming and going from this place is like a tidal wave. And then there are the extras in Arab garb. Attila the Hun could ride in here with a regiment of horsemen and no one would notice."

"Who would want to kill Henry Tippett?"

"I don't know...but I intend to find out," Donovan said, wandering into the hangar set and picking up the bottle of Vichy water that would serve in the show's climactic moment. At least Holland kept that, Donovan thought.

"Please do it soon, Captain," the producer said. "I simply must get this show opened on New Year's Eve."

"Why the big hurry?"

"May I be honest with you?"

"I wish you would," Donovan said, indicating for Moskowitz to give them privacy. The detective complied, strolling back to the apartment set and staring out the false window at "Paris"—a painting of skyline and Eiffel Tower.

"This is strictly confidential," Holland said.

"What do you have to say?"

"This show has cost me over twenty million dollars, not counting the renovation of the theater," Holland said. "I have borrowed heavily from the banks, with the promise I would launch this show with the biggest explosion of publicity ever seen on the Great White Way. This show has to be a hit, or else I lose the building."

"Tomorrow's papers should be interesting," Donovan mused.

"God, I can only imagine."

"KNOCKING 'EM DEAD ON BROADWAY will be on page one of the Post."

"My creditors will go berserk. I'm telling you, Captain, someone is trying to kill this show. That's why three people have died in this theater."

"If someone wants to stop a Broadway show, is killing the actors the best way to do it?" The melody to "Springtime for Hitler" cropped up in Donovan's head.

"It may not be the most sophisticated way to halt a production, but it sure is the fastest. It brought you here, threatening to shut me down. As if you have the authority."

"Well, to be honest with you, I don't. But I can have an army of building and safety inspectors in here in five minutes, and they have the authority. And there's always OSHA—the Occupational Safety and Health Administration. If ever there was an occupational hazard that ought to shut down a workplace, a madman with a crossbow is it."

"You made your point," Holland said, mopping his brow although he didn't seem to be sweating.

"So tell me, who would want to stop this show?" Donovan asked.

"I have made a few enemies over the years," Holland admitted.

"Name them."

"Lucien Schadenfreud, for one."

"Critics don't count," Donovan said. Then he thought for a second and added, "Do they?"

"He does. The man is a maniac."

"The man is a drunk."

"Don't underestimate drunks."

"I don't. But I've seen his hands shake. He can barely hit his mouth with a martini glass. God forbid he should try to hit a difficult target with a crossbow."

"Nonetheless, put him on your list."

"If you insist. At the very least, the man seems to have been involved with a huge number of prominent people who died. What other suspects can you give me?"

"Mala Logan," Holland said, speaking the words with a pronounced sigh.

"The British actress?"

"If you want to call her that."

"I don't pay much attention to show-biz stories, but wasn't she suing you for something?"

"I cast her in the London production of *Casablanca: The Musical* and originally promised her she would star in the Broadway opener."

"But something happened," Donovan said.

"Yes. She demanded three million dollars, plus a percentage, to star in the show on Broadway. So I dropped her and got Elena Jordan instead."

"Who can't sing but is a Hollywood star."

"Well, she's not that bad vocally. I was being facetious when I told you she can't sing. She's been taking lessons like mad and was looking forward, albeit nervously—the poor woman is a wreck—to her singing debut."

"But Elena Jordan only cost you one million," Donovan said.

"Correct. I congratulate you on your memory. However, Mala sued me for breach of contract and I was forced to settle for a million."

"So the Mala affair cost you two million. You're still a million ahead. Plus all that publicity must be worth something."

"I suppose ticket sales haven't suffered," Holland admitted.

"By my admittedly flawed reasoning, Mala Logan made a million dollars off of you for doing nothing. So why does she want to kill you?"

"I bruised her precious ego," Holland said. "No one ever said 'no' to her before. Plus, she would have made a lot more money had I said 'yes.' "

"I still don't see a motive for murder," Donovan said. "And another thing...I saw her on 'Masterpiece Theatre' last year. She doesn't look capable of anything physical. Isn't she about five feet tall and skinny?"

"Five-two, and she has a black belt in tae kwon do," Holland said.

"Maybe that keeps her in shape and offers some protection against muggers, but it doesn't make her a marksman. Sorry, Sir John, but Mala Logan doesn't strike me as your typical mad killer."

"You'll change your mind once you meet her."

"And when will that be?"

"Tonight, after the show, of course. I'm giving a party upstairs. You'll be there, I hope."

"Let me get this straight. Mala Logan is homicidal, and yet you asked her to your party."

Holland shrugged. "She called me and asked if she could come. No doubt she wants to wish me ill. How can I deny the lady? But don't you find it odd she suddenly turns up just as people start dying in my theater?"

"I'm supposed to find it odd a famous actress shows up on theater row?" Donovan asked.

Holland patted Donovan on the arm, and said, "Just meet her. You'll see the hatred in her eyes."

"Okay," Donovan said with a sigh. "Is there anyone else who might want to ruin you badly enough to commit murder?"

"That's all I can think of at the moment," Holland said.

"Try to give it more thought and get back to me."

"We'll talk later," Holland said, making motions to leave.

"Just a minute," Donovan said. "I need your permission, as owner of the theater, to search the entire building, including the dressing rooms."

"What on earth for?"

"A crossbow comes to mind."

"My God, think of the impact on my stars!"

"Would that be anything like the impact of an arrow to the heart?" Donovan asked.

"Kurt may talk rough, but he's a prima donna. Elena is a pile of jangling nerves. No, searching their rooms would give them apoplexy. Search the extras' dressing areas if you like, search our living quarters if it pleases you..."

"Whose living quarters? Who lives in the building?"

"Anton and I both live here. I have a suite, he has a room. Turn them upside down if you like, but stay away from the stars' dressing rooms."

Donovan reluctantly agreed. There was no way Sharkey or Jordan could have pulled that trigger anyway, the captain mused.

When at last Holland had gone, Moskowitz walked over with Bonaci. Several of the crime-scene chief's men were atop the original stairs, taking photos and measurements of the body. Apart from them, though, it was as if no one was taking notice. Stagehands and other theater workers scurried around the base of the stairs, carrying this and that. Not one of them paid attention to the body on the stairs and the policemen working over it. Donovan was reminded of those New York City sidewalk scenes where you could stand on one foot, balancing a bowl of salad on your head and reciting the Bhagavad Gita, and no one would pay attention to you. The reason so many people came to live in New York was you could live anonymously, mostly unnoticed. You could also die anonymously, entirely unnoticed.

"We finally got some good light into that grave," Bonaci reported. "We took samples of the blue-black dust surrounding that impression of a crossbow which, by the way, was by the victim's right hand. According to the lack of dust beneath the outline of the weapon, I would say the bow was removed within a week of our having opened the coffin."

"But after the water main break exposed it."

"Yeah. Somebody was there before us and took it out. And the dart that killed Tippett was definitely Milos's," Bonaci reported.

"He has three left," Donovan replied.

# NINE

## MURRAY HILL 2, BUTTERFIELD 8

THE ROAR OF THE CROWD and the rustling noise it made clambering to its feet for a standing ovation told Donovan two things. One, the show was over. Two, no one ever went broke underestimating the taste of the American public. *Casablanca: The Musical* was going to be the big Broadway musical of the twentieth century's climactic years. As he pondered what the apparent success of the show would mean for American culture, Donovan slipped back onto the stage-left utility stairs. He was looking for the spot from which the killer had fired his most recent deadly bolt.

For ten or fifteen minutes as the curtain calls came and, finally, went, Donovan prowled the utility stairs alone. A few stagehands were around, lowering this and raising that. Some jostled him as he ran his fingers over the aging bricks, looking for clues.

The backstage wall was rife with history. Not just a simple brick surface, it was covered with ancient graffiti. Some scrawlings were measurements, apparently, calculations made for load-bearing ropes. Others were long-gone names or forgotten Manhattan telephone exchanges: MUrray Hill 2, BUtterfield 8, UNiversity 5. Mixed in were attachment points for various types of rigging. Some of these devices were decades old and consisted of heavy cast-iron rings. Others were brand-new stainless-steel fittings that gleamed in the slivers of light that cascaded down from the stage lighting. Every so often a thick, black, iron strap ran for five or six feet down the face of the brick. It was, Donovan thought, as if a giant from nineteenth-century New York was trying to rein in the bulging cage of a beast. Try how he might, however, nowhere could Donovan find a hole from which someone could have fired a crossbow bolt. If there was a beast, most likely it was one able to dress up like an extra, shoot from the catwalk or stairs, and blend in with the dozens—if not hundreds—of on- and offstage personnel wandering about backstage.

After spending twenty minutes running hands over brick, bolt, and strap, Donovan sat down on the crosswalk and waited while the moveable stage came back into view carrying the second stairs. The show was over and the final set—the hangar and the airport—was stowed below. At Donovan's request and with Moskowitz lording over the demonstration, stagehands sent the main floor of Rick's back up. Moskowitz rode the stairs once more, standing at a spot equivalent to where Tippett was felled. The detective stood and played victim for another twenty minutes while his boss tried again to figure out the angle from which came the fatal bolt. In the end, Donovan called off the experiment and tossed his hands up.

"The shot came from the crosswalk or near where it joins the stage-left utility stairs," he pronounced.

Mosko had joined his boss on those stairs and was taking his first look at the murder scene. "I don't see any holes in this wall," he said.

Donovan patted the bricks and said, "This wall is nearly a hundred years old and somebody put cast iron straps on it. You know that six-story building on Canal Street that fell down last year?"

"The vibrations from the subway shook it apart," Mosko said, nodding.

"It had straps on it like these."

Donovan poked a finger at the nearest of the heavy iron bindings. "These are as big as the straps that anchored the rigging on the USS *Constitution*," he said.

"So maybe this place is falling down and that will be the end of the production. And then you and your friend, Schadenfreud, will be happy."

"Building collapse could be the only thing that will end it," Donovan said ruefully. "Did you hear that standing ovation?"

Mosko had. "The stagehands and carpenters on the A-level were all cheering," he said. "They know they're gonna have jobs for six or seven years."

"I need to talk to Derrida about this wall," Donovan said. "Have you seen him?"

"He's not here. A few of the guys downstairs were looking for him. What do you need to ask him?"

"I want to know how thick this wall is and what's on the other side."

Mosko eyeballed the brick edifice, leaning back to appreciate its height, then said, "It's a foot or so thick and on the other side are backstage corridors and stuff. Dressing rooms."

"Not likely," Donovan said. "I paced off the distance between these bricks and the ones on the inside. There's a pace unaccounted for—about three feet."

"Homes for the pigeons, then," Mosko said. "I'll see if I can't reach Derrida at home. While we're on the subject, Bock is nowhere to be found, either."

"That's interesting. He just vanished? We have a body onstage and the man who led us to Milos's grave—from which the murder weapon was taken—has taken a powder?"

"Oh, come on," Mosko exclaimed. "You can't suspect him of being the killer?"

"Why not?"

"He stands to make money off Holland. Why would he do anything to hurt the man?"

"Then where is he?" Donovan asked.

"I can tell you he didn't leave. We got all the backstage exits covered and have been searching the extras' dressing rooms and everyone who leaves."

"How are they taking it?"

"There are a few angry actors out there in Times Square."

"There's a broken heart for every brick on Broadway," Donovan said idly. "Did we find anything resembling a crossbow?"

"Nope," Mosko replied.

"I suppose the killer could have blended in with the audience."

"Not with a crossbow. We were watching that door, too."

"People wear bulky coats in December," Donovan said.

"Yeah, but this is a matinee and it's still light out. Go ahead and convince me our killer is a suburban theater-party member who is hiding a crossbow under her mink coat."

"The man has a point," Donovan said.

The relentless activity backstage—tying back curtains, storing those smaller sets kept on the main stage level—had died down a bit. Yet the stage manager could be seen lurking about the base of the stairs. He seemed agitated, yet reluctant to disturb the detectives in their work. Finally he managed to make himself so much in evidence that, looking down from above, Donovan made eye contact.

"Do you need something from me?" he asked.

"Yeah. If you're done with the stairs, I need to lower the stage."

"We're done with it," Donovan replied.

"Thanks, Captain. Did you know the writer guy is looking for you?"

"Who, Bock?"

Donovan and Moskowitz looked at one another.

"That's him. The one who's writing the book about Sir John."

"Where is he?" Mosko asked.

"In the video booth," the stage manager replied, his tone of voice suggesting it was the most logical place in the world to look for the man.

The detectives exchanged further glances.

"Where's the video booth?" Donovan asked.

The room was located to one side of the projection booth. What was, during the Old Knickerbocker's movie-house days, a complex of three rooms, had been reduced to one projection room and a two-room video studio. What remained of the projection room served to throw black-and-white images of World War II, especially the campaign in North Africa, onto a screen behind the stage at key moments during the show. The newly installed video facility, which included a professional Ikegami camera pointed out a window in the direction of the stage, was used to create tapes of the show for the purposes of public relations and advertising.

Roger Bock sat at an editing console, looking at an image of Henry Tippett caught at the moment of death. The man was in the background and relatively small, even on the tiny screen. Sharkey and his cigarette occupied most of the picture. But the depiction of death remained clear and chilling. Donovan had Bock play it again and again before calling a halt to the demonstration and rubbing his eyes.

Bock turned the room lights back up. "So what do you think?" he asked.

"I think I should have asked whether the show was being taped or not," Donovan replied.

"Do you want a copy?"

"I want the original. You keep a copy."

Bock shrugged and pressed a button. A black plastic cassette popped out of one of two editing decks on the console at which the writer sat. Bock took the tape and handed it to the captain, who frowned at the half-inch VHS tape in his hand. As Mosko watched in admiration, Donovan leaned forward and pressed a button on the other deck. Out popped a three-quarter-inch cassette. Donovan palmed that one, returning the other to Bock.

"This is the original," the captain said.

"Oh, sorry," Bock said. Donovan wasn't prepared to bet the regret was sincere.

"That Ikegami is a professional, three-quarter-inch machine," Donovan said.

"I'm sorry. I'm not a video pro."

"Who shot the footage of the stage?"

"Maurice did," Bock replied, indicating a chubby technician who had taken to hovering near the scene of the inquisition.

"Does that tell you what you wanted to know about the murder?" the man asked, sauntering in closer.

"It confirms what I saw with my own eyes," Donovan said. "Tippett was hit from behind and to his left. Probably from a little above, too. I think the shot came from the vicinity of the catwalk the actors used to get to the top of the stairs. But I'll know better when I get this blown up."

"Can I get the original back when you're done?"

"Sure thing. So tell me, Maurice, where was this guy while you were taping?"

"Beats me," the technician replied. "He came in a while after the murder and asked to see the tape."

"Well, isn't that fascinating," Donovan said.

"Where were you?" Mosko asked Bock.

Taken aback and now white as a cloud, Bock said, "Back-stage."

"Where backstage?"

"I was sitting in Sharkey's dressing room reading the script."

"Was anyone with you?" Donovan asked.

"No."

"How did you know Tippett was killed?"

"I heard people yelling in the corridor and ran out."

"So no one can swear you were in the dressing room when the murder took place," Donovan said.

Bock hesitated, switching gears from astonishment to defiance. "You can't think I had anything to do with the murder," he said.

"You knew where Milos's grave was. The grave had been robbed of the murder weapon. You have no alibi for the time of the killing. After it happened you ran right up here—to run off a dub of the tape and, later, to try to pass it off on me. What were you up to? Seeing if the murderer was caught on tape by some chance?"

Now truly angry, Bock said, "I wanted to see what happened, that's all."

"Where were you the night of December twelfth?" Mosko asked.

"I was home, alone, writing."

"And the night of December fourth?"

"The same."

"You're in trouble, pal," Mosko said.

"I don't have to put up with this," Bock stammered.

"Oh, yes you do," Donovan replied.

"I'm going to speak to my attorney."

"I've known a lot of writers. Most of them can't afford attorneys. But you go out and hire one, if it makes you feel better. We'll talk again when he's around. But you can be sure we will talk again."

"Can I go?" Bock asked.

Donovan said, "Yes," and the man hurried off. When the door had closed behind him, Maurice said, "Wow. I've never seen anything like that before."

"Why did you let Bock just walk in here and take over your console?" Donovan asked.

"Mr. Holland gave him carte blanche. He can go anywhere he wants in this theater."

"And he seems to know a lot about the place. Okay, Maurice, I'll be sure to return your tape when I'm done with it."

"That's good. I mean, I made myself a dub, too, but it's always better to have the original."

When Donovan and Moskowitz were once again alone, the captain said, "Get me Derrida. I want him down here with the blueprints to this dump tucked under his arm."

"You got it," Mosko replied.

The video booth was on the first balcony level. Its door was designed to make it resemble the entrance to an expensive box. The corridor itself was wide and grand, and decorated with lush brown tapestry dotted every so often with paintings of colonial American themes. There was an oil of Wall Street when there still was a wall, and the Canal Street region when water still flowed in the canal.

The corridor curved around the periphery of the theater. They walked along it in the direction of the twin grand staircases that led to the lobby. The theater was largely empty of audience at that point, and the voices of the few who lingered in the lobby carried up the marble stairs and down the corridor. Donovan couldn't make out their words, but the sound made him again aware of the immensity of the building. He tossed the video cassette up in the air and caught it, again and again.

"How did you get to know so much about video?" Mosko asked.

"Once the press has chased you around for enough years, you get to know something about the technology. Besides, do you remember Michael Avignon?"

"The crazy photographer?"

"Videographer. The guy who got in our way when we were chasing that murderer in the Cathedral of St. John the Divine?"

"How could I forget him? He was another of those colorful characters you tend to be attracted to. You sure know how to find 'em, boss."

They started down the grand staircase, their footfalls echoing in the almost-empty lobby. But when they got halfway down and the main entrance hove into view, they could see the crowd of reporters and TV crews being kept at bay outside by uniformed officers. Abruptly and without discussing the matter, they turned around and went back upstairs.

"Lucien Schadenfreud is gonna be another one, isn't he?" Mosko asked.

"Another what?"

"Another weird 'friend of Bill.' "

"Holland thinks the man could be the killer," Donovan said.

"So of course you're gonna pal up with him. I can see it coming."

Donovan said, "When you get Derrida on the phone, tell him to meet me on the catwalk."

"YOU'RE A HARD MAN to please, Captain," Derrida said, spreading a blueprint across the top of the catwalk railing while keeping another tucked precariously under his arm. "I'm on my way to the theater for what promises to be a great party and you got me stopping off at the office first to pick up blueprints. All because you want to know about this brick wall."

"Henry Tippett is dead, which means the body count in this building is now three," Donovan replied. "And I have a deep and abiding suspicion of old and apparently innocent structures in New York City. That's ever since I discovered a whole army of people living in tunnels beneath Riverside Park."

"I agree it's a tragedy about these victims, and I'll do whatever I can to help you catch the man who's doing it. But I can tell you right now there are no secret passages or tunnels in the Old Knickerbocker Theater," the construction chief said.

"Did you tell me there was a body buried in the basement?"

"That's different."

"How is it different?"

"Who could have known?"

"It would seem to me the guy hired to renovate the building should have known," Donovan said.

"If that water main never broke it would still be a secret," Derrida said.

"Convince me this wall is just a wall," Donovan said, pointing at the strap-crossed, fitting-studded structure.

Derrida ran a finger across the blueprint, which crinkled loud enough to be heard over the orchestra—playing at full tilt near the end of act three of the musical's evening performance. "This is an interior, load-bearing wall designed to help hold up the dome of the theater and, at the same time, provide anchoring points for various pieces of stage equipment. The curtain machinery is anchored partly in this wall and partly in its twin on stage right."

"How thick is it?"

"Two feet at parts, widening to four feet where it backs up with various corridors."

"Why is that?"

"To accommodate risers—steam pipes and electrical conduits, for the most part. And there is a system of dumbwaiters that are no longer in use."

"I knew it," Donovan said triumphantly.

"They're bricked up and have been for years," Derrida said.

"Nonetheless, is there one nearby?"

Donovan scanned the wall, searching it for any sign of something hidden behind the apparently imperturbable bricks. Derrida moved the blueprint around to make accessible another part of it. He scrutinized that, and said, "There is a dumbwaiter shaft that goes right by here. If you look down there"—he pointed down to the stage level—"you will see evidence that once there was a small door that gave access to the dumbwaiter. But it's bricked up."

"The shaft continues up and goes right by here?" Donovan asked, imperturbed himself.

"Of course. You would want the dumbwaiter to open where you can get to it, wouldn't you? Not in the middle of the wall twenty feet up from the stage where you would need a ladder."

Donovan stepped to feel the wall where Derrida said the dumbwaiter shaft went by. The bricks were indeed solid. It seemed to Donovan one would need a sledgehammer to break through.

"Is that solid, or is that solid?" Derrida asked, rerolling the blueprint and tucking it under his arm with the rest of them.

"That's solid," Donovan admitted.

"So let's go to the party. We may not be able to bring back the dead, but we can toast their memories."

"You're all heart," Donovan said, but the man merely smiled in reply. Derrida was edging toward the doorway leading to the backstage corridor, and Donovan followed. Below him on the stage, Sharkey was breaking into song. Donovan caught the rhymes "dust" and "trust" as well as "sand" and "friend." He muttered, "I ought to revoke Holland's poetic license," and, in taking one last look at the stage, stepped through the door and into Moskowitz.

"What about a license?" he asked.

Donovan repeated his complaint.

"I always seem to be coming in late on your profound thoughts," Mosko said. He nodded in the direction of Derrida, who was loitering a few paces down the hall waiting for Donovan to catch up.

"You asked me to find out when Derrida was in Vietnam. He was in-country from 1967 to 1969."

"He was what?" Donovan asked.

"He was in-country from—"

"Where'd you get that from?"

"Get what from?" Mosko asked.

"That phrase, 'in-country.' "

"I don't know. That's what people say. If you were in Vietnam, you were 'in-country.' "

"I know a lot of World War II vets. Some of them were in Germany. Not one of them ever told me he was 'in-country' in Germany. And George Kohler, my favorite bartender—pain in the ass that he is—was in Korea, but he was never 'in-country' in Korea. And I guarantee Caesar was never 'in-country' in Gaul."

"Why are you hocking me about this?" Mosko asked.

" 'In-country' is a cliché you got from watching movies about Vietnam," Donovan said.

"So what if I did?"

Donovan frowned and walked over to Derrida, who asked, "News from the front?"

"In a manner of speaking. Tell me, Jack, does the name Tri Ng Dinh mean anything to you?"

"Vietnamese?"

Donovan nodded.

"Nope. Never heard of the man. Who is it?"

"The first victim of this particular crime wave."

"Oh, the Asian in the basement? What about him?"

"Did he work for you?"

"I told you, no. But you can check my payroll records if you like."

"We will," Donovan said.

"You're a suspicious man, Captain Donovan," Derrida said.

"It's part of the job description."

Derrida smiled, and said, "Come on upstairs and let's have a drink on Holland."

No longer willing to wait, Derrida headed off on his own. When he was out of earshot, Moskowitz said, "I don't get the custom of standing around drinking when someone dies."

"Try to think of it as an Irish wake, even though Holland is British."

"It's not right."

"You would rather sit shiva?"

"To be honest with you, yes. On top of there having been a death in the family today, don't all these people hate one another?"

"To the best of my knowledge, tonight Holland only has to put up with one guest who hates him—Mala Logan. I guess we should keep an eye on her. She's supposed to be a black belt in tae kwon do. Can you handle that if the lady turns violent on us?"

"It depends on what degree black belt she is," Mosko said with profound distaste.

"Well, never mind. I can always shoot her if she turns ornery on us. But my guess is this will be a thoroughly phony but essentially harmless event. These are show people," Donovan said. "They'll hug each other, say how sick they are Tippett was killed and how much they adored him, then they'll say 'I hope this doesn't hurt the show' and get on with the main reason they're there—to make dates or deals.''

"I hope you're going to enjoy this as much as I am," Mosko said.

# TEN

## WHO'S DOING IT, WHO'S NEXT,
## AND WHAT'S THIS ALL ABOUT?

WHEN HE STEPPED INTO Peter Minuit's Penthouse, Donovan found a room thick with fashionably dressed bodies and scented with the twin blossoms of fresh flowers and iced whiskey. And, as if to remove any doubt the evening would be memorable, the two people who rushed up to greet him—arms linked—were Sir John Victor Holland and Lucien Schadenfreud.

Donovan and Moskowitz just had time to exchange astonished glances before they were swept into the maelstrom of greetings and machinations. "We must have come in too late for the eulogies," Mosko stage-whispered to his boss, who nodded and said, "Yep."

Holland wrapped his arms around Donovan's shoulders and only a well-timed glower saved Mosko from the same fate. Undaunted, Holland said, "Captain! Thank God you could make it. And Sergeant Moskowitz, how good to see you. What a day. What a day. What a day! Poor Henry. Have you...?"

"Caught anyone?" Donovan asked.

"Moon rockets don't move that fast," Mosko said.

"No, of course you haven't. But the show, you've heard the old saying, 'the show must go on.' It surely did, and wasn't it marvelous? I understand you and Harry Spalding go way back. Wasn't he wonderful? The man is a genius, and to be able to walk onstage in the middle of a great tragedy and perform like that."

"Is he here tonight?" Donovan asked.

"At the piano, of course," Holland replied, sweeping a bony hand in the direction of the sound of playing—a tune from the score, naturally.

"Doesn't he get time off?" Mosko asked.

"Oh sure, he's just enjoying himself a bit. As am I. It's great to have the show open—in previews anyway—at last, and to have all my friends here. As you can imagine, tonight's party is just a warm-up for the big bash in Times Square on New Year's Eve. And you know what the terrible irony is? Henry's tragic death will make this the hottest ticket in town."

He grasped Schadenfreud's hand in both of his and squeezed it. The critic grinned foolishly. He looked like he needed a drink.

Donovan shifted his gaze back and forth from one to the other of the men standing before him. Then he said to the critic, "Well, Luke my friend, what about yon enemy?" Donovan nodded at Holland.

"We made up," Schadenfreud said with a sheepish grin.

"Oh, that was all exaggerated, that stuff about differences between us," Holland added. "We're like a big family, my friends and I. Sometimes we quarrel, like families do. But we always get over it. And there's great news!"

"What?" Donovan asked.

"Guess who The Times has assigned to review *Casablanca: The Musical?*"

"Surprise me."

Schadenfreud raised his hand.

"What happened—the wrestling critic was tied up?"

Schadenfreud blushed, and Holland said, "I have no idea what you mean by that. I'm delighted with the choice. Luke understands my music better than anyone."

"He certainly seems to know it well," Donovan said, recalling how Schadenfreud sang him a verse after claiming never to have heard a note.

"My editor felt John's Broadway music is based in rock," Schadenfreud said.

"I didn't hear any rock and roll down there," Donovan said. "If I had, I would have been out of the theater like a shot—murders or no murders."

"So they asked me to review it. There is a precedent. I've reviewed some off-off-Broadway productions and an occasional offbeat film."

"So you'll be leaving the party to go write the review?" Mosko asked.

"That's not how we do it," Schadenfreud said. "We don't critique previews, exactly. We watch several of them and write a review that's printed the day after the grand premiere."

"In other words," Holland said, "Luke will be in and out of the theater a lot in the next two weeks and then will write a review that appears on New Year's Day."

"Today's performance was the first you've seen?" Donovan asked.

"This afternoon's was," Schadenfreud said.

"You were in the theater when Tippett was killed?"

"Yes. Wasn't that awful? I ran back to the office and filed a story the hard news guys will incorporate into their news coverage of the murder."

"Why didn't you just write the news story?" Donovan asked.

"They wouldn't let me," Schadenfreud said, his voice turning sheepish again.

"I guess there's politics everywhere. So Luke, you're telling me you never heard the score before this afternoon?"

"Never heard it."

"No one who hasn't been in the theater has heard the music," Holland said.

"Fascinating," Donovan replied. "Nearly as interesting as how and when you guys got to be friends again."

Holland said, "This evening we spoke for the first time in—oh, it must be at least fifteen years."

"I called to express my condolences about Henry," Schadenfreud explained.

"And we made up over the phone and I asked him to come here."

"That's very civilized," Donovan said.

"I can't wait to read Luke's review. But I don't want to do anything to influence the man—so, I'm going to get him a big drink."

Schadenfreud emitted a glow of anticipation as Holland snapped his fingers high above his head and called out, "Anton!"

Presently the man appeared, looking harried but stoic. Holland said, "A Bombay martini, very dry, with an olive. And I'll have a Kir on the rocks. What's your pleasure, Captain?"

"Nothing, thanks. I'm going to need all my wits about me to keep up with you guys."

"As you wish. Sergeant?"

"Not unless you can make an egg cream."

"Not a chance," Anton said with a sigh.

"Then forget it."

When the martini was produced, Schadenfreud sipped it—Donovan noticed his hands were rock-steady—and immediately showed signs of relief. A blush came to his cheeks and the apparent tension in his spine went away.

Holland smiled and said, "Luke, if you'll excuse us, I want to introduce the captain around."

"Keep our friend company," Donovan said to Moskowitz.

"You got it. I want to talk over some things with him anyway."

Donovan let himself be taken by the elbow and steered through the packed café. The fashionably dressed crowd parted for Holland, the Paris dresses and Italian suits swept aside by the power of money and celebrity.

Donovan wondered who all those people were. They all looked vaguely familiar, though it might only have been that they acted as if one should recognize them. On either side of him, on both men and women, facial expressions and body language said, "Mere mortals, be in awe." Donovan had been with celebrities before, and generally speaking wasn't impressed. But he had never been amidst such a collection of egos in his life. At the very least, Donovan was grateful he wore his best suit.

Kurt Sharkey had changed from his stage clothes into his Hollywood garb. That evening, his wardrobe included a baggy, black Italian suit cut from some fabric that shined in the artificial light and looked cheap—an affectation, Donovan was sure. Beneath it was a custom-made white dress shirt buttoned at the neck and worn with no tie. Sharkey had rubbed the stage makeup off his earring, though a smudge lingered below his earlobe. He stood a discrete distance from Elena Jordan. The stars were close enough to suggest a relationship, but far enough apart to make it clear that such would never be consummated. They were together professionally—taking calls, as it were.

Sharkey recognized Donovan and a light came into his eyes. It was the light of shared experience. For a fleeting moment, Donovan felt almost a comrade-in-arms with the tough-guy Hollywood star.

"Hiya, buddy," Sharkey said, switching a fat glass from one hand to the other and sticking his palm in Donovan's direction. His voice seemed a bit raspy, and he spoke quietly.

They shook.

"Jeez, what a fuckin' nightmare," Donovan said.

Sharkey waggled the glass, which contained a syrupy, dark brown liquid.

"You bet. This stuff tastes like cough syrup. But I got to take it easy on my voice or I'll never get through the previews."

Donovan had meant the murder, but felt it would be uncharitable—and probably pointless—to tell the man so.

"What're you drinking?" he asked instead.

"Southern Comfort and Coke."

"Another nightmare."

"It's great for the pipes."

"The man has to take care of his instrument," Holland said, a bit sternly, no doubt thinking of the millions he was paying for this man's singing debut. "Captain, I forgot that you know Kurt Sharkey."

"We met in Casablanca, but hardly under the best of circumstances."

"But it is my pleasure to introduce you to the costar of *Casablanca: The Musical,* Elena Jordan."

The woman was tall, thin, and delicate, with fine bones and exaggerated breasts. She was a blond, with large, dewy eyes and pouty lips that curled down slightly at the corners, giving her the mournful look preferred by many fashion models. And she was, more than ever, a nervous wreck.

"Captain Donovan is investigating Henry's death," Holland said.

She placed her hand in Donovan's. It was shaking when he

squeezed it gently, carefully, sensing that to do otherwise would bruise her.

"That was dreadful what happened," she said, her voice scarcely more than a whisper. Either this woman is hiding a booming voice, Donovan thought, or the theater's sound engineer deserves a Nobel Prize.

"Yes, it was," Donovan said.

"I can't stop shaking. Look at my arms." She held them up so he could inspect the goosebumps.

"Let me fix that," he said. Donovan offered a kindly smile as he rubbed her arms to warm them up and make the bumps go away.

"Henry was such a kind man. And to think he could be taken like that, onstage, in plain view of seventeen hundred people. None of us is safe, you know that, don't you? Do you have any idea who's done this awful thing?"

Having just enjoyed a sip of his potion, Sharkey said, "Don't you know, sweetheart? It's the famous ghost of the Old Knickerbocker."

Donovan was certain now that Sharkey's imitation of Bogart was so second-nature that the actor was unaware of doing it.

"There's more? A mad killer isn't enough? Are you telling me that the theater has a ghost?"

"Milos the Magnificent, a vaudevillian," Donovan said.

"A vaudevillian what?"

"Trick shot with the crossbow," Holland said pointedly.

Her eyes widened. Donovan would have sworn that wasn't possible.

"Wasn't Henry killed by a crossbow?" she asked.

"Yes—as a matter of fact, he probably was killed by Milos's very weapon," Donovan said.

This time Holland's eyes widened.

"This gets better and better, doesn't it, pal?" Sharkey said.

"You bet," Donovan said, in his best buddy-movie voice. "Tippett was killed by a crossbow bolt that was buried with Milos the Magnificent in 1933."

"Milos was buried in the basement," Holland said. He sounded like someone who was pitching a movie idea to a studio head.

Donovan was certain that a production based on the long-dead marksman was more than a casual idea.

The actress mulled over this information for a moment, then said, with a trace of a giggle—the sort that frightened people affect in an effort to ease the fear—"I hope he's still in his grave. Oh my, that sounds awful of me to be laughing at a time like this. I'm ready to go home to L.A. and my house in Brentwood, show or no show."

"Don't talk that way, darling," Holland said. "It makes my lawyer nervous."

"As a matter of fact," Donovan said, "We found the grave this afternoon."

Holland gave him a hard stare.

"And he's still in it."

"I'm sure glad to hear that," Sharkey said.

"But the crossbow and bolts aren't," Donovan said.

"They were taken by the killer!" Sharkey said.

"Must be: I don't believe in ghosts," Donovan said.

"I wouldn't be so fast, pal," Sharkey said. "I was standing as close to Henry as anyone and I didn't see a goddamn thing."

Elena looked puzzled. She asked, "If you just dug up the body this afternoon, how did the crossbow get out?"

"We only found the body this afternoon," Donovan said. "But someone got there before us."

"Grave robbers!" Holland said, almost gleefully. Donovan wondered what musical number involving grave-robbing might find its way into the Milos production.

"When could that have happened?" Elena asked.

"Do you remember that water main break?"

"God, yes, I was trapped in the Russian Tea Room all evening and finally had to walk back to my hotel. It was dreadful."

"I understand," Donovan said. "I once got locked overnight in a Blarney Stone and was woken up by rats the next morning."

Sharkey said to Holland, "I like this guy."

"You're joking, of course," Elena said.

Donovan shrugged. "Maybe. The water main break uncovered Milos's grave. Someone found it, took his weapon, threw the broken pieces of concrete back into the grave, and has been using the crossbow to kill people—two that I'm sure of. The questions are, who's doing it, who's next, and what's this all about?''

His audience mulled that information for a moment. At last Sharkey spoke.

"Do you have any suspects?"

"One or two, but I can't tell you who they are."

Elena said, with a nervous laugh, "I hope you're not thinking of me."

"I think of you constantly," Donovan said, adding to the harmless lie a harmless flirt. "But not as a murder suspect."

"You're very sweet. And very charming for a policeman."

Sharkey said, "Come on, honey, it's good business to be suspected of murder. Think of what it's done for O.J. Simpson's career."

"What a ghastly thing to say."

"The man tells the truth," Donovan said. "After all, John Wayne Bobbitt now is a porn star. That's a bit like winning the Einstein Award after having been lobotomized. America has a high degree of tolerance for abberant behavior."

"I wouldn't say 'tolerance,' I would say 'affection,'" Holland noted.

"Who do you think would want to kill people in this theater and why?" Donovan asked.

"Oh, I have no idea," Elena said.

Sharkey offered a quizzical look. "I don't know that much about crime in New York," he said. "Ask me about L.A."

A group of people were rustling about, eager to talk to the stars of the show, and Holland noticed it. So did Donovan, who made motions toward breaking off the conversation. "I'll need to talk to the two of you again," he said.

"You got it," Sharkey replied.

"Any time," Elena said.

"If it's all right, I'll give the captain your phone numbers," Holland said.

That was fine with them, so Donovan let Holland steer him in the direction of a knot of people who were engaged in a noisy conversation near the fireplace. The men there seemed older than those in the rest of the room, and somehow European. One man sported an oldish but expensive tuxedo. His shoulders displayed several flakes of dandruff newly fallen from a balding grey pate. His companion was much younger: a thirtyish woman with a cloud of flaming red hair who was wearing a hot pink, skin-tight dress short enough to show off nearly every inch of her well-muscled legs.

Donovan was a bit disappointed when, halfway to them, Holland stopped and draped an arm around his shoulder, the better to draw him into a conspiratorial conversation.

"Surely you can tell me who your suspects are," he said.

"Why didn't you tell me about the Old Knickerbocker Annex?" Donovan asked.

Thoroughly thrown, Holland said, "What?"

"The building next door. Didn't you buy it when you bought the theater?"

"Unh, no. I didn't need it. Why do you ask me this question? Is it important?"

"I asked it, didn't I?"

"Then I suppose it must be important. But I fail to understand why."

"First you tell me this elaborate tale about Milos the Magnificent, including the information he had a fiancée who was six inches taller than him and that he's buried in the basement."

"So what? The man fascinates me. I may produce a musical about him." Holland added, briefly raising his eyes to the ceiling, "If his ghost doesn't kill me first."

Donovan continued, "But you didn't tell me his agent, who introduced him to his fiancée, lives on in the building next door. Which itself was once part of this building complex."

"Sy Gittelson," Holland laughed, "you found out about Sy Gittelson."

"Wasn't I supposed to?"

"Oh, fine, go talk to Sy if it makes you feel better. He's a character, no doubt. You'll like him. You said you like *Guys and Dolls*. Sy is a true Damon Runyon character."

"Do you like him?"

"Not particularly," Holland replied. "You'll find that he wears off quickly."

"Bock described him as Broadway Danny Rose."

After thinking for a moment, Holland said, "Bock is a flatterer. That's why I hired him to write my biography."

"Another thing you didn't tell me about," Donovan said.

"Do you want to know everything about me?" Holland complained. "I mean, how much of this is germane?"

"Three people have died in your building. There's another body in the basement—I'm talking about Milos now—that was lying beneath a pile of rubble for two weeks. Anybody could have gotten at his crossbow, and someone did. And you're not being honest with me. That makes me suspicious."

"You can't suspect me of these crimes," Holland said. "Clearly they're all designed to put me out of business."

"Apparently designed," Donovan said.

"Oh my God," Holland swore. "I don't believe what I'm hearing."

"I want you to be honest with me," Donovan said.

"All right. All right."

"Tell me everything and I'll throw out what I don't need."

"I agree. Now, who do you suspect?"

"Who did you buy the Old Knickerbocker from?" Donovan asked.

"You're not going to answer my question, are you?"

"Not now," Donovan admitted.

"I bought it from the 987 West Corporation. It's a matter of public record."

"I'll need the names of the principals."

"Can it wait until the morning?"

Donovan nodded.

"Why do you want to know that, of all things?"

"In this vertical city, one thing is more valuable than anything else."

"I sense that you're not going to say 'art,' 'literature,' or 'theater,' " Holland said.

"Real estate," Donovan said. "When somebody appears to be trying to scuttle the future of a historic building, I have to wonder if real estate isn't a factor. The soil atop which this edifice stands would be much more profitable as an office tower or luxury apartment building than it can ever be as a theater. And that's notwithstanding any conceivable success of *Casablanca: The Musical.*"

"You sound like my banker. All right, Captain, let me tell you something. My arrangement with the city and the banks is unique indeed. The city wants to preserve this building, and so forced the 987 West Corporation either to restore it themselves or sell it to me. They chose to sell. But if I can't convince the city and the banks that I can make a go of things, including a faithful and successful restoration, by the first of the year, I have to sell the theater back. I would lose a ton of money—I would, in fact, be bankrupt—and the 987 West Corporation would then be free to tear it down and put up an office tower worth hundreds of millions."

"How does the city define 'faithful and successful?' " Donovan asked.

"A restoration that satisfies the historic preservation people. And advance ticket sales that satisfy the banks. All this by January first. So far I haven't done either, although I'm getting close on both. Now, if you're not going to tell me the names on your list of those who would ruin or kill me, can I steer your wandering attention back to the names on mine?"

"Mala Logan."

"God, yes. She's a beast who would see me dead. That's her in the tight dress." Holland indicated the woman Donovan had eyeballed before. "She's the one showing an unconscionable amount of thigh."

"I noticed."

"You'll meet her in a minute."

"And Lucien Schadenfreud," Holland said, letting out a big sigh.

"Your bosom buddy? The member of your family who you have spats and make up with?"

"You don't understand. The man is out to ruin me again. He cost me millions back in the 1970s with that vicious review of my rock musical, and now he means to do it again by scuttling my masterpiece. I'm certain he maneuvered himself into the position of being the critic of record for my show. I'm also certain he's been snooping around the theater."

"Me too," Donovan agreed.

"You agree? Excellent. What tipped you off?"

"Two weeks ago he sang me a few lines from a song that, according to him, he first heard this afternoon."

"You see? You see? He could have been the one to have taken Milos's crossbow from the grave."

"The thought occurred to me."

"Do you know where he was when Henry was killed?"

"He said he was in the theater, but I would like him to be more specific." Donovan scratched his chin, then said, "Forgive the limited amount of brainpower that I can bring to bear on this issue, but if you guys hate each other, why don't you show it? Forget all the 'my-old-buddy' crap. Just you and Luke go out onto the terrace where the windmill used to be and duke it out. Sergeant Moskowitz and I will stand by to make sure no one gets hurt seriously."

"You're comical," Holland said.

"Add Mala Logan to the fight if you like. If she starts using her alleged martial-arts prowess, the sergeant will handle her. Failing that, I'll shoot her. I just don't get all this phony friendliness."

"You would rather see out-and-out hostility?"

"In a New York minute," Donovan replied.

"I'm afraid that it will never happen. Being polite to one another is very deeply ingrained in show business."

"This is why my Irish ancestors hated the British," Donovan said. "It wasn't so much the armed aggression, land grabbing, and genocide, all of which was straightforward enough. It was the phony charm."

It was Donovan's turn to put his arm around Holland. The captain said, "Sir John, one of the people in this room apparently is out to kill your show...or you, for all I know. Or to kill your show and you."

"If so, all the more reason to keep them where I can see them. And, I might add, where you can see them. No, captain, I will not shun these people. You will simply have to keep this killer from accomplishing his task. I have given you complete access. I promise to be more forthcoming. Now, let's get on with things."

# ELEVEN

## THE MOST VENOMOUS ANIMALS
## ALWAYS COME IN THE GAUDIEST COLORS

HE BROKE FROM Donovan and led him to the actress, who upon seeing the pair left her companion and approached them with open arms.

"John, how good it is to see you," she said in a thick London accent, throwing her arms around the producer.

"Mala, my darling. You look sumptuous. Where did you get that marvelous dress?" He held her at arm's length, the better to look at the creation. At that distance, Donovan noted that it was less a dress than a wrap, one made of shantung that shined nearly as brightly as the fabric of Sharkey's suit. Cheap and flashy must be in this year, Donovan thought.

"From Kristeva, of course. I'm glad you like it." She put her hands on her hips and wiggled. "Does your friend like my dress?"

Holland yielded to Donovan, who said, "I have to get one like it for my lady friend."

"Mala, this is Bill Donovan of the NYPD," Holland said.

"What's that?" she asked.

"The New York Police Department."

"My Lord, a copper!" she exclaimed, affecting a cockney accent. "What happened, John, are they on to you at last?"

He smiled and shrugged. "I guess so," he laughed.

"Will you lead him off in shackles?" she asked Donovan.

"Only after he's picked up the check for this party," Donovan said.

"That's very sensible. Pleased to meet you, Bill Donovan." She held out her hand, which he studied, noting with relief that it was a lot sturdier than the one attached to Elena Jordan. "Do you have a rank that I should know about? Are you an inspector?"

"I'm a captain. I'm head of Special Investigations for the City of New York."

"Which means that he gets to keep me alive," Holland said.

"And investigate the ghost in the basement," Donovan said.

"You're going to wind up in one of his productions, Bill Donovan," she said. "If that happens, I will give you the name of my New York lawyer. You'll need it." She offered a playful smile.

"Ma-la," Holland said, a bit like someone cautioning an unruly child.

"A refreshing burst of animosity," Donovan said. "The air in the room suddenly seems lighter."

"There's no animosity," Mala said.

"Like I told you, Captain, we're all friends."

"Certainly. He screwed me and I made him pay."

"Handsomely," Holland added.

"It happens in the best of families. That doesn't mean we can't talk," Mala said.

"Just don't bend over to pick up the soap," Donovan said.

"I beg your pardon?"

"An American expression that I hope you'll ignore," Donovan said.

"You are an interesting man. Why did you tell me you had a girlfriend? Was it to let me know you're not available or to point out that you're straight?"

Donovan tossed up his hands. "Maybe both. I am straight and I may be available. I called her my 'lady friend.' You changed it to my 'girlfriend.'"

"I was simply seeking to determine if you were sending me a message."

Holland interjected, "Mala checks things out with her lawyer before telling them to her therapist."

"That's a very clever line, darling. If it was original—which I doubt—you must use it in a show."

"I will."

"So, Mala Logan, when did you blow into town?" Donovan asked.

"Another American expression? Um, yesterday."

"And before then you were where?"

"In London, of course."

"For how long?"

"My, you are a policeman, aren't you? Let's see—I did this and that for the past few weeks, I visited my parents in Surrey for a weekend, and I flew to Paris to shop for two days. I bought this...." She displayed her dress again, this time rubbing her thighs together provocatively.

Interesting casting decision, Donovan thought, picking the tall, slender, and mournful Elena Jordan over the short, muscular, and vivacious Mala Logan. Neither of them resembled Ingrid Bergman in the least. He decided that he really knew nothing about how decisions were made in the theater.

"Why are you so interested in my schedule?" she asked.

"I'm trying to rule you out as a murder suspect."

"Oh, that sounds exciting. And my first impression is you were about to put the cop on John. Fair enough. Shoot."

"Where were you this afternoon?"

"Watching the show, of course."

"That means you saw Henry Tippett get killed."

"Um, no, actually. I had repaired to the powder room. I was alone there. No one saw me. At least..." She smiled at Holland. "... I hope no one saw me."

"When my contractor redid the powder rooms he patched up the holes in the walls," Holland said dryly.

"At least in the bathrooms," Donovan said. "Tell me, Mala, where you were on December four and twelve?"

She thought for a moment, then said, "Paris and London, respectively."

"And people saw you in both cases?" Donovan said.

"Absolutely. In the case of Paris I was buying this little number." Once again she rubbed her thighs together. Her pantyhose made a scraping sound. Donovan wasn't able to avoid looking. "So a few people may have seen entirely too much of me."

"And you loved every minute," Holland said.

"John doesn't like me because I'm not demure like his current leading lady, the fashion model."

"You don't like Elena Jordan," Donovan said.

"On the contrary, I love women who are having nervous breakdowns. Did you hear her voice? Did you catch her hands shaking? The woman is coming to the end of her rope and likely to hang herself with the damned thing. I take pity on the creature. If she was on the runway in Paris I would have bought two of these dresses just to keep her in lip polish. That pout must cost her a fortune to keep oiled."

"Ma-la," Holland said again.

Mala pressed a fingertip to Holland's chest and said, "You're bor-ing, darling, like your leading lady. The most exciting thing you've done for me in years is get me interrogated by this charming policeman. I have never been suspected of murder before."

"How do you feel about that?" Donovan asked.

"You have made my visit to New York memorable, Bill Donovan," she said.

"Are you staying long?"

"Another few weeks, I suppose. Some Christmas shopping, and a few other things. I'll be here for the grand premiere on New Year's Eve, of course."

"And then?"

"L.A."

Holland sneered, and she spotted it right off. "It *is* on the tour, darling," she said. To Donovan she added, "British actors come to the States and hit New York and then they hit L.A. That's where the work is. If there were acting jobs in Cleveland, it would be on the tour, too."

"Is there a number where I can reach you if need be?" Donovan asked.

She smiled. "Of course, but only if you give me your number as well."

"Okay." He removed two business cards from his pocket and gave them to her along with a pen. She scribbled a number on one of them and handed it back.

"You're getting yourself in deep, Captain," Holland said.

"John is afraid of me," Mala explained.

"I am not."

"Certainly he is," she insisted. "Why else would he accuse me of being a murderess?"

"I did no such thing," Holland protested.

"But of course you did. There's no other explanation for this man asking me where I was on such-and-such dates."

"Since you're so cool about being grilled in a murder investigation, do you know how to use a crossbow?" Donovan asked.

"Is that what killed Henry Tippett?"

Donovan said that it was.

"Probably I can," she said after thinking for a moment. "Yes, I would say so. I'm fairly athletic. I pump iron. Of course, I don't know how good a shot I would be, but I imagine I could figure the thing out. I've used a bow and arrow. Of course..." She played idly with Donovan's tie. "I much prefer to kill with my bare hands." She smiled.

"What degree black belt are you?" he asked.

"Third. Fairly modest. And you?"

"Nope, not me. My lady friend has ninth in kung fu, however."

"Well, be so kind as to suggest to your lady friend that we work out together one day. And I'm glad to hear you're attracted to athletic women."

"I like women in general," Donovan said.

"That makes you unusual around here," she replied, looking sideways at Holland, who turned away in apparent annoyance.

"We took you away from your friend," he said when he turned back. The continental-looking man with the grey hair was staring at the trio from a distance, perhaps gauging if he would be welcomed into the conversation.

"That's Maurice Sanford," Mala said, implying they should know.

"Who?" Donovan asked.

"The French commercial producer. He wants me to shoot some spots in Provence in the spring. I had better get back to business."

"Nice to meet you," Donovan said.

"And you too, Bill. John, it was delightful as always."

"Likewise," Holland said.

"The best of luck with the show, John. As for you, Captain, go get 'em."

Donovan watched her as she walked away, then turned to Holland and said, "Colorful woman."

Scowling, Holland replied, "The most venomous animals always come in the gaudiest colors. I'm sorry, Captain, but that woman upsets me terribly. I need to be alone for a moment. Would you mind fending for yourself for a while?''

''I think I know how to find my way around a cocktail party,'' Donovan said.

''Anton!'' Holland called out, again snapping his fingers above his head.

The producer's aide rushed over, all the while balancing six drinks on a silver tray. ''Yes, John,'' he said.

''I'm going to my office to lie down.''

''Are you all right?''

''I am a wreck. That woman has done it to me again.''

''Take two Advil and put your feet up.''

''Please see to it that my guests are taken care of,'' Holland said, and rushed off, holding the back of one hand to his forehead.

Donovan and the aide exchanged glances. It was about time, the captain thought, that he paid some attention to the one who seemed forever at Holland's side. ''No wonder the man never married,'' Donovan said.

''No wonder,'' Anton replied dryly. ''Are you okay, Captain? Do you need a drink? We're celebrating here. Would you like a glass of the legendary Piper?''

''I was never a champagne drinker,'' Donovan said. ''Which Piper Heidsieck is 'legendary?' ''

''The 1955, of course.''

''Of course.''

''It's a true classic. Five stars. It was thought to be all gone for many years, but Anders Purslane, our wine supplier, tracked down a case. I can't tell you how much it cost.''

''Tell me,'' Donovan said.

''I was sworn to secrecy,'' Anton replied. ''Suffice to say that I had to go downstairs and sign for the shipment personally when it arrived this afternoon. That's what I was doing the moment poor Henry was killed. You wouldn't have believed the uproar back-stage...so much running around.''

''I was one of the runners,'' Donovan said.

''Then you must be terribly thirsty.''

"But not enough to drink champagne, no matter how legendary it may be."

"Very well," Anton said. "How about a bottle of beer, then. Isn't it Kaliber that you drink?"

"Not tonight, thanks."

"Some *pavés du caves*, then?"

"You lost me," Donovan said.

"Candy—a burnt-sugar confection made to look like the pebbles in the Pyrenees mountain streams near the town of Cauterets, where they are made."

"I don't think so," Donovan said. "But I would kill for a Klondike Bar right about now."

"That I can't help you with," Anton sniffed.

"You'd make a great waiter," Donovan said.

"I used to be one. That's how I was paying the bills when John discovered me. You know how it is in New York. Most waiters are actors or dancers or something."

Donovan nodded. "How long have you been with him?"

Anton looked at his watch, then at Donovan and smiled. "Nearly twenty years."

"And he hasn't found you a part yet?"

"Actually, he cast me in his rock musical. Not a big part, mind you, but I got to sing and dance. Unfortunately, and as you know, Lucien Schadenfreud killed it." Anton nodded in the direction of the bar, where the critic was having a lively discussion with the newly reappeared Roger Bock.

"The show flopped."

"Crashed and burned would be a more apt description. After that I couldn't get any important roles. Sure, I did some commercials. For him, among others." He pointed in the direction of Maurice Sanford, who seemed to be locked in serious discussion with Mala Logan.

"But that work dried up, too."

"I see that you understand. So John took pity on me and made me his executive assistant."

"And here you are still carrying a tray," Donovan said.

"That, regrettably, is part of it. But I'm well paid and, best of all, I'm still in the theater. I literally *live* in the theater. And I get to dress as I please.'' He flicked a speck of dust off the white-cashmere, black-turtleneck combination that Donovan was coming to regard as a uniform.

Trying to put himself in the man's shoes, Donovan said, "I suppose that if I couldn't be a detective I'd want to write about it. Or answer phones in the precinct. Or something."

"You're a very understanding man, Captain," Anton said.

MOSKOWITZ HAD DISAPPEARED. In his place at the bar was Roger Bock, who had steeled himself with a drink the moment he walked into the party and closeted himself in an argument with Lucien Schadenfreud. In that way, Donovan thought, the author could postpone the moment when he had to deal with being suspected of murder. Donovan felt the time had come.

"If this is your attorney," Donovan said, indicating Schadenfreud, "I would suggest a priest or rabbi instead."

"Hey, I would make a great lawyer," Schadenfreud protested.

"Maybe. You already have the mean streak."

"What do you mean, 'mean streak'?"

"You deliberately went out and got the assignment to review this show so you can ruin Holland again."

Schadenfreud giggled faintly.

"Then you used Tippett's murder as the excuse to call Holland and wangle an invitation to this party. You did that so you could rub his nose in the impending bad review."

Schadenfreud sipped his martini; not his first, Donovan observed.

"You want him to sweat for a week. How long is it before New Year's?"

"Ten days," Bock said.

"These will be the best ten days of my life," Schadenfreud said. "Vengeance is mine."

"What did he do to you to get you so mad at him?" Donovan asked.

Schadenfreud sucked in his breath and prepared to deliver a lecture. "Holland is a maggot feeding on the corpse of art in America," the critic said. "Holland..."

"Has gone to lie down because he can't take the stress of having so many friends in the same room," Donovan said.

"Let us only hope that his is not a headache but a coronary."

"And you," Donovan said to Bock, "Where did you disappear to before? You told me you were going to get your lawyer."

"I don't have one," the author admitted. "You scared me before, all that talk about my being a murder suspect."

"Don't try to put things over on me," Donovan said. "You not only insult my intelligence, you piss me off."

"All right. I was trying to hold onto the original of that video-tape because, with the original, I could get a better price out of 'Hard Copy.'"

"You sold the tape of Tippett's murder to a tabloid TV show?" Donovan said.

*"I love New York,"* Schadenfreud sang.

"Yeah, and I got paid less because what I delivered was only a dub."

"How much did they give you?" Donovan asked.

"Twenty-five thousand. I would have gotten fifty for the original. So the way I look at it, you cost me twenty-five thousand dollars. You owe me, Captain."

"That's still not bad for half an hour's work. But what happens when Holland finds out?"

"Surely you jest," Bock said. "Holland loves publicity."

"Even when it's about one of his actors being shot to death onstage?" Donovan asked.

"Especially then. You can't buy this sort of publicity. You have to create it. Ask Sy Gittelson if you want to hear the words of the master."

"I'm getting around to him."

"I told you Holland was a bottom-feeder," Schadenfreud said.

Donovan looked around, trying to spot his partner. Moskowitz was nowhere to be seen. Finally, Donovan asked Bock where the sergeant had gone.

"Your friend went to make a call," Bock said.

That meant he went to make a private call (he had a cell phone). Maybe something was up.

Donovan looked around for other familiar faces. After standing on tiptoes and surveying the room one more time, at last he spotted Derrida's extravagant haircut. The man was having an animated conversation with a black-haired gentleman whose back was turned. The pair were across the room—at least two dozen celebrities and wannabes loitered between Donovan and them—and momentarily inaccessible. For someone so eager to get to the party, the construction chief didn't seem to be enjoying himself.

Donovan returned his attention to Bock. "Did you dig up any dirt on your boss tonight?" he asked.

Schadenfreud looked confused, so the captain elaborated. "Roger is looking for incriminating evidence to put in his biography of Holland—that is, if he doesn't sell it to 'Hard Copy' first."

"The man likes publicity and won't care," Bock said. "But to answer your question, I haven't turned up anything new tonight. But the night is young."

"If you want the lowdown on Holland, let's talk further," Schadenfreud said.

"Sure, sure," Bock said. Donovan sensed that Bock had grown weary of Schadenfreud's perpetual carping about the composer's artistic merit.

"Did you find anything?" Bock asked the captain.

"Well, I made the round of leading ladies and would steer you to Mala Logan. I'm sure she'll have a few tidbits."

"Where is she?" Bock asked, looking eagerly at the crowd.

"Over by the fireplace," Donovan said, pointing the way.

"I'll see you later," the author said, and headed off.

"Nice guy," Schadenfreud said when Bock was gone.

Helping himself to the author's place at the bar, Donovan said, "He seems to have a lot of interests."

"Among them Mala Logan. Who else have you talked to?"

"The stars of the show—Sharkey and Jordan."

Schadenfreud wrinkled up his nose. "The moose and the model," he said.

"I think the moose hurt his throat tonight. He was drinking Southern Comfort and Coke."

"Janis Joplin drank that when *she* hurt *her* throat."

"Who? Oh, the rock star who called you an asshole."

"No, that was Bill Graham, the impressario. Janis called me a bastard."

"You sure got around," Donovan said.

"And I bought her one of those drinks one time. We were at a bar on Fifty-second Street. We were at 21, in fact. I bought her a Southern Comfort and Coke. I had a sip. It tasted like cough syrup. Oh, I was meaning to tell you. The other day I was going through my old files and came across this letter I got in 1970. It read, 'Dear Mr. Schadenfreud. I am writing a biography of the late Janis Joplin and understand that you were with her the night she died....'"

Donovan's eyebrows arched. Schadenfreud saw it.

"But I wasn't with her. I was in New York the night she died in L.A."

"Can you prove it?" Donovan asked, only half in jest.

Schadenfreud looked puzzled for a time, then said, "No one ever asked me that. I would have to crank up the microfiche and look up who I was reviewing that week."

"There's no statute of limitations on murder," Donovan said.

"Janis died of a drug overdose. I told her to stick to booze, but she didn't listen to me. It was the same thing with Morrison. I told him not to mix pills and booze."

Now Donovan looked puzzled.

"Jim Morrison? You don't know who he is? Oliver Stone did a movie about the man."

"I rest my case."

"Oh, come on, Captain. You're putting me on."

Donovan shook his head, then replied, "If I were having a conversation with a leading ichthyologist he wouldn't expect me to know the names of every species of carp."

"Are you comparing rock and roll to *fish?*" Schadenfreud exclaimed, shocked.

"Dead fish. I hate the arrogance of the people who promote pop culture. There are many more people in the world who know something about fish than who know who John Lennon was. And I mainly know about him because he bled to death on my beat."

"You're a tough man, Captain."

"I want to hear your alibi for the night Janis Joplin died," Donovan insisted.

"Now I know you're putting me on." Schadenfreud offered a nervous smile.

"Consider it an official request. And while you're at it, tell me exactly where you were when Henry Tippett was killed. Were you in the audience?"

Schadenfreud said, "And risk having to hear Sharkey sing?"

"Come on, stop kidding around."

"I don't always sit in the audience. Sometimes I stand in back. I like to move around and get a sense of how people in the cheap seats—or in no seats at all—can see and hear the show."

"You like to be able to run to the lobby bar," Donovan translated.

"And to the bathroom, which is where I happened to be when Tippett was killed. I ran back to the audience when I heard the commotion."

"And, of course, nobody saw you in the bathroom."

"Probably not. Holland is too cheap to hire a washroom attendant."

Donovan frowned and said, "So Luke, if I get this biography of Joplin, will I see your name in it, denying having been with her the night she croaked?"

"Nope."

"Why not?"

"The guy never wrote the book. He got the contract to write the first of his *Legends of* books instead."

Donovan frowned, and said, "Is there any chance you're talking about someone we know?"

"Yeah, Roger. Who do you think I meant, William L. Shirer?"

"You knew him before tonight?"

"Of course. There are a lot of writers in New York City, but we're an incestuous bunch. Once you get above a certain level, you know everyone."

"Roger wrote a series of books called *Legends of* something or another?"

"Six or seven, I think."

"How many books has he written?"

"Forty or fifty. That's nothing. I know this science fiction writer who's published close to four hundred novels."

Donovan shook his head. "So that's what's happened to the rain forest," he said.

Schadenfreud nodded. "Roger wrote on it."

"What are the names of some other of his books?"

The critic thought for a moment, then said, "*Legends of American Gangsters. Legends of the Civil War.* That's all I can think of. Oh, and there was one about ships, I think. Possibly a World War II book. Ask him."

"I will," Donovan said.

# TWELVE

## A LONELY CHARACTER FROM A HOPPER PAINTING

DONOVAN WASN'T SURE whether to categorize Bock as a suspect or a source. Any man who knew so much about a variety of things doubtless could be the latter, and Donovan was forever in need of information. But the captain found his attention shifting back to Derrida, whose conversation with the dark-haired man had grown from merely animated to fairly aggressive, so much so that the people close by the pair moved away a bit. But the two men remained across the room, near the exit. At one point the dark-haired man turned slightly so that Donovan caught a glimpse of his face. There was something familiar about it, but in a roomful of people whom Donovan might have seen onstage, on television, or in the movies, Donovan couldn't be sure.

It was then that Moskowitz returned, pulling up to the bar and ordering himself a seltzer.

"Did something come up?" Donovan asked, moving in close for privacy.

"The rooming house in Flushing that's filled with Vietnamese immigrants? Immigration knows about it and says that it's clean. It's simply a place, owned by Vietnamese, where their countrymen live for a time after getting off the boat. Such houses exist."

"And always have. My own grandparents met at a rooming house for Irish on Madison and One-twenty-fifth."

"In Harlem."

"Now it's Harlem. Then it was a place where Irish stayed when they got off the boat. That was about the time this theater was being built, come to think of it."

"Remember that Dinh's neighbors were jittery?"

Donovan remembered.

"We found out why. The Vietnamese cop we sent out there to

talk to Dinh's neighbors? Well, he's part Vietnamese and part Chinese. At least he looks the part and speaks a bit of the language. He broke through."

"Good."

"Dinh was nothing special, an ordinary guy who suffered from headaches, a lot of them. He got off the boat a year ago. What's interesting is the name of the boat he got off: the *Jade Travelor.*"

Donovan's eyebrows bent toward the ceiling. "The boatful of Chinese illegals who were paying ridiculous amounts of money to get smuggled into the U.S.? And wound up on an old rustbucket freighter that ran aground in Dead Horse Bay last year?"

Mosko nodded. "They were Chinese and Vietnamese illegals."

"Dinh's village was near the Chinese border."

"The ship sailed from Haiphong with a few Viets onboard, stopped over in Haikou to pick up the Chinese passengers, and then, after a long and agonizing voyage that hopped around the African coasts, sailed into New York Harbor under cover of darkness."

"I remember it now," Donovan said. "After the cops, the Coast Guard, and Immigration descended on the *Jade Travelor,* the Chinese captain admitted he was trying to sail up the Hudson and unload his cargo of illegals at an old pier. Can you imagine the chutzpah? Anyway, he figured the tides wrong and wound up on a sand bar in Dead Horse Bay. The passengers panicked and tried to swim ashore. Three drowned."

"Those that made it were held in a detention center but were finally allowed to stay," Mosko added.

"Those passengers paid through the nose, right?" Donovan asked.

"You bet. You could have gone first class on the *QE II* for less. The average was about forty thousand dollars. Those that didn't have it promised to pay after they reached the States."

Donovan said, "And gangs working out of Chinatown terrorized the poor bastards to make sure they paid up regularly."

"Dinh worked at a Vietnamese restaurant in Chinatown. We might want to go there for lunch tomorrow. It's around the corner from the office."

Donovan chuckled.

"Dinh was an excellent cook who knew everything about Vietnamese traditional foods," Moskowitz said. "He rode the subway to and from work—the Flushing line to Times Square, where he switched to the BMT for the ride down to Chinatown. Dinh had a legitimate reason for being on the subway platform when the water main broke. He died a natural death—the accident caused the brick wall to fall on him."

"Still, Dinh had seven thousand dollars in the bank," Donovan said. "Maybe he was withholding payments from the men who smuggled him here. Let's run that theory by the Downtown Gang Task Force. It could be Dinh was killed for nonpayment and tossed into the rubble left behind by the water main break."

"Even so, there's no clear connection to Derrida," Mosko added.

"I find it interesting that Dinh was an illegal and Derrida has been accused of hiring them. But, in the absence of evidence of any solid connection between the men, Derrida is off the hook for Dinh. But what about the markings on his body? I have to believe there's more to this than a simple accident."

"The cop didn't know what the stripes might be. The neighbors didn't know or wouldn't say."

"Let's keep an open mind about that. Those markings are weird, but so is this whole case." Donovan pointed at Derrida and his companion. "Can you see the guy Derrida is arguing with?"

Mosko peered and then said, "Not clearly. Who is he?"

"I don't know."

"Does he look like anybody you know?"

"I think I'll find out," Donovan said. He slipped away from the bar and began to make his way through the crowd. Halfway there, a break came in the throng and Donovan got a view of the man's profile. He was dark-complexioned with a sloping forehead and hair black enough to have been dyed that way. This man isn't an actor, Donovan thought, but without being able to pinpoint an identity. Then the man turned suddenly toward the captain—Donovan was sure Derrida had said something—and a look of surprise flashed across his face. He turned and bolted out the exit.

Donovan went after him, as did Moskowitz from another angle. But by the time they could reach the door, the man was gone. The solitary elevator was on its way down; the newly restored brass floor indicator showed floor three and falling.

"Go down the stairs and try to catch it," Donovan said as his aide, way ahead of him, began to run for the top of the stairs.

Donovan turned back toward the crowd and, in so doing, nearly collided with Derrida, who gave the impression he, too, was chasing the man.

"Did you get him?" he asked, breathless and clearly panicked.

"Nope, and unless my friend is faster in the finals than he was in the preliminary heats, we won't. Who was that?"

"He...he's one of the South Bronx Boys," Derrida stammered.

"The group that picketed your construction site?"

"Picketed! They shot it up, is what you mean."

"As I recall the case, your guys shot back. That was the time the mayor of Dodge City went on the air to claim his place was safer than our place. What's this guy's name?"

"He didn't tell me," Derrida said.

"What did he want?"

"What they always want—money. Sure, they pretend they're looking for jobs for their Hispanic members, but what they really want is a payoff."

"How much did he ask for?" Donovan asked.

"Fifty thousand."

"That's all?"

"This week."

Donovan said, "I got to tell you, Derrida, that guy didn't look very much like a cheap hood. He looked familiar, in fact."

"And you don't know any hoods?" Derrida asked, appearing to regain something of his composure.

"Not any cheap ones," Donovan shot back. "How did he get in here?"

"Beats me. I'm not watching the gate. No doubt the bouncer—if there is one—mistook him for a Calvin Klein model. They all look punky and unshaven. It's the thing these days. I'll find out how he got in."

Derrida snapped his fingers in the air and shouted, "Anton!"

"Does everybody here get to boss Anton around?"

"The man is a doormat," Derrida sneered.

When the man appeared he had about him his usual look: half-flustered, half-irritated. "Can I help you, Mr. Derrida?" he asked.

"Is there a guard watching who gets in?"

"In a manner of speaking. There were no formal invitations, and I suppose that anyone who wanted to and looked the part could get in. Of course, you also have to know there is a party tonight, and we haven't advertised. Was there a problem?"

"I was accosted by a very unpleasant man," Derrida said.

"Oh, I am sorry," Anton replied. "Can I get you anything?"

"Another drink."

"Consider it done. Would you like to lie down? If so, you're welcome to use my room. Mr. Holland has already gone to do so in his suite. It's like we're having a little epidemic tonight."

"I know, and here I am working onsite, around the clock, from tomorrow until New Year's to get this renovation done. I'm fine, thanks. Just get me a damn scotch."

Anton hustled off, leaving Donovan to ask, "What was it you said to the man to get him to bolt?"

"Oh, I said, 'Watch out, my policeman friend is here.' That was when he turned and saw you."

"I half-recognized the guy."

"You must have had some run-in with the South Bronx Boys," Derrida said.

"The South Bronx is one place I hardly ever have reason to go. And so far I haven't handled any cases on construction sites. But don't worry, I'll figure out who the guy is."

Moskowitz reappeared, stepping from the elevator with his palms up, barely out of breath. Donovan recalled ruefully the time when he could run up and down stairs without getting out of breath.

"Sorry," Mosko said.

"Did anybody see him go out?"

"The guy at the door said somebody left in a hurry and got into a waiting car."

"What kind of car?"

"Black Lincoln Town Car," Mosko reported.

"The South Bronx Boys must be upgrading their taste in transportation," Donovan said. "My impression is they stole Honda Accords."

Derrida shrugged and accepted a scotch and water from Anton, who hurried off before he could be asked to run another errand. The construction chief sipped it, and as he did a look of satisfaction came over his face. Donovan wondered if the man was happy his alleged tormentor was gone or happy to have gotten away with something.

Derrida said, "I'm not going to lie down, but I think I will find a seat. Do you need me anymore?"

"Not for now."

The man wandered back into the crowd, which in true New York fashion had barely reacted to the tumult of one of its members bolting down the stairs with a policeman in hot pursuit. Donovan watched him go, then said, "It's nice to be able to keep a cool head in the wake of a fifty-thousand-dollar extortion attempt."

"Was that what was at stake?" Mosko asked.

"So the man says."

"And do you believe him?"

"Not for a second."

The sergeant didn't seem surprised. "What, then?"

"Beats me, but I'm telling you I know that man who ran off. Maybe not in person, but the face is familiar."

"Is this worth working up a sketch? We can go downtown and do it now."

Donovan yawned, and said, "Not tonight. I've had enough for one day."

"I'm glad you said that." Moskowitz looked relieved.

"What time is it?" He looked at his watch. "Almost midnight. What's it like out?"

"Pretty warm. Somewhere around fifty degrees."

"Five days before Christmas and it's still in the fifties," Donovan said. "This must be another year of global warming."

"Now that you said that, we're gonna have a blizzard."

"I feel like walking home. Do you want to take my car?"

"Sure. It would save me having to pick up mine from the garage. You really want to walk all the way home?"

"I'll get a cab if I get tired." He handed his keys to the sergeant. "Thanks. In the morning we'll figure out who that guy was who ran."

Donovan nodded and patted his friend on the back. Moskowitz left, taking the elevator down this time.

The captain spent another ten or fifteen minutes at the party. He spoke briefly and informally with those people who had been standing near Derrida and the other man during their argument. No one had gotten the gist of the conversation. He had a few words with Harry Spalding and agreed to meet him later. Then the captain returned to the bar to say goodbye to Schadenfreud, who looked determined to spend the night despite a sickly look. The man had never seemed very healthy to Donovan, but as this night wore on his appearance worsened. He had taken a seat beneath a mini-spotlight and struggled to smile faintly at Donovan, who saw him clearly for the first time. Schadenfreud's skin was yellow; a life spent in concert halls would likely make it only pale. And a hand, left resting on a knee, shook noticeably even when he wasn't trying to use it for anything.

"I see the thrill of tormenting Holland has worn off for the night," Donovan said.

The critic peered through an alcoholic haze and, struggling to regain his normal jaunty demeanor, said, "It will return."

But there was no joy in this proclamation. In fact, the man seemed to be in pain. Donovan reached out and gave him a gentle poke in his upper right side. He winced at the pain in his liver.

"The time has come, my friend, to do something about this," Donovan said.

"I can take care of myself," Schadenfreud murmured.

"Can you?"

The fellow nodded.

"I've been down this road, not as far as you but maybe far enough to be able to help," Donovan said. "Call me if you want to talk."

Schadenfreud murmured, "Thanks," then closed his eyes and seemed to be addressing an inner torment.

Shortly thereafter Donovan was adjusting the collar of his overcoat and waiting for the elevator when he felt a hand on his arm.

Mala Logan had slipped a sable coat over her skin-tight wrap. Atop her head sat a 1940s-style broad-brimmed hat from which projected a long feather. The playful grin remained the same.

"One got away," she said.

"Say again?"

"When I left you before, I told you to 'go get 'em.' From what I can see, one got away."

"This ain't the movies and I ain't Arnold Schwartzenegger," Donovan said.

She squeezed his arm once before letting it go. "What a relief. I hate the movies."

"What happened to Maurice Sanford?"

"He left a while ago. I'm on my own. What was all that fuss about before?"

Donovan shrugged and said, "Everything and nothing. This is New York. People run from the law all the time. Sometimes they get away."

"You're not telling me something, Bill Donovan," she said coyly.

"I don't know what it was about, and that's the truth. Where are you going?"

"Back to my hotel."

"Which is?"

"The Warwick."

"I would have figured you for the Sherry-Netherland, a big star and all that."

"We Brits don't believe in wasting money," she replied. "Besides, an actress on the tour is never in her hotel room. She's always off in meetings, trying to drum up work."

"Did you get any tonight?"

"Maybe. Where are you going? Home to your kung fu friend?"

"We don't live together anymore."

"Oh my, is this a sad relationship?"

"It was once. Now it's just a comfortable relationship."

"It *is* sad, then. You don't look like a man who is satisfied with 'comfortable.'"

"More and more, I am. Look, I'd offer to see you to your hotel but I'm walking."

"I have legs," she said, kicking one out from beneath her coat to prove it.

"Let me get this straight. You want to walk through Times Square wearing a ten-thousand-dollar fur coat?"

"It was ten thousand *pounds*. But I have a third-degree black belt."

"Our muggers have nine-millimeter automatics," Donovan said.

"In that case, I will rely on my police escort. Shall we go?"

The elevator came and they stepped into it. When they reached the lobby, Mala once again took his arm and let him lead her out into the midnight air of Times Square. It was one of those majestic, crisp, autumnal nights where New York was a black-and-white movie with Gershwin music. The air was clean and dust-free, the street-sweeper trucks having moved through earlier, watering down the pavement where the old cobblestones poked through the worn layers of asphalt.

Traffic remained brisk, with two out of every three cars yellow cabs hurrying past then-closed theaters en route to Pennsylvania Station and the Port Authority Bus Terminal. A lone 104 bus turned from Seventh Avenue onto Forty-second Street and chugged crosstown on its way to the United Nations. Outside Hotalings Foreign and Out-of-town Newspapers, a small man in a brown greatcoat scanned his copy of *Paris Match* while waiting for the bus to discharge passengers.

Crawling around the second-story level of One Times Square—the sliver-shaped piece of architectural history formerly known as the Times Tower, from which the New Year's ball would drop in almost exactly eleven days—was a news bulletin about the murder of Henry Tippett. Donovan and the woman watched it in silence while waiting for the light to change at Seventh and Forty-second, then crossed the street and walked north along the west side of Seventh Avenue.

The Jumbotron—the 32-by-24-foot TV set built into the north facade of the tower—flashed an advertisement for Sony CD players. On the far side of Broadway, a gigantic Calvin Klein billboard, made of sheets of colored vinyl, showed the usual picture of half-naked teenagers. Up and down the square, the knife-edged intersection of Broadway and Seventh Avenue was lined with other immense neon and computer-generated signs. Unique among cities, New York required that new buildings in Times Square append to their facades these oversized and glitzy posters. On this cool midnight they fluttered like rose petals caught in a windstorm, advertising financial news, Coca-Cola, Canon cameras, Hertz Rent-a-car, JVC audio and video components, and Boss jeans. The Joe Boxer sign mixed underwear with the Internet. Only the wildly steaming Eight O'Clock Coffee Mug, on Forty-sixth and Seventh, was an old-fashioned mechanical sign of the sort Donovan remembered from his youth.

A long and heavy flatbed truck lumbered down Broadway and turned onto Forty-third, carrying thick rolls of newsprint paper bound for the printing presses of *The New York Times*. Long fond of making utterances that lurked on the edge of incomprehensibility for those not attuned to his stream-of-consciousness way of thinking, Donovan said, "There goes that part of the rain forest that Roger Bock didn't write on."

"Beg pardon?" Mala asked, squeezing his arm to reestablish the connection they had lost while gaping at the Great White Way's electric offerings.

"I was wondering how you planned to get back to the hotel before I came into your life."

"By taxi. There seem to be plenty of them around," she said, pointing out half a dozen that were idling near the at-that-hour empty TKTS booth that, during normal hours, sold half-price theater admissions.

"It helps to speak Pakistani," Donovan said.

"We have lots of that in London these days, so I would manage."

He led her farther up Broadway before crossing the square at Forty-seventh Street, walking in the red glow beneath the fifty-five-ton Coca-Cola sign that stared south toward the Jumbotron. Along the east side of Seventh Avenue, past a row of legitimate theater and movie houses, was a block that recalled the pre-renovation Times Square. A triple-X movie house—two sides, one gay and one straight—squatted between a topless bar and a video and pinball arcade that did a thriving business in fake IDs. Also on the block was an adult book and sexual paraphernalia shop. Mala raised her eyebrows at several naughty nighties draped on mannequins in the window but said nothing. To the right of the triple-X movie emporium (on the straight side) a sullen-looking, unshaven "steerer" smoking a cheap cigar looked for men to whom to hand tiny flyers. He gave Donovan a cursory glance, but seemed more interested, at least momentarily, in Mala's sable. To Donovan the block looked less threatening than desolate. Customers were few and the man with the cigar was a lonely character from a Hopper painting. His time was drawing to a close, and he seemed to know it.

"This reminds me of Piccadilly," Mala said.

"I think someone, long ago, intended it to," Donovan said.

"I hear the city is cleaning it up."

"Yes. Before long all this sweat and grime will be banished to industrial areas of the outer boroughs, replaced by the Gap, Gap Kids, the Limited, Banana Republic, and maybe *yet another* Hard Rock Cafe."

"You sound like you disapprove."

"Let me put it this way. I'm sure the world can do with less pornography, but I'm not convinced it needs another Gap."

"I think I see. You're a romantic—in a bizarre sort of fashion."

They kept strolling along. Donovan said, "That's as good a description of me as I've ever heard," and was going to offer examples of Marcy's opinions of him, when his eye caught a sign on a doorway next to the sexual-aids shop.

"Wait a second," he said, pulling her across the sidewalk toward it.

"Picking up something for the little lady?"

"No. Not the shop. That sign."

She squinted at an eight-by-ten metal sign that was bolted into the brick facing next to a locked door, beyond which was a small entrance with four mailboxes. Mala read out loud: "AAA Amazing Entertainments. So what?"

Smiling, Donovan said, "I just remembered where I saw someone before."

"Who?"

"The man who my sergeant chased down the stairs."

"This person went from John's party and ran up there? Into that dive?"

"Sir John attracts all sorts. I don't know if the man is up there now," Donovan said, then led Mala back toward the sidewalk and looked up. A light shone from the window of an office on the second floor, just above the shop. "But he might be."

"Oh, good, I'm going to see a bust."

"Not tonight," Donovan laughed.

"Why not? You're not afraid of him, are you? What's his name?"

"Anthony Laquidara."

"What is he?"

"A purveyor of random chaos along the waterfront. He owns a lot of piers and buildings in which no good takes place. Among them are porno theaters and like emporiums, including, I guess, this one."

"Is that illegal?"

"Not generally. Ignoring his other activities, the tabloids call him 'the porno king.' "

"It isn't against the law—unfortunately—to be savaged by the tabloids. You should see what the London press does to me on a regular basis. They have me sleeping with everyone from Prince Charles to Manchester United."

"Which one was better? The prince or the soccer team?"

"The prince, of course," she said jauntily. "You don't get to be a king for nothing. Why did that man run from you?"

"Beats me. But I'll be sure to ask."

Mala seemed reluctant to leave, so Donovan put his arm around her and steered her down Forty-seventh Street, toward the diamond district. "Come on, I'll buy you a bauble," he said.

"I can help you arrest that man," she said. "You can deputize me."

"That only happens in westerns, and you told me you don't like movies."

"I lied," she said, giving in and snuggling under his arm and against his body as though she had been molded to fit it.

As at last they made their way up the squeaky-clean concrete canyon made by the new office towers that lined the Avenue of the Americas, Donovan asked, "How did you like singing in Holland's musical in London?"

"A shop question. Okay, I'll answer that: I liked it."

"Why?"

"I assume this is an artistic and not a financial question. The man's music is easy to sing. It doesn't challenge the vocal range of any serious artist, plus all those dramatic crescendos are fun. And you get a lot of attention being in a John Victor Holland musical. It's good for the career."

"But it would have been even better if you were starring in the Broadway production," Donovan said.

"True, and I'd be better at it than Miss Supermodel. But I'm not prepared to kill over the matter. John has been good to me over the years. He could have been better, but welcome to show biz. You don't seriously think I'm responsible for those murders, do you?"

"Did I accuse you of anything?"

"No," she said, but moved out from under his arm nonetheless.

"I ask questions. It's what I do."

"Actors are dramatic people. It's our nature to exaggerate. When we do badly onstage, we say that 'we died.'"

Donovan had heard the expression.

"It's in my best interest to yell and scream at John and, generally, keep him aware he screwed me," Mala continued. "He knows he owes me. Maybe he won't do it again. Besides, I can't write him out of my life altogether."

"Why not?"

"He throws the best parties. I'm looking forward to New Year's Eve, aren't you?"

"I wouldn't miss it for the world."

They stood at last in front of the Warwick Hotel, which occupied the northeast corner of the Avenue of the Americas and Fifty-fourth Street. She turned toward him, looking up, her bright brown eyes glistening in the light from the street lamps. "Are you taking your lady friend?" she asked.

"To the premiere of *Casablanca: The Musical* and the big party thereafter? I hadn't thought about it. But I have a feeling I may be working that night."

"If you're stuck for a date, give me a call," Mala said, giving him a hug and a quick kiss on the lips. The kiss was one of those show-biz traditions, right up there with referring to a bad performance as a death.

"Sure," he said, with a smile.

"I'd ask you up for a nightcap..."

"But I don't drink anyway."

"That too," she said, returning his smile. "Are you walking all the way...where is it you live?"

"Riverside and eighty-ninth," he replied.

"Is that far?"

"About half an hour if I go up Broadway. But since it's still early..."

She glanced at her watch. "One in the morning is early?"

"I've always been a night owl. I just may pull out my thirty-eight and march straight through Central Park."

"Take care whatever you do, Bill Donovan," she said. She twirled, her sable lifting to show a flash of muscular legs. Then she stalked into the lobby of the hotel.

# THIRTEEN

## DARK AS A DUNGEON AND FILLED WITH NOOKS

DONOVAN DIDN'T GO straight home. Instead, once Mala was in the lobby and out of sight, he reversed course and headed back down the Avenue of the Americas. He turned west on Fifty-second, crossing the uptown boulevard again and walking down the block that once held the most famous jazz clubs in New York City. Nancy's Downstairs had never been one of that exclusive company, but it looked the part. Down half a flight of concrete stairs, tucked below an Indonesian restaurant and a shop that specialized in jade sculpture and knickknacks, Nancy's was dark as a dungeon and filled with nooks where couples could hold hands while taking in the trio that noodled away on bebop improvisations on a small stage set against a red brick wall. The club smelled the part, too: wine and cigarettes with an occasional waft of brandy. Donovan slipped into a booth near the kitchen and paid handsomely for a bottle of Kaliber.

Accompanied by a drummer and a bassist, Harry Spalding celebrated his Broadway debut by playing riffs around "Bewitched, Bothered, and Bewildered," his head down and eyes closed, a cigarette sticking from the corner of his mouth. The ice cubes in a glass of rye whiskey jiggled atop the upright piano as he finished the tune. The two dozen people in the room applauded appreciatively as Spalding bowed, offered thank-yous, and gave credit to his sidemen. Then he swept his glass and a pack of cigarettes off the top of the piano and joined Donovan in his booth.

"You know what your problem is, old man?" Donovan asked.

"Tell me." Spalding knocked two Marlboros out of the pack and offered one to Donovan, who shook his head.

"When you've had a couple, you don't know whether to steal riffs from Thelonius Monk or Teddy Wilson."

Spalding laughed and lit up, flicking the match into a heavy glass ashtray stolen, some years before, from the Plaza. "I can't get away with shit with you around, you know that? I'm tired, is what it is. Tired and I feel like playin' some clichés."

"And what would you call what you were doing earlier this evening?"

"Bringin' home the bacon," Spalding said, coughing into a closed fist.

"Is Sir John at least paying you well enough, treating you the way he does?" Donovan asked.

"And how is that?"

"Like the hired-hand piano player who does show-biz parties when he ain't doing weddings and bar mitzvahs."

"Oh yeah, well, about that: I was makin' nice for the boss. But for his next party, he can pay a white man to play his white music. I tell you, Bill, I'm making more a week than I used to make in a whole year back in the old days."

"I'll bet you are," Donovan said. Snatching up the pack of cigarettes, he said, "Gimme one of those."

"I thought you gave it up."

"I did."

"And drinkin'? I heard you went on the wagon. I know because that little place on a Hundred-and-tenth Street where you used to hang out went out of business."

"You bet. But I'll have a smoke with you. Just sitting in this place for half an hour you're inhaling a pack and a half."

"Something or other gonna kill us all. You know what happened after the show? I mean, Henry's body wasn't even cold when Kurt Sharkey—the big Hollywood star, y'see, comes up to me and asks me if I will do a screen test."

"For what?"

"For *Dead Eyes IV*, the action flick that him and Henry were gonna make. Can you believe it, Bill? The man was talking about paying me a million dollars to stand on a sound stage watching while stunt men dressed like me duck fake bullets."

"Go for it. You've earned a break."

"Sharkey says, 'We'll all miss poor Henry, but now that he's gone we've got to think of the franchise.' He was talking about those dumb-ass movies. And not only do I look like Henry, because he got shot to death on a Broadway stage and I filled in for him I'm now a bona fide star. Sharkey said, 'The two of you are linked in the public's mind.' Ain't that somethin'?"

Donovan took a few drags on his cigarette, then scowled at the thing and ground it out. "You've come a long way from Harlem, my friend," he said.

"You ain't kiddin'. I'm sixty-five years old and I've made it all the way downtown to Forty-second Street. And you come a long way, too. I hear you're a captain now, with a big office and a lot of guys working for you."

"I heard that rumor."

"What ever happened to Thomas Lincoln Jefferson, your old right-hand man?"

"He's got my old job as head of the West Side Major Crimes Unit. He's doing well."

"I heard you two had a falling out."

"We...ah, felt it best to work apart for a while," Donovan said. "Make no mistake, I still like Jefferson, and consider him my first pupil. I got a new one now—Brian Moskowitz."

"Brian...Moskowitz. He would be the last of the Irish Jews, right?"

"Yeah, he'd be comfortable with that description. He claims his grandparents were Leopold and Molly Bloom."

"That's terrible about what's goin' on between my people and his people on One-hundred-and-twenty-fifth."

"You would be talking about last year, when the brothers burned down a store owned by Jews and killed seven Hispanic workers in the process," Donovan said.

"All this hate does no good for the world. Our generations—mine and yours—knew that. But what happened to these kids? On one side you got Harlem teenagers ready to torch anything that looks white. On the other side, you got Newt Gingrich."

"At least Tom Jefferson is doing well," Donovan said.

"Well, that's good. I always liked that boy, even if he did dress like a banker." Spalding reached across the table and felt the lapel of Donovan's suit jacket. "I see you've been dressin' better yourself."

"Don't knock the threads. I got to walk Mala Logan home tonight."

"Lucky you. I wouldn't mind having a piece of that myself."

"I only walked her to her hotel," Donovan said.

"And what about...what's her name?"

"Marcy. Marcia Barnes."

"That pretty little girl. Did you ever marry her?"

Donovan made a show of slapping the heel of his hand against his forehead. "Damn! I knew I forgot to do something."

Spalding laughed. "What's she into these days?"

"Quit the force. Runs a restaurant on Broadway uptown."

"You got to write down the name and address for me. Once I get famous in Hollywood, I'll bring all my star buddies around to eat there."

"She'll like that," Donovan said.

"Can she cook?"

"Well," Donovan said sheepishly, "she hires people who can."

Spalding drained his drink, then stuck a slender finger into the glass and twirled the cubes around.

After a minute, he said, "You know, a few years back I reached the point where I could forgive everyone involved in that episode years ago—your dad, her dad."

"Forgive them for what?" Donovan chuckled. "My father got you dead to rights, coming out of that liquor store with a revolver in your hands."

"An unloaded revolver."

"Nonetheless, you're lucky you lived to have that epiphany. And Marcy's father was only the prosecutor assigned to the case. It wasn't like a controversial decision. No one put in a 911 call to William Kuntsler that a black man's rights were being trampled. You didn't have no Johnny Cochran planting the seeds of reasonable doubt in the minds of the jury."

Spalding looked up and offered a toothy grin. "Just the same, I forgave everyone. Is Marcy's father enjoying his retirement?"

"He was, then the governor decided to appoint him to the state supreme court."

"What do you know, everyone's gettin' famous: you...Marcy's dad. Pretty soon her. And me, of course. I still feel torn up about your dad bein' killed the way he was, raiding that drug place. And it's a damn shame they never caught no one.''

"I'm working on that, too,'' Donovan said. "One day I'll get him, whoever he is.''

"I know you will. So, who do you think killed Henry Tippett?''

"I haven't the faintest idea,'' Donovan said.

"I was sitting alone in my dressing room, same as I do every night, including the night that Irish kid was killed, all gussied up in the same type suit Henry was wearing, just in case the worst happened, you know? And what do you know, some gofer came running in and said 'Henry's been murdered! Get onstage!' Did you come here to ask if it was me that killed him?''

Donovan shook his head. "I came for the jazz.''

" 'Cause if you are, you may as well charge me with killing that Vietnamese kid, too, 'cause I was sleeping on the couch alone when that happened. At least I didn't get caught in the damn flood we had that night.''

"I came to hear you play,'' Donovan insisted.

"You come on a night when I've had me some more sleep and I'll play you some real stuff like we used to hear in the old days. You always were the hippest kid in town.''

Donovan yawned and stretched his arms. "I had a good teacher,'' he said.

"I didn't kill Henry,'' Spalding said. "Although I guess it looks bad, me havin' a motive plus a record and all.''

"I guarantee that somebody will think of it,'' Donovan agreed.

"But not you?'' Spalding asked, his voice almost begging.

"But not me.''

Spalding reached across the table and shook Donovan's hand. "A word to the wise,'' he said.

Donovan gave him a hard look.

"Watch out for Mala Logan,'' Spalding said.

"Oh yeah, what have you heard? I assume you're not talking about those nutcracker thighs.''

"She hot, all right, and I know you like athletic women. But the talk about her is that she got a red-hot temper to match that red hair. They say she stalked someone in England a few years ago, and beat her up real bad—bad enough to put her in the hospital."

"Stalked? Stalked who?"

"A rival. Another actress who beat her out for a role in a show."

Donovan said, "Mala Logan stalked and beat up someone? I don't remember seeing this on 'Entertainment Tonight.' ''

"There wasn't enough evidence," Spalding said. "The victim wouldn't press charges or something. It was hushed up. Anyway, that's what people say."

"So what you're telling me is not to cross her," Donovan said.

"Let me put it this way: If you wake up in her bed one morning, be sure to tell her she's the best babe since Cleopatra. And later on, send flowers. Send lots of flowers."

"That's another thing I gave up along with smoking and drinking—chasing women who have attitude problems. I don't know if you heard about the Katy Lucca episode?"

"I read the papers. This rich widow tried to get you killed in order to protect her lover, who killed her billionaire husband. Katy Lucca hot too."

"Not up the river doin' twenty to life, she ain't. Harry, if what you're saying about Mala Logan is true, Elena Jordan should be careful. I mean, Mala doesn't hide disliking her."

Spalding's head bobbed up and down. "Her, yes, and Holland too, 'cause he threw her over for Elena."

"Do you think it's possible that Mala is killing people in the theater as a way of putting Holland out of business?" Donovan asked.

Spalding thought for a moment, then nodded. "How's her alibis?"

"She says she was in London and Paris."

"The good Lord gave us aeroplanes," Spalding replied, "fast aeroplanes."

"And so He did," Donovan agreed. "Let me run one other name by you."

"Okay."

"Lucien Schadenfreud."

"The newspaper guy?"

It was Donovan's turn to nod.

"I've seen his name for years, but never met him before tonight. He came up and introduced himself, at the party while I was playing piano. You know what he asked me?" A grin began to take shape on Spalding's lips.

"What?"

"He asked me what I thought of Jeff Cumins."

"Who's that?" Donovan asked.

"Exactly my words. 'Who's that?' So he tells me, 'the piano player for Ruby Ayelet.' "

Donovan said, "And you replied, 'who's that?' And Schadenfreud said 'I can't believe you never heard of Ruby Ayelet.'"

"You had this conversation with him already," Spalding said.

"No, the man is getting predictable."

"So I says, 'I don't listen to rock and roll, and any rock and roll piano player who's worth anything gets out of it and into an art form that lets him improvise. 'Cause without improvisation there is no art, only dance music for teenagers.' "

"I hear you," Donovan said.

"Can you get the nerve of this guy? Askin' me what I think of some rock and roll piano player? Anyway, that's all I know about Lucien Schadenfreud—other than what you can see by eyeballin' him, which is the man is carryin' around a pack of troubles. What's on your mind? Is he a suspect?"

"Maybe yes, maybe no. I was just thinking that the guy is destroying himself."

"And you were wondering if you could help."

"I know that after you had your epiphany—came to certain realizations about yourself—you got involved with Each One Help One."

"After I got out of jail, yeah, they had that program at my church. It's a good thing. If you've been through something yourself, and someone helped you get through it, you ought to reach out your hand to another. Each One Help One. And on and on, keep the circle going. That's what life is about, you know, circles. After jail, you helped me get my chops back at the piano and keep to the straight and narrow, and for that I am grateful every day. Who helped you straighten yourself out?"

"Marcy. But I already paid her back."

"By not marrying her?" Spalding laughed.

"No. But I let her get away with murder once," Donovan laughed louder than his old friend, if a bit uneasily.

"Do you mean to lend a hand to Schadenfreud?" Spalding asked.

"Yes."

"Help the poor man if you can," Spalding said. "Keep the circle going, for all our sakes. But whatever you do, watch out for Mala Logan."

DONOVAN STUDIED the angry, blunt arrows that, safe from contamination in clear plastic evidence bags, sat in the palm of his hand. "These aren't quarrels," he said. "These are regular bolts."

"What are 'quarrels'?" Moskowitz asked. "Other than any conversations with my in-laws."

"When the tips to crossbow arrows are four-pointed they're called 'quarrels,'" Donovan replied. "In those cases, they're used mainly for piercing armor."

"You've been watching the Learning Channel again," Mosko said.

"I got home late and couldn't sleep, so I logged on to the Internet. There's a lot on the Web about weapons."

"Probably from the same guys who blew up the Federal building in Oklahoma City."

"Far from it. These seem like interesting hobbyists who know all there is to know about ancient and medieval weaponry. A few of them hunt. Some stage mock tournaments. For the most part, they make or collect crossbows. What do guys collect in Canarsie?"

"Parking tickets," Mosko said.

It was ten in the morning, and Donovan and Moskowitz had the Old Knickerbocker Theater pretty much to themselves. Occasional workers—cleaners, mostly—wandered by, leaving footfalls that made tiny wooden echoes in the old and cavernous building. A few evidence technicians, including Bonaci, loitered about, peering into corners and scraping stuff into envelopes. Donovan and Moskowitz sat onstage, on the very stairs upon which Tippett had been shot to death. At their feet a chalk outline of the victim stretched raggedly over four steps.

Donovan held the package up to the light and pointed at the tips of the arrows. "At about three in the morning, I got hold of a guy in Wales who not only is an authority on European cross-bows but knows about Milos. According to my source, our Serbian marksman used a custom-made bow with a thirty-inch walnut stock, twenty-six-inch steel bowstave—"

"Come again?"

"Bow. Bow, as in bow and arrow? The bow has a one-hundred-and-fifty-pound pull. You stick your foot in a stirrup—a loop in the front of the stock—and pull back on the string with both hands to cock the weapon."

"A one-hundred-and-fifty-pound pull...seventy-five pounds per hand....Kind of eliminates Mala Logan, doesn't it?" Mosko said.

"I'm not sure. She told me she pumps iron. Seventy-five pounds is a pretty routine weight to use in the sitting-row exercise. She's also admitted to having used a bow and arrow. But I got a good look at her hands tonight, and there was no line or anything...."

"Which you would expect when you pull back on a bow-string," Mosko said.

"Anyway, my source told me that, for all the hoopla about five and only five bolts, Milos used standard, Port Orford cedar arrows."

Mosko drummed his fingers impatiently on the chalk outline of Tippett's right foot.

"They're from Port Orford, Oregon," Donovan continued. "It's a strong, flexible wood that has a distinct smell of turpentine."

He pulled one arrow partly from the bag and sniffed it, then let Mosko do the same. "Nothing," Mosko said.

"New Port Orford cedar smells of turpentine. Old wood will only smell when you cut it. Are we done testing these?"

"Yeah."

Donovan whipped out a pocket knife, made a small nick in one arrow, and smelled it. "Even after sixty years you can smell the turpentine," he said.

He shoved it under Mosko's nose again, and this time the detective got the scent.

"Milos's arrows were sixteen inches long and tipped with two-edged target blades, and so are these," Donovan continued. "These ones, however, have been worked on recently—sharpened to a razor edge. Now, look at the fletching."

Mosko took the arrows and examined the feathers. "They look new."

"Yes, and another thing. One of Milos's trademarks is he religiously kept to the medieval custom of wrapping a tiny bit of black silk around his arrows, right at the leading edges of the feathers."

"What's that do?"

"Crossbow bolts are so short that they often embed themselves in the target up to and including the feathers. So if you pull them out backwards you wreck the fletching. The silk helps the feathers fold down flat when you retrieve your arrow by pulling it through the target. That way they stay in good shape."

"This killer didn't need the arrows back," Mosko noted.

"Yeah, but a real crossbow aficionado would have wrapped them in silk anyway."

"What are you saying, that Milos's ghost didn't do it?"

"I guess so," Donovan replied.

"You know, you're really hard to listen to sometimes, what with all this 'X-Files' shit," Mosko said.

"I'm also noting that whoever did these murders probably wasn't a crossbow pro. For one thing, both the killings were at short range: ten yards or less for Mooney and about twenty yards for Tippett. According to my informant, that's point-blank range."

"Meaning that you don't have to be a world-class expert," Mosko said.

"You have to be good, but you can learn it in a week with a lot of practice."

Donovan was momentarily distracted when a cleaning person dropped a dustpan far back in the orchestra seats, making a crash that resonated to the ornate dome and back down.

He continued. "I read the forensics report on these arrows. For one thing, they both were shot from the same bow. There's a characteristic scratch running for two-point-seven inches on both. It's faint but viewable under a forty-power microscope. My crossbow expert tells me that sometimes a clip or spring is used to keep the arrow from falling out of the firing groove after the bow has been cocked but before it's fired. You need that if you're firing at a down angle, such as from a horse."

"Or a fire escape," Mosko said, comfortably casting the issue in New York City terms.

"Or that catwalk up there," Donovan said, pointing over his shoulder and up. "Now, about the old wood and the new feathers..."

"Bonaci noticed that the feathers were new," Mosko said.

"And so they are—commercial arrow feathers attached with a cyanoacrylate adhesive."

"Whazzat?"

"A commercial glue sometimes used to close wounds in surgery, but more commonly known as Krazy Glue."

"I got some at home."

"Me too. Anyway, cyanoacrylates didn't come into use until fairly recently. There's no way these feathers were buried with Milos in 1933."

"The killer put them on."

"Undoubtedly," Donovan said. "If you look below the Krazy Glue—and Forensics did—you find traces of an old casein adhesive. This is the kind typically used to glue feathers to arrows years ago."

"It's made from milk," Mosko said proudly.

"How'd you know that? Technology ain't up your alley."

"Casein is a component of milk. I know that because my wife is allergic to it. If she has so much as a schmeer on her bagel she breaks out in hives."

"So what's she put on her bagel?" Donovan asked, with mild interest.

"I'm not sure, but it looks like plastic and tastes like the putty you use to keep your windows from rattling."

"It's probably a cyanoacrylate." He mimicked a Brooklyn accent: "Gimme a poppy bagel with Krazy Glue on it and a cuppa coffee."

Moskowitz laughed.

"So casein was used to bind the original fletching to the arrows, probably by Milos himself," Donovan continued. "The feathers must have rotted away over the years."

Mosko had been flipping through the screens on his notebook, and jabbed at one of them with his fingertip. "Actually, bugs ate them. The same bugs that ate Milos. According to the chemistry report on that blue-black dust in the coffin, there were traces of feather in a part of the depression left behind by the crossbow."

"What was that dust, anyway?" Donovan asked.

"Organic material made up of decomposed flesh, fabric, embalming chemicals, the shellac used on the wood of the coffin, and a laundry list of other things, including feathers—for the dust taken from that depression, anyway. It's pretty distinctive. It's on both of those arrows."

"Really?" Donovan said.

"Yeah." Mosko held up two plastic bags, one holding blue-black and the other holding grey dust. "In fact, Bonaci says you can use both of these—the dust from the coffin and the concrete dust from the water main break—as markers. The blue-black dust contains seventeen distinctive main ingredients. The grey dust contains four main constituents. Bonaci says you can use them to ID people."

"Find someone with blue-grey dust under his fingernails and you find someone who had his hands in Milos's coffin," Donovan said excitedly. "Find someone with that grey dust in his shoes and you find someone who was in the basement after the water main break."

"That's about the size of it," Mosko replied, putting the bags back into the soft leather pouch he used as a carryall.

"Have we found any someplace other than the arrows?"

"Not yet, but we continue to look."

Donovan stood, stretched, and, holding onto the railing, gazed out over the set that showed the main floor of Rick's Café Americain. He sang, not quietly enough, *"I came for the wa-ter, but I'll find love in Casa-blan-ca."*

Mosko groaned. "Just marry Marcy and get it over with, please would you? Enough already with you two."

"I think she's still holding out for a Jewish husband," Donovan said.

"So convert. My mom did to marry my father."

"I don't like organized religion. My idea of spirituality is sitting on a hill looking out to sea."

"There's a nice shul in Brighton Beach," Mosko said. "Close enough."

The cleaning person who dropped the dustpan earlier had moved closer to the stage, near enough for Donovan to see that the white-jump-suited person he had assumed was a woman was clearly a man. He pushed in front of him a two-wheeled cart filled, Donovan presumed, with cleaning supplies.

"Remember that I asked Holland for the names of the principals of the 987 West Corporation?" Donovan asked. "I got the list this morning."

"Is anyone we know on it?"

"Maybe. All the names are of businessmen who commonly deal in Times Square real estate, with one exception. Ever hear of an Andy Carl?"

Mosko thought for a moment, then shook his head.

"Me either, but it sounds familiar. So I ran it through my databases. He's a lawyer in Nassau County who's never done business in New York before—at least not on the level we're talking about."

"Is he dirty?"

"Not personally, but get this. Andy Carl was born Andrew Carlito in Brooklyn. He changed his name after graduating from Brooklyn Law."

"I smell a rat," Mosko said.

Donovan continued, "Counselor Carl is the cousin of—get this—Anthony Laquidara."

"The guy the *Post* calls 'the porno king?' "

"Who happens to be the man you chased down the stairs last night," Donovan said triumphantly. "I told you this whole case could be about real estate."

"Are you suggesting that organized crime, in the person of Anthony Laquidara, has a financial interest in the Old Knickerbocker Theater?" Mosko asked.

"I ain't suggesting it. I'm stating it as a fact. Furthermore, I'm telling you that organized crime has an interest in seeing Holland fail. Or seeing him flat-out dead. You can make a lot more money tearing this edifice down and putting up an office tower than you can by insulting the greatest American movie of all time."

"No wonder Laquidara didn't want to be identified at that party last night," Mosko said.

"No wonder. Two questions remain...."

"What was he really discussing with Derrida?" Mosko said.

Donovan nodded. "And what's Derrida's connection to Laquidara, Carl, and the rest of the 987 West Corporation?"

"He's the front man for the effort to destroy Holland," Mosko said. "In other words, the killer—or the man who plays the killer. No one is in a better position to have dug up that crossbow and set about killing folks with it."

"Yes, and let's keep in mind that Derrida went out of his way to point out that his men were with him when he found Mooney's body. He must have said it three times. He also mentioned something about Dinh being unidentified—at a point when we hadn't released that information."

"Derrida is behind these murders," Mosko said.

"Possibly."

"Possibly?"

"I think that the whole real estate connection is a lot more complicated than you or I know," Donovan said.

# FOURTEEN

## LIKE MICHAEL J. FOX WITH A MUSTACHE

A MAN WHO disliked ambiguity, Donovan's aide sought to change the subject to something more concrete. "Do you want to hear about last night's interrogations?" he asked, scrolling to another page on his notebook.

Donovan did, and sat back down to receive the information.

"I had a sketch artist work with the two stagehands who saw the killer on the catwalk."

"Who saw someone on the catwalk," Donovan corrected. "He could have been an innocent bystander."

"Who ran after Tippett dropped?"

"It's been known to happen."

"The artist also worked with the extra you talked to, the one who was wearing the French police uniform. Here's the result."

Mosko handed Donovan the computer, which displayed the image of a man of about thirty years with thin lips and a prominent brown mustache. A few curls of hair projected from beneath a white djellaba. But there was nothing distinctive about the man.

"How's this going to help?" Donovan asked. "This guy could be anyone. What did they say about height?"

"Medium."

"Age?"

"About thirty."

"This man doesn't look Arab. In fact, he looks like Michael J. Fox with a mustache. Of course, Holland wouldn't go out of his way to hire an Arab actor to play an Arab in the production. Send a note to the Arab Actors' Guild about that lapse."

"Is there such a group?"

"I have no idea. But this is New York, the last bastion of liberal multiculturalism in America, and no doubt there's somebody who will get worked up when the news leaks out that Holland is hiring Anglos to play Semites.''

"It would be a good idea to get the Arabs out of cabs and into the theater, now that you mention it. While we're on the subject, we confiscated all the Arab robes worn by cast members. You should have heard the yowling from the costume department.''

"The Garment District is right around the corner. They can buy cloth and sew more.''

"As it turns out, they had plenty extra.''

Donovan asked, "How many actors wear Arab robes in this production?''

"Twenty-seven,'' Mosko reported.

"And how many robes did you collect?''

"Twenty-eight.''

"Please explain the difference.''

"We talked to all twenty-seven actors. None matched the description. There were three average-height guys with mustaches, but all were accounted for when Tippett was killed. All twenty-seven were in the presence of others, in plain sight, or whatever. They turned in their robes to the costume master when they were supposed to—except that we were waiting there to confiscate them.''

"They were all good little boys,'' Donovan said. "And the other robe?''

"Bonaci found it in a Dumpster in the basement.''

Donovan's eyes widened. "Which basement?'' he asked.

"The bottom one, the B-level, where Milos is buried,'' Mosko said.

"Do you mean that small construction-debris Dumpster near the freight elevator?'' Donovan asked.

"That's the one.''

"Let's go down there,'' the captain said, getting up once more and leading the way down the stairs.

The B-level remained as dirty as it had been the last time he was there. It was as if Derrida's men refused to go to the spot. Donovan was reminded of the old mummy movies where the Egyptian diggers refused to work in the sandy hole that bore the curse of the ancients. Indeed, the lower basement, in the wake of two murders and one pillaged grave, was taking on the aspect of a suburb of hell reachable only by crossing the river Styx.

"Is this place getting creepier, or is it me?" Donovan asked as they stepped off the freight elevator and were met by a blast of cold and musty air.

"It ain't you," Mosko replied, turning up the collar of his coat.

The long hall that ran the length of the lower basement, from beneath backstage to below the front entrance, was dark enough— even at mid-morning—to give the illusion of being filled with the low-lying fog seen in lowland cemeteries on cold and damp mornings. The hastily strung lights that still gave the only illumination seemed haloed, and fell off sharply in brightness as they approached the gravesite, until Donovan could barely see the last one. That was the bulb that Mooney had been hanging when an arrow pierced his heart.

The Dumpster sat between the freight elevator and a utility staircase—not far from the stage hydraulics, which were faintly backlit by a bare bulb in a plumber's lamp hooked onto a pipe fitting. The lump of steel and hydraulic gears, even more dark and massive when silent, loomed over the two men. Red exit lights over the elevator and the stairs cast long and blurry shadows that made the space between the Dumpster and the stone wall, while no wider than a foot, seem big enough to hold a large man. Donovan produced his Mag-Lite and focused the beam on the container; unconsciously, Moskowitz rested his fingers on the grip of his nine-millimeter Penzler Automatic.

Yellow crime-scene tape surrounded the Dumpster, which was filled over the brim with debris: wood, plaster, broken brick, bits of iron support, rusted steel, old electrical conduit, and lead pipe. A few ancient cleaning rags smelled of turpentine, which reminded Donovan of crossbow arrows. He shined the light across the top of the pile.

"The robe was crammed into this hole here," Mosko said, pointing to the spot. A six-inch-wide crevice between several chunks of plaster and an armful of broken wooden slats extended a foot below the brim of the container. Donovan shined the light down there, then to the freight elevator, then to the stairwell door, then back.

"Let's look at this from the killer's point of view," Donovan said. "You want to make a clean escape. The freight elevator is too chancy. Someone might be on it. It could stop at another floor."

"It's too slow," Mosko added.

"You're not in control. Better to take the stairs. How long would it take to run down from the catwalk level?"

"Less than a minute. Actually, running down a couple of flights can be done in well under thirty seconds."

"No one will take particular notice," Donovan said, "Because as several people have pointed out, everyone runs backstage. So you shoot Tippett, stick the weapon back under your robe—which is how you smuggled it up from the basement a few minutes earlier..."

Moskowitz looked around him, his fingers tightening again on the grip of his automatic.

"...and run down the stairs. Anyone who sees you thinks you're late for a cue. You get down here to the empty basement."

"Where no one comes with the exception of cops and coroners, following two deaths and the discovery of a grave," Mosko said, his eyes suddenly flashing to the darkness around the stage hydraulics.

Not noticing, Donovan continued, "You whip off the robe and stash it in this Dumpster. Did we find any plaster or other residue from the Dumpster on the robe?"

"Yeah, on the outside of it," Mosko said, not taking his eyes off the mountain of machinery that sat nearby.

"And the black dust from the coffin?"

"A trace amount...on the inside front. Just where you would hold a crossbow if you were concealing it. Did you see something move over there?"

As he spoke, there was a scraping sound.

"Over where?"

Mosko pulled his nine-millimeter from the holster and used it to point in the direction of the noise. "There," he replied as something fleetingly blocked out the light coming from the plumber's lamp.

Donovan had his Smith & Wesson in his hand. "Police!

Freeze!'' he yelled as a shadowy figure ducked down a small secondary hallway, one that Donovan had yet to go into.

The sound of hard-soled shoes running awkwardly, as if with a limp, echoed along the strange, narrow corridor. Their eyes still unaccustomed to the darkness, Donovan and Moskowitz stumbled in pursuit, but it was pointless. They heard a few more footfalls followed by the slamming of a metal door.

Donovan stopped at the entrance to the corridor and shined his Mag-Lite down it. There was no other illumination but that from the flashlight, which cast spike-like shadows along the outlines of at least a dozen doors. ''It's more of those storage rooms,'' Donovan said. ''More old junk from more old vaudevillians.''

''Did you see which one he went into?''

''No. Get Bonaci and the rest of the boys down here.''

Mosko got onto the cell phone, speaking softly as he followed his boss down the corridor, trying doors. All were locked. By the time they got to the end of the hall, they were facing a red brick wall, filthy with age, that was interrupted by a major vertical structural beam.

''We're at one wall of the theater,'' Donovan said, whispering—for no good reason, as there was no one else around. ''The east wall, I think.''

''The guy went into one of these doors,'' Mosko said, also in a whisper.

''If he did, we got him,'' Donovan said. He had returned to his normal voice.

''Want to bet he turns out to be a plumber who was stealing copper pipe?'' Mosko said. ''You know, like that guy who was caught taking copper off of the Brooklyn Bridge a few years back and selling it to junkyards.''

Donovan stared at the red brick wall and the structural beam for a moment, then kicked it.

''What're you doing, boss?''

''I don't like walls,'' he replied.

''Which is why you never got married. But what's that got to do with right now?''

''Upstairs last night, Derrida tried to convince me the dumb-waiters were bricked up and nonfunctional.''

"He failed," Mosko speculated.

Donovan nodded. "This morning, I wonder what's behind that wall."

"The building next door, I guess," Mosko said, cocking an ear in the direction of the utility stairs, which had begun to resonate with the pounding of police detectives' shoes.

"I grew up in this town and spent enough time in the subway and in the basements of old buildings to know that nothing is what it seems," Donovan continued. "This entire city is an ant hill, a prairie dog colony, a labyrinth."

"You're somethin' else," Mosko laughed.

"See, you grew up in Canarsie, where people live in single-family homes where basements have fake-wood-paneled rec rooms. I grew up in Manhattan, where people live in fifty-family homes and basements are thick with mystery."

Followed by three other men, Bonaci burst into the basement calling Donovan's name. "Over here," Mosko shouted back.

"Whaddya got, Cap?" the crime-scene chief asked, arriving a bit out of breath.

"We came down here to check out the Dumpster and somebody took off on us," Donovan said.

"He went in one of these doors," Mosko added.

"But if he's still in there I'll buy all of you lunch," Donovan said.

"You lose," Bonaci replied. "I been in those rooms. They're filled with junk but there's no way out."

"I want to go to that Vietnamese place where Dinh worked," Mosko added.

"We'll see," Donovan said, and leaned against the wall with his arms folded.

IT TOOK THE MEN twenty minutes to set up lights in the narrow corridor and begin opening doors. It was the same each time: a clink of master keys, a rattling of lock, a precautionary threat from Moskowitz, and a bursting into the room, guns drawn. And in each case there was no reward; the rooms were devoid of life. By the time Bonaci opened the last one, the failure of the mission was apparent. When the final door crashed open to reveal nothing but aging rubble, Mosko sighed and said, "I guess Burger King ain't so bad."

"Where the hell is he?" Bonaci asked.

"Gone," Donovan said, "and I think I know where." He led the way to the back of the room—the part of it that abutted the east wall of the theater, an extension of the same wall Donovan had kicked out in the hall. Unlike most of the other storage rooms, this one held no theater gear. Instead, there were two piles of supplies, both of them dating to the early 1960s. A four-foot pile of rectangular brown metal boxes was separated by a small space from a six-foot pile of brown twenty-five-gallon cans. Smaller clusters of both lay about randomly.

"What's all this stuff?" Mosko asked.

"Supplies from the *Dr. Strangelove* era," Donovan said.

"Come again?"

"Survival food and water in case of nuclear attack."

"You got to be kidding me."

"Poor you, growing up in Canarsie. You never got to play in a real Cold War fallout shelter. This is part of one."

Mosko peered at the rectangular boxes. "Survival crackers," he said, reading the label. "Cool."

"The cans hold drinking water."

"This is the building's fallout shelter?" Bonaci asked.

Looking around him and gauging the size of the room, Donovan shook his head. "It's too small. Something is missing." He squeezed into the passage between the pile of crackers and the pile of water cans, his Mag-Lite again showing the way. Bending over, he said, "I found it."

"What?" Mosko asked.

Donovan grunted and disappeared, leaving behind him a scraping sound and a muffled curse.

"Cap?" Bonaci said.

Donovan's muffled voice replied, "I'm in the building next door. Come on over."

Astonished, Mosko and Bonaci followed their boss. Bending low, they squeezed through a three-foot-high hole in the brick and emerged in a nearly identical room. This one had the same piles of supplies, and added a stack of folding cots. Donovan made his way to the door and flipped a switch. A ceiling light burst on.

"Welcome to the missing half of the Old Knickerbocker fallout shelter," he said proudly.

"Where the hell are we?" Mosko asked.

"I'll bet anything we're in the Old Knickerbocker Annex."

"I ain't bettin' you today," Bonaci said.

"Here's what I want you guys to do. Howard, go back to collecting evidence upstairs. Look for anywhere that dust—either the grey or the black kind—might turn up. Brian, I want you to make calls and find out where all our suspects have been for the past hour. I want to have a word with Laquidara later today. You check on Derrida, Bock, Schadenfreud, Logan, Spalding, and, for the hell of it, throw in Elena Jordan."

"Elena Jordan? You suspect her?"

"I got a feeling about her."

"She looks so soft and harmless," Mosko protested.

"Yeah, but anyone who beats out Mala Logan for the lead role in a Broadway show can't be a powder puff."

"What about Sharkey?" Bonaci asked.

"Sharkey?" Mosko said. "Do you know anybody with a better alibi than Sharkey for the Tippett killing? There were seventeen hundred witnesses."

"Not counting the millions who saw the tape on 'Hard Copy,'" Donovan said. "I agree with Howard. Check him out anyway. He'll be thrilled to be suspected of murder. It will raise his contract price in Hollywood by a million or two."

"Where will you be?" Mosko asked.

"Upstairs in the annex, paying a call on Sy Gittelson."

# FIFTEEN

## IF YOU'RE NEW, POOR, AND TALENTED, YOU HAVE A FRIEND IN LUKE

THE TWO-PERSON elevator dropped off Donovan on a fourth floor, the halls of which were tin that had been stamped with an old-fashioned fleur-de-lis pattern and painted white. Rusting water leaked from bare ceiling pipes that hissed in the winter air, making stains that resembled brown stalagtites on the walls. The floor was made of octagonal marble squares—once quite elegant but now old-timers that cracked and moved when stepped upon, like flagstones set in wet soil. The hall had that smell old New York buildings get at midwinter: too much steam heat cooking the assorted algae that grow during the hot, wet summer.

Only one of the six office doors on that floor seemed to be in use. It was wooden and old, with a cracked, opaque glass panel that bore the legend GITTELSON PROMOTIONS, SY GITTELSON, PROP. Outside it stood a rusting umbrella holder with two umbrellas in it—although it hadn't rained for days or snowed yet that season. Through the door Donovan could hear the AM station that played standards—at the moment, "Begin the Beguine." He turned the handle and pushed the door open.

Sy Gittelson stirred on the ancient couch, once full and plush, now mouse-eaten and tattered, that sat opposite an oak desk that qualified as an archaeological find. The PR man was thin and hawk-faced, with a few wisps of white hair carefully combed over the top of his otherwise bare head. He looked like a man just roused from a long sleep, wiping his eyes as he gaped at Donovan, and struggling to lower his feet to the floor from where they had rested atop a copy of the newspaper. Blue socks partly covered pencil-thin ankles; nearly hairless white skin disappeared up grey woolen pants.

"I'm sorry," he stammered, "I fell asleep. What time is it?" He answered his own question, gawking at a large wall clock. "My God, it's Thursday. I slept all night on the couch. Must have had too much for dinner."

Donovan scooped up the man's black Florsheim dress shoes, which were warm inside, and handed them to the old man. "Here you go," Donovan said helpfully.

Now sitting up, Gittelson bent to tie on his shoes.

"I have got to get a new secretary, but times are tough, you know."

"So I hear."

"My last one, I had to let her go a few years ago. I couldn't afford her, and she was always late anyway. Never could learn how to use the Selectric."

"The what?" Donovan asked.

"The IBM Selectric? The new typewriter."

"Oh, that."

"I always felt that a gal had to keep up with new times if she wanted to be a good secretary, don't you agree, Mr....?"

"Captain Donovan, police."

Donovan was sure that Gittelson was unsurprised. "Oh, a detective," he said. "I was...I was hoping you were a producer."

"Part of my function is to be disappointing...to at least some of the people I talk to," Donovan said.

His shoes now tied, Gittelson got to his feet, groaning as if in pain and pushing at his lower back with one hand. Then he shook the captain's hand and hobbled across the room to his desk, which was piled with papers, including a two-foot-high stack of issues of *Variety*. As Gittelson lowered himself into a high-back chair— like everything in the office, at least four decades old—he lit up a panatela. Donovan helped himself to a seat on the couch and, while his host got his cigar burning properly, picked up and looked at the copy of *The Times*. It was the Thursday paper, the one-dot edition. A bit of newspaper minutia shared by many New Yorkers was that you could tell editions of *The Times* by counting the number of dots between the volume and number on the banner. While it's possible to buy Thursday's paper Wednesday night, it's impossible to buy that particular edition Wednesday night. Gittelson had "slept all night" on an edition that only became available that morning.

"Do you live here, Mr. Gittelson?" Donovan asked.

The man shook his head quickly and profoundly. "It's against the law. Is that what you came to ask me about?"

"No."

"I was working late last night on my new client. I lay down to rest for a minute and I guess I fell asleep."

"Who is your new client?"

Gittelson looked a little sheepish. "Actually, and I'm embarrassed to say this, it's a rock and roll group. They're called Shanghai Love Motel, but you probably never heard of them."

"They're a literate nouveau-punk band," Donovan said proudly. "They opened for Jeff Buckley recently."

Gittelson's black eyes widened. "I'm impressed," he said.

"I like to know a little bit about lots of things," Donovan said. "Including how well you know Lucien Schadenfreud."

Gittelson blew a smoke ring at the ceiling, and said, "I got him to review the band."

"Did he like them?"

"What's not to like? The kids are starting to buy their record, and who am I to argue? Sure he liked Shanghai Love Motel. He likes everything new and fresh and hates everything established and commercial. If you're new, poor, and talented, you have a friend in Luke. If you're old, rich, and stale, he can be your worst nightmare."

"I knew there was something about him I liked," Donovan said.

"Fortunately—I guess I should use that word—most of my clients these days fall into the category of new and poor. I can't tell you from fresh. I do what I can to make sure Luke sees them. So what's he done that a policeman comes to call?"

"Luke? Nothing that I can prove...yet."

"Then what did you come to talk about? It's not whether I live here illegally and it's not what I think Lucien Schadenfreud did or didn't do. I have to think about this. Would you mind waiting a moment while I use the facilities?"

"I'll wait," Donovan said, opening the newspaper as Gittelson got up from behind his desk and shuffled into the adjoining room.

The moment that door closed, Donovan took a small evidence bag from his pocket. He bent over and scraped into the bag some dirt and dust that marked the old carpet beneath the spot where Gittelson left his shoes. By the time the toilet flushed and the old man came back, Donovan was perusing the latest update from Belgrade.

"I remember who you are," Gittelson announced.

"You keep your files in the john?"

"I do my best thinking there, which is a good thing for a man my age. I should be a genius for all the thinking I do. I remembered reading a book about you, those murders in Riverside Park ten years ago."

"Fifteen years ago."

"You're famous, Captain Donovan. What you need is someone to represent you."

"Just for the sake of argument, what can you do for me?"

"Did you make anything off that book?"

"Not a dime."

"Now, that's a crime," Gittelson said. "You should go back to that author and arrest him."

"The statute of limitations has run out," Donovan said.

"So write your memoirs. I'll package the book for you. I'll get you on the 'Today' show. I can even get you on Letterman."

"Doing what, using my service revolver to blow the heads off Barbie dolls?"

"You do what you gotta do. As long as the man holds the cover of your book up so the camera can see it, who cares?"

"Is this the sort of thing you did for Milos Tryvomanic?" Donovan asked.

Gittelson's face lit up, and for the first time in the conversation the man looked like he was enjoying himself. "So that's why you're here, you want to ask me about Milos the Magnificent. In many ways, my greatest client." Moving with amazing speed considering his years, Gittelson scurried across the room and poked a bony finger at a yellowing photograph hung amidst a sea of them. There were jugglers, acrobats, circus musclemen, fan dancers, strippers, models, and actors and actresses. Among the latter were smiling cowboys in ten-gallon hats, dapper Englishmen in bowlers, leering Frenchmen in berets, grinning gondoliers in striped shirts, and more beckoning blonds, brunettes, and redheads than Donovan could count. Most of the photos were signed, and always in bold strokes that suggested the signers were stars of the highest rank. The few that truly were stars, such as Jack Benny, Eddie Cantor, and Fanny Brice, had long since ascended to that big casting call in the sky. All the signatures were addressed to "my friend Sy," "my greatest friend, Sy," or "the best agent in the world."

"Look at my scrapbook," Gittelson said. "The best and the brightest of vaudeville."

"But not much since, to be honest," Donovan said.

"Are you kidding?" Gittelson protested, genuinely hurt. "Look at this photo."

He tapped his finger on an eight-by-ten glossy that showed a chesty blond with big hair and a tiny, silver bathing suit.

Donovan read the inscription: " 'To my best New York pal, Sy Gittelson. Tawny Berkowitz.' Tawny Berkowitz? Named after her grandfather, of the lion-taming Berkowitzes, I guess."

"You're kibbitzing me, Captain. Tawny starred in *Beach Vixens from Mars.*"

"I missed it."

"The movie was on cable, but you can rent it."

"Did you get her on the 'Today' show and Letterman?"

"All a man can do is try," Gittelson said, shaking his head. "Can I get you a cigar?"

"No thanks. Mr. Gittelson, I'm going to ask a personal question."

"So ask."

"Do you make a living at this?"

The man shrugged and tossed his palms up into the air high enough to be juggling coconuts. "I'm eighty-three years old. I've been on Social Security longer than most of my clients have been alive. I get by with a little bit from this one and a little bit from that one. I'm gonna be honest with you, most of my clients are shiksas with big boobs and no brains or else they're rock groups. Sometimes I get them both in one package."

"That pays the rent?" Donovan said, looking around at what amounted to a mini-museum of show biz.

"You see before you one of the last great stories of rent control in the city of New York," Gittelson said.

Challenged, Donovan said, "I have three bedrooms, three baths on Riverside Drive for three hundred ninety-four dollars and fifty cents."

"I can beat that hands down. What do you think I pay for this office?"

"How big is it?"

"This room. Another just like it where I keep my files. And the bathroom."

"A thousand," Donovan said.

"Forget about it," Gittelson said, pronouncing the phrase *fageddabowdit*. "I pay two thirty-five."

"Jesus, no wonder you're the last tenant in the building. The landlord must be going nuts trying to get you out of here. But he can't budge you because you're grandfathered in."

"And covered under the age discrimination laws. And covered under the handicapped act." Gittelson poked at his lower back and said, "My spine is a mess. I'm a tall man and I'm old."

It must have killed you ducking through that hole in the wall, Donovan thought.

"The landlord wants to tear down the building and put up an office tower. He sees these big corporations buying up old buildings in Times Square and turning them into office towers, now that the neighborhood is turning fancy-schmancy. He wants to get me out of here so bad it's giving him agita, but I have my press contacts and the ACLU on my side. Also the Rent Control Alliance. And I got an angel, too. I see myself as being all that stands in the path of the complete obliteration of the glorious history of show business on the Great White Way. Which, let me guess, is the reason you came here to ask about Milos the Magnificent."

Donovan smiled.

"Isn't it, Captain?"

"You're pretty sharp," Donovan said, nodding.

"I've been around a long time. Here, take a look at the man."

Gittelson indicated a yellowing photo of a thin but regal-looking man dressed in a black velvet frock coat topped off by a broad-brimmed velvet hat and a white silk scarf. Tryvomanic was clean-shaven, with narrow, piercing eyes and eyebrows that were thick and curved like scimitars. He was seen in partial profile, looking at the camera with supreme confidence. Clasped to his chest was the crossbow and arrows; on the stock of the instrument stood out a five-pointed star.

"He liked the pentacle," Donovan said.

"Yeah, yeah, but don't make too much of that," Gittelson replied. "The year was 1933. Every other movie that came out of Hollywood was about vampires and werewolves. The pentacle was a gimmick for Milos, no more. It made audiences think of Lon Chaney, Jr. Adopting the pentacle as his emblem was good business for a showman who had an accent that made Bela Lugosi sound like a TV anchorman."

"There was no mystical significance, eh?"

"Not a nickel's worth. So tell me, Captain, the curiosity is killing me, what makes you put Milos the Magnificent in the same sentence with my battle to keep the lease on my office space?"

"It's logical," Donovan replied. "The man saved enough money to buy ten percent of the Old Knickerbocker. He planned ahead well enough to stipulate he be buried in the basement. It was the Depression, when a successful man made every cent count. You can't convince me—as John Victor Holland tried to do—that this same fellow dies without leaving a will. The way I figure it, he left his money to someone. Maybe you, maybe his fiancée, maybe both."

It was Gittelson's turn to smile. "You're worth every penny the city pays you, and if I know New York City that's probably what your salary is counted in. I got Milos as a client from my father when he passed away. I was barely out of my teens myself in 1930 when I took over this business. Milos was a big star in those days. He kept his girl in diamonds and furs—it was the style back then—and still had enough to buy a share in the Old Knickerbocker complex."

"Both buildings?"

"The two of them were originally owned by the Old Knickerbocker Properties office. They were built together and came as a package until fairly recently—five years ago, when the shareholders in Old Knickerbocker Properties agreed to sell the theater to the 987 West Corporation. In the old days, Milos lived upstairs in this building, the annex—he didn't believe in spending a lot on living accommodations, although he kept his girl in a wonderful apartment on West End Avenue. His studio, two floors above this very office, has long been empty, so don't think of going up there looking for clues. Anything important was thrown out by the button distributor that took over the space and then went out of business. I'm the only one left here now.''

"Button distributor?"

"We are around the corner from the Garment District. So to continue the story, Milos did, as you suspect, have a will. He left his share in Old Knickerbocker Properties to Elsie, the chorus girl he fell in love with."

"Elsie what?"

"Klinger with a K. I introduced them, in 1931. She was a beauty—six-foot-one, a lot taller than him, but they didn't care. And she's still a good-looking woman."

"This woman is still alive?" Donovan asked.

"What is it, a crime? You sound like Newt Gingrich. We should all drop dead at sixty-one so as not to use the Social Security Trust Fund and force the twenty-somethings to get jobs and work as hard as we did? Shame on you, Captain."

"Where does she live?" Donovan asked, with a laugh.

"Same place—Ninety-fourth and West End."

"Another rent control success story. I don't feel so unusual. Can I talk to her?"

"Why not? She has ears. If you want her number she's in the book. Tell her I'm still thinking about it and will get back to her in a few weeks. It's a little joke between us."

"Still thinking about what?"

"About marrying her, of course. We've been talking about it for thirty years, but the time was never right. You know, it broke her heart when Milos was killed. She never married. But like I told you, we've been talking about it. She's the angel I mentioned earlier."

"Let me guess—Elsie may have sold her share in the theater, but she won't sell her ten percent of the annex no matter what, unless the new owners guarantee you can stay as long as you like.''

"You got it," Gittelson said. "Although, secretly I think she would like me to retire, marry her, and move out of here. You know, she never would have sold her share in the theater knowing that Milos was buried there, except for the fact nobody knew where the grave was. And most people thought the story of Milos being buried there at all was a myth. I encouraged people to think that.''

"Including Roger Bock?"

"I never told anyone. Elsie never told anyone. And nobody would have known were it not for that water main break.''

Gittelson had drifted back behind his desk, settled back into his chair, and once again was blowing smoke rings at the ceiling, where an ancient ceiling fan that squeaked with every revolution demolished them. "Let me guess," Donovan said. "When Elsie sold her share in the theater to the 987 West Corporation, her place on the board was taken by a nice Nassau County attorney named Andrew Carl.''

"How'd you know that?" Gittelson asked.

"I get lucky from time to time. Do you know who Carl is?"

"He seems like a nice man, but what do I know? He's a lawyer, and I don't trust them as a general rule.''

Donovan cleared his throat, which along with his eyes was burning from the cigar smoke. He said, "Mr. Gittelson, when was the last time you were in the Old Knickerbocker?''

The captain was sure he saw the old man stiffen. Gittelson stubbed out his stogy and replied, "Sometime after the war.''

"Which war?"

"Which do you think? World War II, of course. I was there for a performance by Milton Berle. One of his last before he went into television full time.''

"And you haven't set foot in there since?" Donovan asked.

"Why should I? To me the place was a big mausoleum. Milos spoiled it for me by having himself buried there.''

Donovan was sure the man was lying, but decided not to confront him at that time. Instead, the captain returned to the subject with which he had opened the conversation. He said, "I guess I can see what you mean about the Old Knickerbocker being a mausoleum, although lately it's seemed more like a slaughterhouse. Let's get back to Luke Schadenfreud.''

Gittelson relaxed noticeably. Whatever he was, the man wasn't good at hiding his emotions. "How can I help you, Captain?" he asked.

"I bet you know him pretty well."

"As well as anyone. I've been getting him to review my acts for almost thirty years."

"Why is he so mad at John Victor Holland?" Donovan asked.

"Turning *Casablanca* into a musical isn't reason enough?"

"No. Not for the kind of unreasoning hatred I see. I mean, I don't like it and told Holland so. But I'm not out to destroy the sonofabitch. Schadenfreud is. He seems to take pleasure in torturing the man."

Gittelson sighed, then said, "This didn't come from me. I like Luke."

"So do I."

"I mean, he has some problems, but at heart he's a mensch."

"What did Holland do to him?" Donovan asked.

"It was the early 1970s, when Holland was on a roll."

"Before or after his rock musical?"

"Before," Gittelson said. "Luke doesn't have money. He never did. His father runs an antique shop—more like a second-hand store—on Second Avenue, and not even on a good part of it. Holland always had money, and enough talent as a composer of music to get by. What Holland didn't have, and Luke did, was a way with words."

"I guess you have to be a pretty good writer to work for *The Times*, even if you cover rock and roll," Donovan said.

"In the early 1970s Holland had a falling out with his lyricist. What he did then was to offer the job to Luke. Do you know what writing the lyrics for a John Victor Holland musical makes you?"

"An accomplice?"

"Very good, Captain. You're a funny man. Maybe I can get you on Letterman. No, what being Holland's lyricist makes you is an instant millionaire. All his records go platinum, and I assure you that the way to make a fortune in music is to write the words and music and own the rights. You know 'Stardust?'"

"Of course."

"Every time that song is played on the radio, which is like every ten seconds, the cash register rings at the Hoagy Carmichael estate, even after all these years. And the Beatles? Forgeddabowdit! I wish I wrote the lyrics for 'Yesterday.' I'd buy back the Old Knickerbocker and turn it into a real monument to Milos Tryvomanic."

"I see. So what you're saying is, Holland dangled a bag of gold in front of a starving writer and then..."

"Yanked it away. He made up with his lyricist. Holland even stole one of Luke's lyrics and pretended he wrote it himself. Holland is known for that."

"So I hear," Donovan said.

"Luke had started living as if the money was already in the bank. When the roof fell in, his wife left him. He lost his apartment. He even had to move back in with his parents for a while. And, as I guess you know, he started drinking."

"And has been trying to get even with Holland ever since."

"An eye for an eye," Gittelson said. "Do you blame him?"

"Do you think Luke is mad enough at Holland to commit murder?" Donovan asked.

Gittelson thought for a long while, then shook his head. "At the risk of sounding like a head-shrinker, Luke is a writer. He has an outlet for his anger. He can kill Holland in print."

"He doesn't need to do it in person," Donovan said.

Gittelson fished a tea bag out of a desk drawer and dropped it into a stained old mug that bore the logo of *A Chorus Line*. He asked, "Do you think Luke killed those people?"

"I'd like to think not."

Smiling, Gittelson said, "Let me make you a nice cup of tea."

# SIXTEEN

## KICK THE SHIT OUT OF HIM AND CUFF HIM TO THE RADIATOR IN MY OFFICE.

THE OFFICE OF AAA Amazing Entertainments was newer than Gittelson's, but due to the amazing chaos seemed much older. The hall was lined with cheap wallboard painted some years ago in a light, pastel green—meant, perhaps, to be soothing. But now it looked like one of those interior-design concepts tied inexorably to another time, like mustard-colored kitchen appliances.

There were holes every so often where wiring had been fixed or replaced without patching the hole up afterward. A two-foot length of wrapped cable hung from one of them. A mustard-colored watercooler sat in the hall, making the same noise you get by rattling a ball bearing around in a tin can. Posters from X-rated films appeared at intervals. Like the chesty actresses shown on them, the posters were cheap. The paper yellowed even in the dim light and turned up along the edges.

The office door itself was all glass, made of the sort found in shower stalls. Despite the gold-leaf lettering of the firm's name, Donovan felt he was about to bust into someone's bathroom. "This is like breaking into the steam room at the West Side Y," he said to Moskowitz, who stood to the left of the door with his nine-millimeter Penzler in his hand.

"I'll bet this is less gay."

"We'll see. Is the guy in there?"

"According to Surveillance, he got here an hour ago."

"Before then?"

"He left his house in Marine Park, Brooklyn, at five, had dinner alone at the Galatian Diner on Flatbush Avenue..."

"Is that one of your places?"

"I've been there. It's not bad. After he ate, Laquidara took the

Belt Parkway to the Prospect and up there into the Brooklyn-Battery Tunnel. He got to his office on West Street near Fourteenth…''

"In the wholesale meat and gay-bar district."

"Yeah. That's the place he runs his waterfront properties from. He got there around seven, stayed for an hour, then drove up the West Side Highway to Fiftieth and came crosstown. Like I said, he got here an hour ago."

"Is he alone?"

"Yeah, apart from the secretary, a young woman."

"The secretary works evenings?" Donovan asked.

"I don't think they keep bankers' hours in the porno trade, boss. As a rule, Laquidara's driver stays with the Lincoln, at the garage down the block, until he's called. We're keeping an eye on him."

Behind Moskowitz were half a dozen other detectives, like him wearing blue, bullet-proof vests marked NYPD.

"Is Laquidara dangerous?" Donovan asked.

"Not personally, according to the Organized Crime Task Force. But with these guys you never know."

"Go ahead," Donovan said.

He stood back—Donovan had promised Marcy to avoid getting shot at whenever possible—and watched as the door to AAA Amazing Entertainments flew open. The secretary screamed as the door hit the front of her desk and vibrated like a stop sign shaking in a hurricane. Mosko led the way into the office, followed by the other officers. Donovan heard another scream, and then two barked commands: "Wait outside with the officer, sweetheart!" and "Hang up the phone, asshole!" Proud of his protégé, Donovan strolled into the office and looked around.

The girl was a bottle blond, with big hair that was teased into a bullet shape that circled her head about six inches out from it and fell below her shoulders. Were her face even slightly angelic, it and her hair would have resembled one of those bathtub Marys—the Virgin Mary stuck in a bathtub that had been inverted and dug into the front lawn of a home, often in Brooklyn. But large breasts pushed out a red angora sweater that was belted over silver tights, and she chewed gum furiously as a detective ushered her toward the door.

"What's going on?" she wailed.

"Is your name Donna?" Donovan asked.

"Sure," she replied, calmed slightly by having been asked a question. "How'd you know?"

"Do you drive a Camaro?"

"I used to, but it broke down."

"Well, guessing right half the time is still pretty good," Donovan said. "What do you drive now?"

"I got a Corvette," she replied, both proud and perplexed.

"A secretary's pay must be up these days," Donovan said.

"Mr. Laquidara has been good to me."

"I'll bet you been pretty good to him, too," Donovan said. "Wait with the detective."

Laquidara sat in an inner office, the walls of which—like all of the office—were decorated with X-rated film posters as well as with autographed photos of their female stars. He was arguing with Moskowitz, who stood with impressive forearms crossed over massive chest, looking scornful.

The outer office was filled with filing cabinets, grey metal desks used mainly to hold piles of newspapers and magazines, and more blowups of porn stars. A detective said, "Hey, Cap, check this out," and drew Donovan to an eight-by-ten that showed the bare back of a young man who cowered on his knees in front of a leather-clad dominatrix holding a horsewhip. A pattern of bruises crossed the man's back. The words over the picture read WENDY THE WHIP WOMAN.

"Are you thinking what I'm thinking?" the detective asked.

Donovan nodded and went to confront the proprietor—who, upon seeing the captain, bellowed, "Are you in charge of this harassment?"

"You ran from us last night," Donovan said.

"Last night? What are you talking about?"

"Do you read Stephen Jay Gould? No, of course you don't."

"Who's he?"

"I'm a member of a predatory species, Laquidara," Donovan said. "You run—I chase. It's an instinct with me. I can't help myself."

"I don't know what the fuck you're talking about," the man said, made even madder by hearing Donovan talk over his head.

"Do you own pier one-seventeen?" Donovan asked.

"Pier what? No—that's a city pier. One that's falling down, too. You came here to talk about docks?"

"Among other things. So you don't own one-seventeen, but you do own one-sixteen. True?"

"Yeah, such as it is, I own it. You wanna buy, Captain? I been looking for a buyer for a year."

Donovan said, "That would be ever since the captain of the *Jade Travelor* ran aground in Dead Horse Bay while en route to discharge a load of Chinese and Vietnamese illegals from his old rustbucket freighter onto your pier one-sixteen."

"I got no idea what you're saying," Laquidara said, poking nervously at bushy black hair—Donovan was sure it was a toupee—that covered his otherwise tanned scalp. Three gold chains glimmered below a silk shirt open halfway to the waist, just the point where the man's stomach began to flop over his patent-leather belt.

"The captain told the Coast Guard and Immigration that he was headed for a rendezvous on pier one-seventeen, which is interesting because it's falling down and not on the charts except as a hazard to navigation. So I figure he was really bound for your one-sixteen."

"What has this got to do with anything?" Laquidara asked.

"Does the name Tri Ng Dinh mean anything to you?"

"What's that, a chink?"

"A Vietnamese."

"If you seen one slant you seen 'em all. No, I never heard of the guy. Who is he?"

"A man who was found dead in the basement of the Old Knickerbocker Theater on Monday, December Fourth. Interesting that you knew the gender, by the way. Upon hearing that name for the first time, I wouldn't have assumed it was a man. Anyway, I'll need to know where you were the night of December Fourth, and at a few other times as well. The sergeant here will ask you."

"Never heard of the bum."

Donovan perched himself on the corner of the man's desk. He

said, "Let's talk about the 987 West Corporation, which owns the Old Knickerbocker."

Laquidara thought for a moment, then said, "I want to talk to my lawyer."

"Oh, so now you want a lawyer. You don't need an attorney to discuss a Vietnamese man who had his brains knocked out of him in the basement of a building you used to own. But when we move up to a simple discussion involving the executive suite, suddenly you need a lawyer."

"I'm entitled. Besides, I don't own that theater."

"No, but your lawyer, Mr. Carl of Nassau County, does. That's Andrew Carl, a/k/a Andy Carlito of Brooklyn, who changed his name once he got sprung from Brooklyn Law but who never quite left the family."

"He's my cousin. I guess you know that."

"I know he represented you half a dozen times in the Nassau County Court in Westbury, and once in Brooklyn Superior Court. I want to ask you a question."

"I want a lawyer," Laquidara said again.

"What's Jack Derrida got to do with all this?"

"You keep askin' me about guys I never heard of."

"I saw you with him last night, and so did a dozen other people."

"You were there, pal," Moskowitz added, unfolding his arms and then folding them again.

"I think the two of you are nuts."

Donovan said, "Derrida was so afraid of being seen with you, he lied and told me that you were a Puerto Rican punk from the South Bronx who was trying to shake him down."

Laquidara laughed despite himself.

"You know what, Laquidara?" Donovan said. "I think I'll book you on the charge of trying to shake down Derrida for fifty thousand bucks last night."

"That's a bullshit charge that won't stick," the man replied. "This Derrida—whoever he is—won't press charges. I guarantee."

"So what? I think I'll do it for the sheer joy of making you spend the night in a holding pen and making Mr. Andrew Carl drive all the way in from Nassau County to bail your sorry ass out."

"I'm gonna sue you for all you're worth," Laquidara spat.

Donovan poked himself on the chest, and said, "See this S on my chest? It stands for 'Should I care?' The City of New York indemnifies me for a hundred million dollars against nonsense like that. I'm like a U.S. Senator speaking on the floor of Congress. You can't touch me. So go ahead, waste some more of your money. I'll get a kick out of that, too."

Laquidara sighed. "Whaddya want, Donovan?" he asked.

"I want to know what you and Derrida were arguing about," Donovan said. "It can only be two things—the Vietnamese body in the basement, or how Derrida and you are going to sabotage the restoration and get the Old Knickerbocker back."

Laquidara laughed; it was a scoffing laugh. He said, "I heard a rumor the 987 West Corporation sold that building."

Unfazed, Donovan said, "To John Victor Holland. Yes, I know. The city's historic preservation people made you—and I do mean you—do that. But there's a catch. If Holland can't make a go of it, including a faithful and successful restoration, by the first of the year, the building reverts to the 987 West Corporation. And with that you will be able to develop the property as office space, which we all know is much more lucrative, especially now that Times Square has gone upscale."

This time there was no laugh, scoffing or otherwise. Still, Laquidara was tough. He said, "Let me get this straight. You think I'm killing people in the Old Knickerbocker as a way of getting the building back?"

"Is that what Derrida and you are doing?" Donovan asked.

"You're a card, Captain, that's what you are. I want to talk to my lawyer. Not another word until I do. Now charge me or get the hell out of here, and take your Mr. Tough Guy with you."

Mosko clenched his fists and took a step toward Laquidara, but Donovan restrained him. "We'll be seeing you," Donovan said, and led his assistant out of the office.

Once out on the street, Donovan said, "Let's get down to the theater. I want to talk to Derrida before Laquidara gets to him."

"I'll call Laquidara tomorrow and get those alibi dates from him. He'll have calmed down by then."

They got back into Donovan's car and drove south on Seventh Avenue, moving slowly in the heavy traffic that jams Times Square late each evening when the theaters let out. In addition to what seemed like a thousand taxis, the square was bumper-to-bumper with cars bearing license plates from New Jersey, Connecticut, and even Massachusetts and Pennsylvania. The electronic signs blazed so brightly and in such a cacophony of colors Donovan swore he could nearly hear them. But most startling were the shoppers. They piled up on corners waiting for lights to change or looking for cabs, arms full of packages.

"Do you believe this?" Donovan asked.

"What, Jersey plates on cars that aren't here to buy drugs?"

"No, Christmas shoppers in Times Square. They're spilling over from Fifth Avenue. You can't tell me those red-and-green boxes are full of sexual aids."

"Like it or not, boss, the neighborhood is changing," Mosko said.

Donovan nodded, tapping his fingers on the steering wheel in time with a picture of David Letterman flashing on the Jumbotron. After a moment of reflection, he said, "I guess it's for the better."

Mosko looked at him. "Are you okay?"

"I'm fine," Donovan said with a smile.

"If you want to go someplace and rest..."

"Stop mothering me. I'm just coming to the conclusion that progress is inevitable and desirable in this case. I just hope they leave a few of the gyro and souvlaki joints so a guy can still get something to eat for a couple of bucks. Or will it all be fifteen-dollar-burger places?"

They pulled up behind the Old Knickerbocker, leaving the car right behind the stage door. The usual Derrida Construction trucks and vans were parked—illegally, of course—in the fire zone behind the theater, and the usual night security guard watched the stage door, quietly nursing a steaming cup of coffee. Forty-first Street was empty, save for an occasional New Jersey car racing toward the entrance to the Lincoln Tunnel. The two detectives showed their credentials to the guard, then walked down the stairs to the A-level basement, where the renovation was supposed to be concentrated during the final week before the grand opening.

Donovan was struck not so much by the bustle of activity, but by the absence of it. There were but a handful of workmen in the Derrida crew that night, when the men were supposed to begin working 'round the clock until New Year's. And those men seemed to be working in slow motion—those who weren't on what looked like a permanent coffee break, one that included a boom box that blasted out music.

Mosko collared the first guy he could find and said, "Where's Derrida?"

"Ask Del," was the reply.

"Who's that?"

"The foreman. He went downstairs to the lower basement ten minutes ago."

"How come you guys never finished cleaning up down there?" Donovan asked.

"Ask Del," the man said again, this time adding a faint smile.

"Don't tell me you're afraid of a ghost?" Donovan said.

"Mooney got killed down there," the man replied. "But that wouldn't stop us. We've all worked on high iron, and if you want to talk about danger, we had that shootout down the block last year. We could always put up plenty of lights and finish the lower basement in no time. If you want to know why we haven't, ask Del."

Donovan frowned, then said, "Derrida told me that the renovation job was going full blast, twenty-four hours a day, starting today. What I see is more like the Great Snail Race."

The man's faint grin broadened. He sucked in his breath and was about to speak when Donovan said, "I know...ask Del."

"Right," the man replied, exhaling the big gulp of air he had taken in.

"Has he got a last name?" Mosko asked.

"Wilcox."

Donovan and Moskowitz returned to the stairwell and walked down another flight, descending once again to the B-level basement in which so much had happened already. They found it darker than usual; that seemed appropriate as the hour neared midnight, but on this occasion the gloom was thick enough to grasp. The few ceiling lights were the same ones Donovan had seen several times before. If any work had gone on there, it was impossible to tell. But there was a light—from a large flashlight being trained at the ceiling down the main corridor a bit.

"Del?" Donovan called out.

"Who's there?" The light flashed around, quickly and with some fright behind it, until it picked out their faces. "Oh, the officers. Jesus, you guys scared the shit out of me."

The three men met near the stage hydraulics, in a part of the sub-basement supposed to have been completed long ago.

"Del Wilcox?" Donovan said.

"You got him."

"Bill Donovan and Brian Moskowitz. You're the guy who was with Derrida when Mooney was killed."

"I was with him, all right. He couldn't have done it, if that's what's on your mind."

He shined the light on their faces, then turned the beam upward so that some light illuminated them all. Upon closer inspection, Wilcox was a wizened old bird, tough in the arms and tattooed up and down, with a particularly nice rendering of a pigeon on his forearm.

"It wasn't," Donovan said. "But thanks for telling us anyway."

"What brings you here this time of night?"

"We're looking for Derrida," Donovan replied.

"You just missed him."

"How long ago did he leave?"

"About fifteen minutes."

Donovan said, "I thought he was going to be here around the clock until New Year's."

"Me too. But he got a call on his cell phone and took off like a shot. He didn't say where he was going."

Donovan and Moskowitz exchanged knowing glances. "We're too late," Mosko said.

"He also told me that the whole renovation project was being speeded up," Donovan added.

"He said that, did he?" Wilcox added, with a smile.

Donovan nodded.

"It don't look like it, do it?" Wilcox said.

"No, it sure don't."

"In my thirty years in construction, I never seen a job like this. You work like mad, then all of a sudden you stop. You do everything by the book, then all of a sudden the book..."

"Gets thrown out the window," Donovan said, taking the flashlight from Wilcox and using it to point out several ribbons of greyish material that hung right over their heads.

"You noticed that, too, huh?" Wilcox said.

"What is that stuff?" Mosko asked. "It's hanging all over the place, like Spanish moss."

"Asbestos," Donovan replied.

"It was put in here thirty or forty years ago as fireproofing," Wilcox added.

"Isn't that stuff dangerous?" Mosko asked.

Donovan nodded. "It causes lung problems, including cancer. Del, tell me one thing."

"You got it."

"How long would it take OSHA to shut down this building if they knew about this friable asbestos?"

"About a minute and a half," Wilcox replied.

"Friable? Whaddya mean, 'friable?' " Mosko asked.

"Easily crumbled, such as by brushing against it. The stuff isn't dangerous just sitting there, only if you disturb it and it gets into your lungs." To illustrate his point, Donovan pinched the end of an asbestos ribbon.

"Hey," Mosko exclaimed, jerking his head back.

"And how long would OSHA shut the building down for?" Donovan asked the construction foreman.

"They come in here with machines that test the air. If there are too many particles floating around, they shut down the place for as long as required to remove the stuff. In some buildings, if you can seal off the contaminated area you can stay open. But theaters aren't built that secure. You'd have to shut down until the asbestos is cleaned up."

"And how long would that take?"

"Working days only, about three weeks. Working around the clock, all shifts, including the Christmas holiday, one week. I put the price at about fifty grand, assuming you go twenty-four hours a day.''

"So it can be done in time for Holland to open his musical on New Year's Eve?''

"Yeah, it can be done. We were gonna subcontract with a certified asbestos-abatement firm to do it, but all of a sudden today, the boss says 'forget about hiring someone, don't worry about it, maybe OSHA won't notice,' et cetera and so forth.''

"Why are you telling us all this?'' Mosko asked. "Derrida is your boss.''

"And Hitler was Eichmann's boss,'' Wilcox said.

"Meaning that the 'I was only following orders' excuse hasn't worked in some time,'' Donovan said.

The foreman nodded, crossing his arms and squeezing them together until the pigeon in his tattoo seemed about to suffocate. "I like my job, but you see, officers, if I knowingly conceal information about the committing of a crime that could result in serious injury or even death I am liable for prosecution under various laws, not the least of which is the RICO statute.''

Donovan smiled. "I like you,'' he said.

"I got my future to think about,'' the man said with a shrug. "This is New York City. You can't get away with shit no more. You try to conceal an asbestos problem and...bam, you're on page one of the *Daily News*.''

"I remember all the fuss a couple of years ago when that Con Ed steam pipe released some asbestos on the East Side,'' Donovan said. "You said that OSHA could shut this building in a minute and a half?''

"If that long.''

"What would it take to get them down here to inspect the building and shut it down?''

"One phone call. Whether you make it, or I make it, or the man in the fuckin' moon makes the call don't matter. All OSHA needs is an anonymous tip there's a major health hazard in a theater seating thousands of people and this production is history.''

"And the building reverts back to its former owner, the 987 West Corporation,'' Donovan said.

"I wouldn't know about any of that,'' Wilcox said.

Donovan led his assistant away for a moment, then asked, "Now do you see the connection between Derrida and Laquidara?"

"Laquidara paid Derrida to sabotage the renovation so he could get the building back. Probably there's a family connection someplace. You know how it goes, the mob and the construction industry."

"Derrida was getting paid by both sides," Donovan said. "Holland was paying him to renovate the theater. The mob was paying him to sabotage the work by causing a deliberate health hazard. I'll be surprised if OSHA hasn't already gotten the call and is on the way down here."

"You know what this also means?"

"Yeah. Derrida wasn't killing people to shut down the production. Someone else must be doing that. Let's take Derrida off our suspects list."

"You got it," Mosko said, relieved that at least one aspect of the case had gotten clearer.

"Send men out and pick up Derrida," Donovan said. "Find him wherever he is, kick the shit out of him and cuff him to the radiator in my office."

Mosko smiled. "You don't have a radiator," he said.

"I'll run down to the Bowery and buy one," Donovan replied.

As his assistant walked to the privacy of the stairwell to call the office, Donovan returned to Wilcox, who was still brooding about the condition of the basement, shining his flashlight here and there along the ceiling, gauging the extent of the cleanup.

"Is the asbestos just in this basement?"

"Mostly, but there's some in the backstage area near the dressing rooms. You know, I told Derrida over and over we got to get on the stick and subcontract out the job. But he kept stalling and I could never figure out why. I'm gonna retire soon, officer, and I want to go out with a clean record. You know what I'm saying?"

"Did anything change in the past day?" Donovan asked.

"Yeah. Right after that party last night the boss decides to forget about the asbestos altogether. 'No one will find out,' he said." Wilcox threw up his hands. "So here we are," he added.

Donovan thought, That's what the argument last night was

about; Laquidara told Derrida it was time to shut down the production. It was getting too close to New Year's.

"I got to go talk to your boss," Donovan told Wilcox.

"You didn't hear nothing from me."

"Not a word."

"Don't spend too much time down here," Donovan said. "It's not safe."

"No shit," the man replied.

Donovan joined Moskowitz and together they started back up the stairs.

"I sent guys to Derrida's house on Long Island," Mosko said. "There's no answer on the phone."

"Where's Laquidara?"

"Holed up in his office."

"No doubt Donna is getting her Christmas bonus," Donovan said.

"You have an emergency call from Schadenfreud," Mosko reported.

"What's his problem?"

"He didn't say, just that you come to his apartment ASAP. It's an emergency. Are you gonna do it?"

They walked through the A-level basement, past the largely idle Derrida construction workers, and out into the early morning air.

"Yeah, why shouldn't I?"

"With Derrida out of the picture, it's more likely that Schadenfreud is the killer."

"Only one way to find out," Donovan replied.

# SEVENTEEN

## WHATEVER GETS YOU THROUGH THE NIGHT

SCHADENFREUD'S ADDRESS was impeccable: in a landmark building with a famous, curved facade that wrapped around the corner
of Riverside Drive and one-hundred-sixteenth Street. The latter
was a broad, short boulevard that led from Riverside Park up the
hill to the main gate of Columbia University. The spot had but
one drawback—ferocious winter winds that swept up from the
Hudson and, channeled into One-hundred-sixteenth Street, made
January an adventure of antarctic proportions. Otherwise, it was
hard to do better than One-sixteenth and Riverside when choosing
a West Side residence.

Schadenfreud's apartment was less than perfect, however. It was
in the back of the building, on the second floor, and the only light
it got was at the bottom of a tall airshaft. The sun shined for but
twenty minutes a day at the height of summer, when a sliver of
sunlight landed on one windowsill. Otherwise, it was nearly impossible to tell midnight from noon by looking out any window.
Moreover, when opened the apartment door let in a fierce breeze
that blew papers off the kitchen table and sucked the curtains—
such as they were, made of colorful bedsheets that Schadenfreud
had attached, with broad hems, to curtain rods—out into the airshaft, where they flapped in the darkness.

When Donovan knocked on the door, it creaked open. He could
feel the wind at his back as the air rushed through the small, one-
bedroom apartment and up the airshaft. (As was true with most
buildings that faced the Hudson, including Donovan's, the heat
was kept so high that it was impossible to close windows even on
the coldest night.) The door opened into a foyer barely large
enough for a man to take off his coat in, and then there was the
living room. From the doorway Donovan could see it was lined

with homemade shelves—even the couch was like a cubbyhole in them—holding yard after yard of recorded music. There were deep shelves lined with LPs, and small ones glistening with compact disks. Opposite the couch was an ancient oak desk with a maroon leather top that showed the results of years of wear. On either end of the couch sat gigantic speakers. Schadenfreud sat in a straight-backed kitchen chair that had been placed at the focal point of the speakers. An LP had run out; the stylus scratched out the same pattern of static, over and over again, as the critic sat staring at the wall and clutching his knees until his knuckles went white. A white telephone sat in its cradle on the floor at his feet.

Donovan's hand slipped to his holster, at least for a moment until he got a better look at the man. Then he closed the door behind him and stepped into the room.

Schadenfreud was wearing cut-off jeans and a white T-shirt. His fingers dug into his knees, leaving imprints like dinosaur tracks.

"Luke?"

Schadenfreud's eyes flashed toward Donovan, back to the wall, then to the captain again. He said, "I can't move." His voice was a stammer; his lips quivered as his jaw moved.

"Are we alone?" Donovan asked.

Schadenfreud's head bobbed up and down; the movement was jerky.

"Mind if I check?"

He shook his head. Donovan slipped into the bedroom, bath-room, and kitchen, then looked out of the airshaft windows. The apartment was neat, aside from the clothes closet, the contents of which spilled out onto the floor. The two men were alone.

Donovan shut off the record player and walked to Schadenfreud, who had tears glistening in the corners of his eyes. "I'm sorry," he said several times.

"It's okay. I offered to help."

"I'm mortified you're seeing me such a wreck."

"I guess you think you're the first one I've seen," Donovan said. "Did you go see your doctor?"

Schadenfreud nodded. It was still an effort for him to keep his mouth from shaking when he spoke, and his hands remained af-fixed to his knees.

"I had a checkup this morning. He said I'm okay. There's no permanent damage. My liver is all right, so far as he can tell on the first visit. But my blood pressure was through the roof—two thirty over one ten."

"Ouch," Donovan said.

"He gave me an antihypertensive and called in a prescription for Xanax, but I couldn't fill it."

"Because your hands were shaking too much to go out in public, right?" Donovan said, grabbing Schadenfreud's desk chair and pulling it over.

"Rrr...right," the man said, bobbing his head awkwardly.

"Be grateful your job doesn't involve firearms."

"The doctor told me, 'You've been lucky so far because you're active and you eat well. But you're still a prime stroke candidate.' In other words, there will be no romantic, artist's death like so many I covered. There will be no peaceful closing of the eyes and waking up dead. Instead, my death would be drawn out and painful. I might even be paralyzed and linger in pain indefinitely. That man scared the shit out of me."

"Here...I brought you something."

"What?"

Donovan went into the kitchen and returned with a glass of water. He said, "Valium. They're Marcy's." He pulled a bottle from his pocket and twisted off the cap. "It's the same kind of drug and will make you feel better until you get your own prescription." He popped one into Schadenfreud's mouth and held up the glass of water for him. "How long has it been since you had a drink?"

"Last night, around midnight. Maybe one in the morning. I lost track."

"Well, you made it for nearly twenty-four hours," Donovan said. "How does it feel?" He tossed his coat onto the couch.

"Terrific," Schadenfreud said, laughing nervously.

"You're having a panic attack. My suspicion is you'll survive it."

"I don't know."

"What would you like to hear?" Donovan asked, going to the turntable and taking off the record that was on it.

"That again."

"*Sgt. Pepper's Lonely Hearts Club Band?*" Donovan said, holding up the LP. "Who did that, the Beatles? How long ago did that come out?"

"Nineteen sixty-seven."

"My friend, it was rock and roll that got you into this mess."

"It was my review of that LP that interested The Times in hiring me."

"All ancient history," Donovan replied, walking to the receiver and switching the function knob from turntable to radio. He found WQXR, the classical music station, and turned it on low. A harpsichordist was playing Bach's "Goldberg Variations." "No one gets over a panic attack while listening to rock and roll."

Schadenfreud seemed to be loosening up a bit. He relaxed his grip on his knees somewhat, then let go entirely. The marks on his legs did, indeed, resemble dinosaur tracks.

"I wonder if it was like this for Joplin, Morrison, and the rest," he said.

"Who? Oh, the dead ones? I doubt they ever got to the doctor part. So, did you do what I asked?" Donovan sat in the chair facing Schadenfreud.

"What's that?"

"Check your alibi for the night Janis Joplin died?"

"Oh, that," Schadenfreud said, laughing a bit less nervously. "Actually, I did. I was reviewing Muddy Waters at the Limelight. Do you want to see the proof?"

"I'll take your word for it," Donovan replied.

"I think I'm starting to feel better." Schadenfreud flexed his hands, then looked down at the marks on his legs. His cheeks reddened in embarrassment, even as the color was returning to his legs.

"How long have you been sitting here?"

"Three hours, I guess. God, I have to take a leak."

"Can you walk?" Donovan asked.

"I think so." To prove it, Schadenfreud stood. He was shaky, and stayed bent over until he got his balance. But within a minute he straightened up.

"Is there any booze in the house?" Donovan asked.

"I threw it all out last night."

"Good man."

Schadenfreud hobbled off to the bathroom, walking carefully, in fact walking with less spring in his step than Gittelson had. But when Schadenfreud returned a moment later, his gait had improved.

He sat down on the couch. Donovan swiveled around to face him.

"How do you feel?"

"Better. I feel better. I don't know how to thank you."

"I can think of something."

"Anything."

"In a day or two I'll ask you a few questions, and I'll expect you to be honest with me," Donovan said.

Schadenfreud nodded silently, then fell silent for several minutes, listening to the music. At last he stretched his arms and said, "I definitely feel better. If only I can get to sleep tonight. I'm terrified I won't be able to sleep."

"You'll sleep. You look exhausted now."

"One of the reasons I drank is I'm deathly afraid of having a heart attack and dying in bed. I lie there and I can hear my heart beat and it just scares the hell out of me."

"What did the doctor say?"

"He said I'm healthy. I have to stop drinking and lose weight."

"So you have nothing to be afraid of. This heart thing is another excuse. What's the longest you've been without a drink?"

"This is it," Schadenfreud said sheepishly. "Since I was eighteen, this is the first time I've gone a whole twenty-four hours."

"You'll make it."

"How long has it been since *you've* had a drink?" Schadenfreud asked.

"I went five years without a drop," Donovan said. "But about a year ago I began having an occasional glass of wine. At ceremonial occasions, weddings and bar mitzvahs and the like. The five years was to prove I don't have to drink. The occasional glass of wine is to prove I'm strong enough to be sensible about it. This whole thing we're talking about is learning how to be sensible."

"At the moment, I just need to learn to sleep without booze. What happens if I have a heart attack and am all alone?"

Donovan stood, straightened his pants, and said, "Come with me and stay at my place tonight. You can sleep on the studio couch in my den."

"You would do that for me?" Schadenfreud asked.

"Marcy is staying with me tonight," Donovan said. "She's a licensed paramedic. If you have a heart attack, she'll resuscitate you."

"Okay."

"Sit there while I round up some clothes for you."

Donovan searched the apartment, found a plastic garbage bag under the kitchen sink and took it into the bedroom. Moving quickly, he packed up every pair of shoes he could find—including boots that seemed especially dusty—as well as several pairs of pants, a few shirts, and a sweater. Then he went back to the living room and handed the critic an outfit. "Get dressed and we'll go," Donovan said.

An hour, a shower, and another Valium later, Schadenfreud was wearing jeans and a sweatshirt and seemed to be feeling much better, almost relaxed. He prowled Donovan's studio, looking at his Gateway desktop computer, examining the shelves and shelves of books, and at last coming to the captain's collection of records and compact disks. These he examined as closely as a microbiologist studying a germ. He was looking—Donovan could feel it—for evidence that the captain's loudly proclaimed hatred of rock and roll was not borne out by his possessions.

Donovan sat on the edge of his desk, listening to the winter wind rattle the old windows. The lights of New Jersey were reflected in the shimmering water of the Hudson River. Fifteen stories below, the occasional taxicab wandered down Riverside Drive in an early morning quest for passengers.

"Aha!" Schadenfreud exclaimed.

Donovan squeezed his eyes shut for a moment, then sighed and opened them.

"Guess what I found under *R*?" Schadenfreud asked.

"I don't suppose you mean *Rampal plays Bach.*"

"Rolling fuckin' Stones. Their sixties album: *Let it Bleed*. What do you say to that?"

"I was a kid once. Hire a lawyer and sue me."

"And...lookee here...under *D* we have Bob Dylan. Two LPs! *Bringing it All Back Home* and *Highway 61 Revisited*."

"Like I said, I used to be young. I also watched 'Captain Video' and, a bit later, wanted to be James Garner in 'Maverick.' I grew out of it."

"Well, I can tell you—and you're hearing this from the expert in the field—that your taste in Dylan is impeccable."

"As I recall, the man wrote some interesting songs. The main thing I require of life is that it be interesting. I liked the man when he was playing a guitar and singing. But I lost interest in him a short while after he started to sound like a country and western band."

"So did lots of folks," Schadenfreud said, sitting down on the studio couch and letting his shoulders slump.

"Tell me," Donovan said. "What got you into writing about rock bands?"

"It was the only way I could get a job at *The New York Times*. They needed someone to cover the subject, so I sold myself as the authority. After a while, I became it."

Donovan smiled.

"What's wrong with that?" Schadenfreud asked. "The alternative was doing a ten-year apprenticeship at the Cleveland *Plain Dealer* or something like that. Who needed the aggravation? Who had the time?"

"You were a man on the move," Donovan said.

"And I had this fantasy about them recognizing my talent and letting me write the 'About New York' column. You know that one?"

"I read it all the time."

"It's a prestige spot, a career-maker. Every so often I made a pitch for the job, and the response was always the same: an amused smile followed by some variation on, 'Very nice, Luke; now would you mind catching the Moody Blues at the Garden Saturday?' "

"Is that a band? Has anyone died in it?" Donovan asked.

"Not that I'm aware of."

"Who was the last rock star you knew who immolated himself?"

Schadenfreud thought for a moment, then said, "Jesus, why not just ask me to explain the theory of special relativity? Uh...Kurt Cobain...no, Jerry Garcia in 1995. But I didn't know Jerry that well."

"No doubt that's why he lived so long."

"We had a beer together, backstage at Woodstock. My God, my whole life has been measured in drinks." He fell silent for a while, then said. "Drinks and deaths."

"Mine, too," Donovan said. Then he added, a bit ruefully, "More of the latter recently."

"Come to think of it," Schadenfreud said, "most rock stars are self-absorbed, self-destructive assholes."

"What a coincidence," Donovan said. "So are most felons."

Schadenfreud said, "They profess to identify with the downtrodden, but in real life they loathe the poor, including their fans. They claim they live for their art, but most of them can't put three words together without sounding like complete idiots. Anyway, I wanted to get my byline in *The Times,* so despite the drawbacks I became a critic. Why did you become a cop?"

"It got me out of Vietnam," Donovan said, straight-faced.

Schadenfreud laughed out loud for the first time that evening. Donovan sensed it was for the first time since he had his last drink. "You got to be kidding," he said.

"It was one of the reasons. Another was that my dad was a cop. A third was that I was a Catholic-school boy, and that was what you did in those days. You had three basic career options: cop, priest, or hoodlum. I always liked girls, so being a priest was no option. Since my father was a policeman, becoming a hoodlum seemed too Freudian."

Schadenfreud smiled.

"And besides, I sort of thought as a cop I could make a difference. It was the sixties. Making a difference was important. I realize that caring has become passé, if not an actual impediment to your career."

"So here you are a few decades later, a famous detective with a Jewish girlfriend. You've come a long way yourself, Captain."

"She's only half Jewish, but then I'm only half famous. At any rate, thank you," Donovan said, trying without luck to hide a yawn. It was nearing two in the morning.

"I'm a little tired myself," Schadenfreud said, watching as Donovan went to the window and stuffed a rolled-up matchbook in the crack. The rattling calmed down, although the whistling continued. "But I'm still afraid of falling asleep."

"You're worrying for no reason," Donovan said. "The doctor said you're healthy. What you're feeling now is biochemistry; your body wants the booze. Fight it for another day and you'll be in good shape."

Schadenfreud hoisted his feet up on the studio couch, and was about to lay his head on the pillow when Marcy came in, bearing a platter.

"How are you guys doing?" she asked.

"Good, I think," Donovan said.

"Good," Schadenfreud agreed.

"I brought a sure cure for your insomnia—butter cookies and milk. This is whole milk now, which I don't normally serve. But the butterfat is an essential part of the cure."

"It is?" Schadenfreud said, taking a bite and yawning.

Donovan added, "There's an interaction between the nucleic acids in the butterfat and the maltose molecules in the cookies, producing an endorphin surge that acts like a natural tranquilizer."

Marcy slipped back out of the room and Donovan dimmed the lights. He leaned against his desk while Schadenfreud finished his snack. When the man showed signs of impending sleep, Donovan shut off the radio. Then the critic lay his head on the pillow and said, "I'm just going to shut my eyes for five minutes," he said.

"You do that."

Soon he was sound asleep and snoring lightly. Donovan turned off the lights and closed the studio door. Then he propped a chair against the door in such a way that it would fall over and make a noise should the man try to get out.

Marcy was in the master bedroom, sitting up in bed and brushing her hair. "Is he asleep?"

"He's sleeping like a baby."

"The cookies and milk worked."

"Whatever gets you through the night," Donovan said. He began pulling off his clothes and hanging them in the closet.

"How did I do?" she asked.

"You were perfect. He bought it hook, line, and sinker."

"Was that true, what you said about nucleic acids and the rest?" she asked.

Donovan shrugged, balled up his T-shirt, and tossed it across the room and into the hamper with a perfect hook shot. "I made the whole thing up. But it sounded good, though."

Marcy put her hairbrush on the end table and pulled down the covers on his side of the bed. "How did you handle his fear of having a heart attack and dying in his sleep?"

"I told him you're a paramedic and will bring him back to life."

She frowned.

"What will we do if he has a heart attack?"

"Call 911," Donovan said.

"Honey, what if he *dies?*"

He smiled, and said, "Then we'll bury the sonofabitch in the basement, like Milos."

Donovan got under the covers and pulled them up. "Did the courier from Forensics come while we were in there talking about my record collection?"

"Yeah, and as usual Forensics is in awe of your ability to get around the search-and-seizure laws. If the dust from Schadenfreud's boots proves to be from the basement of the Old Knickerbocker…"

"It will. I'm sure of it."

"…does that mean he's the killer?"

"All I can say is it makes things look bad for him," Donovan said, with a yawn. "But then, if the dust from Gittelson's Florsheims also comes from the basement of the Old Knickerbocker, and it will, things will look bad for him, too."

"Eighty-three-year-old Jewish men don't kill people with crossbows," Marcy said. "How hard do you have to pull to cock that thing?"

"Seventy-five pounds. And you span a crossbow, you don't cock it."

"We'll see if you can span seventy-five pounds when you're that age," she said.

"I'll bet I can," he said. "Since I'll still be putting kids through college then."

Marcy plucked a piece of paper off the end table and scrutinized it. It was the marriage license. Donovan looked away.

"We have two weeks left before this one expires," she said.

"We'll do it first thing after New Year's," Donovan said.

"Uh-huh."

"I mean it. We'll find a justice of the peace."

"My mom wants a rabbi," Marcy said. "My dad wants a preacher."

"Can't your dad just perform the ceremony in between trials?" Donovan asked.

"Isn't that a conflict of interest?"

"This whole marriage thing is too complicated," Donovan said.

Marcy said, "I've been thinking—maybe if we get married *before* trying to have a baby it will change our luck."

"Now you sound like a Pat Buchanan," Donovan replied.

She put the paper away and was silent for a moment while he stared at the ceiling.

"I *told* you why Sy Gittelson was in the basement of the Old Knickerbocker Theater," Marcy said. "You know I'm right."

"We'll see," Donovan said. "Hey, what do you mean, 'Forensics is in awe of my ability to get around the law?' "

"They are."

"I don't just get close to an occasional suspect because I'm trying to weasel information out of him," he insisted.

"How close have you gotten to Mala Logan?"

"Not very."

"Good."

"But she was overseas during two of the killings, and so isn't a serious suspect."

"Ever hear of airplanes?" Marcy asked.

"Harry Spalding mentioned them."

"How is Harry?"

"Good. He asked about you. What can I say, the man won the lottery. He deserves it. But I still don't get close to people just because I want to get something on them. Look, once I can prove these guys were in the basement of the Old Knickerbocker, I'll ask them about it. I resent what you said."

Donovan slid down under the covers and yawned once more.

"I'm sorry," Marcy said, snaking an arm around his neck and pulling his head against her. "Lay your kepi down."

"I genuinely like these guys. Sy Gittelson reminds me of your uncle. And Luke Schadenfreud reminds me of myself in 1968."

"He's fifty years old."

"Some people grow up faster than others. I think he's on his way. I think he's gonna make it."

Marcy said, "He reminds you of yourself ten years ago, is what it is."

"Before I grew up."

"Before you gave your rock and roll records to the kid, for one thing," Marcy said.

"I kept a few," Donovan replied, rolling toward her.

After a moment, Marcy said, "Is this guy going to wake up from the cookies and milk and try to kill us?"

"He's not armed. I checked. And the crossbow isn't in his apartment. I searched."

"I asked you a question," Marcy said.

"If he does, you can take him," Donovan replied.

"You're the man of the house."

"You're the black belt."

"You know what, we sound married already," she said, reaching for him.

A while later they were snuggling comfortably, listening to the sound of a police siren wailing as it moved down the West Side Highway, when the phone rang. Groaning, Marcy said, "I've been to this movie."

Donovan picked up the phone as Marcy rolled away from him. "Yeah?"

He listened for a moment, then said, "Is there any reason I have to be there?"

Marcy rolled back. More silence was followed by, "Okay, take a snapshot of the corpse for me and I'll see you in the morning at the office.''

"Is that Moskowitz?" she asked, before Donovan could hang up.

"Yeah."

"Have him pick up a dozen bagels at that place under the el in Sheepshead Bay."

Donovan relayed the message, said good night, and hung up.

"Who and where?" Marcy asked.

Donovan replied, "Jack Derrida, in his car, on Canarsie Pier, two shots to the back of the head. All who are surprised please raise their hands."

# EIGHTEEN

## AND THEN THERE WERE TWO

MORNING ARRIVED with no loss of life in the Donovan household. Lucien Schadenfreud slept like a baby until six a.m., when he was awakened by another, mercifully smaller panic attack—that he dealt with himself by taking a third Valium, which put him back to sleep until eight. That was the hour Donovan woke the man, congratulated him on having successfully negotiated the first night of the rest of his life, fed him an egg-white omelet on rye toast, then sent him packing—along with his plastic garbage bag full of clothes—to keep an appointment to interview the original members of Cycle Sluts from Hell. Donovan had made a friend and, very likely, a convert to healthy living and mature thinking. The captain was proud of himself. He had gone way beyond the police commissioner's order—presented along with his captain's badge—that he stop insulting reporters. And Donovan had kept his promise to Harry Spalding, with whose life Donovan's personal and professional history was so closely entwined.

After breakfast, Donovan sat down at his Gateway and spent an hour doing computer searches relevant to Schadenfreud, Bock, Sharkey, and Logan. At nine-thirty Donovan drove Marcy to her restaurant, where a delivery truck was waiting with a load of supplies. Then he headed down Broadway for the half-hour drive to his office in lower Manhattan. He was stuck in the usual bottleneck at Seventy-second Street—buses turning onto Broadway tied up traffic at the narrow intersection—when the call came on his cell phone. All hell had broken loose at the Old Knickerbocker Theater.

Donovan flicked on the siren and barged through the traffic jam, driving partway onto the sidewalk to do it. As he roared down Broadway, the nighttime security gate was still closed on the Hotsy

Totsy Club and the news ticker at One Times Square was describing the latest mass grave dug up in Serbia. As he pulled to a halt behind the theater, Donovan found his usual illegal parking spot taken by a black Cherokee bearing the logo of the Occupational Safety and Health Administration. Several other such vehicles took up the remainder of the fire zone. Donovan double parked next to them and left the emergency flasher on as he ran into the building.

The stars of *Casablanca: The Musical* were onstage arguing with one another and with Holland, who looked even paler than he had two nights before when he had had to lie down. Moskowitz stood slightly off to one side pondering the scene, which took place on the main set of Rick's Café Americain. Wandering around the orchestra and behind stage (and, Donovan presumed, in other parts of the building) were OSHA inspectors carrying what looked like geiger counters. All in all, the combination of uniformed presence and artistic chaos on that particular set made Donovan think of the scene in *Casablanca* where the patrons rise as one and sing the Marseillaise. He draped his overcoat over his arm and strode out onto the stage, quietly singing *"Allons, enfants de la patrie, le jour de la gloire est arrivé."*

Mosko hurried over, intercepting him before he could reach the gesticulating actors. Donovan pointed at an OSHA inspector and said, "I bet you thought government regulation ended the day you voted Republican."

"This is nuts. The inspectors are everywhere. They've already sealed off the lower basement—strung up plastic sheeting to prevent asbestos in the air down there from contaminating the rest of the building."

"Was it bad?"

"The operative word seems to be 'Chernobyl.' "

"That sounds serious. I guess I'll take the street entrance if I go see Gittelson again."

"Good idea," Mosko said. "And tell *him* to stay out of the basement, too."

"So he was down there," Donovan said.

"His shoes carried particles of the grey dust, like you suspected."

"But not the black dust?"

"No, he was standing near the grave, not in it."

"Nonetheless, he lied to me, the old weasel. He told me the last time he set foot in the Old Knickerbocker was to catch Milton Berle's act."

"I still refuse to believe a man his age is our killer," Mosko said.

"Has the analysis come back on the dust from Schadenfreud's boots?" Donovan asked.

"It's too early. But I'm expecting a report soon. Here's your photo." He presented a Polaroid that showed Derrida's body splayed across the front seat of his Mercedes. "Your bagels are in my car," Mosko added. "You owe me four eighty-five. You know, I can name six places that make better bagels than that shop under the el."

"But not bigger ones, and I have an appetite. So, Derrida got two in the base of the skull."

"A professional job," Mosko added needlessly.

"Does anyone here know?"

Mosko shook his head.

"Laquidara doesn't like to be messed with. Who called OSHA?" Donovan asked.

"It was an anonymous tip. Considering this is a major Broadway theater with thousands of people coming and going each day, the Feds moved fast."

"What about Laquidara's movements last night?"

Mosko consulted his notebook computer, then said, "He stayed in his office until two in the morning."

"Donna must have gotten two bonuses."

"At least. Laquidara kept her there until half an hour after the ME says Derrida was shot."

"How convenient."

"Yeah. Then they went their separate ways, with him being driven home to Marine Park."

"I consider this part of the case closed," Donovan said. "If the organized crime boys have any interest in it, pass it along. But the last thing I need now is to get sidetracked by a mafia hit. Especially since I'm convinced it has nothing to do with the crossbow killings."

"Except that it takes two suspects off the list," Mosko said.

"Leaving us mainly with Bock, Schadenfreud, Logan, and Gittelson."

"What about your friend, Harry Spalding?"

"He's incapable of murder," Donovan said.

"He has a record."

"Don't argue with me on this point. I know that man."

Mosko remained silent on the matter, though his expression made clear it wasn't closed. Instead, he said, "I guess your critic friend had a peaceful night."

"He seemed grateful. I hope he sticks with the program."

"I'm glad he didn't kill you and Marcy. Where is he now?"

Donovan said, "As long as it isn't a bar, I couldn't care less." He gestured at the pack of actors, who were clustered about Holland either arguing with him or glancing warily at the OSHA inspectors. He noted with some pride that Harry Spalding was right in there with the stars, and looking as if he belonged, too. "What's the powwow about?" Donovan asked.

"The stars are pissed about the asbestos, for starters," Mosko said.

"What bothers them most—that they may be breathing a carcinogen, or that they may be out of work?" Donovan asked. "That's if Holland can't get the place cleaned up by New Year's."

"Actually, I think they're maddest about their dressing rooms being violated. The inspectors found asbestos in them, too. Elena Jordan has convinced herself she's been poisoned." Mosko added, "She's a Hollywood type."

Donovan shook his head. "This asbestos thing has to be Milos the Magnificent's revenge. The body in the basement reaches up to touch everyone who disturbed his resting place."

"You remember that Holland wouldn't let us search the stars' dressing rooms?"

"Oh yes."

"Well, I took it on myself to have our guys slip into the rooms along with the inspectors. Holland hasn't noticed."

"Good idea," Donovan said.

Holland had begun waving at him, so Donovan wandered over there and soon found himself at the center of a knot of artistes.

"What's happening?" he asked Holland, watching as Moskowitz disappeared into the backstage area to check on the search.

"What's happening? What's happening!? The world is coming to an end, that's all." He appeared to Donovan to be hyperventilating.

"Somehow I always knew it would happen in Times Square," Donovan said, maneuvering the group a few paces across the set so he could lean on Sam's piano.

Sharkey guffawed and lit up a cigarette, striking the old-fashioned wooden match on the sole of his shoe. Then, noting that Donovan had watched the movement, said, "The props department cooked this up for me. Pretty neat, huh?"

"Outstanding," Donovan replied, as the actor struck a pose against the other side of the piano.

Elena Jordan said nothing. She was pressing a handkerchief to her nose and breathing through it. On her face was the panicked look of someone trying to escape a burning building. Donovan saw that she had been crying. "Hi," he said, but she didn't acknowledge him.

Harry Spalding sat down at the piano, flipped up the keyboard cover, and stared silently at the ivories.

Holland said, "They found asbestos in the basement, and in the dressing rooms, too."

"Yeah, I heard about that."

"This is unreal," Elena sobbed into her handkerchief. "First that worker dies in the basement. Then Henry is murdered. Now they're trying to kill us all with this chemical."

"Take it easy, sweetheart," Sharkey said, again the tough guy.

"You take it easy. No wonder my throat has been burning. You smoke anyway. What do you care if your lungs rot?"

Trying to be helpful, Donovan said, "Asbestos will only kill you if you breath it for years."

"I remember when they said not to worry about AIDS if you're not a Haitian, homosexual heroin-abuser," she cried.

Holland said, "I paid Derrida good money to handle problems like this. Where in hell is he?"

"Probably not too far from the watercooler," Donovan replied.

"I beg your pardon."

"Derrida's dead. We found his body in his car early this morning."

"Oh my God," Holland said, slumping down onto the piano stool. Spalding hastily moved over to make room.

"Another death?" Elena said.

"Jeez, what a fuckin' nightmare," Sharkey replied.

Donovan said, "Derrida was shot to death in his car on Canarsie Pier. That's in Brooklyn."

"With a crossbow?" Spalding asked.

"No. With a gun."

"But why, why?" Holland asked.

"This is how it looks, Sir John," Donovan said. "Derrida was playing both ends against the middle. He was taking money from you—"

"Good money, very good money."

"—to refurbish the theater. But he was also taking money from the 987 West Corporation to ignore the asbestos problem until it got so big it ruined you."

Holland hung his head so low he appeared to be inspecting his zipper.

"The 987 West Corporation kills people?" he said.

"They have a little mafia problem," Donovan replied. "Consider it an interlocking directorship. The mafia kills people."

Rubbing her eyes, Elena mumbled, "Death by crossbow, death by asbestos, death by gun. I'm sorry I ever left Brentwood."

"Death by having your throat slit," Sharkey added, using his Bogie voice.

"I feel weak," she said. "I have to sit down."

Holland quickly stood to make way for her. Elena sat next to Harry Spalding, who sought to calm her by playing "As Time Goes By." That didn't work.

"Oh, *please*," she wailed, and he stopped.

Holland said, "I don't know what to do. Can you help me, Captain? Do you know if asbestos can be removed by New Year's Eve? The OSHA inspectors tell me the theater has to stay shut until the asbestos is cleaned up."

"Talk to Derrida's foreman, Del Wilcox. I suspect he was about to blow the whistle on the contamination when I figured it out on my own."

"Del Wilcox," Holland said, taking out a pen and notepad and scribbling a note.

"According to him, a crew working—really working, this time—around the clock can get the job done," Donovan said. "But it will cost upwards of fifty grand."

"I've had more expensive dates," Sharkey said.

"Agreed. That's not much money, all things considered. I'll get right on it." Holland snapped his fingers high in the air and yelled, "Anton!"

No response was forthcoming, and the producer looked around in irritation. Instead of his redoubtable aide, he saw Moskowitz emerging from backstage, looking grim and carrying an evidence bag. With him were two other detectives. Donovan also noticed the procession.

Holland asked, "Sergeant, have you seen my assistant?"

Mosko said, "No," then handed Donovan the bag.

The captain turned the bag over and over in his hand, inspecting the crossbow bolt contained therein. The arrow was one of Milos's, identical with the first two found in Mooney and Tippett.

Holland, Sharkey, and Spalding gaped at the murderous dart. Elena looked at it quickly, then turned away, her face a whiter shade of pale.

"And then there were two," Donovan said.

"What?" Holland asked.

"The killer has two arrows left." To Moskowitz, Donovan asked, "Where'd you find this?"

"In his dressing room," Mosko replied, clamping a beefy hand on Spalding's shoulder to prevent him from rising. "If you look closely, it has traces of black dust on it—the kind of dust found in Milos's grave."

Elena's pouty lips fell wide open, and her eyes went as big as quarters. She jumped to her feet, screaming, "No! No! Now there's a killer a few doors down the hall!"

Donovan moved to comfort her, but she backed away from them all. "I quit!" she yelled at Holland. "You can sue me if you like! But I'm going back to L.A.!"

Then she ran off the stage.

"Let her go," said Holland.

"She can't sing anyway," Sharkey growled.

Donovan looked at his friend, Harry Spalding, who returned the gaze, imploringly.

"That's not mine," he said of the arrow.

"I know," Donovan replied.

"I didn't kill anyone. I'm being set up."

"I know."

"I told you something like this would happen. Because I have a record and all, and because I stood to benefit from Henry's death, that someone would accuse me of being the killer."

"I might add, speaking as your friend, that your alibi stinks," Donovan said.

"If you're so innocent," Moskowitz asked, "Then how did this get in your dressing room?" Skepticism notwithstanding, he released the grip on the man's shoulder once it was certain he wasn't running.

Spalding said, "I got no idea. All I can say is, that's only been my dressing room for a day or two."

"Where in the room did you find it?" Donovan asked.

"In his piano," Mosko replied.

"You have a piano in your dressing room?"

"Sure I do. An upright, like this one." He patted the top of the instrument. "But I played it last night after the show. And again this morning. About an hour ago, in fact. I would have known if there was anything in there."

"Where in the piano was it?" Donovan asked.

"Right on top of those things that connect the keys to the strings," Mosko replied.

"No way," Spalding said. "I would have known right off." He turned again to Donovan, saying, "Bill...I'm being set up."

"You sure are," the captain replied.

"You can't be guilty, Harry," Holland said. To that, Sharkey added, "We're behind you, buddy."

"How can you be so sure about this?" Mosko added.

"Because I know the man. And also, if you're doing a production of *Casablanca*—musical or otherwise—the last place you want to hide a key piece of evidence is in Sam's piano."

"You got that right," Spalding said.

"Even the piano in his dressing room," Donovan added. "Unless, of course, you want it to be found."

"Who would want it to be found?" Holland asked.

"The real killer," Sharkey said.

Donovan nodded. "And that person had to know one thing—that OSHA, followed by my men, would be searching the stars' dressing rooms." He turned to Moskowitz. "How old is that information, Brian?"

Mosko checked his watch, then said, "About an hour, boss."

"With your permission this time, Sir John," Donovan said, "I would like this building sealed off until we count every nose in it."

"You go right ahead, with my blessings."

"Apart from the workmen and the inspectors, who is in here this morning?"

Holland looked around, and said, "No one should be, really. There's us, Anton of course, and..." He smiled, awkwardly at first, then sheepishly. "Oh well, you would find out eventually."

"Let me guess," Donovan said. "Mala Logan."

"Anton!" Holland yelled, louder this time, snapping his fingers in the air twice.

# NINETEEN

## ANOTHER ONE WHO DOESN'T READ
## STEPHEN JAY GOULD

"HOW COULD YOU possibly know about Mala?" Holland asked.

"You theater people are so transparent a normal person can read a magazine through you," Donovan said. "In the short time I've known you, you get very upset at the least thing going wrong. But a few minutes ago, your leading lady stalks off in a fit. And you say..."

"'Let her go,'" Holland admitted, his sheepish grin turning into a whole flock.

"And Kurt here says, 'She can't sing, anyway.' So I assumed you had already made the decision to dump Elena, had talked it over with Kurt."

"The woman really *can't* sing," Holland said. "I had hoped she could rise to the occasion, given enough motivation and coaching. But it never happened."

"Besides, she was falling apart," Sharkey said. "And on top of that was a lousy kisser. Forget about those famous lips—they're all show. That and injectable collagen."

"So you made sure Mala flew into New York and hung around until the opening. Her explanation for spending so much time in New York wasn't really very good."

"I asked her to be here in case she was needed," Holland said. "And, as it turns out, she was."

Mosko said, "Uh, before we let Elena out of the building, are you guys prepared to swear she was with you for the past hour?"

"She was right here," Holland said, "for every awkward minute." He then smiled broadly, and added, "Sergeant, *you* were here."

"But not onstage with you for the whole time."

"Where were you when you weren't onstage?"

"Backstage," Mosko said, the realization striking him that he, too, could alibi Elena Jordan, Sharkey, Holland, and Spalding on the arrow-planting matter.

"That's good enough for me," Donovan said.

"Captain, I'm going to seal off the building and count noses. Let's find out once and for all who could have done something and who couldn't."

"Go ahead."

Mosko looked at Spalding, then at Donovan. "Are you okay with this guy just sitting here?"

"Yeah. The sonofabitch aimed a gun at my father once..."

"It was empty, and I didn't aim it at no one," Spalding said.

"So I have no problem with shooting him if he acts up."

Smiling ironically, Spalding laid his hands on the keys and tickled out a few bars of "What a Wonderful World."

Moskowitz went backstage, taking the two other detectives with him.

Holland said, "Think of it, Captain: I got a zillion dollars worth of publicity when I dumped Mala for Elena. Now that I'm dumping Elena for Mala, the publicity will be worth two zillion."

"And, of course, there's the headlines you got when Henry Tippett was shot to death on the grand staircase," Donovan said. "That came on top of all the fuss in the papers after Mooney was found dead in the basement. Do you keep any business records down there, by the way, or is the B-level just a reliquary for old vaudevillians?"

"Um, I do have some files down there, now that you mention it," Holland said. "Very old files, going back twenty years or more. Why do you ask?"

"I was just curious. Let's return to the issue of publicity. You told me once that Americans have an affection for aberrant behavior..."

"And so they do. Watch 'Hard Copy' or any of a thousand talk shows where average citizens display their dirty linen for all the country to see."

"And you," Donovan said, looking at Sharkey, "pointed out that being suspected of murder can be great for your career."

"As long as you aren't convicted," the actor replied nonchalantly.

"So I imagine that having Harry here accused of being the crossbow killer will do wonders for ticket sales as well. As long as I can be counted on to get him off the hook. You know how this country was fascinated with the O.J. Simpson trial. I guess that people will line up for miles to see a show in a theater where a couple of murders have taken place already and in which the chief suspect is one of the stars."

Spalding, Holland, and Sharkey exchanged nervous glances. Then Holland said, "All you say is true. *Casablanca: The Musical* will run forever." He added, as an aside, "That's assuming I can get the asbestos cleaned up." And he knocked on the piano for luck. "But none of us killed anybody, and I can assure you none of us planted that arrow in the piano. We were all together, right here, onstage. Ask Elena, if she isn't halfway to the airport by now. Ask any of these federal inspectors who have been scurrying around."

"Three of them have already come up and asked for my autograph," Sharkey said. "And one of them tried to hit on Elena. These guys are big fans of my movies—the movies Harry and I will be making." He patted Spalding on the shoulder. "It's not like we've been invisible."

"Who the hell else has been in this theater for the hour?" Donovan asked.

"Anton would know," Holland replied. "Where the hell is he?"

"Here I am," the assistant replied, scurrying across the stage with his arm around a cocky Mala Logan. She looked like the Cheshire cat that ate the canary, dressed for rehearsal in a several-times-too-large sweatshirt emblazoned with the lettering SAVE THE NATIONAL ENDOWMENT FOR THE ARTS. Her sinewy legs were shrink-wrapped in white tights that disappeared beneath grey leg warmers and cross-training sneakers.

Holland and Sharkey embraced her as they might a long-lost sister—or lover. Even Harry Spalding, who Donovan felt didn't know her that well—if at all—took part in the hugging, kissing and general revelry. Donovan watched their performance with deep suspicion, finally signaling it by draping his overcoat over the top of Sam's piano and folding his arms disdainfully. Before too long, Holland noticed.

"What's the matter, Captain?" he asked.

"This reminds me of the Nixon White House," Donovan said.

"Whatever do you mean?"

"There's something *wrong* with this happy little clan, and I know what it is," Donovan said.

Mala went to him then, and wrapped her arms around him. It was like the night he walked her back to her hotel, only her body felt softer with fewer clothes on it. "You're a suspicious man, Bill Donovan," she said. "But it's good to see you again."

She kissed him, and this time it was more than the perfunctory kiss he got outside the Warwick.

"You guys seem pretty pleased with yourselves, considering the road to your particular revelation has been paved with three bodies so far, and I have every reason to believe at least one and possibly two more are coming."

"Captain, all we are is relieved that Elena is gone, Mala is back..."

"And Harry is accused of murder," Donovan said.

"But no one believes he could have done it," Holland said.

"I hate to argue, but *someone* does. This is a highly public case. You don't seriously think they—they being my superiors—will let me say, 'Oh, hell, I like Harry so I'll ignore the fact a murder weapon was found in his dressing room.' "

"We have faith in you," Sharkey said. Mala had gone to him and linked arms with the actor. The attraction between them was palpable. Probably it had long been there, Donovan realized, but they only just decided to let it show.

"Anton, just who is in this theater beyond us, the workmen, the inspectors, and the police?" Donovan asked.

"Nobody."

"Not a soul?" Donovan asked. "No extras in Arab robes?"

"No nobody," Anton replied. "Between the OSHA inspectors and the police, this building is sealed tighter than a drum."

"What about the sub-basement?"

"No one can get in or out of there," Anton said. "The inspectors taped up plastic across the stairwells and locked out the elevators so they don't go there.''

"Which reminds me," Holland said. "Anton, we must contact a Del Wilcox, who worked for Jack Derrida. The captain tells me Wilcox can solve our contamination problem for us so that we can open on schedule.''

"Thank God.''

"On schedule and at last with the right leading lady," Holland added.

With that Logan and Sharkey kissed. Holland and Anton applauded. "They like each other," Holland said, blushing.

"I know," Donovan said.

"You can see?''

"I got it off the computer first thing this morning.''

All eyes turned toward him.

"What do you mean?" Mala asked.

"You told me you were in Paris on December fourth, buying that dress you wore the night before last," Donovan said.

"I was. That was the day I got the Kristeva.''

"But her fashion show wasn't on the fourth, a Monday. It was on the third, a Sunday, which also happens to be the day that Kurt took a fifty-thousand-dollar hit on his American Express card—also in Paris.''

Sharkey looked over in astonishment.

"That was the expensive date you bragged about a few minutes ago," Donovan continued.

"Is it legal for you to have this private information?" Sharkey asked.

Donovan shrugged. "Is it legal for you to lie to me during a murder investigation? All of you have been lying to me. That tends to piss me off.''

Turning his attention back to Mala, Donovan said, "You used your card to book two seats on a flight from Paris to New York, arriving early in the morning of December four. In case you forgot, that's the day bodies started turning up in the basement of the theater.''

"You're not suggesting Kurt and I are responsible for these killings, are you?" Mala said.

"You lied to me," Donovan said. "People who lie to homicide investigators don't look very good."

"Why would we want to murder anyone?" Sharkey asked.

"It scared the hell out of Elena, and now Mala has her job back," Donovan said.

"That would have happened anyway," Holland said.

"Maybe," Donovan said. He opened his briefcase, set his notebook on the piano, and called up a screen.

"What are you looking for?" Mala asked.

"A clip from *The Hollywood Reporter*," Donovan replied, taking note of how that name made Sharkey wince. "Here it is...November thirteenth. 'Sources report a rift between buddy-movie megastars Kurt Sharkey and Henry Tippett that developed after Tippett demanded two million dollars to reprise his role as Sharkey's sidekick in the forthcoming action flick, *Dead Eyes IV*. Sharkey's production company owns that franchise, and so the star is reported balking at the high fee.' What did you tell me he offered you, Harry—a million?"

Spalding bobbed his head up and down.

"Renegotiate," Donovan said.

Sharkey scuffed his foot on the stage floor, and looked down at it.

Donovan continued, "One crossbow bolt and Mala has a job. Another crossbow bolt and Kurt saves himself a bundle on sidekicks. I see a pattern emerging."

"How am I supposed to have killed Henry Tippett if seventeen hundred people were watching me as he got hit?" Sharkey asked.

"Not you," Donovan said, "Her." He pointed at Mala.

"Mala?"

"Dressed as an Arab extra, wearing a fake mustache. We never did find the 'man' matching that description seen running from the scene of the crime. She could have shot Henry, hidden the crossbow somewhere—I still have my eye on certain dumbwaiter shafts—and stashed the robe where we found it, in a Dumpster in the basement, before returning to her seat. She says she was in the bathroom."

Moskowitz scoffed at that suggestion.

"Mala doesn't know how to use a crossbow," Sharkey said.

She tossed up her hands, and said, "Sorry, darling, I already confessed to the captain a certain expertise in archery. I can figure out how to use a crossbow, and he knows it."

"You also have a reputation for violence," Donovan continued. "You stalked another actress and beat her up."

"It was a cat fight, darling," she said, "same as women have had since we all lived in caves. The London tabloids made more out of it than it deserved."

"You put her in the hospital."

"A ploy to strengthen her lawsuit, which I settled for peanuts. I'm not really violent, but the press thinks that because of the black belt."

Changing the subject, Sharkey said. "Look, Donovan, why would I frame Harry if I'm using him to save all this bread?" Sharkey asked.

"There are a lot of black men who can play piano and sing," Donovan said, adding, "Sorry, Harry. Almost certainly Sharkey can get someone for scale once you're behind bars."

"You forget that Harry is famous now," Holland said. "Famous is worth a lot in Hollywood."

"Harry is worth more as a fall guy," Donovan snapped.

"Okay, okay," Sharkey said, lighting another match on the sole of his shoe and touching it to a cigarette. "You got us on the charge of being in love with each other..." He was back in the Bogart accent, and pulled Mala to him. "...and of being heartless bastards to everyone else, especially Elena Jordan. But we didn't kill anyone, and we certainly didn't plant that arrow in Harry's dressing room."

"That's right," Mala said.

"And I can't prove I'm telling the truth on this next point," Sharkey continued, "but I really intend to use Harry in my movies. And if he wants to up the ante a bit, I can deal with it."

"Just don't push your luck," Donovan said to his old friend.

"Not me," Spalding agreed, shaking his head aggressively.

Mala said, "Can I be honest with you, Captain?"

"I wish you would."

"We flew straight here from Paris so we could be in New York fucking our brains out."

"What's wrong with Paris for that? I thought romance was the big attraction of the burg for those who don't go there for the surly waiters."

"Paris ain't New York," Sharkey growled. "Besides, I had to start rehearsals."

"I didn't invite you up to my room at the Warwick that night because Kurt has his clothes there and he himself was on his way," Mala said to Donovan. Then she turned to Sharkey and added, "I mean, I didn't want to ask him up anyway, but I didn't because...oh, you know what I mean."

Donovan said, "She means we'll never have Paris."

Sharkey squeezed her waist.

"I'm sorry I lied to you about being in Paris. But I thought it would look bad if you knew I was there with Kurt, what with Elena being on her way out and all that. Do you see what I'm saying?"

Donovan nodded.

Holland added, "None of these people you see standing before you has killed anyone. I have no idea who's responsible for these terrible crimes. I was afraid at first that the killings would shut down the show. Now it looks like the killings are just making ticket sales go through the roof and asbestos may shut us down."

"Talk to Del Wilcox," Donovan said. "He seems to think there's time."

"I wish I knew who the killer is and why he's doing it," Holland said.

"Or why *she's* doing it," Donovan said, making Mala's eyes widen.

"Maybe it is the ghost of Milos the Magnificent, punishing me for disturbing his resting place."

Donovan said, "There are other possibilities."

"Like what?" Holland said.

"Like...hold on." Donovan said this as a ruckus came up the stairs and across the stage from the backstage area. Accompanied by the same two detectives as before, Moskowitz dragged a protesting Roger Bock across the set. The man had his hands cuffed behind him, and his *Town & Country* appearance seemed to have been dragged through a ditch. His expensive suede jacket was covered with grey dust, which also coated his hair and the side of his face. There were a few scratches on his cheeks.

"Like him," Donovan said.

"Roger!" Holland exclaimed.

Mosko let go of the man, and he fell to the stage floor at Donovan's feet.

"What have you got here?" Donovan asked.

"Another one who doesn't read Stephen Jay Gould," Mosko said.

"What are you talking about?" Holland asked.

Donovan translated. "He ran. My friend chased him. This one didn't get away. Brian, was he the only other pigeon you found in this coop?"

"He's the rara avis," Mosko replied.

"This is outrageous," Bock sputtered, struggling to get his legs in a position that left him more comfortable. A small trickle of blood ran from one of the superficial cuts on his face.

"Who's this guy?" Sharkey asked. "I remember seeing him around."

Holland said, "This is Roger Bock, author of *Legends of the Broadway Theater* and the man who will—at least I think so—write my biography."

"To paraphrase the late, unlamented President Nixon," Donovan said, "You can do a lot of good writing in jail."

"Jail!" Bock exclaimed. "What do you mean?"

"Where'd you find him?" Donovan asked.

"In the basement," Mosko said. "Apparently he came in through that hole you found in the wall."

"Hole? What hole?" Holland asked.

"The one that's been allowing Gittelson, Bock, and, I'm pretty sure, Schadenfreud, to get in here whenever they want, by way of the annex, and poke around," Donovan said.

Holland's mouth fell open.

"You're right about Schadenfreud, boss," Mosko said. "I got the word backstage—Forensics connected the dust on his shoes to the grey dust in the basement."

"Exactly where in the basement was Bock?" Donovan asked.

"Trying to break into those filing cabinets we found over near where Milos is buried. I heard a noise down there and went through OSHA's barrier to investigate. Bock took off and tried to beat it back into the fallout shelter. I caught up with him, but we knocked over a pile of cans of survival biscuits.''

"Fallout shelter? Fallout shelter?'' Holland asked.

"That's where the hole is between this building and the one next door,'' Donovan said.

Holland looked like he felt faint again. He slumped back on the piano stool next to Spalding.

"You have no right to handcuff me,'' Bock said. "Sir John gave me the run of the building.''

"Not to break into my files,'' Holland said. "What were you looking for?''

"He's been trying to dig up dirt on you,'' Donovan said. "He said he's researching some of your—he called them your 'ethical lapses'—but says he meant only to confront you with them and get your permission to touch on the controversy in the biography.''

"What lapses?'' Holland asked angrily.

"Oh, you know, the *Huck Finn* thing,'' Bock said.

"Oh that,'' Holland said, "That's old hat. Time magazine took me to task years ago for not crediting Twain. Sure, he can write about that if he wants. But Roger, you didn't have to break into my files.''

"The *Huck Finn* thing wasn't what he was looking for,'' Donovan said.

All eyes were on the captain again.

"Bock was looking for the Luke Schadenfreud records,'' Donovan said. Again consulting his computer, he said, "In 1976, ASCAP—the licensing agency that handles your songs—took note of a letter of grievance filed by Lucien Schadenfreud that accused you of having stolen certain song lyrics that he wrote and having published them as your own.''

Holland's skin went whiter yet.

"These were songs for a certain rock musical,'' Donovan continued. "Among them was a ditty originally about lust in the dust in Sahara. If you will forgive my singing voice, which is worse even than Elena Jordan's...''

Donovan cleared his throat, said, "Harry, feel free to jump in,'' and sang, *"I came for the wa-ter, but I'll find love in Casa-blan-ca."*

Spalding tickled out a few notes before realizing that his boss, sitting next to him, looked on the verge of a coronary.

Donovan looked triumphant. He said, "Schadenfreud and Bock are friends. I suspect Gittelson is a kind of aging scout leader for both of them. The old man showed them how to get into the basement of the Old Knickerbocker whenever they wanted. At first, Schadenfreud tried to find records proving that you had, in fact, stolen his words. I found dust from there on his boots. But he was in no condition to do anything, his hands were shaking so badly. So Bock stepped in, taking over the job of breaking into your files. No doubt that was what brought him to the basement in the first place, where he stumbled over Milos's grave."

"And took the crossbow and arrows," Mosko said, turning to the accused. "One of which you just planted in Harry's dressing room."

"I did not," Bock said, struggling to his feet. "I did find the grave, but I didn't touch it. In fact, someone got there before me. Besides, I don't know anything about crossbows."

"You just lied to me," Donovan said.

It was Bock's turn to go pale.

"What do you mean?" Holland asked.

Donovan said, "You ran away from my partner and you lied to me. This is not a good thing."

"I'm sorry," Bock said. "Okay, so I *do* know a little about crossbows."

Mala stared at him intently, but without letting go of Sharkey's arm.

Donovan said, "Bock wrote a whole series of *Legends of* books, among them..."

*"Legends of Medieval Weapons,"* the author admitted.

"Which includes three chapters on crossbows," Donovan said. "The Welsh crossbow expert I met on the Internet referred me to them."

"Bock, you're fired," Holland snapped.

"But I never used one," Bock argued. "In fact, I never held one in my hands. You really don't think authors actually have to know a subject to write about it, do you? All it takes is imagination."

"Why did you start to kill people, Bock?" Mosko asked. "So you could sell the tape to 'Hard Copy?' "

"What?" Holland said.

"He sold a dub of the Tippett-killing tape to them," Donovan said. "It got him twenty-five thousand."

Contrary to what Bock had predicted, Sir John was not amused. He said, "Take him away, Sergeant. I want him out of my theater."

"Or did you do it to cover up stealing records from Holland's files?" Mosko asked.

"What would stealing records be worth to me?" Bock asked.

"Let's see, share of a successful theft-of-intellectual-property lawsuit against a man of Sir John's status would be worth a couple of bucks," Donovan said.

"I didn't kill anybody," Bock wailed. "I never touched a crossbow in my life. So I tried to help my friend Luke get the goods on Sir John. But I never expected to benefit from any lawsuit."

Donovan said, "No, you'd just blackmail Holland with the information. You'd tell him, 'Pay me a lot more to write your bio, or else the truth comes out.' Bock, you were in the perfect position to have taken Milos's crossbow from his grave. You have no alibi for any of the murders. You were acting suspiciously the day of the Tippett killing. Moreover, you were the only one on my list of suspects who could have planted that arrow in Harry's dressing room."

Bock hung his head, but said nothing.

"Get him out of here," Donovan snapped.

"I want to see a lawyer."

"Yes, this time, please do," Donovan said to the man's back as the two detectives led him away.

"Wow," Mala exclaimed.

"Way to go, buddy boy," Sharkey said, taking Donovan's hand and pumping it.

Holland added, "I took that man into my family, almost, and he turns out to be a killer. Captain Donovan, you're every bit as good as your reputation. You must be very proud of yourself.''

"I'll be happier when we get a search warrant for his apartment and find the crossbow," Donovan said.

"Is that necessary? I mean, can't you convict him without it?"

A twinkle came to Donovan's eyes, and he said, "I got good news and bad news."

"What's the good news?" Holland asked, in a better mood now and willing to play along.

"Hitler didn't die in the bunker. He was found alive in Argentina."

"That's the good news? What's the bad news?"

"He's being tried in L.A.," Donovan said.

Holland laughed. "The point being?" he asked.

"That it helps to get a conviction if you have the murder weapon. It scares me that a very lethal crossbow—with two bolts remaining unshot—is out there someplace."

"I'm sure you'll find it when you search Bock's apartment," Holland said, standing and stretching his long limbs. "Everyone— I think we have reason to celebrate. We'll get this theater cleaned up and open as planned on New Year's Eve. At last count, tickets were being sold for the year 2001. This grand opening will usher in the New Year amidst the most glorious night Times Square has even seen."

"I'll drink to that," Sharkey said, slipping into character. He waved an imaginary drink at Spalding and said, "Play it, Sam."

Spalding began to play "As Time Goes By."

Smiling and shaking his head, Donovan walked away from the little gathering with Mosko. But Mala broke away from Sharkey and caught up with Donovan, taking him by the arm the way she had that other night.

"I guess I can't make good on my offer to accompany you to the grand premiere party at the Hotsy Totsy Club," she said. "I'm sorry. I did mean it...sort of."

"There're a lot of 'sort ofs' in your life, aren't there?" Donovan asked.

"I admit it: I'm a bitch—sort of," she laughed.

"Well, Bock looks like our killer, and it appears all we have to do is find the crossbow," Donovan said. "So I guess I won't be working on New Year's Eve after all—*Casablanca: The Musical* appears to be safe from mad killers."

"You'll be there, then?"

"I'll bring Marcy, if she can find something to wear. The poor woman hasn't had the chance to go shopping since she opened her restaurant."

"Oh, well, then I can help. What size is she?"

"Seven."

"And how tall?"

"Five-seven."

"She can borrow the Kristeva. You know, the little number you walked me home in the other night? Is that her style?"

"If you mean tight and short, yes, she, too, likes to show off her legs."

"That's absolutely fabulous," Mala gushed. "We leggy babes salute you for your good taste."

"She's a few inches taller than you."

"So she can let down the hem, if she's shy. I'll get it for you to take to her."

"You're a good woman," Donovan said, then sent her back to her lover and started across the stage toward the door. He didn't get far. He was met by a contingent of police brass that arrived in a convoy of official vehicles heralded by massed sirens.

"Trouble," Mosko said.

"Pilcrow," Donovan replied.

# TWENTY

## IF YOU GET HARRY SPALDING TO LOOK
## WHITE AND THIRTY, MAZEL TOV.

"MY TAKE ON THIS is Harry Spalding is spending the night in the Tombs," Donovan said to his partner, who nodded grimly.

The highest-ranking black in the New York police department, Deputy Chief Inspector Paul Pilcrow was a much-honored man with a difficult job. For one thing, it fell to this highly visible African-American to act as the calm voice of reason and caution when high-profile cases touched on racial matters. That meant getting between the combatants in Crown Heights a few years back, when the blacks and the Hasidic Jews were at one another's throats. That also meant playing the role of the smooth-talking moderator on One-hundred-twenty-fifth Street—the main commercial drag of Harlem—a few months earlier when a black hothead burned down a Jewish-owned discount store, killing eight Hispanic workers.

Pilcrow was good at his job. But being the spokesman for black crimefighters also made him something of a straight-laced, humorless, by-the-books prig when it happened that a prominent black man was accused of something. Donovan often referred to Joyce in calling Pilcrow "a control freak and scrotumtightened neatness nut" whose goal in life sometimes seemed the destruction of everything unconventional or rough-edged. Pilcrow hated the untidy; Donovan was his favorite target because the captain was unconventional yet brilliant and, in recent years, the city's most successful solver of homicides.

Whatever lingering irritation sent his testosterone through the ceiling that day, Pilcrow was mad. And when that happened, he looked like the twin brother of Supreme Court Justice Clarence Thomas. That made it hard for Donovan—a confirmed West Side

Democrat, one of whose old buddies was a political strategy adviser to President Clinton—to avoid laughing as he gave the man a cursory handshake.

"Hello, Paul."

"Captain Donovan, I hear you have good news."

"I guess you're not referring to a bad joke I told a minute ago."

"I never liked your sense of humor, Captain."

"What's on your mind?"

"I understand that you're ready to charge Harry Spalding with the murder of Henry Tippett, with the presumption he's responsible for the rest of the murders."

"What 'rest of the murders' are those?" Donovan asked.

"Why, the Irish kid, Mooney, and the Vietnamese boy, of course."

"Dinh—the Vietnamese man—was killed by the water main break. He had no gang involvements. He owed no money. He has nothing to do with my case."

Pilcrow seemed surprised. "You're sure?"

"Absolutely positive."

"What about those torture markings on his skin?" Pilcrow asked.

"I don't know about those, yet. But Dinh's presence was coincidental. What he did in his spare time to account for those markings is none of our business."

"I read the reports," Pilcrow went on. "Doesn't Laquidara make sado-masochism films?"

"Among other things."

"And you don't see a relationship?"

"I have no information that Dinh appeared in porn films," Donovan said. "The man was a cook."

"So you're charging Spalding in the Tippett and Mooney killings, then."

"No, I'm not," Donovan said assuredly enough to blunt the expected onslaught.

"I was hoping you weren't going to say that," Pilcrow said, "But I'm not surprised. Captain, Spalding is an ex-con with a history of violent crime. He pulled a gun on your father, for God's sake."

"It wasn't loaded. Harry was lucky my old man didn't blow his fool head off. It was that scare that allowed him to change."

"Nonetheless, Spalding was sent to jail. Now, I understand that he's your friend."

"My dad helped him get straight. Teaching me to appreciate jazz was part of the cure. It worked. Harry hasn't had so much as a parking ticket in thirty years."

"Spalding has no alibi for either the Mooney or the Tippett killings," Pilcrow pointed out.

"True. He was in his dressing room both times."

"Spalding stood to gain from Tippett's death. I heard about that movie offer. What's he getting to become a movie star, a million?"

"I advised him to renegotiate," Donovan said.

"Spalding could have put on an Arab robe, posed as an extra, and shot Tippett before running back to his dressing room, where an arrow was found."

"The man witnesses described was a white man, about thirty years old, with a mustache. If you can get Harry Spalding to look white and thirty, *mazel tov*. You should become a plastic surgeon and go to work for Michael Jackson."

Seething, Pilcrow asked, "What about the evidence found in Spalding's dressing room?"

"There are two points I would like to make," Donovan said. "The first is that at the time of the Tippett killing, Spalding occupied the stand-in's dressing room, which we searched and found nothing in. At the time the arrow was found this morning, he occupied the star's dressing room. That evidence had to have been planted this morning."

"By who?"

"I'm assuming by one of my principal suspects—Sharkey, Logan, Bock, or Holland. Sharkey, Logan, and Holland all alibi one another as regards planting the evidence, but you must have seen *Murder on the Orient Express*."

"Who was in it? Was that the one with Albert Finney?"

Donovan said that it was.

"I saw it. What's your point? That they're all guilty and in it together?"

"It's a possibility," Donovan said.

"What's their motive?"

"They're all getting rich. Tickets are sold out through the year 2001."

"Oh, and that would also be why you included Holland in your list of suspects," Pilcrow said.

Donovan nodded.

"I hope he's not involved in the killings," Pilcrow said. "The man is a major player in this city's financial future. The mayor expects his show to draw in enough tourists to make Times Square as safe as a suburban shopping mall."

"And about as interesting," Donovan added.

"That's not your call," Pilcrow said. "I know if you had your way, Times Square would always be a Wild West show."

"Wrong. I just hope in addition to the family-entertainment theaters, ten-plexes, Gaps, Banana Republics, and All Star Cafes and other fifteen-dollar burger emporiums, they keep an occasional Greek gyro joint, sloppy pizza place, Blarney Stone where you can get meat loaf for $2.99, and, yes, the odd cigar store/magazine stand where you can buy X-rated stuff. Let's not forget the free-speech issue."

Pilcrow looked at Donovan with the sort of distaste proper citizens usually reserve for serial killers.

"You mentioned Bock," he said at last.

"We just hauled him off," Donovan said. "He's a much better suspect than Harry Spalding. Let me tell you why."

And that's what Donovan did, filling in the Deputy Chief Inspector on what had transpired before he got to the theater. When he had told his story, Donovan noticed a look of renewed irritation appear on Pilcrow's face. It was like the morning's breakfast sausage had finally fulfilled its promise and brought on an ulcer attack.

"Are you charging Roger Bock?" Pilcrow asked.

"I'm not sure. I may hold him while I get a search warrant for his apartment."

"If you're not charging him, why not?"

"He's my best suspect, but he's far from a perfect one," Donovan said. "For one thing, Bock didn't seem to be hurting for money and was about to make a good deal more off John Victor

Holland. Why, then, go around the man's theater killing people? It would be like killing the golden goose.''

"I see."

"I can only think of two motives for killing people in this theater. One is the real estate motive, which Derrida had."

"I read that in your report," Pilcrow said.

"But Derrida found a less messy way of stopping the production."

"Asbestos. A contractor would know that was a sure-fire way to empty out a public building."

"Yeah, and he nearly got away with it," Donovan said.

"What's the other motive for murder in this case?"

"Sheer, blind hatred of John Victor Holland," Donovan said. "Now, I have heard it told there are eight million theater lovers who qualify. One of them could be skulking around this building with a crossbow under his djellaba."

"What's that?" Pilcrow asked.

"An Arab robe."

"I suppose you learned that word during your years in the French Foreign Legion," Pilcrow said acidly.

"Nope. I got it out of the dictionary."

"Sharkey, Logan, and Spalding don't hate Holland."

"Not noticeably. In fact, I see a grudging admiration, the way Yankees fans sometimes admire George Steinbrenner."

"But wouldn't be caught dead admitting it."

"Exactly. Schadenfreud hates him, but has an impeccable alibi for the Mooney killing. His hands shook too much for him to hit anything but the bottle anyway."

Pilcrow elevated his eyes to the ceiling, and breathed a big sigh. "Thank God you're not charging the New York Times critic with murder," he said.

"Not so fast. I still haven't let him off the hook for Jimi Hendrix."

"Say again?"

"A little joke between the two of us, Deputy Chief."

"Well, you know how I feel about your sense of humor."

Donovan shrugged. "Gittelson doesn't hate Holland and is too old to be a murderer. There are uncaught Nazi war criminals younger than Sy Gittelson, and they can't do more than sit under trees in Argentina and weave baskets. Bock stood to benefit from Holland. So here I am, uncertain just who may be doing the murders. But Bock is my best suspect."

"I disagree, Captain," Pilcrow said, delivering a pronouncement that Donovan felt had been brewing for some time.

"You're telling me that Harry Spalding is the killer."

"He has motive—he got the job and will become a star. He had opportunity and no alibi. He's a convicted felon. And one of the arrows was found in his dressing room." Pilcrow looked triumphant. "In his favor, all he has is that the investigating officer is an old friend."

"Why would Harry kill Mooney?"

"To make it look like the work of a madman. To drag up the ghost thing."

Donovan shook his head sadly. "This is such an obvious frame," he said.

"You're wrong, Captain," Pilcrow said. "I want you to let Roger Bock go—the man is a respected author—and charge Harry Spalding."

"Are you taking this case away from me?" Donovan asked.

"Do I have to?"

"If you want me to charge Harry—yes."

"Captain Donovan," Pilcrow said formally. "You have done a magnificent job in identifying Harry Spalding as the murderer of George Mooney and Henry Tippett. On behalf of the New York Police Department, thank you. I'll take it from here."

"You're making a mistake," Donovan said. "You're going to get someone else killed."

"By who?" Pilcrow said.

"Whom," Donovan said, unable to prevent himself from raising the easily baited man's blood pressure.

"Whom," Pilcrow said, taking the bait. "The ghost of Milos the Magnificent? The joke around One Police Plaza is that you're bucking for transfer to 'The X-Files.'"

"There is no ghost," Donovan said, "merely the loitering superstitions of some old vaudevillians."

"Take some well-deserved time off, Captain. Enjoy the holidays. Will you be celebrating Christmas with Marcy?"

"Christmas, Hanukkah, and, if her dad gets in a playful mood, Kwanzaa," Donovan replied. "It's a complex family."

"Nothing about you is simple, is it, Captain?" Pilcrow said.

"I don't like simple," Donovan said.

Maybe Donovan seemed to imply that Pilcrow was feeble-minded. Certainly the captain thought that, but was pretty sure nothing in his tone of voice said as much. But that must have been how the Deputy Chief took it, for he fell back on an old threat involving Donovan's raucous past. The unspoken understanding with which he was given the captain's badge was that he stay on the wagon. Thus, since his promotion, Donovan had been waiting for a particular shoe to drop; it was Pilcrow who dropped it.

"You seem under stress lately, Captain," Pilcrow said. "That wouldn't be liquor I smell on your breath, would it?"

Donovan thought, I could knock this jerk into next week, but it wouldn't help me very much, would it? And he held himself back. Nor could Donovan protest the accusation, for on the subject of alcohol, in the politically correct world of New York City a loud denial was an admission of guilt.

"It wouldn't be," Donovan said.

"I didn't think so," Pilcrow said. "Take some time off and enjoy the holidays—whichever ones you're celebrating."

And the man walked off to slap the cuffs on Harry Spalding. As he did so, Donovan watched from the sidelines, exchanging silent glances with Spalding and listening to Holland, Sharkey, and Logan issue promises of support:

"You'll be out on bail in an hour."

"We're behind you, buddy-boy."

"We know you're innocent, Harry."

"We'll get the trial moved to L.A."

"I'm calling the lawyers now, pal."

And when Moskowitz came over to commiserate, Donovan told him to take the rest of the year off.

IT TOOK LONGER than an hour to get Harry Spalding out on bail. It took, in fact, until the middle of the afternoon. But considering the nearness of the holiday, the bare-minimum case papers forwarded to the court by Donovan's office, and the sudden appearance of $1 million in bail from Holland, Spalding was back on the streets in time to play with his trio at Nancy's that night. Roger Bock never made it to jail at all, and disappeared into the depths of the concrete city. Donovan was on his way home for a rare holiday break, a custom Kristeva draped over his arm. And the Old Knickerbocker Theater was being torn apart, double-time, around the clock, to get all the asbestos removed and the hall ready for its grand premiere on New Year's Eve.

As was his honor every year, Donovan climbed a stepladder and placed the Star of David atop the Barnes family Christmas tree. Marcy let down the hem on the Kristeva an inch—which still left the dress much shorter on her than it was on its owner. In a trial run, she wore it at the neighborhood holiday party she gave each year at Marcy's Home Cooking. Even George Kohler showed up for that annual event and, as usual, was complaining—this time about the long hours and lack of interesting customers among the tourists who came in to the Hotsy Totsy Club.

By the time New Year's Eve had arrived, and the crowds began to form in Times Square, the case of the crossbow murders seemed to have faded into the mists of yesterday's news. Pilcrow had worn out his welcome on the front pages, alternately taking credit for the arrest of Harry Spalding and bellowing about the man's release on bond. Times Square was renovated, scrubbed, polished, and looked, in fact, like the Mall of America, Times Square Substation. The theater was open and magnificent, with clean air to match its sparkling appearance. As if in celebration, ticket sales had reached into the year 2003. Such was the power on the American musical stage of having multiple murders in the theater and an accused killer in the cast.

And it came to pass that, just as the curtain was about to fall on the official opening of Casablanca: The Musical, Donovan convened an extraordinary gathering in the office of Sy Gittelson. The captain looked resplendent in a freshly pressed tuxedo. Marcy was radiant in her trashy but expensive Kristeva. Gittelson wore a new cardigan—a present from Elsie Klinger to keep him warm through the winter months. And Lucien Schadenfreud looked rosy-cheeked and full of life, having dropped ten pounds as his new life completed its first week.

As he popped the cork on a bottle of alcohol-free wine and poured four glasses, Schadenfreud proposed a toast: "To health and good friends."

"*L'chaim,*" Gittelson replied, in practiced Hebrew.

"*Sláinte,*" said Donovan, in halting Gaelic.

"May *Casablanca: The Musical* run forever," Gittelson said.

All eyes turned to Donovan for the expected torrent of abuse. It never appeared. He shrugged and said, "What the hell. This is America. Everything comes with a tune."

"And one of them in this show is mine," Schadenfreud said, proudly waving a show poster that included the words MUSIC AND LYRICS BY SIR JOHN VICTOR HOLLAND; ADDITIONAL LYRICS BY LUCIEN SCHADENFREUD.

"How much is that line worth to you?" Donovan asked.

"Two percent....more, if Barbra Streisand records it, which I hear talk about. Enough to let me quit reviewing rock concerts and write my novel," Schadenfreud said.

"And another bite is taken out of the rain forest," Donovan said. "I thought Roger Bock already used most of it for his books. Where is he, anyway?"

"Disappeared," Schadenfreud replied. "I guess he was embarrassed at having been handcuffed. Roger is easily hurt and has vanished before. There's this little town he goes to on the Maine coast when he wants to let his wounds heal. Personally, I would head west if I wanted to chill out."

"I never been west of Eighth Avenue," Gittelson said. "I had a cousin who died on Ninth, but I met the funeral cortege on Eighth and we buried him on Broadway and one-fifty-fifth. God grant him peace. Where did you get this wine, Captain?"

Donovan poured a second round from an old and venerable-looking bottle, then held it up to show off the label. "This is a very rare, nonalcoholic Chevalier Montrachet," he said.

"You didn't get that at the A&P," Gittelson said.

"Hardly," Donovan said proudly. "This bottle comes from Anders Purslane, the wine merchant who supplies Holland. I was in is office this morning—a long-dangling loose end I wanted to clean up."

"And did you clean it up?" Gittelson asked.

Donovan nodded. "I sent Pilcrow an e-mail about it, but he'll just reprimand me for not minding my own business."

"How do you feel about having tonight off?" Marcy asked Schadenfreud.

"I'm delighted that *The Times* won't let me review a show I have a song in. Let the regular guy do it. Anyway, the inside line is he likes it. He mentioned something to me about buying a Porsche."

"Holland will be happy," Gittelson said.

"You know what I'm even happier about? Tonight I don't have to exude a few platitudes about 'Dick Clark's New Year's Rockin' Eve,' and tomorrow night there's a concert by Nine Inch Nails that I don't have to go to."

Donovan smiled.

"How do you feel about having your case taken away from you?"

"It's happened before," Donovan said. "John Lennon comes to mind."

"Ah yes, John Lennon—in 1972 he accused me of collaborating with the CIA and the FBI to try to get him deported," Schadenfreud said.

"At least he lived another eight years after tangling with you," Donovan said. "What did you do to him?"

"I reported he was here making a record."

"That could get him deported?" Marcy asked.

"He was here on a tourist visa," Schadenfreud said. "No working allowed."

"Sometimes I think that politics is everything," Donovan said. "There's a lot of it in this city; Pilcrow has had it in for me for years. But don't worry, I'll get even. I have something planned if he insists on ignoring me."

Schadenfreud reached into his tuxedo jacket and pulled out a small, brightly wrapped package. He handed it to Marcy. "This is thanks," he said.

"What is it?" she asked, ripping it open.

"A new Valium prescription to replace the one you gave me last week."

"Your doctor gave it to you?"

He smiled, and said, "Let's just say that a man doesn't review rock concerts for thirty years without making a few connections."

"Thank you," she said, giving him a hug and a kiss.

"You look great in that," he said, nodding at the Kristeva, which clung to her long legs as if lacquered on them.

"While we're clearing up old business," Donovan said, "I have something for Sy." He took from his pocket one of the small stones he had found at Milos's grave. He dropped the rock into Gittelson's palm.

The old man saw it and turned red. "I'm sorry I lied to you," he said.

"That's okay. You didn't want to admit you've been making occasional visits to Milos's grave to honor his memory."

"If I had any idea an Irish cop would know Jews leave stones on the grave to show they've visited I would have told you the truth. You're a very wise man, Captain."

Donovan pointed at Marcy, who acknowledged having been given credit for the information. She said, "It's not that he's so smart. He reads a lot and asks questions. This afternoon I found him with his nose in *The New England Journal of Medicine,* of all things."

"There were dried flowers down by the grave, too," Donovan said. "From Elsie Klinger?"

"Yes. A wonderful woman. I brought the flowers to Milos for her."

"You should marry her."

"I'm getting around to it," Gittelson said. "One of these days, I will."

Marcy gave Donovan a look, so he changed the subject. "If you guys can do without us for a few minutes, I want to take my girl to the theater."

"You never take me anywhere, except maybe crime scenes and

occasionally the morgue,'' Marcy said. ''Did you get tickets to the show? This show that's nearly over?''

''Not exactly,'' Donovan replied.

''Then how will we get in?''

''Follow me.''

# TWENTY-ONE

## MOST MEN CARRY CREDIT CARDS OR CONDOMS WHEN THEY GO OUT ON NEW YEAR'S EVE

DONOVAN URGED Marcy through the hole that connected the annex to the Old Knickerbocker. Through it, they could see a floor covered with boxes of survival crackers—the ones scattered when Moskowitz tackled a fleeing Roger Bock. The B-level basement was much better lit than before, the asbestos-abatement company having strung lights everywhere, even in the many storerooms, while doing its work. But bending low to see through the opening in the brick, Marcy still had the feeling of being dragged into a subdivision of hell.

"You take me to all the best places," she said.

"If you bend a bit lower you can avoid snagging the mink," Donovan said, putting a hand over her quarter-length fur jacket to shield it from the brick.

"Remember the body on the pier?"

"Yes," he said, urging her through the hole by giving her a pat on the backside.

"Remember the mobster who washed ashore on Breezy Point?"

"You weren't with me that day," he replied as he followed her through the opening.

"But you invited me," she said, brushing some red brick dust from the shoulders of his overcoat. "Now you're taking me to see the grave of a trick-shot vaudeville artist who died more than twenty years before I was born."

"That's not where we're going," Donovan said.

"Oh, where then?"

"To see Sabah, the Wild Man of Borneo."

"Great," she replied, taking hold of Donovan's arm so he could lead her there.

Even well lit, the B-level basement had about it the gloom of death. The show was over upstairs so there wasn't even that faint sound—a far-off wail of brass or thrum of strings—to hint at life. There remained only the recently scrubbed tomb that the sub-basement had become.

Walking arm in arm, Donovan and Marcy found the storeroom devoted to the old stuff from Sabah, the Wild Man of Borneo, including the shrunken heads. The door was open a crack and, not expecting to find anyone inside, Donovan pushed it with his shoe. It creaked open, sending a shaft of hall light onto the collection of slatted packing crates marked with the place names Sarawak, Sulawesi, Java, and Bali. The old boxes had been moved around since Donovan was last there, the asbestos removers having relocated most everything in their last-minute, very expensive cleanup effort. The phony palm trees were stacked neatly against the rear wall, and the board from which hung the shrunken heads had been laid neatly atop them. The ceiling was scrubbed clean; stains from a detergent of some sort crept down all four walls. On the wall to the right, a still-wet trickle of solvent ran around a square, hinged metal plate that previously was hidden by crates.

"Shrunken heads," Marcy said. "Cool."

Donovan found the switch for the newly hung utility light and flicked it on. Freed from the relative darkness at last, he looked more closely at the long-stored artifacts.

"Are these real heads?" Marcy asked, leaning tentatively over them, but still holding onto Donovan's arm.

"I think they're early Trader Vic's."

"Painted coconuts?"

"Possibly. Look over there."

"Where?"

"To the right. That wall." He pointed at it.

"It's a wall," she replied.

"It's too thick."

"It looks like a wall."

"This whole room is spatially displaced," Donovan said. "Remember 'Dr. Who?'"

She thought for a moment, then said, "That means it's larger on the outside than on the inside, right?"

"The other way around," Donovan said.

She sighed. "I slept through most of those shows," she said.

"I went through this with Derrida while going over the blue-prints as they pertained to the catwalk level—about two and a half stories above here. This is the same load-bearing wall I looked at. There's a dumbwaiter shaft up there."

"Dumbwaiter shafts tend to run to the basement, don't they?" Marcy said.

"I heard that rumor," Donovan replied, walking to the metal plate and yanking it open.

It sprang away from the wall with nary a squeak. The hinges were freshly oiled. Donovan shined his Mag-Lite into the shaft.

"What are you looking for?" Marcy asked. "You established that the killer got up and down from the basement using the stairs. Remember the djellaba Bonaci found in the Dumpster?"

"I'm looking for the place the killer hid the crossbow," Donovan said. He stuck his head inside the shaft, aiming the light here and there. Then he said, "And I think I found it."

Donovan pulled a plastic evidence bag from his pocket and popped something into it.

Marcy said, "Most men carry credit cards or condoms when they go out on New Year's Eve. My man carries evidence bags. What did you find?"

He showed it to her. "It was stuck on the bricks in there, where the killer hid the crossbow—a clump of fibers recently pulled off a white cashmere sweater."

"Who among your main suspects wears white cashmere?"

"None of them," Donovan said.

"When he's not dressed up like Bogart, I would imagine Kurt Sharkey wears torn T-shirts."

"Yeah, well, he goes back and forth between Bogie and Brando. The man honors the classics. It's *Anton* who wears white cashmere sweaters. When Holland mentioned the shrunken heads to me one time, he let slip that it was Anton who told him about them. This is a man who is so much a piece of the furniture around here that nobody notices him anymore."

"Who the hell is Anton?"

"Holland's long-suffering personal aide, who has a room upstairs...."

"He lives here? Did you search his room?"

"We searched every room," Donovan said. "Anton's alibi for the time Henry Tippett was killed was that he was signing for a shipment of rare, 1955 Piper Heidsieck."

"And?"

"I talked to the wine merchant this morning. His records show Anton signing half an hour before the killing. The sonofabitch lied to me, probably thinking I wouldn't check."

"Why would Holland's assistant want to hurt or kill him?"

"Derrida called Anton a doormat. That's exactly how he gets treated, and it's been going on for twenty years."

"That's a motive," Marcy agreed.

"And I guess Anton also would like to kill Holland for the same reason eight million New Yorkers would want to do it," Donovan said. "Making a shambles of the Broadway stage, specifically, making a Hollywood extravaganza out of *Casablanca*."

Marcy nodded, then pointed up in the direction of the now-silent hall. "The curtain went down some time ago," she said.

"Everyone is at the party by now," Donovan replied. "They're going to the Hotsy Totsy Club in costume, which means..."

"Arab robes big enough to hide a crossbow under," Marcy said.

"And Anton has two arrows left."

DONOVAN SLIPPED and allowed himself to think that getting from the Old Knickerbocker Theater on Forty-second Street to the Hotsy Totsy Club on Fifty-fourth would be a snap. Twelve blocks could be walked casually in twelve minutes, he knew, and run in three—even in evening clothes. Driving or taking a cab was out of the question; traffic flows downtown through Times Square. You could easily wait twenty minutes for a subway train. So running was the fastest way to get to the club. What Donovan had momentarily forgotten was that it was nearly midnight on New Year's Eve.

Upward of half a million souls paved the intersecting boulevards that night, wearing funny hats, blowing paper horns, waving colorful rattlers, and gazing up at the luminous ball that soon would fall to mark the coming of the new year. The noise was earth-shattering, louder than any jet airplane. The racket seemed to shake everything—the towering electronic signs that flashed madly in a thousand colors, the Jumbotron that took a portion of the celebrating crowd and magnified it a hundred times normal size, and the several stages set in front of One Times Square. Atop the latter were several ongoing TV shows—"Dick Clark's New Year's Rockin' Eve" was one of them and, atop another stage, Kathy Lee Gifford appeared to be singing "Those Were the Days," although only the audience at home could hear it. Far above them, a newly refurbished New Year's ball dazzled the crowd with 10,000 watts of light, 12,000 rhinestones, and a gross of strobes.

Police barricades along each curb nominally kept the crowd off the sidewalks, leaving the latter free for those who felt like walking. But the sidewalks were packed with pedestrians who jostled along, hip to hip, guarding their wallets against the pickpockets who the Times Square renovation people had failed to legislate into the outer boroughs.

"My God," said Donovan, gaping at the task ahead of him.

"If you have any plan to sprout wings, now is the time," Marcy said.

"Let's go." He flipped his badge onto his overcoat's breast pocket, grabbed Marcy's hand, and pushed his way across Forty-second Street.

The crowd was a living thing, throbbing and noisy. Keeping to the sidewalks along the west edge of the square and shouting "police" every few strides, Donovan and his companion made their way slowly, enduring the occasional sneer of disbelief at the spectacle of a man in evening dress and his designer-clad sweetheart bruising their way through the throng behind a badge.

After two blocks, however, Donovan was recognized by a patrol sergeant. That officer recruited two street cops and together they formed a flying wedge that moved faster along up Broadway, clearing a path. Before long the scene attracted the attention of the Jumbotron camera operator who was picking out crowd scenes to show the world. He focused on Donovan, Marcy, and their escorts and briefly projected them onto the facade of One Times Square.

Then he shifted his focus to the mayor, the Roman Catholic cardinal, and other dignitaries, who stood in a group at Forty-fifth Street waiting to press a button to fire a laser beam that would, in turn, start the ball falling.

The Hotsy Totsy Club was at the northern end of Times Square, and for the last block the crowd thinned out. Shedding their escorts, Donovan and Marcy ran up the middle of Broadway and past the two sky-sweeping spotlights parked in front for the grand opening party of *Casablanca: The Musical*. A knot of paparrazi lingered outside, occasionally popping a flashbulb when a costumed celebrity happened by a window. Some had broken away to set up their cameras to shoot the ball falling on the old year, an event that was only minutes away when Donovan and Marcy rushed up.

Flashbulbs lit their faces. The assumption was that they were celebrities. Donovan had grown into a dignified sort of confidence, and Marcy was forever being mistaken for someone famous. He ducked into the club, brushing aside the bouncer with a practiced move that simultaneously shoved a badge into his face and an elbow into his chest.

The room was wall-to-wall with actors and hangers-on, nearly every one in costume. There were a dozen French policemen, their kepis bobbing proudly atop carefully coifed heads. There were three dozen Arabs in white and black djellabas, and as many westerners dressed in 1940s evening wear. But it was the profusion of robes that stood out.

"This is like the Dome of the Rock in here," Marcy said, shaking her head.

"Where the hell is Anton?" Donovan swore, looking around.

Several small, ceiling spotlights picked out Sharkey, Spalding, and Mala Logan by the bar. The light spilled over onto the scowling countenance of George Kohler, who looked like the captain of the *Titanic* shortly after she hit the iceberg. Holland stood near them, beaming with the pride of one whose fame and, particularly, fortune were assured for the foreseeable future. A few non-theater people were sprinkled about. Prominent among them was Deputy Chief Inspector Pilcrow, whom Donovan discerned was having a crisis deciding whether it was smarter to be where he was or out in the street sucking up to the mayor and cardinal. Pilcrow seemed to have decided to stay in the club, where he could take action lest Harry Spalding bolt for Mexico.

Pilcrow spotted Donovan, saw he was heading for Holland, and jumped to head him off. "I didn't expect to see you, Captain," he said, nodding at the same time to Marcy, "but I'm glad you're here."

"I know who the killer is, Chief," he said. Donovan didn't stop but continued pushing his way through the crowd. Marcy was still on his arm, and Pilcrow joined in the rush, elbowing his way to the captain's side.

"I'm talking to you," Pilcrow said, his voice rising above the sound of the Holland-Schadenfreud score, which blared over loud-speakers. "I want you to know I'm thinking of charging Laquidara as an accessory in the murder of Tri Ng Dinh."

"Dinh was killed by the water main break," Donovan said. "Have you seen Anton?"

"Who's Anton? I'm telling you, Dinh was murdered after taking part in a sado-masochistic film," Pilcrow insisted.

"Chief, Dinh wasn't in any film. He got those marks from 'coining.' "

"Coining? What's that?"

"A traditional Southeast Asian remedy that Dinh was using for his headaches," Donovan said. "You rub a coin across the skin in a striped pattern. This morning I found the photo of another 'coining' victim in *The New England Journal of Medicine*. The marks are just like those on Dinh; they're sometimes mistaken for abuse by American doctors. That's the exact mistake the medical examiner made. I'll have the details on your desk Tuesday."

Pilcrow grabbed Donovan's shoulder, stopping him. The captain spun around and said, "Anton is Holland's assistant."

"Oh, the doormat. I haven't seen him. So what, anyway? Harry Spalding is the killer," Pilcrow insisted.

"I found the place Anton hid the crossbow. All I can say is it ain't there now, and Anton is among the missing. Unless..." Donovan looked around at the teeming throng of actors and extras who filled the club to the brim. "He's dressed up in one of these goddamn robes."

Donovan tried to pull away from his boss. Perhaps sensing he was about to be upstaged, Pilcrow tightened his grip. Donovan warned, "Someone else is gonna get killed," and wrenched away.

Pilcrow growled "Donovan!" and would have said more, but Marcy got a knee in the back of his knee and an elbow in his gut that sent him sprawling onto the floor. The move also sent a long rip up the seam of the Kristeva. As Donovan hurried off toward Holland, Marcy grabbed Pilcrow's hand. "God, I'm sorry, Chief, this dress is so tight I can't keep my balance." Holding the dress together with one hand, she helped him, scowling but unable to prove anything, to his feet.

Donovan's eyes moved quickly from face to face, trying to find Anton. The captain pushed through the crowd to where Holland stood, surrounded by his stars. Donovan burst into the inner circle, followed closely by Marcy. Holland's eyes met Donovan's and lit up. "Captain! The show's a hit!"

"Where's Anton?" Donovan shouted.

"I don't know."

"Is he here?"

"If he is, he's fired. He's been missing all day."

Sharkey stuck his hand out for a shake, saying, "Good to see ya, pal."

Donovan's eyes flew across nearby faces and shapes, a blur of Arab robes and French police uniforms. Behind them, George Kohler saw the only friendly face of the evening and, in a rare burst of charm, held aloft a bottle of Kaliber. "The drink's on me," he said, a proclamation that at another moment would have left Donovan speechless.

Mala and Marcy eyeballed each other, looking up and down and making judgments—involving the torn dress and other things—that neither would ever reveal. Then from the back of the crowd Pilcrow stumbled up, madder than a bumblebee that had been flicked off its flower. Short of breath from the shot to the stomach, he fumbled in between Donovan and Holland and said, "Captain Donovan..."

In that instant Donovan saw, behind Pilcrow and behind Holland's shoulder, a flash of white cashmere beneath a black djellaba. Donovan said, "Anton," and reached for his revolver. But Pilcrow

was jammed chest-to-chest with him and the captain's arm was
pinned. Then Anton's arms moved and his robe widened out as
the old crossbow was moved into the hip firing position. An angry
male voice growled and there was a sharp sound, like the limb of
a young tree snapping in a winter storm.

Holland's body shook and his eyes shot open and then blood
spurted from the corners of his mouth and down his chin. His
body jerked forward against Pilcrow. The deputy chief inspector
shuddered and gasped, and then he clawed at his back with both
hands.

Pilcrow fell forward against Donovan, and as he did so the point
of the arrow pulled out of his back. As Pilcrow and Donovan fell
away from him, Holland gaped down in desperate, dying amazement at the several inches of Port Orford cedar that projected,
dripping blood and muscle, from his chest. Then his eyes rolled
back into his skull and he fell straight down onto the floor.

Anton was triumphant. His eyes blazed and he looked down at
his handiwork for an instant, before jumping over the body and
barreling through the crowd and out the door. As the sound of
music was replaced by the wail of screaming, Donovan rolled the
wounded Pilcrow off him and scrambled to his feet.

Sharkey stared at Donovan and started to say, "Jeez..."

Donovan held up a finger. "Don't say it," he snapped. Then
he pulled out his Smith & Wesson and ran after the killer.

# TWENTY-TWO

## THIS TIME IS NO TIME FOR HIM TO START MAKING ENEMIES

IT WAS TWO MINUTES to the new year when Donovan burst back through the crowd of paparazzi outside the club door. If the photographers had any idea one man was dead inside and another was nearly so, they didn't show it. It was only the revolver in Donovan's hand that startled them, and then the bulbs didn't start to go off for a few seconds. In that time, Donovan said, "Where'd the guy in the robe go?" then looked south as several photographers turned their heads that way. As the lights flashed in his face once again, he ran toward the throbbing mass of a half million souls that packed Times Square.

If there was one thing that stood out on that shoulder-to-shoulder night, it was a man running. Donovan spotted Anton two blocks to the south, as he bowled his way through several partying couples. Two men were left gesturing angrily after him as he forced his way into the increasingly thick mob. Donovan ran after him, and soon closed the gap to half a block.

Shouting "police," Donovan moved into the crowd. Anton's pace was down to a crawl, and he accomplished that only with a lot of yelling and pushing. Then Donovan heard several women's screams and a shout of "Watch out!" as his quarry shed the robe and brought the crossbow out into plain view. Now, in Times Square on New Year's Eve, as in New Orleans on Mardi Gras or in Rio de Janeiro during Carnival, it's possible to ignore a lot of things. Everyone wears funny hats and most are in costume. Many carry assorted fake weapons. No spectator is really frightened. But a crossbow is a serious piece of killing equipment that can be mistaken for nothing else. There are no toy crossbows like there are rubber swords or plastic guns. A crossbow looks thick, dark, and angry, like a piece of medieval torture equipment—especially when it's being spanned.

In unison, the crowd started to count down the final sixty seconds to midnight. As the countdown began, Anton tired of fighting the crowd and squeezed between two police sawhorses and into the lane for policemen and emergency vehicles that planners had carved down the middle of the celebration. There was a pair of cops every block to prevent what had just happened—an interloper going beyond the barricades. But no one had planned on an interloper with a crossbow.

The two cops who first spotted Anton saw him, as Donovan did, coming out of the crowd with the weapon held over his head. They moved toward him, hesitated at the sight of the crossbow, drew their weapons, then stopped in their tracks when they saw the captain duck under a barricade half a block away.

The emergency lane reminded Donovan of the main aisle of the Old Knickerbocker Theater, which he had dashed up when Henry Tippett was killed. It ran from Forty-seventh Street to One Times Square. Donovan looked down it and saw the mayor and celebrities clustered about him as he awaited the moment, 11:59:30, when he would push the button to start the wildly lit ball falling stories above. The cops stationed every block along the corridor turned toward the confrontation fast developing to the north.

Anton spun around, scanning his diminishing options. Five hundred thousand people surrounded him. Those closest wore blue uniforms and pointed guns. And Bill Donovan, who had been after him for weeks, was closing in. "I want him alive," Donovan bellowed at the nearest uniform, who used his radio to pass the word. Anton whirled in his direction. The crowd, mostly unaware of what was going on in its midst, counted down to forty-five seconds.

Donovan knew from his research that an experienced crossbowman could use a weapon of the type Milos made famous to get off four or five shots a minute. That meant that spanning the bow, pulling back the string, and setting the trigger took at least ten seconds and perhaps longer—when done by an experienced man. Anton wasn't experienced—at least Donovan didn't think so—and could need several times as long to make himself, once again, armed and dangerous. In that time he could have a hundred bullets in him, for Donovan and half a dozen uniformed cops were moving in. But any gun would have to be shot with the knowledge that a miss would certainly hit, and possibly kill, an innocent reveler. Donovan wondered if the man who had successfully plotted and executed three murders would realize that, in a strange and frightening way, he was in the center of a standoff.

The crowd counted down to thirty seconds. A block away, the mayor pressed the button. A laser beam shot to the top of One Times Square, setting off the 10,000-watt light, 12,000 rhinestones, and 144 strobes, which blazed brightly to the roaring approval of the half million in Times Square and perhaps 300 million watching on television and through the Internet. A ton of confetti began to snow down from open windows around the square. Sky-sweeping spotlights, including the pair outside the Hotsy Totsy Club, went into high gear. In Central Park, visible up Seventh Avenue, fireworks lit the sky. The gigantic glowing ball started its descent.

His Smith & Wesson at his side, Donovan started walking toward Anton, moving at a brisk pace. The man looked at the captain, then at the other officers surrounding him, and decided to take the chance and arm the weapon. He lowered the crossbow to the pavement and stuck his left foot in the stirrup.

"Don't do it," Donovan yelled. He had no idea if he was heard. He had even less idea that the Jumbotron cameraman had found him again and decided that the confrontation, not the mayor, not the cardinal, not Dick Clark, and not any of the other celebrities, was what the world truly wanted to see as one year gave way to another.

Anton slipped the ring on the butt of the weapon onto the belt hook he wore and bore down with his foot as he pulled up on the string with both hands. The string started to come back to the firing position.

"You'll be dead before you hit the ground," Donovan yelled.

The crowd counted down to fifteen seconds.

Donovan saw the other cops looking to him for guidance. He raised his revolver. "Anton!" he yelled.

The killer looked up and their eyes met. The crossbow was now ready to fire. He took his foot out of the stirrup and slipped the butt off the belt loop.

Donovan yelled, "Live to tell the world about Holland!"

Donovan swore he saw Anton's eyes mist over. But the man raised the crossbow nonetheless.

"Dammit," Donovan swore, and shot him once in the middle.

The man crumpled to the pavement as the crossbow slipped from his grip and fell, still ready to fire, onto the concrete.

The crowd counted down to zero as the glowing, pulsating ball reached the bottom and touched off a gigantic electric sign spelling out the new year. The crowd roared, the lights all around flashed or swept the sky, the horns blared, and the confetti fell. The mayor, the cardinal, and several other dignitaries, who had seen their roles in the ceremony preempted on the big screen and around the world, walked toward the spot where Donovan knelt alongside the killer and his weapon.

Anton writhed in pain, clutching the hole in his middle. He looked up at Donovan and said, "Is Holland dead?"

"Dead as a doormat," the captain replied.

"And that black detective?"

"He's no detective, and unfortunately I think he'll live. Why Mooney?" Donovan asked.

"Practice," Anton moaned, but with no sign of remorse.

"Why Tippett?"

"I thought killing a star would shut down the show and ruin Holland. When it only made more people buy tickets, I knew I had to kill the man."

"Okay," Donovan said, "Why Holland?"

"He treated me like garbage for twenty years," Anton said. "Exactly how he treated the Broadway stage. Someone had to stop him."

"And Harry Spalding?"

"Tell him I'm sorry I made him the scapegoat," Anton said.

By the time he reached the end of his explanation, his speech was slurred and Donovan recognized the signs of incipient death. A paramedic had run over and was setting up his equipment. Donovan picked up the crossbow. He held it up and turned it around and around, inspecting it in the brilliant artificial light.

"Why a crossbow?" he asked.

"I found it after the water main break," Anton said, fighting the words past the attempt of the paramedic to put an oxygen mask on him. "I thought having a ghost do the killing would confuse the police and buy me time."

Confetti was landing everywhere, on Anton, on the paramedic, and on the shoulders of the police. Donovan stood and handed the weapon to a sergeant, instructing the wide-eyed man to be careful. It was then that the dignitaries arrived, and with them at least fifty more police. Assured that no further deadly force was in the offing, the mayor and the cardinal, old Catholic-school stickball buddies before their lives took different paths, walked up and watched as the paramedic, now joined by two more, worked to keep Anton alive.

The mayor looked Donovan in the eye and, after glancing around to make sure no reporters were present, said, "You upstaged me in front of half the world."

"Sorry, your honor," Donovan replied.

"Donovan, I'm curious, and my wife wants to know this about you: Are you planning to run against me next year?"

"With all the skeletons in my closet?"

The mayor thought for a moment, then smiled and said, "Well then, you can keep your job. Nice shot, captain. I'm glad you didn't hit any innocent bystanders."

"There was little chance of that, sir," Donovan said.

"And why is that?"

"No one is innocent in Times Square on New Year's Eve."

"Thank you for sharing that thought," the Mayor replied.

The cardinal eyeballed the rapidly slipping killer, then asked, "Is this man a Roman Catholic?"

"Beats me," Donovan replied.

"Even if he isn't, I'll give him last rites. He must renounce the devil."

"This is no time for him to start making enemies," Donovan said.

Holding his Bible solemnly between two hands, the cardinal stooped to administer last rites to the dying Anton as a thick crowd of policemen encircled them. Donovan and the mayor walked a few, respectful paces away. The mayor said, "My regards to your father-in-law."

"Marcy and I haven't gotten married yet."

"Get married and settle down," the mayor said. "I'll perform the ceremony myself."

"You can really do that?" Donovan asked.

"Of course. I'm like the ultimate justice of the peace. Not that I've ever had to exercise that function. But I've got a tough ree-lection campaign coming and I'll do anything to keep you out of the headlines."

It was then that a corridor formed in the blue wall of police around them, and through it burst Marcia Barnes. She had the torn side of the Kristeva clutched tightly in one hand, but despite the effort the better part of the left side of her body was visible in the flashing neon light. Her eyes sought only Donovan.

"Are you okay?" she asked.

"Yeah, I'm great. Say hello to the boss."

She recognized the mayor then, and the red-robed cardinal, and blushed while desperately trying to cover herself.

"Happy New Year, your honor," she said.

"Same to you, Sergeant Barnes."

"Retired Sergeant Barnes," she corrected.

"I like the outfit," he replied. Then a wicked smile came over the mayor's face, and he looked at the cardinal, who rose from having finished his ministrations and was walking over.

"The poor man is gone," the cardinal said.

The mayor replied, "John...while you're in an official mood, maybe you could..." Then the mayor looked at Marcy, thought for a second, and said, "No, never mind. Better I handle this."

With that he snatched the cardinal's Bible and brought Dono-van's and Marcy's hands together atop it.

"Do you take this man to be your lawful wedded husband?" he asked her.

"Uh...what?" she asked, astonished.

"Yes or no."

"Yes...yes, I do."

The mayor looked at Donovan and said, "Do you take this woman to be your lawful wedded wife?"

"I do," Donovan replied.

"I now pronounce you husband and wife. You may kiss the bride."

Donovan did just that, and she let go of the side of her dress to wrap her arms around his neck as the wall of policemen cheered and the Jumbotron TV operator focused in. The cheers of millions seemed to be for them alone.

When they pulled apart, Donovan looked at a triumphant mayor and said, "I'll bring the papers around on Tuesday for you to sign."

"That will be fine," the man replied. "Now, Donovan, settle down. Buy an easy chair and put your feet up. In fact, that will be your wedding present. Raise a family. Raise *three* families. But whatever you do, get outta my face."

THE DEBATE went on for hours and left all the participants exhausted. Should the brisket newly added to the menu of Marcy's Home Cooking be served with a sauerkraut or a cranberry sauce? Marcy had a recipe for the former from her mother and preferred it. Donovan wanted the latter. George Kohler, newly reinstated as cook, wanted to restrict the menu to burgers and salads, which he had no trouble preparing—especially as Marcy did the salads.

"Nobody likes sauerkraut with anything but hot dogs anyway," Donovan said, using a tone of voice that he thought lent finality to the matter.

"You like the taste of fruit and meat together," Marcy said. "If it were up to you I'd be running a Chinese or Thai restaurant."

"There's nothing wrong with that. You liked that Vietnamese place I took you to the other day."

She said, "I would have liked it more if that poor man, Dinh, were still alive to cook the food. They said he was the best cook they ever had."

"And he did it despite the migraines," Donovan said. "Anyway, I heard that his family in Vietnam is suing the city of New York for a hundred million dollars."

"That's all?" George asked.

"They're claiming that the city was negligent in not having replaced that water main in ninety some-odd years," Donovan said. "They'll wind up settling for ten million and bring all the aunts, uncles, and cousins over. There will be a whole Dinh colony out in Flushing. Maybe one of them can cook and you can hire him and that way I'll get my brisket with cranberries."

It was ten on a Sunday evening in mid-January. Winter had at last arrived in the form of a blizzard that raged up I-95 from the Carolinas and Virginia, dumping snow like mad: thirty inches in Washington, D.C., twenty-six inches in Baltimore and Philadelphia, and twenty-four inches in New York City. The restaurant was still open for dinner, but almost no one was there. Regulars hardy enough to tramp through snow-covered sidewalks were let in to eat whatever was available. In attendance were mainly the bar customers, principally Jake Nakima, Marcy's partner, who was studying the sports pages, and Richard Marlowe, who was using Donovan's notebook to construct a crossword puzzle based on puns and wordplays. Every so often he would lean in the others' direction and ask a question such as, "How's this for a clue: 'Avian attorney?'"

"Parrot-legal," Donovan replied in that case.

"Too easy," Marlowe would answer, and lapse into silence for another ten minutes.

Harry Spalding and Luke Schadenfreud sat at the old upright Marcy kept against the brick wall, trying to invoke the spirit of Cole Porter. The two of them were Donovan success stories. Anton had lived long enough to absolve Spalding of any responsibility for the murders and Schadenfreud remained on the wagon after three weeks.

"I think I'll go with brisket and brown gravy," Marcy said at last.

George apparently approved. "Can I get it out of a can?" he asked.

"No. But Mom has a recipe." She closed the steno pad on which she planned menus and poured herself a glass of red wine.

"I'm glad to have you back," she told George.

"I'm glad to get the hell out of the Hotsy Totsy Club," he replied. "In fact, I'm lucky to get out of there alive. It was like the days of Legs Diamond had come back. The tourists were six deep at the bar, all asking me to autograph their Zagat restaurant guidebooks. Did I mention that the management kept the chalk outline that your men put around Holland's body? They made it permanent, using real paint, then invited the guy in the bear suit from the Letterman show in so they could get on TV.''

"I guess death sells after all," Donovan said. "About these blood-hungry tourists, how did they tip?" In asking that question, he was sure he was cutting to the heart of the reason for George's departure.

"Like they were home in Oshkosh having flapjacks at the IHOP," George said. "But I'll tell you, they love Times Square. The place is nearly all whitewashed now, the hookers have been pushed so far west they have one leg in the Hudson, and nine out of ten of the porno palaces are playing in Brooklyn and Queens. Next thing you see is, the three-card monte dealers will be playing hearts."

"And still the tourists come for the thrill and the danger," Donovan sighed.

"The Madame Tussaud's version," George agreed.

"Maybe Pilcrow was right," Donovan said. "Maybe I would be happier if Broadway were still a Wild West show."

"How is the deputy chief inspector?" Marlowe asked.

"Roosevelt Hospital sent him home the other day," Donovan replied. "They patched up that rib the arrow broke, sewed up the hole in his peritoneum, and scared the hell out of him with that AIDS test."

"Why an AIDS test?"

Donovan shrugged. "One of the big ways AIDS gets transferred is that a needle with one guy's blood gets stuck, accidently or otherwise, into another guy. Well, my favorite boss got stuck with a crossbow bolt that went all the way through someone else."

Marlowe shook his head and George grimaced.

"I hadn't thought of it that way," Marlowe said.

"There was a piece of Holland's aorta nailed to Pilcrow's rib cage," Donovan said.

George poured himself a draft beer and looked away.

"Anyway, Pilcrow managed to come off smelling like a rose. He depicted himself as rushing to the assistance of a trusted detective, me, and getting seriously wounded in so doing. This assures him a full-salary pension if he ever retires.''

"But he still hates you," Marcy said.

"More than ever," Donovan said. "And he's sure you knocked him on his ass deliberately, but he can't prove anything. So you're on his shit list, too."

"I should have hit him harder," Marcy said. "He never would have gotten in the way of that arrow."

"Remember that for the next time," Donovan said.

"Was Mala Logan upset about that rip in her dress?"

"If she was, she didn't say anything to me. The lady is too busy making money and sleeping with Sharkey."

"The celebrity life is exciting," Marcy said. "I'll always remember how much I enjoyed running around Times Square in my pantyhose."

From across the room, Schadenfreud said, "Roger Bock resurfaced this morning. He was up in Maine, like I thought, and got over his emotional wounds by writing the outline for another book—*Legends of Broadway Murders*. He wants to interview you for it."

"Not a chance," Donovan said. "I don't like Bock, and I don't help writers who can afford suede jackets. If you want to write a book about this case, I'll be glad to help out."

"Really?" Schadenfreud said, ceding the piano to Spalding and walking across the room.

"Sure. All I require is that you stay on the wagon..."

"I'm never going to drink again," Schadenfreud agreed.

"...and I want fifty percent."

Schadenfreud laughed, then said, "I happen to know that's pretty standard, but tell me this—I thought you didn't need money."

"We're going to try to have a kid," Donovan said, getting up and walking out back into the kitchen.

He opened the freezer. It made a click that, considering the hour, sounded as loud as Times Square on New Year's Eve. He heard her voice calling, "I hope that's the oysters you're getting out of there."

The piano suddenly starting resounding with "The Party's Over," and that was followed by Spalding's hearty laugh.

Donovan returned to the bar carrying two Klondike Bars. He tossed one to Schadenfreud. "Sensational," the man said, tearing it open. "Since I stopped drinking, I've had this incredible craving for sweets."

"It will pass after a few years," Donovan said, biting into his own ice cream bar.

"What else are you keeping in my freezer?" Marcy asked. "Why do I have this feeling my place is becoming a locker room for you and the usual suspects?"

Donovan then showed her the fifth crossbow bolt, the one never fired at him that night in Times Square.

"You kept that in the freezer?" she asked.

"Yeah. I want to keep it as clean as possible before I take it home and put it on the mantel. I just thought I'd show it to you so you didn't mistake it for a frozen eel and sauté it."

"Another souvenir," she moaned.

As he walked out back to return the bolt to the freezer he said, "Hey, the sergeant who saved this for me nearly had a coronary figuring out how to get it off the crossbow without killing someone. So the thing has even more of a history to it."

When he came back, he said, "It will be safe there."

"I don't want it on the mantel at home," Marcy said. "Put it in the shoebox with the rest of your old stuff."

Spalding laughed and said, "Anything you two lovebirds want to hear?"

"Surprise us," Donovan replied.

The man began playing "Autumn in New York." Out in the street, the traffic went on relentlessly, ceaseless despite the blizzard. That part of Broadway was more than forty blocks north of Times Square and light-years less noisy, but the buzz of activity was endless. The drunks and lonelyhearts loitered in the Dunkin' Donuts across the street, next to the Off-Track Betting parlor and the blizzard of torn-up betting slips and marked-up pages from *The Racing Form*. Clattering up Broadway, a *New York Times* truck stopped for ten seconds to toss a bundle of newspapers on the sidewalk beside the newsstand. Steam hissed and billowed from the manhole covers. A snowplow rumbled and scraped along, making graceful turns around the BMWs double-parked outside the twenty-four-hour fruit-and-vegetable markets. On the concrete bench in the mall in the middle of Broadway, a lone man sat huddled in a brown parka and a blue knit cap, blowing frosty breath into a harmonica.

Marcy reached up and kissed her husband on the cheek, then whispered, "I love you" into his ear.

"I love you, too," he whispered back.

"I like being married," she said.

"Me too. And so will Sy Gittelson, I guess."

"He proposed to Milos's ex?" Marcy asked, excited.

"Yeah, he called this afternoon to tell me. They're getting married in June. He's trying to book the old Variety Actors Benevolent Association Hall on Forty-fifth for the reception. It's a second-story billiards parlor now."

"How quaint," Marcy said, making a face. "Tell them they can have it here."

Spalding stopped playing and sat staring out the window at the traffic. Schadenfreud had taken to flipping through the pianist's fake book, searching for inspiration.

"Did your wedding present from the mayor arrive yet?" Marlowe asked.

Donovan nodded. "Two leather recliners and a big bag of popcorn."

Marcy said, "I found a new doctor. He's a specialist in high-risk pregnancies for women my age. And, guess what?"

"You got me," Donovan said.

"He's on your medical plan. He's one-hundred-percent covered. Did you eat the oysters like I told you?"

"What oysters? I thought that was a joke."

"I bought them for you," she insisted.

"Can't I just take more vitamin E?" he asked.

"Go and get them out of the freezer. George, slice up some lemons and get me the hot sauce."

Donovan had begun to march dutifully toward the kitchen when from that darkened room came a crash and the sound of a large brass cookpot rolling across the tile floor.

"Who's back there?" George asked, whipping his head around.

"Nobody," Marcy said.

Donovan pulled his Smith & Wesson as Richard Marlowe ducked down, using the bar as shield. Spalding and Schadenfreud hid behind the piano. Nakima had run over to the numbers joint.

Pausing at the entrance to the kitchen, Donovan heard a sound—he swore it was hard-soled shoes running awkwardly, as if with a limp—echoing around the tiled kitchen.

"Who's there?" he called, but the only response was the sound of a door opening and closing.

Donovan flicked on the lights and hurried into the kitchen, his revolver in front of him, Marcy just behind. There were many cabinets and storage areas, but none big enough for a man to hide in without being easily seen. A kettle of chicken barley soup bubbled quietly alongside a steaming cauldron of Manhattan clam chowder. On the floor below was the copper pot they heard fall. It rocked back and forth, still in motion.

Donovan stepped over it and hurried to the back door, which he knew led to an alley where he sometimes kept his car. He threw the door open and looked outside and up. No one was on the fire escapes, and the chain-link gate, topped with barbed wire, that blocked exit to the street, was locked. He returned to the kitchen.

"Did you see the burglar?" Marcy asked.

"Nope. He disappeared into thin air."

"Well, I don't think anything was taken. Maybe it was just a homeless guy trying to get out of the cold. But there's something wrong in here. What's that smell?"

Donovan sniffed the air. "Garlic," he said. "Lots of garlic."

She yelled, "George, did you put garlic in the barley soup?"

"No," was the reply.

"In the chowder?"

"You got to be kidding."

"Come in here a minute."

This time the voice was louder and more insistent. "I ain't settin' foot in that kitchen until Donovan gets rid of the arrow," George said.

A voice like a child crying came from a dark corner. Donovan flashed his mag-Lite into the spice pantry. Nothing was there but jars and cans of spice. A few sprigs of dried basil hung from nails driven into the ceiling, looking very much like desiccated bats suspended from a cave roof.

"We must be hearing things," Marcy said.

"We must," he agreed.

"Where's the garlic smell coming from?"

"Milos was nuts for garlic," Donovan said with a shrug.

He put away his light and, on an inspiration, went to the freezer in search of the arrow. He pulled open the lid, but found no cross-bow bolt. The stash of Klondike Bars on top of which he had left it was intact, but the Port Orford cedar arrow—the one nearly fired at him in Times Square on New Year's Eve—was gone. Gently, he closed the lid.

"Where is it?" Marcy asked.

Donovan shrugged and said, "There are two possibilities. The burglar I thought I chased, though I didn't see anyone, took it. Or Milos's ghost came and snatched it back."

"Which explanation do you like?" she asked.

He shrugged. "I don't care. Pick one that appeals to you."

When they got back into the daylight of the bar, a number of pairs of eyes met theirs. "Well?" George asked. "Did Mr. and Mrs. Charles find anything?"

"I think it was the ghost," Marcy said matter-of-factly. "He took the arrow and left."

"Oh, okay," Marlowe said, and went back to his puzzle.

Schadenfreud said, "As long as he left the Klondike Bars," and turned his attention back to the Cole Porter songbook perched on the piano's music stand.

"Anybody want soup?" George said, heading for the kitchen.

Donovan and Marcy looked at each other, proud of their friend's unflappability. Then he asked, "Do you ever regret living in New York City? 'Cause if you do, the mayor will probably pay for us to leave."

"Not for a New York minute," she replied.

# COUNT YOUR ENEMIES

# PAUL NATHAN

## A BERT SWAIN MYSTERY

Gaia World Institute is an ecology think tank, research facility and holistic retreat where controversy and politics are just a part of saving the planet. But now its director, Anne DeVilliers, is receiving threatening faxes. Bert Swain, media director for a New York hospital, and amateur sleuth, is asked to look discreetly into the matter.

Aided by his precocious teenage daughter, Swain discovers a hotbed of infighting, jealousy and blackmail dominating a place devoted to peace, harmony and a greener world.

*Available May 2000 at your favorite retail outlet.*

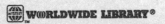 W(O)RLDWIDE LIBRARY®

Visit us at www.worldwidemystery.com          WPN348

# AILEEN SCHUMACHER

## A TORY TRAVERS/DAVID ALVAREZ MYSTERY

# FRAME WORK FOR DEATH

When a ceiling collapses in an El Paso home, two dead women and a baby are pulled from the wreckage in what at first seems to be a bizarre accident. But to engineer Tory Travers and detective David Alvarez, when a secret room is discovered and the strange connection between the victims emerges, it begins to look suspiciously like murder.

Armed with her code books, calipers and clipboards, Tory determines the means of the murder, and Alvarez uncovers the motive, as a surprising twist, strange revelations and an unlikely killer create a solid framework for death.

*Available May 2000 at your favorite retail outlet.*

WORLDWIDE LIBRARY®

# JONATHAN HARRINGTON

## A DANNY O'FLAHERTY MYSTERY

# the Death of Cousin Rose

# WHEN IRISH EYES ARE DYING

Irish-American Danny O'Flaherty hears the call of his ancestors' homeland and the unanswered questions about his roots. Leaving New York for the Irish village of Ballycara, he arrives in search of his long-lost cousin Rose. Unfortunately, Danny finds Rose bludgeoned to death in her garden.

Worse, Danny is also the chief suspect. To clear his name, Danny opens a Pandora's box that lies within this quaint village and uncovers a generations-old scandal…and a secret that someone will murder to protect.

*Available May 2000 at your favorite retail outlet.*

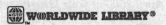 **WORLDWIDE LIBRARY®**

# DEAD
## ON HER
## FEET

A STELLA THE STARGAZER
MYSTERY

# CHRISTINE T. JORGENSEN

Unfortunately for Stella the Stargazer, providing astrological advice for the lovelorn is not very fruitful for the pocket. So she's moonlighting as the assistant director for a local theater production. She should have known there would be problems: an anxious producer, a temperamental cast, a stage mother from hell.

Then Barbara Steadman is found barely alive and tied to a prop. A second "accident" nearly kills the director. When a real corpse makes an appearance, the show takes a dramatic turn to murder.

*Available April 2000 at your favorite retail outlet.*

**WORLDWIDE LIBRARY®**

Visit us at www.worldwidemystery.com WCTJ344

# C.J. KOEHLER

# PROFILE

### A RAY KOEPP MYSTERY

Dr. Lisa Robbins is being stalked by her own patient— a man who may be responsible for a rash of serial killings. But as a psychiatrist, ethics prevent her from talking to the police. Then another murder occurs.

Detective Ray Koepp asks Dr. Robbins to listen to the recording of the man who anonymously reported the homicide. Neither could have predicted the chilling turn of events: the voice on the tape is Lisa's husband.

*Available April 2000 at your favorite retail outlet.*

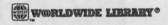